Dead Cat Bounce

Kevin Scott

TP

ThunderPoint Publishing Ltd.

First Published in Great Britain in 2017 by
ThunderPoint Publishing Limited
Summit House
4-5 Mitchell Street
Edinburgh
Scotland EH6 7BD

This book is a work of fiction.
Names, places, characters and locations are used fictitiously and any resemblance to actual persons, living or dead, is purely coincidental and a product of the authors' creativity.

Front cover image: © studiostoks/shutterstock
Back cover image: © Leonid Andronov/shutterstock

ISBN: 978-1-910946-18-3 (Paperback)
ISBN: 978-1-910946-19-0 (eBook)

www.thunderpoint.scot

Dedication

For Lisa

Acknowledgements

This novel, like all others, was once a scribble of a scrap of an idea. For helping that idea gestate and grow into something more I am forever indebted to the University of Glasgow's Creative Writing department, who above all else, made me realise that all you have to do to be a writer is write.

For their helpful feedback, encouragement and general tremendousness, the G2 Writers Group; and for responding to questions as though partaking in a pub quiz, the Want To Work Here collective. And thanks to BJR for fielding the more technical questions about trading.

Also Seonaid and Huw at Thunderpoint for believing my writing was worthy of an audience, and for illustrating that independent publishing in Scotland is thriving.

To my mum, for her unstinting support and encouragement.

And finally, to Lisa and Elliot – you make every day more enjoyable, more exciting, and more full of love, laughter and plot twists than any novel.

1

I wonder if coffins are as comfortable as beds. Lying on my back, following the faint spirals of the Artex ceiling, this is what I think about. With morning beginning to leak through the curtains, the pattern becomes clearer, along with the contents of the bedroom where I spent my childhood. Almost all the furniture is in the same place I left it twelve years ago. Even the shitty wee digital clock that I loved so much is still there. Its bright red digits, which once told me it was time for school, now tell me that there are just over twenty-six hours until Nicky's funeral.

As the headache I've been anticipating arrives with the punctuality of last orders, I come to the conclusion that if a coffin is comfier than a bed, then mankind has failed somehow. In the end it's just a box. Six bits of wood, nailed together. I wonder how many boxes like the one Nicky's currently lying in have been constructed in the history of mankind. We're talking nine figures, maybe even ten. It's a solid business model, that. One that's not going to dry up in a recession. Man, I need water.

My fingertips massage my head while outside a dog barks and cars start. Seconds become minutes without pausing in respect. The wee man would already be out in the garden kicking a ball off the wall and noising up Mum. What she'd give to sweep up pebbledash now.

Somewhere on the floor the muffled sound of the guitar intro to Oasis' Rock & Roll Star starts up. Answering my phone means getting up. It means turning on the light, finding my jeans, choosing a pocket. If it's important they'll phone back.

They do, seconds later, looping the riff around my neck like a noose and forcing me out of bed. I open the curtains enough to let a beam of light reveal the whereabouts of my jeans, giving me time to answer just as Liam's snarling vocal kicks in.

'What do you mean he's missing?' I say, after exchanging good mornings with the undertaker and discovering the reason for his call.

He talks slowly, quietly, deliberating over how to phrase his admission.

'I see what you're saying Mr. McAllister, but I'm not asking how my brother vanished, but more what you're doing about it. I mean, how do you lose a fucking coffin?'

Naked and too shocked to find clean boxers, I perch myself on the corner of the bed and cover my balls with my free hand. 'No, I won't apologise for my language, I think it's the least you can fucking expect. I'm phoning back in ten minutes. I'd be very grateful if you could locate my brother in that time. He's only eleven; he's not very street savvy.'

I throw my phone onto the duvet as if the call never happened. Maybe it didn't. Or maybe the universe is seeing just how far up the arse it can fuck me.

I lie back down and allow the information to settle. Coffins don't vanish. They've just made a mistake, and it's one that needs resolved without Mum finding out, so the quicker I get down there, the quicker it's fixed. Mum will think I'm still sleeping. No drama.

I pull on my jeans and almost catch my cock in the flies when the phone starts ringing again. Unknown number. Bit early for that carry on. I leave it. It rings off then begins again almost immediately. I concede with a hissed 'Hello'.

'Hello Matthew, haven't caught you at a bad time have I?'

The gruff accent sounds more irritating than usual, but the run-in between cock and fly means I'm alert enough to maintain politeness.

'Bradley, hello. As it happens, it is a wee bit of a bad time. Can it wait?'

'Not really pal, no. What could be so important that you can't spare a few minutes for Bradley?'

'My brother's funeral's tomorrow, Bradley.' Only cancerous ballbags refer to themselves in the third person, Bradley.

'Of course, sorry. I was reading about that in the paper. A tragedy, Matt. A fucking tragedy.'

I imagine him reclining in the soft leather chair behind his mahogany desk, sunlight streaming through the bay windows that frame the view of his Merchant-Ivory garden. Wanker.

'Yeah. It is.'

'Thing is Matt, dead brother or not, you owe me fifteen grand.'

'Not today Bradley, please.' I sit back down. My legs seem unwilling to carry my weight. I desperately want to hang up but the repercussions of such an act would put a missing coffin in the sort of context normally reserved for lost pen lids.

'How come you're so much older than your brother then, if you don't mind the intrusion into your family's affairs? No disrespect, but you must be pushing thirty?'

'I'm thirty-one. He's my half-brother.'

'Was, Matt. Was.'

I don't say anything. I can't.

'Your other brother up for the funeral?' says Bradley, not allowing the silence to intrude on whatever it is he's playing for here.

'Of course he is. Why?'

'This brother of yours, he's got a good job, eh?'

'So?'

'He must be worth a few quid.'

Textbook Bradley, incapable of just getting to the fucking point. 'I imagine so, I don't really speak to him.'

'Are you being lippy with me, Matt?'

'No, sorry, not at all. It's just a bit of a stressful morning.'

'Well, either way, you'll have to speak to him today because – and Matt, I don't like being the bearer of bad news, especially at such a traumatic time, but unless I get my money by tomorrow morning there's not going to be a funeral.'

The dots join with magnetic force. 'No. You didn't.'

'I fucking did.' He laughs down the phone. 'Speak to your brother and call Woody when you've got the money. Speaking of which, I had to employ the services of some associates, the cost of which I fully expect you to meet, so the fifteen is now twenty. Okay?'

I push the phone between my thighs and clench them until I'm content I've choked the bastard.

'Don't worry, I've got faith in you Matt,' says Bradley as I lift the phone back to my ear.

'You even think about opening that coffin and I'll put you in

3

one of your own.'

'Easy, Matt. I know this is tough. Don't worry, the young man is being treated with the utmost respect, it's not like I've got my coffee sitting on the fucking thing. Now, you've got a day, and I'm being generous because there's been a death in the family.'

'I'll get it.'

'I know you will. And Matt, don't you ever fucking threaten me again.'

The phone goes dead and I stare at it for a full minute. No one calls back. There's no mistake. I begin to shake. It starts with my fingers, spreads like a frost – teeth chattering, knees knocking; it's all I can do to keep breathing.

I leap to my feet, open the curtains, the window, gulp in cold air until it hurts.

I stare blankly at the few red leaves left clinging to the sycamore tree. Dad planted it when me and Pete were wee. He was always proud of it, despite doing nothing with it other than sticking a sapling into a hole in the ground. *My kind of gardening,* he'd said.

Beyond the tree, the slates on the rooftops fade into low-lying clouds that turn Glasgow even greyer than its natural gloom.

Nicky is out there somewhere. I stop shaking and start thinking.

Padding down the stairs, gripping the bannister, the smell of frying sausages takes me back to the Sunday mornings of my childhood. Me and Pete would race down to the kitchen, eager to fill our bellies before the boredom of church. When Dad died, the sausages kept being fried but Mum's faith was buried along with her husband. *God spare me if I'm wrong boys, but I don't think He's been watching over us of late, so I don't see why I should keep devoting my days to Him,* she'd said over breakfast the first Sunday we missed church.

The haste with which her faith was restored upon the arrival of Nicky ten years later, and two weeks before her forty-second birthday, was as unexpected as the wee man himself. Unfortunately for Nicky, she's spent the time since making up for her years in the spiritual wilderness. Now though? Now her faith will be gone for good and if losing him in a mortal sense can do that, losing him in a physical sense could be the end of her. Fucking Bradley. She can't find out. No one can.

I need a plan, and so I stand in the hall, bracing myself. On the other side of the door, Mum's probably nursing a cup of tea, heavy-eyed and weak shouldered, sausages likely burning in the pan. I can handle the tears, the cries of why and the ever-increasing sense of injustice. But I can't fill a silence, can't pull together the words she needs to hear. I picture the airport, a window seat on the plane, straining my neck to see Scotland disappear forever. This isn't fair.

I open the door and greet her with a grunted good morning as I sit down at the table. It's been cleared of the remnants of dinner that I now remember promising to wash and put away before going to the pub.

Mum is facing the cooker. Family pictures hang on the wall between the window and the back door. Dad is absent, his legacy locked away in a drawer as if he never really existed. There's one with me, Mum and Pete. She's slim in it. Terrible hair, but she's alive. Back then she'd have been darting about the kitchen, keeping everyone's mug full of tea. Man, she'd have been doing that last week.

'And how are we this morning?' she says, turning to me.

'Good. Well, y'know. How about you?'

'You'll be hungry,' she says, nodding to the pan.

Beneath the pictures are the marks where me and Pete were measured every birthday. Mum stopped measuring at our insistence when we each turned sixteen, and it's always annoyed me that I've only grown two inches since then, while Pete's rocketed by about five. Some way beneath the tallest marks on the wall are the green scores that marked Nicky's progress. 'Nicky: 11' says the last one.

I try to move my thoughts into a slower lane, but they slip between Nicky being dead and Nicky being missing. I keep hearing him whenever the house shifts in the wind. When someone dies they don't disappear right away. Floorboards creak and it's them, door handles turn and it's them. It was the same after Dad.

Mum turns round again, fish slice pointing in my direction. Nicky disappears. 'How is it that I went to my bed having watched you drink nothing more than a glass of wine with dinner and yet three hours later I heard you shouting down the phone like a common drunk?'

'That was a private call.' The desperate pleas I made to Siobhan while sitting on the stairs after the pub come bounding back to me. Mum's still got a way of making me grimace as if she's found my first porn mag.

'If you want privacy go to your room and keep your voice down. Poor girl. How is she anyway?' She's trying to sound pissed off, but the energy drains from the words too quickly.

'You're not helping.'

I want to argue, because it's normal, but she turns away, puts four slices of white bread in the toaster. She moves slowly. It's like only half of her is here.

'Can I have tea please?' I say.

Somewhere in my head the parts of a plan are spinning around like planetary objects destined to collide and fuse into a new world. Who steals a coffin? It's deranged and Bradley is too calculating for that.

'I'm pretty sure you can, Matthew, given that you know where everything is kept.'

There's irritation in her voice this time. It warms me. She shakes the frying pan and squeals as a little ball of fat leaps onto her arm. We never know where our next wound's coming from. Sometimes even the possibility of pain is enough to damage us. Fucking McAllister. He's been Bradleyed. Threatened, blackmailed, waterboarded, fucking something that has persuaded him to lie about the whereabouts of my little brother. I stand up. My headache hasn't improved any but I feel better.

'Be a good lad and get me one as well, would you?' says Mum. Her eyes are glazed again.

Nicky's safe. I just need to convince McAllister that Bradley is all talk. I put the kettle on then put my arms around Mum as she faces the cooker. It's the type of hug she gave me when I was a boy, the type she said put us both in a bubble where nothing could hurt us. She needs this too. I pull her tighter and let my head rest on her shoulder, just as the doorbell rings.

'That'll be your brother,' she says, shrugging me off and turning the tap on to wash her hands.

'Already?'

It's as if I'd never hugged her in the first place. She's smiling an actual smile. Tease me, please him. Story of my fucking life.

'Some people maybe set their alarms in the morning,' she says, drying her hands on a dishcloth. 'Some people probably didn't get drunk last night either.'

'My alarm was set as well,' I shout after her. A faint tut comes back in reply.

I should have known that six sausages were too many for just me and Mum.

Returning twice a year from London with his expensive teeth and perfect family, he always manages to become the centre of attention for the two or three days his conscience deems sufficient to spend with his mother. Helen will be with him this time, no doubt trying to keep the twins away from me, as if I'll somehow infect them with a sense of social justice. Well, this visit is about more than them.

As footsteps come back up the hall I grab a sausage from the pan and make for the back door. This business with McAllister is more important than breakfast with Pete. I only realise I'm in my bare feet when my soles meet the cold, wet path. I'm about to go back inside when I hear the side gate swing shut and see wonderboy coming around the corner. Impatient prick.

'Pete. How's it going?' I meet his eye then glance at his hairline for long enough to let him know I'm measuring how much it's pushed its way back onto his dome since the last time I saw him.

'It's Peter. What you doing out here?'

He's standing there with his fucking teeth and the top three buttons of his white shirt undone, big woolen overcoat soaking up the rain.

'I'm just…' I take a step forward. The sausage is beginning to burn my hand. 'How was the drive? Hotel all right?' I trail off again.

'Yeah, fine. Where's Mum?'

'Answering the door, Mr. Impatient.'

He glances down at the sausage again. This is bullshit. Now I need to explain why I'm barefoot in the back garden, holding a sausage, while his reasons for not waiting for the front door to be answered will never be questioned. I grip the sausage tighter, imagine it resting on my plate with its pals, surrounded by scrambled eggs and toast.

'I was about to have a smoke,' I say, moving away from the window. Mum will be back in the kitchen, wondering where I've gone.

'Thought you'd stopped. Again.'

'It's been a pretty stressful few days.'

Pete smirks. 'So stressful you've started smoking sausages?'

It's a decent comeback. Shite. I look at the tip of the banger emerging from my curled fist and laugh. In the moment of clarity that comes with it I realise it might be better if he's the one to call McAllister's bluff.

'Look, something's happened, there's a problem.'

'It's not nine o'clock yet, how can there be a problem?' Pete folds his arms.

'You'll have to ask the undertaker. He's managed to lose Nicky.'

As I study the change in Pete's expression, I take a bite of sausage.

2

It was as Peter was trying to work out why Matt had no shoes on that he became aware of the sausage poking out his brother's clenched fist. While his brain could understand complex financial algorithms it toiled when it came to the inner workings of his older sibling. Then, even as he tried to draw a conclusion to the improbable, along came the unfathomable. He would have assumed it was a joke were it not for the sheepish look that accompanied the news.

'How does a coffin get lost?' he said.

Answer: It doesn't. So, Matt must have fucked up in some capacity. The chances of this being the undertaker's fault were next to nil. Where there's a Matt, there's a mess.

'God knows. I'm about to head down there,' said Matt, the sausage meat in his mouth doing its level best to escape.

'With no shoes on?' There was nothing more irritating than someone talking with their mouth full.

'Wait here a minute, it's better if Mum doesn't see you.'

'That's why I'm here.'

'Fuck that. I need you to come down the funeral parlour with me, help sort it out. Half an hour tops and we're back for breakfast.' Matt started shepherding Peter down the side path.

'Don't drag me into – '

Matt put his hand up. 'Please. Half an hour.'

'I rang the bell. She knows I'm here.'

'She's not seen you. I'll come up with something on that front.'

Peter's cheeks filled with air. 'Put some fucking shoes on then. I'll phone Mum and tell her I'm running late.'

Back in the Range Rover, as he waited on Matt, Peter pressed his fingers deep into his trapezius muscle, wincing at the pain. Mum's medicine drawer would have to wait. He glanced at the Breitling he'd chosen for the trip. It wasn't five past nine yet and

9

Matt had managed to turn the day entirely. Peter hadn't even had a coffee yet. Okay, he wasn't exactly looking forward to his mum's wet eyes staring back at him, but it would be easier than the phone calls, the muffled sobbing as she held the handset away from herself. Christ, how were you meant to respond to that? Nicky was just seven years older than the twins. They'd not seen each other for nearly a year, but the wee man had been so protective of his nieces. Peter remembered how Nicky would hold both their hands as they crossed even the quietest of roads.

His mum was beyond repair. Thankfully, he was parked far enough away that she wouldn't be able to see his car from the window but it had still felt strange phoning her while looking at her house. She had accepted with a crestfallen groan the lame excuse that the girls were being difficult and he'd have to push breakfast back. He'd apologised and meant it, his guilt being exacerbated by the sound of Matt's mock outrage as he stomped about the kitchen.

Maybe it was the undertaker's fault. Maybe he'd been harsh on Matt – he'd taken the whole thing pretty badly judging by their phone calls. Peter looked down the road towards the football pitches, imagining Nicky running along the pavement, ducking out to cross the road and then the noise of his body shattering the car's windscreen, the screeching of brakes and that second of silence after the car stopped but before the body landed. He pictured Nicky lying on the tarmac, blood quickly pooling around his head. But then it wasn't Nicky. It was… one of the twins. Who? The face, twisted… bloody… he couldn't make out which daughter... her hair, matted red, a yellow dress… the body, rolling over and over and flashes of flesh and bone and yellow and red and… Peter blinked hard, his heart pounding. Fucking hell.

He turned the engine on and rolled down a window. His mum's hedge was unruly, mangled. She needed a gardener. He'd need to book her a holiday in a couple of months. Get her away from it all, away from Matt for a while. Give her peace.

Peace. He shut his eyes. His brother's company over the next two days was always going to be trying – even before this fuck up at the undertakers. Peter usually tried to time his visits north to coincide with Matt's absence. This time was different. And not just because of Nicky.

He thought of the investment bank where he'd spent his entire career, his empty desk, the voicemail light flashing on his phone. The stocks he was holding for investors, both institutional and private. There was a chance he would never be back there. The gloom Peter usually felt in Glasgow had intensified to the point of nervousness. It was as if all eyes were on him, wet with grief and expectant. The city he'd abandoned would want to know how he'd react, what he'd learned. What his fate was. He wouldn't mind knowing that himself.

His thoughts retreated when Matt opened the door and climbed into the passenger seat.

'Right, go,' he said, leaning forward.

As he slowly pulled away Peter frowned at his brother. 'What are you doing?'

Matt was hunched over, his head gently rapping against the dashboard as the 339 brake horse power 4x4 crept its way out of the estate towards the main road.

'Fixing my shoe. I didn't get it on properly.'

'Christ Matt, it's not that tricky.'

'Leave it will you. Just drive.'

Peter accelerated sharply then tapped the brakes, causing Matt to roll back and bang his head more forcefully on the dashboard. He cried out.

'Focus,' said Peter. 'You need to explain what's going on. Coffins don't just get lost, especially when there's someone in them.'

Matt sat back, rubbing his head. 'Fuck's sake, what did you do that for?'

'You look like a bag of washing. You stink of booze. Seriously, what sort of ineptitude am I about to walk in on here?'

'The creases in my t-shirt are of little fucking concern right now.'

Peter looked at his brother, hoping his face adequately translated his thoughts. 'Aye, okay,' said Matt. 'The bare feet, the sausage. I know. It all looks a bit surreal. Can you blame me? I feel like shit, she's in there trailing about like a ghost and I've just been told Nicky's missing. Is it surprising I'm a bit at sorts?'

The clouds were moving across the sky with a purpose. The

rain was on for the day. That much Peter knew.

'What did he say, exactly? It can't be missing.'

'It's missing Pete, that's what the man said.'

'I know, but what were his words? How did he say it?'

'What difference does it make? We're on our way, you can ask him yourself. Left at the junction here,' he said, pointing forward.

Peter said nothing. He felt his work phone vibrate. He couldn't answer with Matt there.

'Can I smoke?' said Matt.

'This is an £95,000 car. No, you cannot smoke.'

'I never asked how much your car cost.'

'I'm just saying, you can't smoke.'

'Well, just say "don't smoke" then.' Matt leaned towards Peter, his breath minty with mouthwash. 'See just for the now, just until this is over, how about you don't act like you're better than everybody else.'

Peter looked Matt in the eye. 'This isn't about me. And for once, it's not about you either.'

'Watch the road.'

Peter squeezed his brakes as he approached the lights, gripping the wheel as if it was Matt's neck. He had no control left anywhere. Peter delivered what was demanded, and expected the same of everyone. The people that entrusted him with their investments knew how capable he was. He'd clear his name. It was simply a matter of working out how.

The lights changed. Peter drove on silently, waiting to see what Matt would do next. Within seconds he'd started fumbling at his jeans and pulled out his phone. Peter tried to glance at it, but the unfamiliarity of the roads he once passed his test on demanded full concentration. The car in front was a red Mazda, a tiny wee effort that barely looked safe enough to take to the shops. He wondered who would drive such a thing.

'You ever wonder if the guy in front is the guy that hit him?' he said, before he managed to stop himself.

Matt stopped texting. 'What?'

'The guy that hit him, where he is? He wasn't arrested was he?'

'Well he's not been charged with anything. Ron knows a guy that knows him.'

'Who's Ron?'

'He was in your year at school. Ronnie Graham. He's Ron now, for whatever reason. I saw him in the pub last night.'

'So the guy is what? Just going about his life?'

'Nah,' Matt shook his head. 'He's fucked. Shaken right up. Hasn't left the house apparently. His missus has been trying to get him to go to the docs but he just sits there watching the telly. So Ron says.'

'So Ron says.'

'Look, you asked a question. The answer is, it's not the guy in front of you. It's a guy with two kids, probably about Nicky's age. He went out to go to B&Q or something like that and before he got there he'd killed somebody. It wasn't his fault.'

'That's for the courts to decide.'

'Mum's not looking for that so neither am I. She reckons he's got his sentence, same as her.'

'She never committed a crime though.'

Matt shook his head. 'We don't know he did either. Punishing someone's not going to bring him back, it's not going to make her feel any better. You know what she's like, she'd just feel guilty.'

Peter felt as distant from his family as he ever had. He thought it would be straightforward – find out who was driving the car, hire the right lawyer, get them locked up, end of. Of course it would be different to lose your own child than a brother, and that was what was eating at him. It didn't feel like he'd lost a brother. The whole drive north he'd tried to flick the devil off his shoulder, but there was no getting away from the fact that Nicky's death had confirmed something Peter had denied for so long. Something he'd felt since the day his mum told him she was pregnant again.

'Where now?' he said, pushing the memory aside.

Matt had returned to his texting.

'Matt, where have I to go, there's a crossroads coming up.'

'Fuck's sake, Pete, you grew up here as well. Just go straight on. In about two minutes you'll come to the railway bridge, first left after that,' said Matt, turning back to his phone.

On the pavement, pensioners shuffled along as if stuck in the past. The few shops still in business looked fucking horrific. Peter hoped they'd didn't sell meat or any other perishable stuff. It shocked him that this is where he came from.

13

He missed the lights, again. Matt tapped away on his phone, breathing heavily as if he was calming himself. The text was probably a distraction to avoid conversation. Words were difficult. They were spat out like squadrons of midges, nipping at the other's skin, but never penetrating deeper.

'How you feeling about it all?' said Peter, always the one to rise above it.

'It's their mistake, right? Whatever it is, we'll – '

'I mean about Nicky.'

The lights changed.

'You don't need to do that.'

'What?'

'Act like you give a shit.'

'Fucking hell, Matt. Am I in the habit of asking questions I'm not interested in hearing answered?'

Silence. Then Matt sighed. 'I miss him. I got him a wee phone for his birthday. He texted me every day. I think he'd worked out it was costing me money every time he hit send, the wee shite.' He laughed a little. 'It's horrific, the worst thing I've ever known. Worse than Dad.'

Was it really? Worse than not knowing why Dad wasn't at work anymore, then why he couldn't get out of bed. Then him just not being there. Matt, offering hugs because Mum didn't have the strength. Peter was seven. He'd cried non-stop until days after the funeral. He remembered not speaking, seeing a doctor. He just hadn't felt like saying anything. Nearly two weeks it lasted. He hadn't thought about that in years.

'I don't imagine it's been easy,' he said. Either way, Matt looked worse than he ever had.

As they passed under the railway bridge Peter eyed up the turning. 'This us, then?'

Matt nodded.

The parlour sat on the corner, separated from the deserted street by a wrought-iron fence. It looked like a bungalow, its front facing the main road with the 'McAllister & Son Funeral Services' livery the only thing that revealed its true purpose. The entrance was on the side street, presumably for reasons of sensitivity. Across the road, railway arches housed workshops and showrooms for all manner of cheap tat.

The car came to a stop. 'Look, whatever happens with this guy, we'll get it sorted. Don't worry,' said Peter.

'What a fucking start to the day this is,' said Matt, opening his door.

Peter climbed out and looked the place over again. He'd never considered what a funeral parlour should look like, but surely it shouldn't look like a house. The vision he'd had of the sinister sounding 'under taker' where his dad was prepared was a sanitised basement where men in white coats moved like ghosts as they prepared the world's dead for heaven. The vision came back to him as he locked the car and he felt that same anxiety crawl over him again. It never occurred to him that the place where Nicky was being kept was a shitty bungaloffice with cracked pebbledash walls on a street that reeked of deprivation.

He sucked in his stomach and stuffed his shirt back into his jeans. 'You ready then?' he said.

'Let me do the talking,' said Matt.

Peter nodded, content to observe. This was not his world, it had different rules, and if he didn't know the rules, he didn't know how to bend them.

3

Now I'm facing the parlour my assumptions about McAllister being blackmailed and Nicky being safe begin to unravel and I'm becoming convinced that Bradley put the heel of his shoe through his moral compass as soon as he learned to walk. What if he did steal Nicky? And what will he do if I can't get the money? Jesus, what will Mum do?

SO THERE YOU GO,
THAT WAS THAT

That's what I think I'll have on mine; on that cut of rock that others will remember me by. It'll last far longer than I will, before it yields to shoots of grass that will brush its face and push it back or forward at their will while years of rain and wind fade the carefully chiselled typeface. The text will vanish and the stone will follow. By then, I'll be gone, even my smirking skeleton will have decomposed and there will be no sign I ever existed. Eventually, there will be no sign that any of us ever existed. Sometimes I just wish it would hurry the fuck up and happen.

Pete looks at me as if I've not got on a bus I was waiting for.

'I need a minute,' I say.

'What happened to "let me do the talking"?' he says.

I smile a smile that tells him he can fuck off as far as he likes and lift a cigarette to my lips. They're dry and it sits there like a plank overhanging a ship's bow. I draw a match to it and suck. The smoke ghosts through my veins and I keep sucking, filling my whole body with it. A quarter of the fag is gone by the time I exhale. Ash drops onto the wet pavement and sizzles. I hope Nicky's not outdoors.

Nicky. He's there again, as if he's playing hide and seek with me.

nickynickynickynickynickynickynickynickynickynicky

This isn't the sort of place Nicky would find much fun. Nicky.

Cracked pavements and a pot holed Nicky road, empty except for a rusty Transit and someone unloading rugs from a clapped out Nicky Volvo estate. If the wheels are still on Pete's car when we come out, I'll be surprised. And a bit disappointed.

'Are you coming then?' says Pete, who's standing at the door. I throw my fag into the gutter. There are three main objectives to this sham of a meeting:

1. Finding out if McAllister is being blackmailed
2. Ensuring Pete doesn't find out the truth
3. Ensuring neither of them phone the police.

I nod at Pete and he opens the door, inviting me through first. It's cold inside. I guess it needs to be. A tinted window looks out onto the main road, lighting the room with a sepia filter that makes the whole place seem even quieter. It's as close to a church as an office can be.

The girl sitting behind the reception desk looks up from her computer when the door clicks closed.

'Mr. Fletcher? We've been expecting you,' she says.

I'm not sure which one of us she's talking to, but Pete confirms she's right either way. She's got a look on her face that suggests she either doesn't know or doesn't care why we're here. It must be the latter – surely the panic has reached every corner of the company? She's young, early twenties, blonde hair tied tight in a ponytail that's about as formal as her dull black dress. She looks like she could shine if it was a Friday night and not a Thursday morning. She probably gets wrecked after work on a Friday. I'll need to try and catch her name at some point, see if there are any decent photos of her on Facebook. Can't be much fun working in a funeral parlour; every time you answer the phone it's another mourning relative telling you their mum/dad/husband/wife/son/daughter has just died. At least we're providing her with the sort of theatre she won't have dreamed of.

'Hold on one minute,' she says, before heading off down a corridor. She returns seconds later, stern-faced, followed by McAllister. I've met him before, when I came down with Mum two days ago. He's wearing the same morning suit and is still staggeringly tall – like six and a half feet. At least he'll get a discount on his coffin; he'll need a fucking huge one when he pops off.

'Matthew, hello,' he says, offering his hand. I shake it. I tell myself Nicky's through the back, resting easy.

'And you must be…'

'Peter.'

'Yes, yes, I'm sorry. Peter, of course. It's just that with everything that's happened this morning, my head isn't quite where it ought to be.'

I watch McAllister's face for a tell, but even his blinking is mechanical.

'I'm sure. Can you explain exactly what's going on?' says Pete, refusing to replicate the man's pleasant tone.

'Please,' he looks around the empty room, 'come on through to my office.'

I look at the receptionist. She's staring out the window, not blinking.

'Jenny, can you do coffees, please – none for me,' says McAllister.

Jenny. Jenny what though?

Pete and I say thanks simultaneously. I budge past him to get in front. He's not controlling this until I want him to.

The office is impeccably tidy – soft lighting, plush powder blue carpet that my feet sink right into. Makes me want to slip off my shoes. His desk is this huge old oak thing with an Anglepoise lamp sitting alongside the usual computer and stuff.

He gestures to the two chairs on our side, and goes around to sit down. I catch him before his arse is on the chair.

'Where is he then? Have you moved him? Or is he still in the back?'

McAllister looks at me as if I've enquired as to the cost of fucking the dead. 'I don't follow… sorry… When we arrived this morning the coffin containing Nicky was gone. There's no other way to say it.' He's muttering. Nervous.

'What do you mean?' says Pete.

I wish I'd brought a notepad or something to make me look like I'm investigating this thoroughly, put the shitters right up McAllister.

'I… I… well – '

'Are you suggesting Nicky's actually gone? That this isn't some clerical error?' says Pete.

'I'm afraid so, Mr. Fletcher.'

'Has anyone spoken to you about Nicky?' I say. 'Perhaps threatened you in some way?'

He looks appalled at the thought. If he's bluffing, he should take up poker; I wouldn't fancy playing against him.

'There's been no threats, no sign of forced entry. I've spoken to everyone and no one moved your brother.'

He seems visibly upset. I push harder. 'Well somebody did, and I doubt Burke and Hare have risen from the dead and jumped across the M8 to diversify into a new market.'

'I don't know what to say, Matthew.' He's on the verge of tears, the daft old prick.

'You must have a theory,' I say. My eyes don't leave his. He's wearing these perfectly round glasses with a gold rim, looks like he was born wearing them.

'Frankly, I'm at a loss. I can't even begin to explain how upsetting this is for us all. I've sat behind this desk since my father retired forty years ago and I've never had this conversation.' He takes the glasses off and rubs his eyes.

He's not lying. They fucking did take him. Shit.

'Well, you're having it today,' says Pete.

I hate McAllister right now. Fishing for sympathy. He allowed this to happen. I should be at home, eating breakfast, dealing with this hangover. Where's that Jenny with the coffee? I lean back and leave Pete to interrogate McAllister. I want him ruffled up. I want him lowered out a fucking window by the belt on his trousers.

Pete has started quoting laws he doesn't understand in an attempt to intimidate a man who's probably perfectly versed in his legal position. It's not the right angle, but I feel dizzy. I can't concentrate. This is where Bradley wanted me. I listen as Pete goes at McAllister. He doesn't aim for the wall and miss. There are still two points on my agenda for the meeting.

There's a knock at the door and Jenny comes in with a tray. She's taller than she looked sitting down, her legs in black tights to go with her black dress. Makes me wonder why she dyed her hair blonde. She's off the hook anyway; if he's not bluffing, she's certainly not. Her expression when she puts the tray down is one of abject boredom. It's shite for her; she shouldn't be cooped up with all this darkness.

Both mugs are black, so is the little milk jug she places between us. I've never seen a black milk jug before. Everything here is the colour of death.

'Thanks,' I say. Pete just stares at McAllister. Whatever they were talking about, he looks mighty pissed off.

The last thing off her tray is a sugar pot, black, obviously. She catches my eye as she retreats, but her expression remains blank and I wonder for a second if she's a ghost.

I spoon five sugars into my coffee in the hope that the sweetness will makes its way to my brain and obliterate this headache.

'Christ, are you trying to make tablet?' says Pete, lifting his own mug. It's the first time he's glanced my way since we sat down.

'Look, there's three times this much in a can of fizzy juice – I don't know why everybody makes such a big deal about it.' I take my own sip. Filter coffee always reminds me of working in an office. Pete places his mug back down and pushes it away. Dead black coffee clearly not good enough for him. It'll do for me.

'As I was saying,' says Pete. 'We both want the same thing here. The problem is we want it for different reasons.'

'Mr. Fletcher, I – '

'I've not finished.' Pete's voice gets louder, making me burn my top lip. 'You phoned Matt an hour ago. What have you done since then to find him?'

'We've turned the place upside down.'

'He's not exactly going to be at the back of a drawer. I don't think you're treating this with an appropriate level of urgency.'

'We're doing all that we can.'

'No, you're not. If you were, then this discussion would have taken place out there because you wouldn't have had time to sit down, and she wouldn't have had time to make this.' He flicks his mug with his middle finger and coffee spills over the edges onto the desk. Go on, Petey. 'If you can't find him, the police can,' he adds.

Shit, he's crossed the line now. 'Easy there, Pete,' I say.

'This is a very sensitive matter, Mr. Fletcher,' offers McAllister. So it was his fucking reputation that stopped him calling the rozzers. I should be thankful, but it makes me even more pissed off.

'Listen to the man, Pete. Think about Mum. Neither of us wants this to get out.'

He ignores me and steadies his stare on McAllister. 'Sensitive? What you seem to be missing here is that I'm not phoning the police to report you, but to assist you. If you were more interested in our brother than your reputation, you'd have phoned them yourself. I, on the other hand, have about as much interest in your reputation as I do in finishing this piss water you call coffee. In fact if you never saw another dead body in your life it would be a just conclusion to this fucking debacle.' Pete's half on his feet, now, practically spitting.

McAllister's tiny eyes seem to swell up behind his glasses, his mouth is hanging open as if he's had a stroke.

I try again: 'Look, it's only half nine, Pete. Calm down. Let's give the guy a couple of hours. If the police get involved, Mum gets involved. She doesn't need that.'

Pete stands up, his sticking chair making him stumble a touch. He picks it up and slams it down, the thick carpet silencing any effect he was looking for. 'You don't just lose a coffin! It doesn't just fucking vanish!' He's proper angry, nostrils flaring. Overreacting. He pulls out his phone. The mute McAllister doesn't budge. It's me against Pete.

'Two hours, Pete. Come on, please?' Reasoning is the only option I've got left.

'You're pleading with me on this?' He points his phone at me. 'Why are you so certain that a man capable of losing a coffin is capable of finding it?'

Why did I ask him to come down here? 'It's just Mum. She can't – '

'Nah, it's not Mum. I know you.'

I stand up to face him. 'What does that mean?' He knows nothing about me, nothing about what's happening. Brings down the gavel then hears the evidence. And he wonders why we never speak.

'What have you done, Matt? Come clean.'

I put my hands up. 'Nothing. What are you looking for here?'

McAllister surprises us both by standing up. Defeat surrounds the bastard. He still says nothing. Pete shakes his head like only he can. Nothing I say can alter his actions so I reach out and grab the phone from his hand.

He fails to snatch it back. 'What are you doing?'

'You can't phone the police.'

'Why the fuck not?'

'Just let Mr. McAllister do what he needs to do.'

'Give me the phone, Matthew.'

'Now, gentlemen, I know this is a difficult time,' says McAllister.

We both pause. He's turned a similar shade of grey to his jacket. Of course there was no blackmail. Bradley wouldn't risk it backfiring. He's too thorough. So is Pete. The meeting is over.

'Look, I can't, Pete.' I say.

'What do you mean you can't?'

There's nowhere to go. I could have scripted this fiasco from the car. Stupid move. Should have left him to eat my sausages.

'Give me the fucking phone, Matt. Now.'

'Fuck you.' I push him in the chest. He stumbles backwards, grips the back of his chair, hard. McAllister does likewise, I suspect for entirely different reasons. 'You can't tell me what to do, Pete. I'm not one of your minions. I don't want the police involved, so they're not getting involved.'

I say it like I mean business, like I'm simply stating what's going to happen. I think that's what pushes him over the edge.

He runs at me, all red-faced. Fat prick. I try to get out his way, but he's on me before I can stop him and I wince as my back slams up against the wall. I try to push back but he shoves me into the wall again. And again. The fourth time the wall shudders and my shoulder blade takes the brunt. I try to break free, but he's got a good grip. There's still muscle beneath the flab. I shove the phone into my jacket pocket and stamp on his foot. The shock weakens his grip and I push him back and get away from the wall, circle around him. He comes for me again and I'm bracing myself to try and deflect a punch when he ducks and drives his head into me as if he's a fucking rhino. As I career backwards I start punching his back. He roars forward, lifting me off my feet and slamming me into the carpet, his colossal weight dropping on top of me. I try to sit up but can't so I swing aimlessly, every punch blocked but keeping his arms busy. Then McAllister's voice bellows through the room. 'Enough!'

We both freeze, eyes inches apart, chests heaving. Pete has menace in his eyes. He always was a dirty fighter. I'm fucked if I'm conceding though. I narrow my eyes, throw him off me. He stands up, straightens himself out.

McAllister has his desk phone in his hand. 'I'm calling the police. This is too much. We can ensure that – '

'Woah, hold your horses there, old yin,' I say, dragging myself off the carpet.

Pete turns back to me, primed. I'm outnumbered now. There's no way round this. This is what my life coach Phillip Turnbull would call *cornering the cul-de-sac* – a point where one must acknowledge their mistake, turn to face the consequences, and begin to deal with the repercussions.

'I know where he is,' I say. And there's silence at last.

4

So, Peter was right. Again. He'd fucking known something was up with Matt. Still, the shock of his brother's admission had hit him harder than that realisation he'd been involved in a fight in the middle of an undertaker's office. How the fuck? He felt the room expand and contract with his breathing. He needed to get out, back to his own world. He was finished with Matt for good. But still, curiosity demanded answers.

'What do you mean you know where he is?' he said.

Behind him, McAllister held the phone half way between his ear and the desk.

'Well, I don't know where he is, but I know who's got him,' said Matt.

Peter clenched and unclenched both fists. 'Got him? What the fuck does that even mean?'

'Please, language,' said McAllister. Who the fuck did he think he was?

'Give me a minute,' said Matt.

'You don't have a minute. What are we even doing here?'

Peter took in as much of the stale air as he could. His head pulsated. Everything was fucked. Everything.

He watched his brother return to the desk, sit down, straighten up and take a sip of coffee as if he was in the middle of a business meeting. 'Please...' he motioned to the two empty chairs.

McAllister sat down robotically. If he was asked to suck his own dick he would probably have gone along with it such was the vacant look on his face. Peter remained where he was, arms folded. What was the next lie going to be? Matt began with more pleas to McAllister about why he couldn't phone the police.

'I need answers, Matt.' Peter slapped the desk, stinging his palm. 'Now!'

McAllister motioned him to calm down.

'Look, Pete – this isn't easy, right? You think I like the fact

24

Nicky's missing and we're down here while Mum's stuck at home, alone again?' Matt rubbed his eyes and leaned back.

Peter had seen this pathetic theatre to squeeze sympathy from his audience countless times. 'Dry your fucking eyes, Matt.' He sat down. 'You brought us here. So whatever fuckery you're mixed up in, get it out, on the table, now.'

Matt sipped at his coffee, the mug shaking as he held it. 'It started a few months ago when my guru made me a business offer.'

'Sorry, did you say your "guru"?' Peter leaned in, cupping his ear. He pictured Matt dressed in robes, sitting cross-legged, trying to *om* his way out of trouble.

'Just listen, will you.'

Peter laughed. 'Fire away, please.'

Matt explained how he'd met some charlatan called Phillip Turnbull, and how he'd 'gone into business with the guy'. The weak and foolish were fooled every week, thought Peter.

'It was the deal I've been waiting for but the banks wouldn't entertain me,' said Matt.

'There's a reason for that.'

'Too right there is, and it's not the reason you think. They're never there for people like me, never there to...' he paused, 'anyway, they knocked me back. But I couldn't not invest in this, so I went where I had to.'

Matt was reckless, but this was new ground. 'Is this about a loan shark?'

'No. It's not like that. He's an acquaintance. But he's fucked me over, demanded early settlement. Then this morning, literally two minutes after you phoned me,' he nodded at McAllister, 'my guy called to say he had Nicky. I thought he was bluffing, that he had blackmailed you. I hoped... well, it doesn't matter now.'

Peter felt a headache land like a helicopter without a rotor. They'd been getting more frequent, more intense. He reached for his coffee then thought better of it.

'We have to phone the police,' said McAllister. He was looking so pale he was becoming transparent, as if he was just fading from existence.

'Really?' said Matt. 'So you fancy this all over tomorrow's papers? Your phone ringing off the hook and a bunch of arseholes outside trying to take your picture? Your business ruined. Or do you want to get in your car and drive Nicky to the crematorium? It's your choice.'

'How much do you owe this guy?' said Peter, against his better judgment.

'I'll explain later.'

'How about you explain now?' Idiot, thought Peter. How could they even be related?

When Matt turned his eyes to the floor and admitted he owed twenty thousand pounds, McAllister issued what sounded like a mini-shriek. Peter's collection of watches must have amounted to at least double that, Christ, he went on twenty grand weekend breaks. Nothing on Earth was as relative as money though, and that meant Matt would turn to him at some point. Well, fuck that. Not after this shambles.

'I don't know what to say, Matt. Genuinely. I mean, you've left me speechless before, but this? This is something.'

'It's not past the point of no return. We can do it,' said Matt.

And there it was. 'Did you hear the "we", there Mr. McAllister? The "we". "We can do it." He means us. You see, he's right, if this gets out, your business is fucked.' McAllister grimaced again, every expletive like a blow to the kidneys. 'And it'll finish off my mum. But here's the thing, she'll ask me why I didn't help him, why I never gave him money for whatever scheme he's being scammed with.'

'I'm not being scammed,' said Matt.

Peter pointed furiously at his brother. 'You shut your mouth and listen.' He turned back to McAllister. 'Now, she's my mum, so I can hardly turn round and say "I never stepped in, dear Mother, because your son's pockets are like a fucking sinkhole for cash," so I have to take my share of the blame, which I'll be doing no matter the outcome of this crushingly fucked up debacle.' Peter stood and moved his chair back into place. 'Therefore, this is not my problem.' He turned to Matt. 'As for you, if I don't see you later, I'll see you tomorrow morning. You're on your own here.'

He crossed the office and opened the door. He was about to slam it but saw the dim looking receptionist smiling vacantly at him, so just let it click behind him. He passed her, returning the smile and seconds later was starting up the car. When he reached the junction he turned left into what little traffic there was.

It wasn't about the money. For years he'd heard nothing from his mum but 'poor Matt' and how all the family's luck had landed at Pete's feet. Matt's countless employers clearly disagreed with this theory and from what he'd heard, it sounded as though Siobhan had finally also had the sense to see him for what he was. It was time their mum did. Let this one fall apart. It was a dripping tap compared to the burst dam he was dealing with in London. That was what demanded his concentration.

The morning Peter's world fell apart started brightly enough. From the office window, eighteen floors up, London's splendour was beginning to reveal itself as the sun rose. He enjoyed those moments of being wide-awake while the city was still rubbing its eyes. So much would happen across its streets while the sun arced over the sky. Peter wished he could see it all. Saying that, he would settle for seeing inside the heads of the fuckers that sat around him. He turned to survey the empty trading floor that in an hour would be alert, air frenzied with traders, brokers, sales people, all revealing their thoughts on the morning reports, logging onto Bloomberg terminals, seeing how the foreign markets had performed overnight; all ready to make money by whatever means necessary. Each had a moral ambivalence to match their ability to spot a deal. It was a battlefield and it was Peter's playground.

He sat at his desk and typed in his password, watching all three of his huge monitors spring into life – like any other day it would end with a profit or a loss. Into the black or into the red. He occupied a corner spot on a twin row of twenty. At the next desk was Stuart Morgan – twenty-two, six months into the job and craving every day like a man who's been told he'll be a millionaire by the time he's twenty-five. Next along was Alan Wood, a mid-forties alcoholic who just couldn't move on. He was the Keith Richards of the floor – three wives, two heart attacks and in the market for more of both. No one normally lasted beyond thirty-five. If you hadn't crashed and burned, you'd cashed in and run. They all knew that. Except Al. If Al stopped he would be dead inside a month. The desk opposite Peter was empty; Craig had chucked it three days shy of his thirtieth birthday and eloped with his brother's wife. His replacement was starting the following week. Next to Craig's desk was Kim – the only woman in the row. She owned some of the boys, using her mouth to deceive them while her body distracted them. Her throaty laugh would have brokers on the end of the phone wanking into their wastepaper baskets as she confirmed trades. So she boasted anyway. Peter respected her more than anyone else, and therefore he watched her closer. Further along, the rest of the trading unit was packed tight as battery hens, golden eggs expected to drop out their arse every time they made a phone call.

Behind Peter, Thomas Matheson's glass-partitioned office looked out on them all, surveying their manoeuvrings while he permutated the markets and read every report he could get his hands on.

By eleven o'clock, Peter was feeling twitchy. The Euronext derivatives market was sluggish and some of Peter's positions had been meandering south for days. Some new client had been brought on board by one of the sales guys; a fund manager that had asked, by reputation, for Peter to personally execute his trades, which made Peter only too happy to oblige until he saw the strange nature of the positions. Still, almost every pussy tasted funny at first so he had measured the risk and bought the options. To hedge against the likely failure of said options, Peter had short sold a shit tonne of common stock in the hope that a downturn in the FTSE would balance his Profit & Loss. A political summit in the Middle East was key – plenty of traders expected it to have a positive impact on the market, but oil and gas was as volatile as, well, the fucking Middle East, so if the talks went well and the whole market bounced, he'd sell the futures contracts quicksmart and the new client would be happy; if the talks went badly and the market dropped, at least he'd temper the losses from the option withdrawal through the short. He'd borrowed the shares from a broker for a fee and sold them into the market. To make a profit he needed the market to fall so he could buy back the shares he'd borrowed for less than he'd sold them for. He'd then close the short with the broker and that was that. Short selling was frowned on more than ever after the 2008 crash when traders were driving down the price of even the banks themselves to line their own pockets, but if it was still a legitimate instrument for hedging then by fuck, Peter was going to keep doing it.

As it stood, the FTSE was up slightly, making his positions in both markets look less than impressive. At this rate his daily P&L report would be fucking toilet paper.

The other thing making him nervous was the three calls from Matt to his personal mobile. He'd ignored them of course; Matt never called to chat – he was likely in London and needed something. That was not a request that would be heard, never mind granted.

He was about to put in a call to one of his favoured dealers when his desk phone rang. He picked it up hoping for good news.

'Pete, it's me,' said a Glaswegian voice.

'What… is that you Matt?' It didn't sound like his brother. It sounded like the steam-rollered soon-to-be-corpse of his brother calling to say his goodbyes.

'It's me, yeah. It's… it's Nicky.'

'How the fuck did you get this number?'

'He's dead, Peter.'

'What? Who?'

'Nicky. He's dead. He's been killed.'

What the fuck was Matt on about? He didn't need this. Work was a place for work, not attention-seeking ballbaggery. 'Whatever game you're playing, pack it in,' he said. 'What do you want?'

'He got knocked down on his way to football practice.' Matt's voice was shaking. Was he for real? Peter didn't reply. He turned away from his screen, his eyes stopping on an under-watered plant in the corner.

'Pete?'

'I'm here.' Peter slid back in his chair. 'You're not at the wind up?'

'It's a school holiday. Police came to Mum's. We're at the hospital, but I don't know why. It was instant, apparently.'

Around Peter, everyone continued to perform, fluid and controlled; standing, sitting, shouting, typing – each of them locked in their own battle: whatever it took to win. Whatever it took.

Peter said he'd be in touch and placed the phone back on its cradle while Matt was mid-sentence. He barely knew the kid. He'd moved out soon after Nicky was born. The fact he had a half-brother seventeen years his junior had always embarrassed him. It was something his colleagues knew nothing of.

He heard his name being shouted, but ignored it. The voice was miles away.

'Peter, are you fucking deaf?'

It was louder now, practically in his ear. He wiped spit from his cheek and turned to face Matheson, the man who for the last thirty-odd years had diligently run AMJS with red-faced rage and a will that each member of staff had to match. He didn't do second chances. Somehow he looked ten years younger than he was, his suits as well cut as his aging body, skin tight and tanned, wavy hair still where it should be.

'Sorry, did I wake you? Get up and get in there.' Tom pointed towards his office.

Peter followed his boss. Had he heard Matt right? It felt as though the conversation hadn't even happened. Tom's office was too hot.

'Sit,' said Tom.

Peter stood, the pain forcing his left eye to close over.

'What the fuck is the matter with your eye?' The volume of Tom's voice was like a slap in the face.

Peter sharpened up. 'Nothing. Just a headache. What's going on?' He sat down as Tom leaned forward over his desk. His boss's musky aftershave crossed the divide. Tom's greying hair was swept in a side parting as neat as his shirt. His tie, navy to match his suit, swung from side to side as he animated his sentences. 'I just took a call on my mobile. My fucking personal mobile,' he said. 'Some joker calling himself Barton. Says he knows you?'

Hearing the name caused Peter to forget everything that had just happened. How had Barton got Tom's number, and more importantly, why the fuck had he phoned him?

'Well? Does he?'

'Yeah, I know him. Well, I know of him. He's a hedge fund

manager; we've never actually met.'

Barton was a ghost. Since hearing the name for the first time nearly two years ago, he had failed countless times to set up a meeting and yet Barton had become the only man in the City Peter answered to, other than Tom. Until last week.

'I ask him what he's on about, who the fuck he thinks he is, then he says the strangest thing. He tells me to wait five minutes and I'll find out, says 11.27 quite clearly, then hangs up.'

'Sounds like bullshit to me,' said Peter. 'A crank maybe?' His watch told him it was 11.24. He noticed he was shaking. *Don't say no to him,* Barton's dealer Cillian had warned Peter just days before. *You don't know what he's capable of.*

Peter brought the car to an abrupt halt, almost enjoying the pain of the seatbelt cutting into his chest. The doorman arrived before he had taken the key out the ignition.

'Is breakfast still being served?'

The doorman nodded. 'Until 10am, sir.'

Peter thanked him, pressed a fiver into his hand, and took the wide stone steps up to the hotel entrance. The marble floor of the lobby harked back to a time when things were done properly. Ornate lights hung high and red upholstered seating offered a resting place to watch guests come and go. Peter loved the detachment of hotels; they were like airports without the urgency. Everyone was a stranger. A blonde receptionist flashed a smile at him. Eight out of ten, easy. He gave her a nod and felt the tension begin to lift. He turned left and made his way down the red-carpeted stairs into the restaurant. It was half full of guests in various stages of breakfast.

Peter chose an empty table for four and placed an order for poached eggs and sausage. While he waited for his meal he drank two cups of mercifully drinkable coffee and scanned his emails. It was an unremarkable day so far. In the City, at least. No sign of the fallout yet. It had been five days since Barton called Tom, since the mayhem that followed. Peter felt like he was in a car with no brakes, waiting for the cliff to appear on the horizon. He shouldn't have lost control in the undertakers but Matt could bring out the worst in anyone. What sort of people was he caught up with? If Peter ever got hold of them he'd snap their fucking legs off and force-feed them their own bone marrow.

His meal arrived and he cut into a sausage before stabbing it repeatedly into the poached egg until it was smeared with yolk. He reminded himself Matt's problems were not his problems and nor would they become his problems.

'Peter?'

Just as he was raising his fork to his mouth, Helen's voice shrilled through the restaurant. He looked up and saw a smile cross her perfect face before fading just as quickly. At her side, the twins looked far less confused by their Dad's appearance than their Mother did.

5

I stare at the door long after Pete closes it. What a dick. I should have walked first. Typical. So fucking typical. 'I'll see you tomorrow morning.' Fuck does he think he is? So he gets to spend the whole day hanging out with his kids while I'm bursting my arse trying to pull together a sum of money he probably spunks on a pub lunch?

Behind me, McAllister clears his throat. 'Matthew, you have pressing issues to deal with, no?' His expression isn't too dissimilar to a rock.

I try to smile but suspect I look like I've just been kicked in the balls.

'You misled me.' He's back on his feet. 'This business has been in my family for seventy years, dammit.' He punches the desk. Looks sore. 'I will not allow you to ruin it. All you've done is lie to me, led me to believe that somehow my staff have been responsible for this, and become tangled in a brawl in my office. Enough is enough.'

He looks as though he's about to have a heart attack, but sadly all he does is lift his phone.

'We've been through this. You can't phone the police. We'll never see him again.'

He begins to dial.

'Look, these are not normal people. I know how they work. You get nothing if you phone. The only thing you'll be burying tomorrow is your business.'

The handset hovers, midway between half a chance and complete defeat.

'One of your staff must have let them in. Think about it. You're guilty by association.'

He just stares at me.

'My mum will never be able to say goodbye to her son.'

Nothing.

'Come on. I'm right and you know it.'

He slams the phone down, his face reddening. 'Get out.' He points at the door.

'Does that mean – '

'Out!'

His tone is one I've rarely heard since leaving school so I leave without another word. The phone is in its cradle. Positives, man, it's all about the positives.

The receptionist is looking at her screen, but there's no way she's working.

'Thanks for the coffee, Jenny,' I say. She smiles without actually smiling. I pause to catch my breath and realise I'm sweating.

'So are you one of the McAllister clan then?' I say.

'We're one big happy family,' she says, utterly straight-faced.

So she is a McAllister. Noted.

I'm gripped with an urge to sit down and explain to her how this happened, how it's not my fault, that if things had gone according to plan it would never have come to this, that the ten grand I originally borrowed from Bradley was going to set me up, that it still can. Still will. I want her to nod in agreement, tell me it'll all be okay.

'I'll see you another time,' I say. There's that non-smile again. She's mastered the art of being polite and judgmental with the briefest twitch of a jaw muscle. She's fucking gorgeous.

Outside, the rain's on and sure enough, Pete's car is away. Looks like no one stole his wheels then. I head towards the main road and light a fag. When this is over I'm going to chuck it again. Properly this time. Go and see the doctor and everything, get patches, gum, whatever. Clean mind and clean clothes. Then a new start. One day Scotland will be nothing more than a memory for me – a damp cloth of a country that seeps up all the pish around it and wrings it out on a compliant population who justify this by occasionally driving past a field and commenting on how fucking green it is. Give me a scorched desert any day. Vegas. That's where you'll find me, living in a wee apartment just off the strip. Shit like this wouldn't happen to me there. It'll be a woman a week, steaks for dinner and staking my fortune – which will begin arriving as soon as Turnbull turns up and our business

34

gets underway. The night's darkest before the dawn, so they say. Well the sun better be ready to show itself.

The bus stop is mercifully quiet. I eye up a slab of glistening meat in the butcher's window next to the stop. It's that deep shade of pink that can only be found on something that was once alive. Nicky's accident flits through my mind and I yak, my stomach tightening as it pushes vomit up my throat and out onto the pavement. I cough and it makes me sick again, and again. I notice chunks of sausage from earlier, smoothed round the sides from my body beginning to process them. Seeing them makes me retch in a horrific self-fulfilling prophecy that may end with my actual intestines on the pavement.

When I finally stand up the butcher is glaring at me from inside the shop. I take a draw of my fag to dilute the taste in my mouth and glare at some old woman who's eyeballing me as if I'm a tramp. How the fuck did I get here? Pete's a prick. Such a fucking prick. I doubt he sees his entire visit as anything other than an inconvenience. I wipe my mouth with my sleeve. I will not phone him. There's a solution somewhere in my head. I just need to get to the flat, to think. It will come to me.

Behind me, a kid in a white apron has appeared from the butchers and is pouring water on my sick. I start walking to the next bus stop, rain hitting me in the face at an almost impossible angle. At least the next stop has a shelter.

When I was wee, Mum would take me and Pete out to the shops with her on Saturday mornings for the weekend's food shopping. After church on Sundays, while we got changed out of our best gear and played with toy cars, she'd make soup, and a roast on the first Sunday of the month. The last Sunday dinner we had was the worst. Dad could barely stand to carve the meat. I was ten, Pete seven. We just thought he wasn't well, that he'd be fine after a few days in bed, like us when we had the cold. He'd told us it was a great cut of silverside, the best Mum had ever found, but he never ate any, just pushed it about his plate until Mum started crying. Then he forked a single chunk and she fled the room. I remember wondering why they were fighting because it was a really nice dinner. She never bought red meat after he died, not even when Craig moved in. It was always roast chicken. I forgot how good steak was until I moved out. I wonder if Nicky had ever even tried roast beef.

The bus is eleven minutes late and there's not even that much traffic. When it arrives I pay my fare and try not to look at anyone's face while finding a seat. It's a single decker, which limits my options. More problematic is the fact I'm not that far from Mum's and there's easily a chance some jobless balloon I went to school with is on the bus. They're bad enough at the best of times, but the news about Nicky will be all over the place. I see an empty seat about half way up on the left and sit against the window, clearing condensation with my jacket sleeve. As the bus thunders along I scan ahead of me. I've pulled the average passenger age down by about twenty years. There's a smell of dampness and thrush. This is why I don't get the bus.

'Matt, is that you?'

Shite. He's on the seat before I can even deny I'm me. I turn towards the owner of the voice. The face is bloated and the hairline pushed back but I knew it was Andy before he finished his sentence.

'You all right, Matt? I heard about Nicky. Tragedy, man. Utter tragedy. What you doing on the eighty-seven, mate? Some day for the rain, eh? Some day.'

I blink once for every question and tilt my head to see if he's quite finished.

'Aye, it's me, Andy. What's happening?'

'Just getting this stuff for my ma.' He holds up a blue poly bag. He's taking up about two-thirds of the shared space, his jogging bottoms soaked and cold against my jeans. Fat folk in tracksuits, defining irony since the mid eighties.

'I meant in a more general sense,' I say.

'Ah, okay. With you. With you. Not much, mate. Same old. So, see Nicky, have you – '

'You working?' I cut him off. Some old dear in front of us has heard the word Nicky and turned her head. I can sense some rusty cog clicking in her ancient brain. Nosy cow.

'No, I'm just getting these messages.'

'Not the now, Andy. I mean, do you have a job?'

He laughs, ignorant to his ignorance. Plaque cements the gaps between his teeth; his breath is sharp, bitter. 'Well, kind of. You know, bit of cash in hand for my dad's mate. He's got this car valeting service.'

'That's good Andy. Decent work that – folk are too lazy to wash their own cars these days. You'll have a busy time of it.' I feel something shuffle at my feet and only then notice that Andy is wearing a lead like a bracelet. 'Who's this little bugger?' I ask, reaching down to tickle the dog's ears. It's a wee black terrier mongrel thing; looks just like the dog Andy had when we were growing up. He called it Andy, which he never lived down. Every day in school he took pelters. He couldn't ever see why we thought it was funny.

'You're at it, aren't you?' he says. 'It's Wee Andy. Do you not recognise him?'

The thing has barely registered me.

'Fuck off,' I say, a bit too loud. The nosy woman turns her head again. There's no way that's the worst thing she's ever heard on the eighty-seven. Andy laughs and slaps my shoulder.

'Say hello, Andy. You remember Matt?' He lifts the wee shite up onto his lap. Sure enough, it's the oldest looking dog I've ever seen. Its eyes look weary. A life with Andy and my eyes would be the same.

'Are you taking the piss, Andy? How old is he? Dogs don't live that long.'

'He's eighteen and still going strong. Aren't you, pal? He kisses wee Andy's crown and ruffles his ears. The dog looks up and licks him. I remember why I used to be mates with Andy – he's like a dog himself, unflinchingly loyal, never aware enough of anything to take offence. Even now, ten years since I last saw him, he seems void of stress, happy to simply exist. Bumping into me will keep him going for days. Wee Andy licks my hand. I wonder if he remembers the night he stayed with me. We've got a bond, me and this mutt.

'You know, if it wasn't for me and your big pal here, you wouldn't have seen your first birthday,' I say to wee Andy. I figure the bus is going to take at least twenty minutes to get into town and I'd rather spend them with my head in the past. I can't believe the pair of them have been together for eighteen years.

It started at school, as most things did when you're thirteen. One lunchtime, Andy was distracted from a game of football by something in the field behind the baize pitch. Given he was in goals and Big James had stroked home into an empty net to give the fourth years a five-nil lead, we weren't that happy with Andy going walkabout. He was crouched over at the fence, looking like he was inspecting the grass on the other side.

While our team kicked off under duress from the fourth years, me and Sammy ran over to drag Andy back and saw he was tickling this tiny wee pup. It was black with wavy hair – like an inverted west highland terrier with a dose of something else in its DNA.

'It's a dog,' stated Andy, which earned him a dead arm from Sammy.

'So fuck if it's a dog – there's a game going on.'

'It's not got a collar,' said Andy, ignoring both the punch and the reprimand. 'If you find a dog with no collar you get to keep him, I heard.'

'How do you even know it's a him?' said Sammy. His hair was stuck to his forehead, wet with sweat.

'Because he looks like one.'

Sammy started to laugh. 'They all look the same, you absolute trumpet.'

'Fuck off, Sammy. It's been abandoned.'

'Aye, come on, Sammy. The wee thing's shivering,' I said, kneeling down. Sammy stopped laughing.

'I'm going to call it Andy,' said Andy, picking it up. Me and Sammy burst out laughing.

'You can't call a dog the same name as yours,' I said.

'I can call him whatever I want, he's mine now.'

'Aye, I'm sure your ma and da will let you,' said Sammy, between chuckles. 'Andy. Aha-ha! Andy's not even a dog's name.'

He became more resilient as we walked back to the pitch, Andy cradling the puppy like a baby. The game of football stopped. Everyone conspired to find a way for Andy to hide Wee Andy until home time.

My door went around seven o'clock that night. We'd finished dinner and Mum was watching telly. I was doing the washing up and Pete was in bed, most likely doing homework under torchlight, the total gimp that he was. Mum was beyond strict about bedtimes. She always reminded us that Dad said a minute less than we needed was never enough to function. That was why he had spent half his Saturday mornings in his pit, presumably.

Crafty bastard.

I jumped up to answer the door and Andy was standing there, his jacket half open and this wee black head popping out the side. His cheeks were red.

'You're not coming in here with that,' I whispered.

'I need your help.'

'Who is it?' shouted Mum.

'It's Andy,' I shouted back.

'Well tell him to get in or get off the doorstep. I can feel the draught from here.'

I beckoned him inside and hurried him up the stairs, closing my door behind us. He tipped the dog onto the floor and sat down on the bed. The dog started sniffing about my toys before it became distracted by the dirty school uniform rolled into a bundle that Mum hadn't picked up yet.

'They won't let me keep him.'

'We told you that, Andy. You were lucky the teachers never found him.'

We'd hidden him in the toilets and taken turns at pleading for a pee to make sure he was still there. Everyone accepted pretty quickly that Andy had dibs on him – but that was mainly because everyone else knew they'd get a doing for bringing a dog home.

'Dad slapped me a dillion when I showed them. He'd been down the pub.'

'What did your mum say?'

'They told me to take him up the moors.'

'What?' I was pacing while Andy leaned back against the wall, but this made me stop.

'That's where they think I am. They told me to let him loose up there and get back home.'

The moors were a good forty-minute walk away so it would be dark well before he'd get home. I didn't blame him for not going, but I don't know what he expected me to do.

'You're always good at coming up with plans,' he said. 'How can I make them let me keep him?'

I lifted the wee thing up and held him close to my face. He licked my nose and I started laughing.

'You really can't call him Andy.'

'He answers to it now, I can't change it.'

I knew this was rubbish but when a mate's lost you don't spin him round until he's dizzy. I let the name slide and sat down with the pup. I teased it with a shirt from the washing pile until it grabbed a sleeve in its mouth. Andy had kicked his shoes off and was lying back on the bed. The puppy yelped a little when I pulled the sleeve and I shushed him. I imagined he was my dog and how long he could stay hidden, how I could make Mum want him too. I watched the plan as it came together – it was like fragments, these unidentifiable shapes floating through this vacant space in my head, bumping off the sides until finally coming together and revealing their form.

'Here's what we're going to do.' Andy sat up in a shot. 'You're going to hang about here until Mum chucks you out – which will be in about half an hour. Go up the road on your own, leave Wee Andy here. I'll keep him tonight.'

'How will you keep him quiet?'

'I'll worry about that. You just get home, make sure your trainers are muddy. Trample them through the hall. Your mum will put them out the back garden – that's important. Make sure she does that. You'll get a slap but they'll believe you were at the moors. Act all upset, be in the huff with them. Whatever you do, you need to convince them you ditched him. What time do you have breakfast at?'

'Dunno,' he said.

'Think. I need to know.'

'I dunno. I leave for school at twenty to nine.' He stares at the ceiling, 'so twenty past eight.'

'Right. At quarter past eight I'm going to sneak round to yours and I'll leave the dog in the garden. When you go down for breakfast, look out the window, but don't say anything. Let your mum see him first. Here's the important thing – don't believe her. She'll be raging at you, calling you a liar, but ask her why she's winding you up. Tell her she was out the back with your trainers the night before and he wasn't there then, was he? When she starts doubting herself, that's when you go out and grab him, bring him in and say you can't believe he made his way back. She won't believe it either but pass him over to her. She'll be sold in seconds, and with her on side, your old man will crumble.'

'I don't understand.'

'You don't need to. Can you remember all that though?'

'I think so.'

'You better.'

I dropped Wee Andy on Andy's lap. 'You want to train him to fetch until Mum chucks you out?'

I can't believe the dog is fucking eighteen. It must be the oldest dog in the world. There's a lot of sense in that saying, it's a dog's life. I've dealt with more crap in the past hour than Wee Andy has had to put up with in his entire life. All he's ever had to worry about is why his dinner's not in front of him.

'You think he knows who I am?' I'm stroking the thing now, desperate to just make myself happy. Nicky loved dogs. He always wanted one. Mum would have killed me, but I should have got him one. One like Wee Andy, that wouldn't have needed too much walking. It would have gone with him to football training, maybe he wouldn't have

'Course he remembers you, look at him,' says Andy.

I used to be close to Andy, we had our first drink together, we dreamt of who we'd shag and what we'd do with our lives. I tended to be the one that did most of the talking right enough. We drifted before I even started university – there's this age around fifteen or sixteen where you begin to see the potential in the world and gauge how much you can lock into it. I could see for miles, still can. There's something to be said for being blindfolded to the world beyond your postcode. Andy will almost certainly sleep easier than me tonight. Contentment isn't an easy thing to measure.

'Where are you heading?' he says.

'Fucked if I know, Andy,' I say. 'Better to ask me that tomorrow.'

'But I'll not see you tomorrow.' He looks confused.

The underground station is coming up. 'My stop, mate,' I say.

He stands up and drags Wee Andy out of the way to clear a path for me.

'It was good seeing you, Andy.'

'We should have a pint, soon, eh?' he says.

Fuck that, I think. 'Definitely. Talk about the good old days. I'll be in touch,' I say and walk towards the door before he gives me his phone number.

When I step onto the pavement I'm dazed, nauseous and want to punch someone, but the journey has given me clarity: if I'm going to get through this I need Woody onside. It's him I've to call when I've got the money. Bradley trusts Woody, that's why he leaves him to look after things. There's no doubt he's the one that got hold of the coffin, or at least directed proceedings. That means he knows where it is. I need to play on his conscience. *With the right words, you can make your message clear enough to convince anyone.* Turnbull told me that we already know the words that will help us, that they're in our basic vocabulary. The key is to put the right words in the right order. Since Turnbull came into my life, finding order has been easier – it's not just about words, it's about the way he approaches the world, the way he helps me see potential in place of problems. *Every problem offers future fulfillment*, he says.

You, Yes You. That's the title of his first book – the one I bought and he signed after a lecture he gave in Glasgow. There's a picture of him on the cover, pointing out at the reader. Everything in the book made sense. It made me see what a negative person I'd become and how I could control my future by refocusing my mind.

Over two years later and he's my closest ally, my confidant and business partner. Saying that, for someone so keen to promote the mutual benefits of our business, he's been awful fucking quiet of late.

The phone rings out, his warm voice almost pleading with me to leave a message.

'Phillip, it's Matt Fletcher. Something's come up and I really need to speak to you. I'm not sure if you got my message about Nicky, my wee brother, but… look, I'll explain the details when we speak. Just give me a call.'

I walk down into the underground station and try to straighten my posture. For the first time today I've got options. One of them needs to come good for me because sure as fuck there's no one else to turn to.

6

Peter watched the girls break free from Helen's grasp and run towards him, their cries of *Daddy, Daddy* turning the heads of curious breakfasters. Both were wearing tan-coloured dresses and white tights. Jess was in a grey cardigan and Sam a white one. Helen always tried to ensure their outfits were at least a little different – unlike every other set of twins in the world, as she constantly reminded him.

As the girls closed in on him, he glanced down at the egg-soaked sausage on his fork, and rammed it into his mouth, savouring its warmth and flavour.

'Dad's eating, girls. Don't jump,' he said, as they clattered into him.

'Don't talk with your mouth full, Daddy,' said Sam.

'That's rude,' said Jess.

'But how can I tell you how much I love you if I can't talk?' said Peter, showing them the mushed food on his tongue.

'Peter, please.' Helen hadn't taken a seat.

Peter swallowed. 'I assumed you'd be getting these little monsters ready.' He ruffled their heads. 'I was just going to shovel this up and come get you.'

'What are you doing back here?'

'Long story.'

'Does it involve Matt?'

'Beginning, middle and end.'

Helen shook her head. 'What's he done?'

'Just sit down, will you. You too girls.' Peter began to cut his sausage.

'Can I have some, Daddy?' said Sam.

'Me too, can I have some?' followed Jess.

Peter looked at his wife and smiled.

She softened and took a seat opposite him. 'Girls, you'll be able to get breakfast soon. Cereal and fruit, thank you.'

43

The girls sighed and sat down.

'Is everything okay? Is your head sore?' said Helen. She was wearing black jeans and brown boots with a thick black cardigan. Her hair hung loose, just below her chin. It was gleaming with whatever product she'd run through it, not something she generally did on a weekday morning.

'You're going to knock this city for six,' said Peter.

She took his hand. 'Are you going to tell me what happened?'

Not a fucking chance. 'I need to nip to the loo, I'll explain when I get back. Order me a fresh plate and we can eat together.'

He stood and placed his hand on her shoulder. She gripped it, though he could see the puzzled look on her face.

'Are there any painkillers in the room?'

'Why didn't you just… In my bag, there's some different ones. Take whatever you need.' She smiled again. 'And, talk to me, okay?'

He kissed her forehead. It tasted of moisturiser and foundation.

In the lift he began scrolling through his emails, hunting for any sign of unrest. He was still looking when he entered the room.

It was a riot. Helen had always had an incredible ability to make a hotel room look as though it had been burgled. Clothes were strewn across the unmade bed. The curtains were half open, and the steam in the bathroom hadn't yet evaporated. Four pairs of children's trainers lay at his feet, almost tripping him as he made his way to the window. Why did the kids each have two spare pairs of trainers? They were only there for three days, one of which would require formal shoes. A future of teenage demands and abandoned treats flashed before him. They'd agreed the girls would never be spoiled. They would appreciate the fortuitous world into which they'd come to exist, where they would work not to survive, but to pursue success in whichever field they fancied. Or at least, that was the plan.

He fully opened the curtains and looked out at his home city. He could barely see the clouds for the rain. The hotel overlooked a green square surrounded by townhouses that were home to scores of small businesses, their logos plastered on every window: solicitors, surveyors, engineers, PR firms. It was hardly London. He'd always heard good things about what Glasgow had become, but he was a stranger in the city. Having left for Exeter at eighteen with a bag full of promise and ambition, he'd never got to know the place. He never would.

Within a minute he'd unearthed two handbags, but found no painkillers. It was like there was a needle on the inside of his head, pushing its way out through his eye socket. He lay back on the bed, his feet dangling off the edge. In the corner of the ceiling a web had been missed by the cleaners. Some small thing was in the midst of a slow, crushing death. The spider was nowhere to be seen. It had no thought for the torturous death of its breakfast. No conscious thought meant no moral responsibility, a freedom that, ironically, animals were incapable of appreciating. Peter's phone rang. It was Stuey.

'What's happening, buddy?' said Peter, sitting up.

'Shotgun, how's Glasgow?'

'Wet.'

'Well, you're about to join it. Tom's been raided.'

Air left Peter's lungs as if they'd been punctured. Fuck.

'Did that register?' said Stuey.

'Affirmative, mate. What the fuck?'

'No idea. Compliance appeared half an hour ago. They're still fucking in there.'

'Where's Tom?'

'He's not been in.'

In the silence, Peter couldn't hear the hiss of a headset. Stuey must have left his desk to make the call. That made it more of a warning than an observation. Did Stuey know anything about Barton? No, that wasn't possible, but still, the fucker couldn't be trusted.

'I'll try Tom, okay?' said Peter. 'I'll let you know if I get hold of him.'

'Is there something I need to know?'

'I got to go, Stuey – family shit, you know?'

'Peace, bro. Best to them.'

Peter stared at his phone. The homescreen wallpaper was a picture of the twins in Tuscany, smiling in the garden of the villa Peter had bought last year on the back of his deals with Barton. If compliance had found their way to Tom that meant they were tracing a path from last week's catastrophe and Barton had made sure the red button was sitting square on Peter's desk.

When the kids were afraid of something, Peter told them to picture a scene where everything had worked out and they were telling the story of what had happened. He made them describe it until they'd forgotten what had scared them. If they could defeat their fear, he said, they would be stronger than anyone. As he waited for the lift, he tried to focus on his life continuing as it was, but it wasn't something he could rationally imagine. The only way to save himself was to find Barton.

After breakfast, Peter quickly shepherded everyone into the car and headed for his mum's for the second time that morning, feeling as if the dimension and not just time had shifted. Just two hours earlier Matt had yet to invade his day and Stuey hadn't rolled a grenade under his feet.

He'd sucked up Stuey's news and returned downstairs, ignoring any thoughts as to the whereabouts of Matt. In the end breakfast had felt normal, as if they were on holiday, in another hotel in a dryer, hotter country. He'd explained to Helen that Matt had dragged him to a meeting with the undertaker and he hadn't seen his mum yet, which in essence, was true. Presumably she put his distance down to the whole Nicky thing.

As they drove, the twins gazed out the window into the rain as Peter humoured their endless questions on the city. They did this every time they were in Glasgow. Now four and a half, they were old enough to feel a connection. Peter may have had no love for the place but the more Helen ran down the city her husband had escaped from, the more he felt compelled to defend it, to highlight its successes, himself included. He wanted his children to know their past, how their genes had made it this far. He remembered the time Sam said she wanted to live in Glasgow when she was bigger. Jess had loved this idea and the pair of them got excited about buying a house just round the corner from their Gran Fletcher. Helen quickly used the weather as a weapon to extinguish the plan, which Peter thought unfair, even though the city kept giving her ammunition.

'Look, it's raining, girls. Remember what I told you, your dad didn't know what sunshine was until he met me,' she said, winking at Peter.

The twins giggled. 'Does it ever stop, Dad?'

At the traffic lights, heavy blobs beat off the roof and reminded him of wakening in a tent.

'Remember the time we went camping in the Highlands, and all the hills were really bright green, and there were loads of mountains and stuff?'

'Yeah,' said the girls.

'If it wasn't for the rain, it wouldn't be nearly as beautiful. You know how your mum always tells you to drink enough water because it makes you healthy and your skin shine?'

'Yeah.'

'Well, Scotland's the same. It's pretty because it gets so much rain.' He winked back at his wife. The camping trip had been a disaster, Peter's inability to put the tent up properly leading to a soggy awakening on their first morning and a subsequent two-night stay at the nearest spa hotel.

'Girls, you must remember that this isn't a normal trip to Gran Fletcher's,' said Helen. 'She's going to be very upset, so you must be quiet and respectful.'

'She doesn't need them sitting there on their best behavior. A bit of a distraction will do her the world of good.'

'Will Uncle Matt be there?' asked Jess.

'I bloody hope not,' muttered Helen, loud enough for just Peter to hear.

He wondered where Matt had gone when he left the undertakers. With Matt, it was generally better to know exactly what he was doing – a bit like keeping a dog on its lead at the beach. How does someone with no money attempt to raise twenty grand in a working day? Presumably by dicking about for hours then admitting defeat and asking your brother.

There was a time when twenty thousand seemed like a fortune. When he was at university twenty was the number he'd had in his head for a starting salary. In the end Tom made him an offer of almost double that.

When he discovered the world of derivatives in his second year at Exeter, Peter knew how he would make his fortune. He learned about futures – how you could agree to buy specific quantities of commodities or assets at a future date for a specific amount and then make your money by hedging whether or not the value of the contract would go up or down. He became obsessed with how this market worked, consuming economics theory alongside biographies of bankers who'd been celebrated and shamed. He devoured the subject; its history, how it worked, how it could be manipulated and sculpted. So, when he convinced his senior lecturer over an otherwise laborious dinner party a year later that his career lay in trading and not accountancy, Dr. Hamilton agreed to put him in touch with a former colleague who ran a small private investment bank.

The following week, in a slick, contemporary office high in one of The City's new skyline-defining towers, where modern art adorned the walls and black screens with cascading numbers dominated every desk, Peter met Thomas Matheson and was immediately drawn to the man's appetite for, well, pretty much everything. Upper-middle class, skin colour that was more Mediterranean than metropolitan and in great shape for his age, Matheson had a proud head of wavy hair and handmade shoes that looked more expensive than Peter's car. He told Peter that his glowing reference had been impressive, but that references made not one cuntflap of a difference on the trading floor.

Peter nodded sharply, taken aback by such blunt language from the sort of accent he usually only heard on the BBC. He concentrated on what he knew, explaining that when he began to pull away from his maths classmates in second year at school he realised he was gifted. By the time he was fifteen he saw that this gift was one that could guarantee wealth far beyond the station he'd been told he belonged to. He knew that when people spoke of investment banks that they were quick to reference the 80s boom that resulted from the Reagan/Thatcher deregulation of the industry, but to him it was about much more than just getting rich. It represented the very genesis of trading beyond mere trade – supply and demand taken to another, more prosperous level. He spoke of the Greeks, how fucking Aristotle himself had written the story of Thales, a man who could predict olive harvests and who bought future stocks at a low price because farmers were willing to hedge against the possibility of a bad crop. He told how he fell in love with the idea of predicting the value of commodities, currencies, share indexes themselves. For as long as it took Tom to drink an entire coffee, Peter reamed off a polemic on the power of the markets and why they were the key to global finance.

When he finally stopped, Tom told him he could write a book on investment banking. 'With respect, sir,' Peter had replied, 'after ten years working for you, I don't believe either of us will have to consider working again, never mind slogging over a book.'

Tom had laughed his cheeks red and shaken Peter's hand. 'This is the nuclear reactor of banking, son,' he'd said. 'It has the ability to fuel the world's economy cleanly and efficiently, but in the wrong hands it could be the most destructive force in the country. We run a clean plant here. We create energy, not bombs. You remember that, and yes, I think in ten years you might be doing okay.'

Peter graduated in 2006, two years before the sub-prime bubble burst with such an explosion that the cracks in the system widened enough for Lehman Brothers to fall right into while plenty others were left clinging to the edge, Governments themselves reaching down to grab outstretched arms. Everything felt exposed, every decision subject to hindsight and head shaking.

Since then the rules had changed. The City was more conservative, risks more considered and capital less abundant. It could still be manipulated though, and over the last couple of years Barton had shown Peter just how much.

The morning of Barton's 11.24 phone call, Peter left Tom's office determined to sort it out with Barton's dealer. Hedge fund managers rarely spoke to traders directly so whatever Barton's notion, he instructed Cillian, who would pass requests on to Peter, who then bought or sold contracts as required. Of course, Peter didn't just await commands. He'd put ideas Cillian's way too, and even though Barton never followed Peter's advice, he'd made plenty of other investors considerably wealthier. Peter's foresight was down to his ability to read the markets quickly, with a mathematician's mind, to interpret and predict trends, to pay attention to the analysts he trusted, all washed down with a syrupy dose of good fortune. At the morning meetings before the market opened Peter would gather all evidence and instinct and tell the sales guys what to push to their clients. That morning he'd been shouting about options in copper, based on a report one of the analysts had been particularly excited about. Nothing had come of it yet though and he made a note to explore things after this mess was fixed.

Cillian picked up just as the clock turned 11.27. He curtly reminded Peter that he worked for Barton and not with him and therefore knew nothing of what the man did. Nothing else happened, there was no mayhem, no earthquake.

He was about to end the call when Stuey jumped to his feet. 'What the fuck is going on?'

'Holy shit,' followed Kim.

In an instant, Peter watched the entire floor rise to their feet. He'd witnessed moments of chaos before, but not on this scale. The numbers on his screen were turning red with abandon. This was more than a glitch. Every share price was plummeting at an unprecedented rate. By the time he'd got to his own feet the FTSE had dropped by just under ten percent – £150 billion wiped off its value in under a minute. Everyone was scanning the floor for an answer. Seconds later Tom came running out his office as if being chased by a bear. 'Get fucking moving, people, NOW!' Peter saw his boss glaring at him, head shaking. 'I mean fucking now! Someone tell me what the fuck is going on!'

The floor became louder than it had been all day as traders grabbed their phones; this was the buzz Peter usually craved. He could feel the entire floor exhale, the sound almost operatic.

'You have fun out there.' said Cillian, his Irish accent halfway to gleeful. Peter dropped the handset and focused on the numbers tumbling down his screen. Fun? Fucking hell, this was all the fun of the funfair. *Who likes short shorts,* sang Peter under his breath as he punched in the number of one of his brokers. With the scale of everyone else's panic, he was able to buy his short stock back for a fraction of what he'd paid. The broker had flapped like a three-winged goose, but Peter repeated his instruction, slowly, firmly. He was off the phone in thirty seconds. It was perfect. A beautiful thing. Helter fucking skelter.

'The Prime Minister's been stabbed,' shouted a voice. 'He's dead.'

Heads turned to the man; Peter didn't know him, some ass pirate from sales.

'Source?' said Al.

'Looks like Reuters. Twitter's gone berserk,' said Kim.

Once again the floor fell silent. As they took in the news, Peter's thoughts were elsewhere. Some helter skelter. It was 11.28.

When major news broke the markets wobbled but not like this, not this quickly, not this deeply. This was the fucking Mariana Trench of dives. This was the work of the algos. Why did he... fuck. The computerised algorithms that did much of the City's trading automatically were programmed to monitor news sites. They were locked into placing orders based on the traffic created by newswires. They didn't panic; they just did what they'd been programmed to do.

'It's a hoax,' shouted Tom. He was patrolling the floor, a mobile phone at each ear. 'Everyone calm the fuck down and let the market bounce back.'

No one calmed down. Instead, confirmation that no one had in fact brought an end to the Prime Minster seemed to galvanise the floor. They returned to making calls, trying to work an angle, minimise their losses. The volume grew. The voices seemed to coalesce into the rumble of machinery. Peter sat motionless, a statue in a room of robots.

Have fun? Shit. He walked away from his desk, from the noise, tried to calculate his profit, too many numbers, too little room. He shook his head, looked outside at the people below, walking, thinking, unaware. They weren't living in the same world.

He sat back down and watched numbers, breathed with them.

Ten minutes later, as Tom predicted, the market had indeed bounced back to just below where it had been; losses were bad, but containable. News quickly spread that the flash crash had been caused by someone hacking Reuters' Twitter account and announcing that the PM had been assassinated.

It was fine. Fine. It would be fine. Others would have shorted, others would have made the call he made. He knew as much as anyone else and Cillian's advice to have fun could not be interpreted as anything else than a friendly send off.

Tom was addressing the floor with both barrels. 'Some whizz-kid in his bedroom with no fucking idea of the chaos he was creating. This has caused more problems than the fucking AIDS monkey. The algos just went crazy...' He stopped, looked around and swept his hair back with both hands. 'I've never seen anything like that.' He was standing over Peter's desk, a hundred people crammed into earshot. 'This is the problem with these systems, we make them quicker and quicker, microseconds, nanoseconds. How can we control what we can't fucking see? The whole market is in their hands and when they fail it's a cunting catastrophe.'

If Peter had bothered eating lunch he suspected it may have made a bigger comeback than Christ at Easter.

'They wouldn't cause that though,' said Stuey. 'Not on that scale.'

'You bet your fucking life they would, you pubescent little shitstick. You just saw it happen. The algos are too volatile. I've said it since day one. And today was nothing. Worse will come. Mark my words. It'll fucking end us all. Right, back to it.' He walked off towards his office, head still shaking. 'Peter, a word,' he added.

For the second time that morning, Peter found himself trailing after his boss. In the moment he executed the trade he had no idea what was happening. It was instinct. He tried again to do the sums – his brain was numb, but they came to him this time. They were big numbers, the sort that compliance red-flagged when something so unprecedented happened. Trade patterns were checked, phone records, the contents of his bin, of his fucking bowels. The repercussions were career-ending. Fuck, they were family-ending. Would Helen wait around for the two years he could spend in jail if he was charged with insider trading on this scale?

He slumped into a chair, his entire body shaking. There was no question that Barton was the mystery new client. When someone asked for a trader personally, it was better to do some background than knock one out in the toilet in celebration of how fucking great you were. He could never prove it was coincidence. He'd been hedging against contracts that he could now see were never meant to move the right way. He was exactly where Barton wanted him to be.

'11.27 that tweet was sent, Peter. That was no kid in his bedroom. Just who the fuck is this Barton character?'

Peter replayed events for the thousandth time as he took the final few turns though the estate he had grown up in. Cillian was the only person who could vouch for him, but there was as much chance of Barton coming forward himself.

'We're here,' he announced and parked in the spot he'd vacated just two hours earlier. With the rain relentless, they made a run for it, huddling in the porch while his mum made her way to the door.

'Grandma, Grandma,' said the girls when the door opened, each hugging a leg.

'Hello my beauties,' said Betty, hugging them both. 'And Helen, hello.' She leaned forward and slapped her wet lips on Helen's cheek, while Helen's pursed lips kissed the air. Peter smiled.

'Hi Betty. I'm so sorry,' said Helen, stepping into the hall and placing a hand on Betty's arm.

'Hiya, Mum. How are you?'

'Come in, come in,' she said. 'Where's your brother?'

He's out trying to find twenty grand so the racketeer he's in debt to will give him back your son. 'No idea, Mum. He said he had something to take care of.'

'He's always taking care of something other than himself,' said Betty. 'Siobhan's split up with him again. One of these times it'll be for good. I've told him as much, but that's…' Betty trailed off and walked towards the kitchen. 'I'll get the kettle on. Helen, I've got some of that peppermint tea for you. Will that do?'

'Just water is okay, Betty,' said Helen, hanging her jacket on the coat stand. Peter prodded her in the side. 'Actually, I will have a cup, thanks. That would be perfect.'

The girls spun out of their coats and ran off after their gran.

'She looks fucking awful,' said Peter.

'Have you booked a restaurant for tonight? We should get her out of here for a while.'

'Let's see how she's doing first, yeah?'

Peter led Helen into the kitchen. Betty was standing at the sink, facing the garden, ignoring the girls.

'Come on, girls,' said Helen. 'Your dad's going to help Gran Fletcher get drinks,'

'But I want to help,' said Jess.

Peter lifted her up and she wrapped her arms around his neck. 'You're on holiday, young lady. That means you get looked after, so why don't you go and get a seat next door and we'll be in soon.'

'I want to make tea.'

Peter kissed her cheek. 'You can help make lunch.'

As Helen ushered the girls out the way, Peter joined Betty at the sink, looking out at the garden he'd had a nostalgic compulsion to visit just a couple of hours earlier. Matt had been standing there as still as a clothes' pole. If only Peter had waited at the front door.

'Some day, eh?' And people thought he didn't make bad decisions. It was all he'd done of late. 'Mum?'

'Tea, yes. Sorry, son. Can you get the kettle and I'll get the bags?'

'I want to know how you're doing.'

Her eyes looked as if they were still looking at last week's world. 'I can't even think, Peter. The days are all just one long blur. I'd rather just get on with making tea.'

'I'm sorry about breakfast,' he said. The dishes were drying on the draining board, the food likely warming the bin.

'Not at all, it's a long drive. They'll have been tired.'

Peter filled the kettle and switched it on. The new kitchen he'd treated her to last year made the room feel as if it was in another house. He'd spent countless hours there, eating family dinners, then after Craig moved in, grabbing his plate and heading for his room. All memory of his dad had been erased from the house by then – it was no wonder he rarely spoke of him, he hadn't been allowed to. He wondered if Craig would be at the funeral, if he had even heard. If he did show his face… well, that was a problem for later.

'Nicky looked up to you, Peter. I always told him if he worked hard enough he could be just like you, with a big house and a busy life.'

'It's just a life, Mum,' said Peter. 'I'm sorry. I just mean – '

'Don't pussyfoot about. You're in your own home. I wish you wouldn't treat it like it was made of eggshells. I know what you meant. Now, what will the girls drink. Wee drop of lemonade? Nicky always liked....' She seemed incapable of finishing half her sentences.

'I know he did. Bit early for that though. Have you not got any fresh orange or anything?' He felt his phone vibrate in his pocket. Stuey? 'I'm sorry. I need to take this call,' he said, lifting it out.

His mum shooed him away. 'It never stops with you does it?'

Peter noticed she hadn't taken the tea bags out the cupboard. He glanced at the phone. It was Stuey. He stared at the name until it stopped ringing.

'Come on, let's get some tea made,' he said.

7

The flat's a fucking riot. Being back at Mum's the last week has just reminded me how good it would be to have a cleaner. Even in her darkest moments she's managed to pick up plates of crumbs. She'd have a fucking fit if she ever saw this place. Stiff washing covers every radiator and newspapers are scattered as if the living room is the bottom of a budgie's cage. I can't even remember going through the papers – what was I looking for? The 'Queen of Fucking Everything' mug that I bought Siobhan but she included in my boxes is sitting on the table. I'd just made coffee when Mum phoned. I remember that much. It seems like so much further in the past. Mould is beginning to grow in the mug. It can wait. I need to get back to Mum's. I need to make things happen.

Pete was right about McAllister; he failed in his single duty and he needs to take his share of the blame for this shambles. He deals in managing the most tragic aspect of human existence. That carries with it a fuck load of responsibility and it is not something he can just call theft, as if he's the victim. Old fucker. Nicky should never have been left alone overnight. He's just a kid. He's the victim here, along with me and Mum and even Pete. And I'm the one who's spending the entire fucking day trying to fix McAllister's mistake? Well, if he wants his bill settled he can stare up my arse until I start shiteing fivers.

The place is cold and utterly empty. It's felt terminally ill since the day I moved in. I hung pictures on the wall but they're like flowers at the bedside of the dying. What did I say to Siobhan last night? I need to get hold of her, make her see sense. I look at my watch and pour a whisky anyway. It's a bottle of 15 year-old Glenlivet that Siobhan's dad got me last Christmas. I even opened it on the night to give him a nip. He wasn't fucking shy in taking it either. She needs to know how much I miss her. She'll answer. It's the funeral tomorrow.

Sure enough, she picks up after three rings.

'What is it, Matt?'

I consider telling her everything. 'I'm sorry about phoning last night.'

'I'm at work.'

She'll be sitting there, that rocket Emma across from her, earwigging. I wonder what Siobhan's wearing, both on top and underneath.

'I know, I'm just saying, I shouldn't have called you at that time of night.'

'You shouldn't be calling me, full stop.'

She's breaking up a bit, must be on the move, away from Emma. Good. 'Look,' I say. 'I want to talk to you tomorrow after – '

'You're pathetic.'

'What, I'm – '

'Do not interrupt me, Matt. I will be there tomorrow for Betty, she needs all the support she can get. But what I will not do is listen to whatever it is you're currently planning on saying to me. I'm not going to pretend I know what you're going through, but you can't use the situation to – '

'Fuck you for thinking I would do that. That's not on.' I slam the arm of the couch, as angry at my reaction as I am at her suggestion.

'I'll see you tomorrow.'

'Look, I'm sorry, I didn't mean to – '

'I'm at work, Matt.'

She hangs up. That's three phone calls today, not counting the voicemail to Turnbull. I've still got Woody to get hold of but I feel like setting my phone on fire.

I stare out the window. Second floor tenement, twenty odd feet from the ground, and the only thing in sight is other tenement windows, all cast under this grey sky that's so dark it feels like perpetual twilight.

I refill my glass with about an inch of whisky and turn on the stereo, pulling a Stone Roses CD from the rack next to the fireplace and skipping ahead to track nine. If me and Siobhan ever get married, *This is the One* will be our first song. The first time I ever saw her it was playing. Upstairs in The Garage was

ɔtty little enclave of sweaty indie dancing and for a
was fucking amazing. I was twenty-one, still clinging
.y youth, back home after six months in Barcelona and
.er two in Paris. Everything was possible – especially after
a . .w beers with the boys – and that night I was just made for
dancing. Everything felt right. Okay, it could be that the huge
cumulus cloud of nostalgia has distorted reality, but I swear when
that song started up I saw her face on the first note. She was
blonde, her hair cut short and sharp, perfectly framing her smile.
She had straight teeth and a pair of Converse on and was holding
a glass of something clear above her head while she danced. That
was more than enough for me. By the time the chorus kicked in
we were singing to each other, being squashed together and
pulled apart at the crowd's want. Arms flailed, drinks spilled and
whenever she passed under a light, I felt as though I was being
punched in the stomach. I never spoke to my mates for the rest
of the night. I texted her from the taxi, told her our first date
would be spectacular.

I know all the words that will bring her back, I just need to put
them in the right order and get them out at the right time.

I'm fucked if I'm going to be sitting here this time next year
planning the next plan. I'm going to harness everything that was
amazing about Nicky and make it work for me. He will inspire
me and I will make life better for everyone, make Siobhan happy,
and Mum. I've got it within me. All I've ever needed was a bit of
fortune, and Turnbull has shown me where to find it.

Today is a setback. *Setbacks are challenges. Challenges are
opportunities. Opportunities are open doors.* I close my eyes and hold
my breath, like Turnbull taught me. I hold it until I can feel my
heart beat heavier. My shoulders are straight and body in
alignment. While my body is starved of oxygen I think of what
is going to happen next; how I'm going to get Bradley to see
reason; how Woody will return the coffin to McAllister; how
we'll do right by Nicky tomorrow and the room will cry and I
will hold Mum and let her let everything out, before we dig into
steak pies and eulogise on the impact Nicky had on us all; how
I'll tell Siobhan that the fog is lifting and all I can see is her and
me in a house in Australia or America or some fucking place,
making money and giving our own kids a better life than we had;

how we'll plant a tree for Nicky in his school's playground.

I exhale, controlled, through pursed lips, opening my eyes and seeing the shapes that filled the gloom sweep away as the light returns.

I need to stay this relaxed until the plan comes to me so I flip open the laptop and head for Facebook. In the search bar I type 'Jenny McAllister Glasgow'. Bingo. She's there – a proper smile on her face too. I click on photos. No holiday snaps but there's a load of nights out. I begin to flick through them, hoping they'll do the business. I begin to squeeze my cock through my jeans, just to waken it up a bit. As I focus on a particularly sexy pic of Jenny where her ruby lips are blowing a kiss at the camera, my cock begins to squeeze back. Just a five-minute distraction before I get on the move. A wee bit of Matt time. There we go; that's the stuff. I put the laptop on the arm of the couch and begin to undo my belt, but there's a scratching sound at the door that's distracting me. If it's the postman, why doesn't he just post the fucking letters and be done with it.

I close the laptop, quietly make my way to the hall and look through the peephole. I take a step back in fright when I'm met with the top of a shaved head bent over my lock. The footsteps squeak and when I look back my visitor has straightened up and has their ear turned towards the door. It's fucking Woody. I hold my breath and keep perfectly still despite my heart's best efforts to give the game away. Saves me a phone call I suppose, but there's more to worry about here than my monthly minute allowance. It looks as if he's trying to break in for a start. Like they've not stolen enough from me for today. After a few seconds he returns to whatever he was doing to the lock.

There's a console table next to me but the only thing that's going to give him a fright is the ashtray that I empty my loose change into. If I lift it he'll hear the change rattle and so I go for the quieter option, a paperback copy of A Tale of Two Cities that I've not started reading yet. It's thick enough to do some damage. I hold it aloft and wait. And wait.

Woody is footering about with some sort of pick, which occasionally pokes its way through onto my side. I feel like grabbing the thing and yanking it through. It scratches, slips, scratches, slips. Man, I want to just opening the fucking door, but I need the element of surprise. I can hear his breathing while I hold mine tight in my chest. He scratches, there's no slip this time and I hear the lock click.

As he opens the door I take a step back, ready to lunge, screaming head first into revenge. He looks up in surprise and I throw the book at him. It sort of bounces off his forehead and flops to the floor. Why the fuck did I throw it? At least it took him by surprise. I run at him and push him up against the wall – realising that it's still morning and I'm in my second fight of the day. He easily overpowers me and when he pushes back, I see him lift the ashtray. Change flies everywhere as he swings it. I manage to block it with my elbow, which fucking screams out in pain. It feels as if the bone has shattered. Then I see blood. I swing a punch at Woody and he ducks, coming back up with a blow to my belly that winds me and knocks me back against the wall and he's getting the better of me, until I glance down and see that the blood is coming from his hand and not my arm. I ram my head into his chest, Pete style, and run until he clatters into the front door, slamming it shut. He grimaces, but not as much as he does when I grab his hand.

'Fucking hell, Matt!' he shrieks. 'Don't fucking hold a guy's hand when you're fighting him.' He breaks free and pushes me away, but doesn't come again. He stands leaning against the door, holding his hand up to inspect it. 'Jesus, fuck.'

The cut doesn't look too bad – it runs for about an inch down from the side of his pinkie. The blood's trickling, not gushing.

'Don't fucking break into people's houses then,' I say.

He glares but doesn't respond. This is all a bit shite. I don't mind Woody. He's a decent guy. He likes his music and his cars. Beyond that he's not really into conversation, but get him on either of those two and he's yours for the day. He's one of those odd guys that has a full head of hair but decides to shave it. I guess when your job is to be a hardman it helps to look hard.

'You're in some pretty deep shit this morning, pal,' he says.

'You want a whisky?'

'It's eleven o'clock, Matt.'

'I've had a bit of a tough morning, like you say. Come on.'

I head for the kitchen. Turning my back on him is bold, but I need him onside. If I'm still conscious by the time I take the half dozen paces into the room, I'll know he's on Team Matt.

I've known Woody a couple of years now and he's always treated me with respect. He might work for Bradley, but he's made for more than breaking into folks' houses and making threats on behalf of a man with marble floors in his bathroom. I've even encouraged him to take up a trade. Not that he has. We've had enough drinks together to make us more than acquaintances though. And I'm going to need him if I'm going to get today back on track.

In the kitchen I pull a chair out and throw Woody a dishcloth. The room's small. Units hug the walls, with the sink under the window and a table tucked in an alcove.

'Probably a good idea to get that cleaned up,' I say, stopping short of a full apology.

I get the whisky from the living room. There's no noise from the kitchen. I check to see if Turnbull has phoned. He hasn't. Neither has Pete. On the way back through I put the Dickens back on the console table. Ineffective heap of shite.

'I've got a question for you, Woody,' I say as I pour two whiskies. My last one gave me a bit of a ping so this will need to be the last. I can't be doing with Mum thinking I'm drunk at lunchtime. Woody says nothing. 'Why exactly were you trying to break in?'

He raises his glass and takes a sip. The dishcloth is wrapped in a tourniquet around his other hand. 'Information.'

'Are you fucking serious? Information on what, exactly? What happened this morning is not cool, man. Seriously. You need to fix this.'

He raises his hands. 'I don't know nothing about that. I told Bradley it was off limits.'

I sit opposite him and take a long sip, tasting the whisky this time, trying to slow everything right down – there's that hallmark clay note on the Glenlivet that gives way to plum, malt and a little dry tobacco. And swallow. Magic. 'I appreciate that, but he's crossed a big fucking line, even by his standards.'

'Watch what you're saying about Bradley. I might sympathise with you here, but remember who pays my wages.'

He's void of emotion. Complete professional, always has been. Type of guy that fell in with the wrong crowd when he was a kid, was tempted down a path to easy riches and found himself knee deep in the foulest smelling shite imaginable.

'What if you could help me get Nicky back, and keep Bradley happy?' I say.

'I don't know where he is, Matt. I swear.'

'Well, why did he tell me to phone you when I've got the money?'

'I'm trying to help you, mate. Bradley doesn't know I'm here. I handed over ten grand to you not so long ago – that money's gone somewhere. I want to know where. If you owed someone, tell me who.'

'You could have phoned and asked me that.'

'Nah, people say what they want on the phone. When I'm sitting in their lounge and they come in the door and see me comfy on their couch, they tell the truth. You're fucking stupid at times, Matt – no offence – but I can't believe you've got yourself in this deep. I figure if I can persuade whoever you owed to give you it back on a short-term basis, this can all go away, until after the funeral at least.'

Ten! I never thought of bartering. Fuck, this changes everything. The five in my bedroom on an evens horse and it's sorted – no need for me to disrupt the plans with Turnbull, definitely no need for Pete. Thank you very nicely.

'I can get ten for you in a couple of hours.' I have another long sip of whisky. I hold it in my mouth. It doesn't feel like this morning anymore. An hour ago I was waiting on a bus in the pissing rain – now I've got options. Lunch is going to taste a lot sweeter. I check my watch, it's just before half eleven. I top up my glass. Woody places his hand over his.

'So who did you owe?' he says.

'It's not like that. I needed it for legitimate business reasons. I told Bradley that. You know that guy that's been helping me out, Phillip Turnbull?'

'The guy with all the positive thinking pish?'

'It's not pish. Your attitude relative to your environment helps define who you are and what you can achieve.'

'Aye, it's working out pretty well for you so far.' He stands up and goes over to the sink, runs his hand under the cold tap.

'How the cut?'

'It's fine. Have you got a bandage or something though?'

I go to the messy drawer and start sifting through it, unearthing a first aid kit I had no idea I owned. I hand it to him. 'So, anyway. Phillip says to me he's got an idea – he's spreading himself too thin, I mean he's had three books out, he's in demand. They want him to do an Australian lecture tour, but he doesn't want to abandon what he's started in Britain, right? Says he can't spin plates in one room while he's in another. Wants me to do the spinning for him.'

'He offered you a job?'

I shake my head. 'Better than that. He offered me the chance to go into business with him, to launch these self-starter workshops that can take place anywhere across the country. I'm client services. I'll get an office to work from, the lot.'

Woody's leaning back on the counter, soaking it all up, processing it. I can tell he's impressed because he's not interrupted me.

'First off, how much have you given this clown? Tell me not the full ten? Tell me you at least lost five on the tables.'

I ignore the insults. He just doesn't get it. He'd rather break into someone's house to make his presence felt. 'We founded a company and each put in £10,000. We're equal partners.'

'Equal? All due respect, Matt, what have you done to convince him you're his equal?'

'I'm an agent for him. I represent him.'

'Sounds like you'd have done that for a fucking biscuit. He's hoodwinked you, mate. If he's in Australia – which I very much fucking doubt, he's larging it up on your ten, and now you owe Bradley twenty.'

It's easy for those who haven't yet grasped the possibilities of Turnbull's teachings to dismiss them. That's exactly why they work, exactly why we're going to succeed. 'You asked me where the money went, I've told you. Beyond that, what you think is your business.'

'Don't get tetchy with me, Matt. Remember your place in the order of things here. You're in debt to my boss, a serious amount of debt, and the repercussions of that are pretty fucking clear.'

I glance down at his bandaged hand. He's not made a particularly good job of it, but I'm not helping him now.

'I need to go to my mum's for lunch.'

'Does your brother know?'

I nod my head, wishing more than ever I'd gone to McAllister's without him.

'Do yourself a favour. Don't ask him for help unless you have to. We both know his sort.'

'I'll phone you at four. I'll have the ten. You can speak to Bradley.'

'And if your horse doesn't come in?'

I drain the rest of my whisky and put the glass in the sink. 'I've got to go.'

I show Woody out without another word. He glances at the fragments of ashtray lying on the hall floor.

'Anybody else would have snapped you in two, Matt. Don't forget that.'

He makes his way down the stairs. I wait until I hear the close door shut before moving. Lunch beckons, but first I top up my glass, and go into the bedroom. I move my shoes out of the wardrobe and feel for the envelope.

The image of watching the curtains close on Nicky's coffin is all I need to see now. Mum wailing her objections against the comforting melody from the organ pipes will be a triumph next to the alternative.

I take out the cash, bundled tightly with an elastic band, and flick through the notes – fifties and twenties – exactly five thousand pounds. I know because I counted it twice the night I won it. With this much there's not a corner of the world I can't reach in twenty-four hours. That poolside seat in Vegas, bikini-wearing hostess heading my way with a pint on a tray. It's within reach. This, all this, gone. Fuck. I slam the wardrobe door shut.

Back in the kitchen I put the cash on the worktop. *Patience and serenity are the binding roots of confidence. With them, you know you can achieve your goals.* I open the laptop and close Facebook. Sorry Jenny. I look at the day's races. It doesn't take long. General Catalyst, 2.45 at Carlisle. He's 6/5 and looks good value for it. After lunch I'll get down the bookies. Then everything's in the hands of the Gods – good luck versus bad. I've totted it over the years and it owes me, it owes me fucking big. Today's the day it's going to pay out.

8

Carrying two glasses of concentrated orange juice that he hoped Helen would take for freshly squeezed, and an instant coffee he knew he'd have to drink, Peter followed his mum into the living room. She'd made Peter get the step out to retrieve the good cups and saucers from the top cupboard, something Peter reckoned happened only on Christmas Day and whenever Helen was there. Even the minister wasn't granted the Wedding China. That she'd bothered on today of all days struck Peter as absurd.

In the living room, the girls were sitting either side of Helen on the three-seater. Their little legs were dangling off the edge while Helen sat as though the back of the couch was a blanket of pins. His mum had actually done a decent job of decorating the room: walls a neutral colour that wasn't quite magnolia, a painting of Pittenweem harbour hanging above the old fireplace, flatscreen TV, at last. She'd called to thank him for that one. It's even got the internet, she'd exclaimed, before admitting that Nicky had been the one to point that out.

'I do like this peppermint stuff,' said Betty, pulling out the smallest table from a nest and placing the cup and saucer on it.

Peter gave the girls their juice before joining his mum on the two-seater. The girls took small sips and held their glasses with both hands. He hoped Helen wouldn't check to see if the juice was freshly squeezed.

'Now let me look at you properly,' said Betty. 'You're both getting so big. Can you remember the last time you were here?'

'I'm sorry Uncle Nicky is dead,' said Sam.

'Me too,' said Jess.

'Girls,' said Helen.

Peter put an arm around his mum's shoulder. He felt his phone vibrate again. He quickly checked the number – Stuey. Shit, he needed out of there. Time was moving faster while he was distracted.

'We're all very sorry, girls.' said Betty.

Peter sipped at his foul coffee, his eyes willing Helen to say something. Even one of his mum's pointless stories would have done, but there was nothing. It had become the sort of silence that had to be smashed open. Until they were lost in conversation, Peter wouldn't be able to find out what Stuey had to say.

'Girls, I think Gran needs hugs today,' he said.

'Peter,' said Helen, her arms preventing the girls from jumping off the couch.

'Och, Helen, they're not going to break me in two,' said Betty. She always pronounced her *T*s like a Scottish actor trying too hard when Helen was around. It was one of the reasons why the two of them circled one another, looking anywhere but in the other's eyes.

Betty opened her arms out and the girls ran over, clattering into their gran and jumping onto the two-seater, Peter taking one stamp in the balls and two in the stomach in the process.

'Girls, I'm not a cushion,' he said, moving over to the big couch to join his wife.

He patted Helen's thigh. 'Will you relax,' he whispered.

Her smile didn't reveal much. She hadn't touched her tea.

'Is Uncle Nicky really in heaven?' said Sam.

'That's right,' said Betty, pulling her granddaughters tight around her. 'And he's going to make sure he's looking after all of us from now on – our guardian angel.'

'My Grandma Ellison is my guardian angel,' said Jess.

'You can have two,' said Sam.

'Don't be silly.'

'You can have two, if you're a very lucky girl,' said Betty. She rubbed Jess's arm.

'But how can he watch you and me at the same time?'

'Oh, that's what you can do in heaven. You can look at everything all at once if you want to. Everyone has a lot of people to look after at the same time – just like your mum has to look after both of you at the same time. I had to do that too.'

Betty smiled at Helen. It was often misplaced but Peter knew she would never stop trying. The smiles would still be there in twenty years. Perhaps by then Helen would have finally

66

forgiven her.

'And down here we can look after you, Granny, can't we?' said Jess.

'That's right. You're a very clever girl. You take after your Dad.'

Peter felt Helen's thigh tense beneath his hand. Christ, anything could, and would, be perceived as a snipe.

'Girls, why don't you ask Gran to tell you a story,' he said, before that particular hole got any deeper.

'The wedding, the wedding,' the twins said.

Peter would never tire of hearing their voices in unison. A prison visit flashed through his mind, the girls quiet, too shy to speak with the guard hovering behind them; Helen, looking well, a different wedding ring on her finger.

'That's a big story,' said Betty.

Peter winked a green light. He jumped up and took the girls' glasses over to them, taking care to grab a couple of coasters from the fireplace.

'Okay then... well, the day your mum and dad got married I thought I would die it was so warm. There we were, dressed up in all our finery at a beautiful castle out in the country and the sun was shining so bright. Your mum looked prettier than I think anyone has ever looked. And do you know why?'

The girls shook their heads even though they knew fine well. Peter sat back down and smiled at Helen, who thankfully reciprocated.

'Because you were both inside her tummy. You were tiny in there, so small that no one knew you were there, not even me. It was as if you were hiding, already looking after your mum.'

Peter wondered if Betty's barbs were as innocent as they appeared.

'Anyway, your mum and dad kissed like a prince and princess and then everyone had a huge feast. You should have seen it. The room was white. White tablecloths, white chairs, white drapes. And when all the food was over, we watched the bride and groom – do you know what a bride and groom is?'

'A bride is a mummy and a groom is a daddy,' said Sam.

'Clever girl. You drink your juice up.'

'It tastes funny,' said Jess.

Bollocks, thought Peter. 'Just let Granny tell her story,' he said,

67

gripping Helen's leg tighter. She tensed back in return. These little touches usually communicated sexual appetite; in his mum's presence they were a series of coded warnings. He took a long sip of coffee and spat half back into the cup. He had fucking phone calls to make.

'The bride and groom danced across the room as if they were gliding. They were so happy. It was the most perfect wedding.'

Helen crossed her legs, brushing Peter's hand off. Shit. Did everything have to be tainted? He knew then that she wasn't thinking about *It Had To Be You*. Her mind would be later in the evening, when Matt had pretty much drunk the bar dry on his own and decided to tell Siobhan that she was pretentious. Siobhan handled it all with the sort of dignity that made Peter question why she ever had anything to do with Matt, but the damage was done. He'd stumbled across the dance floor, bumped into Helen, almost knocking her down, and proceeded to trip over a chair and land on his arse at the feet of some old aunt of Helen's that Peter couldn't remember the name of. Whatever it was, Matt clambered to his feet and dragged the cadaverous woman up for a dance. When Peter had been ordered to get him out, he'd tried to defuse the situation by telling his bride of a mere six hours to 'calm down'. Betty's nod of agreement had seemed unending, like that fucking nodding dog the kids wanted for the car.

'I'll get some biscuits, shall I?' Betty stood up and wiped her eye. 'And I'm going to make sandwiches later, just how you like them Peter.'

Laced with a gram of coke? thought Peter, watching his mum head for the kitchen. He lifted his phone from his pocket. Helen's legs remained crossed, her foot dangling away from him. Fucking nothing from Tom. Not even a text. Where was he? Surely Peter would be the first person he'd call. And what did she mean anyway, just how he liked them? That better not have been a dig about nutrition. They were his fucking children.

'Can you speak, please?' he said to Helen. 'Just get involved in the conversation.'

'It is not an easy situation. I don't know what to say. She can't help herself can she? Even today.'

'I know. But just be yourself.' He smiled.

'It's just so awkward. I keep thinking of him.'

'Course you do, we all do. Just say what comes to mind. And if that happens to be Nicky, talk about him. I'm going to see if she's okay. Just take their lead,' he said.

That vision again, of Nicky lying in his suit in a box in some random fucking hideout. He wondered where Matt was, if he was managing to talk his way out of it with promises that everything would work itself out later on.

He stood and kissed the girls, trailing his hands across their heads as he passed them.

In the kitchen, his mum was leaning on the sink, staring out at the back garden.

'You okay?' he asked, hoping for a closed response. Instead she said nothing.

The lawn badly needed cut and bushes were beginning to encroach on the path.

'Garden's looking decent, isn't it?' he said. A pointless lie, but it was words.

'I've not missed Craig for a long time, but I wish the bastard was here today,' said his mum. 'Not the one that left us, but the one that lived here before Nicky came along. He was a good man back then. I know you and he never connected, and that was my fault.'

'It wasn't your fault, Mum. It was his.'

'I know where my faults lie. I've had plenty of time to think about what could have been done differently. I don't know why you and he never got on, but I never did anything about it. He got on well enough with Matthew and I suppose I thought the pair of you would just work things out. It was lazy of me.'

'You're a lot of things, Mum. Lazy isn't one of them.'

'Your father would disagree.' A laugh grew from her throat that she seemed to capture and swallow. Peter wondered when it would escape. 'I wouldn't change it you know,' she said. 'I loved your dad more than anything. Not like you three – you're different. You're part of me, physically. He was another part entirely. More than Craig ever was. I never want you to think that I loved Craig as much as your dad.'

'Mum, don't worry yourself about stuff like that, it's long in the past.'

'But you have to know. I wouldn't have kept your dad. If I'd kept him I would never have had Nicky, and he was my baby, Peter. My baby. He was the last thing I ever gave the world, and the world had no business taking him back.'

She slumped forward and Peter grabbed her, taking her weight as her legs buckled. As she sobbed into his shoulder, a wretched, piercing cry coming from deep within, he tried to remember the last time he had hugged her, but all he saw were pecks on cheeks. He caressed her head and smoothed her hair the way he did when Jess or Sam were upset. It felt coarser than theirs.

As she wept, he wondered if she felt guilty. She'd done nothing wrong. You couldn't keep them locked up – he'd learned that lesson in A&E one particularly cold night the previous winter after Sam had slipped in the garden and needed four stitches on her hand. Falling down is part of growing up, the doctor had told him. She'll be smarter tomorrow than she was today.

He rubbed his mum's back and straightened her up. Her eyes were wet and bloated and her mascara was running, taking sharp turns where wrinkles blocked the route south.

'I'm so sorry, Peter,' she said. 'I don't know what came over me.'

'You're fine. You'll be fine. I promise.' He let go, keen to see if she could support herself.

'I just want to go back in time. Just a week. A week's nothing.'

Peter thought of Cillian's warning, of the repercussions of ignoring him. 'A week would be good, Mum.'

She sighed. 'You look after those girls, you hear me?'

'Of course I will.' He looked down, then back up. 'Look, I need to make a quick call. Work is badgering the life out of me. Go and get the girls to tell you about Tuscany. I'll only be two minutes.'

She wiped her eyes with a dishcloth. 'For God's sake, why can't they just leave you alone – do they not know why you're here?'

'They don't care.'

It was the most sincere thing he'd said to her all morning. She closed her eyes and for a moment he thought she was about to start again. 'It's okay, I'll just be a minute,' he said, squeezing her shoulder.

He turned into the hall, inhaling slowly, deeply. By the time he reached the top of the stairs he was through to Stuey's voicemail. Unreliable prick. Peter needed phones answered. He needed answers full fucking stop. Tom was a stickler for Profit & Loss management, always checking his senior staff, and when Peter had completed his P&L the day of the flash crash Tom's red face lost some of its colour. *You might find yourself answering questions over this*, was all he had said. Not a word on the million-plus Peter had just earned the company as everyone else counted their losses.

He dialled Tom and heard his boss's familiar voicemail message. Compliance hadn't made it as far as Peter's desk yet; Stuey would have revelled in passing that information on. That was still a guess though, and guesswork was the preserve of the ignorant. Facts needed to enter the mix. Using his personal iPhone, he flicked to 'Tom Personal' and dialed. Voicemail. Answers did not emerge from silence. The window at the top landing had steamed up, heightening the claustrophobia that was beginning to gnaw at him. He wiped it with his shirt sleeve and peered out at the slate roofs across the back, rainwater rushing down them and filling gutters. The point of no return had passed a long time ago.

Peter's memory of hearing the name Barton for the first time was hazy at best, even if the context was unforgettable. He had been invited to Miami by a hedge fund that had just relocated there from New York thanks to Florida's encouraging income tax rates of precisely fuck all percent. The hedges were moving south like pensioners and wanted to announce themselves in style, and so one Friday evening Peter kissed his sleeping toddlers, waved goodbye to Helen and stepped into the back of a waiting Jaguar. The driver hadn't been talkative as the car bolted along the M25 to Biggin Hill airport and Peter had spent the journey gazing out at London's suburbs. The stress peeled itself away as if the trip was an exfoliation. Arriving at the airfield, he met up with the half dozen other London traders invited on the jolly. Two glasses of Krug later and the Cessna took to the sky, leaving behind London and all she demanded of him.

From the manufactured perfection of the cabin crew and their white-toothed smiles, to the smell of leather and weight of the crystal glasses, everything on board was something Peter coveted. Stretching out on his chair, Champagne flute in hand, he quickly found common ground with his fellow guests as they downplayed their excitement, treating the private jet's luxury as if it was something they did every week.

It was only in the seclusion of the bathroom that Peter could look in the mirror and allow his smirk to widen into a beaming grin of enormous self-satisfaction. Flying private. He focused hard on his reflection and promised himself it wouldn't be the last time. It was little wonder those at the top of the ladder baulked at *flying commercial* like Peter did at the prospect of having to use the bus.

As the hours passed the drinks kept coming. With every popped cork the enthusiasm grew, to the point that one of the cabin crew eventually flipped at the constant clawing and lewdness, scolding the arse-grabbing culprit and transforming rogues into schoolboys, aside from one particularly obnoxious prick, Davis something or other, who had claimed he'd have her sacked before they landed. It was around this point Peter decided to take a nap. By the time they touched down he had slept off the Champagne and got drunk again.

After checking into the Mandarin Oriental on Brickell Key they met their hosts in the hotel's Azul restaurant, where around twenty Wall Streeters were already doing their best to work their way through an impressive wine list. The restaurant was darkening as the sun set across the south beach. From the island they were ensconced on the sea looked vibrant blue, with yellow and orange lights shimmering in its reflection. Yachts dotted the keyside, and beyond the coastline, mainland high rises sat back from banks of palm trees, each apartment window a whole world waiting for the night to start. Peter looked out at the city coming alive and felt as content as he'd ever done.

Their host, Bernhard Lieberman, was chief executive of the hosting hedge fund. He was a small man, but muscular for someone in his fifties. Peter knew him by reputation, though they'd never met. Lieberman had a net worth way north of a billion. If he could do it, what was in Peter's way?

Introductory speeches out the way, the dinner flashed by; more Krug, fucking handfuls of Beluga caviar being gobbled down with no appreciation of whatever flavours were meant to come though. The steak on the other hand was something Peter did savour; each mouthful washed down with an Archaval Ferrer Malbec that was bursting with cherry undertones. Peter noted the name; it would be worth sourcing back home.

'I want to meet this cow's mother and buy her a fucking drink,' he told the guy sitting next to him, who laughed too hard in response. Frankie was a Wall Street trader with the look of someone born into privilege who spent their life sliding off the rails in sub-conscious self-loathing. Peter knew enough Frankies to be guarded. Unlike the Davis guy from the plane, who was just an arrogant wank, Frankies were like unpinned hand grenades when they stepped off the trading floor. Still, the school trip atmosphere along with the constant flow of four hundred dollar wine kept him relaxed.

Two hours later, their huge table, pristine with white tablecloth and gleaming cutlery upon arrival, was covered in spilt wine and discarded food. With a clap of his hands, Lieberman was soon leading the full crew through the lobby, a nearby nightclub the next stop. '*The* fucking club,' according to Lieberman, who stopped at the front of the fleet of people carriers waiting outside. As each cab filled and drove away Lieberman slapped the roof and greeted the next group of bodies with a huge grin. The world's first billionaire taxi marshal.

Peter followed Frankie into the back of a seven-seater, having been unable to shake him off, and found himself in a headlock before he sat down.

'Peter Fletcher, fuck me. I mean Jaysus, what the fuck are you doing out here?'

He recognised the rural Irish accent and broke into a grin as he wrestled himself free. 'Cillian, you wee shite,' he said, wondering how the laughing leprechaun had managed to stay hidden throughout dinner. He hadn't seen Cillian since he left London for a job as a dealer with Lieberman in New York; that must have been, Christ, at least two years ago.

'Haha, well done, Shotgun. I thought I might have had you puzzled there.' As the car drove off Cillian grabbed him in the sort of hug a kid gives Santa. He was already higher than the jet that had likely brought him south from Wall St.

'You kidding, you're the only broker in the world that sounds like a fucking sheep farmer,' said Peter.

The taxi erupted in laughter and high fives served as introductions.

'So, Shotgun?' said Frankie. 'I gotta hear how you got that one?'

Cillian slapped his thigh. He was always reckless after just a couple but he would have been reckless if he still lived in the village he grew up in. No scruples, no pretense. He was just a nutter, and that was as close to comfort as Peter had found in the City. The less complex the individual, the more you could read them. That was why Cillian was one of the few people Peter had trusted. Well, trust wasn't the word, but if he was hanging from a window ledge Peter felt confident Cillian would drag him back inside while everyone else queued up to stamp on his fingertips.

'Six months into the job and Shotgun here fat fingered two trades in three days, a bit too quick off the mark when he saw a good deal. How much did you cost your firm again, Peter?'

Peter began to laugh. 'It was safely into six figures.' The taxi erupted again. 'Never did it again, I'll tell you that much.'

He looked into the rear view mirror and locked eyes with the driver, who turned away in what Peter couldn't decide was disgust or pity.

The nightclub was exactly the type of place Peter had been expecting. Whisker Kings was famous for being the biggest strip club in the world. Looking like a faux-Roman temple from the outside, the interior had even less taste. Whatever Lieberman was doing, he'd called this one badly wrong. It was the size of a warehouse, flashes of violet and pink neon crossing the room in time with the music. The main stage was fucking enormous, like a west end theatre. Booths and long bars dotted around it – making even London's finest establishments seem amateurish in their efforts. The party trooped through in a conga line, whooping at dancing girls who blew kisses and beckoned them with teasing fingers. Peter joined in, happy to leave however many fucks he may have given about the tackiness of the place tucked in his pocket. They made it to a private Champagne Bar with the loss of only a couple of casualties. Whatever taxi Lieberman had climbed into had gone elsewhere but his MD stood on a table and lifted a bottle to the air: 'Tonight, gentlemen, is on Mr. Lieberman. Welcome to Disneyland.'

As he said it, the doors opened and a team of girls entered, sparkling dresses glued to their synchronised bodies. Trays of Champagne were carefully balanced in each hand, their arms thin and tanned, too fragile almost for the weight they bore. The timing was perfect. Everything was perfect; the Yanks couldn't do it any other way.

'I've had enough of that stuff for the now,' said Cillian, nudging Peter and tapping his nose. 'Shall we?'

Minutes later Peter was crushed in a toilet cubicle staring down at a plump line of cocaine with a rolled up $100 bill in his hand. He snorted hard and shook his head. It was fast, heavy – his head instantly seemed to float free of his neck a little.

'Holy fuck,' he shouted. 'Yes. Fucking YES!' He high-fived Cillian and took a deep breath.

Cillian laughed and tapped out a line for himself. He mopped it up and dabbed a finger into the residue before rubbing it on his gum and roaring like fucking Tarzan. 'Shall we take a seat for the show then?' he said.

As they moved back through the throng Peter's eyes took in the club's moving parts. And there were a lot of parts moving. This was it. Here. Now. There were easily forty girls dancing. Moving. Sliding. Glistening in the light. Others were chatting up the clientele as if they genuinely wanted to be taken out for dinner. The men were either suits like Peter's crew or tourists fresh from the golf course. He caught the eye of one girl; she looked about twenty. Gold bikini top. Matching mini-skirt. Little Roman pixie. Stunning hazel eyes, big and innocent. Her smile was huge. He wondered where she'd gone to school, how she did in her exams, where she lost her virginity. For a second he wanted to ask her how she'd ended up wasting her smile on such sordid men. It was business though. It was all just fucking business. He was here because he'd earned the right to be entertained. It wasn't some seedy back street hovel. These girls would have whooped ecstatically when they got their job offers. Yes. This was it. Here. Now.

He and Cillian sat at a small table and ordered Cognacs while two girls danced for them. Peter watched them closely, one eye closed over thanks to double vision setting in. The room slowed down as they moved. The blonde's tits were fake and when the brunette squeezed them they held firm, like buoys out in the bay. He preferred the brunette; she didn't have tan lines for a start, her tits were smaller, pert - the opposite of Helen's fun bags. He decided he'd shout this brunette over for a private dance when she'd done with her performance. Just a wee holiday present. He turned to speak to Cillian and saw he was alone. Laughing, he sipped his drink and sank back into the comfort of the chair as his pulse felt like it was synching into time with the pounding of the music.

'Daddy, Gran Fletcher says you've not to work today.' Sam stood at the bottom of the stairs with her sister.

Peter was sitting on the top stair like a scolded schoolboy sent upstairs with no pudding – he'd made it as far as his old bedroom door then returned to the stairs, reluctant to invade Nicky's private space, even if that space had once been his own.

'I just need to make one more call, little miss,' said Peter.

Jess began to climb the stairs, always bolder despite her sister's bossiness.

'Come on, Daddy, we're telling Gran Fletcher about Italy.'

Italy. Peter wished he was there now, watching the girls swim as Helen, eyes shaded from the Tuscan sun with those huge sunglasses of hers, dozed by the pool.

He allowed Jess to drag him down the stairs. When they reached the living room he waited until they ran back to their seats before holding up two fingers to Helen to indicate how long he would be. She nodded with no hint of impatience. When it came to work she knew the score; that was what kept her in designer sunglasses after all.

He attempted to take the stairs two at a time and was shocked to find his legs couldn't manage it. Not only that, but the exertion caused the dagger in his head to reappear – just for a moment, but enough to close his eye over again. This time he didn't stop at the landing. He turned not into Nicky's bedroom but the spare room. It stank of hangover. He kicked Matt's crap into the corner and opened the window.

When Cillian returned to the table his hair was all over the place and the smile on his face was as wide as the Clyde. Peter shook his head at the old saying. It was something his dad had always said. He drained his glass.

'We should work together more,' said Cillian.

'Definitely,' said Peter, laughing.

'Not because of the view you daft bastard. Listen, keep quiet in front of the rest, but I'm moving back to London. Fucking Miami. Not a chance I'm living down here – fucking college kids and pensioners. It's not for me, Peter.'

'So what you going to be doing?'

'Dealer for a new hedge fund. A lot of capital, your kind of people. Fuck, would you look at that.'

On stage, the brunette had peeled down the blonde's thong and was bent over at an impossible angle, running her lips over the top of her pal's thigh.

'I'm always open to new experiences,' said Peter.

Cillian slapped his back. 'Guy running it is this fella called Barton. Serious fucking player. He's asked me to find a trader I can trust. I can trust you, Peter, eh? You're a good guy.'

Peter agreed and turned his attention back to the show. Cillian grabbed his shoulder and spun him round.

'Forget the fucking girls for a minute, would you. I mean, can I trust you, properly?' Cillian's eyes had lost their bravado. He was laying himself bare here. He was like Peter – no privilege in his past, no hereditary arrogance. All self-made, right down to the flaws.

'Course you can. What is it?'

'We've done enough together in the past that you know I wouldn't fuck about with you.'

'Get to the point. I'm losing my semi here.'

'I'm serious.'

'You're fucking high is what you are. Does this look like the sort of place to be serious?'

'What would you say if I asked you to do a wash trade for me?'

Peter forgot about the girls. There were any number of reasons for doing a wash trade, none of them particularly ethical. 'I'd ask you why the fuck you were being so stupid.'

He turned back to the girls, point made. Blonde was honing in on Brunette's tits, while Brunette's head was thrust back in pleasure. As her tongue flicked over a dark nipple, Blonde's eyes were focused on Peter, enticing him to join her.

'I told you Barton needs a trader he can trust. Look on it as a test of faith.'

Peter was getting annoyed now. Blonde signed off by dipping a finger inside Brunette's thong and walking off stage sucking her finger. Brunette was left grinding against the pole, beckoning Peter with a long-nailed finger of her own.

'If you hadn't met me tonight I wouldn't even be on your radar, mate. The coke's making you too bold.'

'Well look at it as fate then, my friend.'

'Why would I do a wash trade for a guy I've never met?'

Cillian's grin reappeared. 'Because in return you'll get a trade you can retire on.'

Peter shook his head. 'Watch the girls, Cillian. Watch the girls.'

Back in London, after his head had cleared, after he'd cleaned up the sick on his hotel room floor while the sun passed over the bay outside, after the tour of Lieberman's offices and the lines of coke in the company toilets to stop the shaking, after another night of mayhem and a flight home in complete silence, starlight peppering his golden reflection in the window, Peter couldn't shift Cillian from his mind. A bad run over a couple of weeks moved his thoughts from *maybe* to *why not?* Tom was getting on his back. It was like he'd been cursed. Every hunch was wrong, every black number turning red. Peter didn't like the principle of wash trades though. For starters they were technically illegal, although they did happen. Generally, stock was bought and sold simultaneously for the same price and everyone ended up where they started. They were only ever carried out by investors wanting to get the value of a stock temporarily off their balance sheet, or to generate interest in a particular stock to prompt other investors into buying the position.

It would only be the once though; it might be worth a punt. Everyone would see some commission, but not enough to red-flag it. Not only would it get Tom off his back and cease the jibes from across the floor, but he'd also find out just how much this Barton character had to invest.

He should have left the entire idea in Miami with the memory of the brunette's lap dance. He should never have called Cillian.

Since that day all he'd managed to do was lose control. Fuck, what was in his control? Not his wife's coldness towards his mum, not the twins' future.

Matt's room was appalling, truly. At least he could do something about his surroundings. He left, slamming the door behind him, and walked down the short hallway.

Nicky's room – his room – was serene compared to Matt's, but it felt alien. Nothing was where it should have been, the wallpaper new, the curtains and matching bedspread not how he remembered then. Saying that, he couldn't quite recall what colour they had been in his day. If only we could control which things we remember, he thought, sitting down on the bed and beginning to sob.

9

Decent single malt is too precious to be gulped down as anesthetic for the mind, so I've filled a mug with gin. It bites but slides down without digging its teeth too deeply into my throat. I've never know this couch to be more comfy. With my eyes closed I imagine it swelling in size as I shrink until I've disappeared into the security of its cotton folds. Just for a moment or two. I've got my money, I've got my horse. I'll get my brother back. I will settle the score with fate. *Visualise and reprise your desires until they become real and true.*

I might believe in Turnbull, but my mind doesn't always want to pick the right side. I weaken it with another gulp of gin. In the time it took me to have a piss it turned against me. Well it's my fucking mind. I am the one who makes the decisions here.

It was in an advert in some shit newspaper at the doctor's I first saw the name Phillip Turnbull. I'd fucked my knee and was trying to get decent painkillers. Doc was running late and it wasn't even ten o'clock. In a wee quarter page panel near the back of the mag there was a picture of a guy in a suit with an open collar. He had a thin, confident face. He wasn't smiling or anything cheesy, just looking at me.

Make your tomorrows today

was the tagline. Under it was his name, the dates of a lecture tour and venues across the UK. He was playing Glasgow that afternoon. Fuck it, I thought. I was out of work at the time, Siobhan on at me for it. Things were not as I'd planned them to be. Serendipity. I don't know what made me pick up that paper, what made me flick to that page, but I left the doc's empty-handed and limped off to get the subway into town. I didn't tell Siobhan, I just went, fannied about for a while, picked up some over-the-counter painkillers, had a pint, then paid my £8 and took a seat in an auditorium in some hotel that had seen better days. It probably held two hundred but it was less than half full, mostly middle-aged couples and students. There were twenty or so people there on their own. Most were women in their 40s – I wondered if they were divorcees then felt guilty. I took a seat somewhere towards the back and shut my eyes. It was comfortable, like being early for the cinema. I must've dozed off because there was this huge bang that shocked me back to the present. Dry ice was rolling off the stage like a rough tide and a guitar was rocking a solo through the PA. Then this guy walked out wearing the same suit as I'd seen in the advert. He waved and stood dead centre, his legs further apart than looked comfortable. He seemed such a dick.

'Thank yourself for coming here today,' he said, the sound carrying through some ridiculous Madonna mic he was hooked up to.

Everyone sat still. I felt like punching myself, never mind anything else.

'If you can't thank yourself, you can't better yourself,' he added.

A few folk murmured thanks. I held my own counsel on this one. I wasn't thanking anyone until I knew what the fuck the guy was going to do with my eight quid. Then he started talking, beginning with how he was bullied in school and devised a method, 'The Grater Power,' he called it, to take all the negative memories in his life and grate them, 'like cheese', every night before he slept. When they lay there in shards they could do nothing to him. He said he'd been doing it every night since he was ten. I didn't know whether to laugh or burst into applause at the absurdity of this image. My knee was killing me though and I was getting annoyed that I'd left the doctors, so I sat through the whole spectacle; the anecdotes of growing up in Nottingham, of his career in sales and how he'd drive home every night, lost in the sounds of his car engine, wondering why his life couldn't be as efficient as the parts that powered his journey. He wanted to power his own journey, he said. He spoke in phrases rather than sentences, his every uttering rehearsed and calculated. There was something in it though, a resonance: I wanted to power my own journey too. Beyond the foggy razzmatazz of the dry ice was the outline of an answer. I hadn't been looking for anything other than a distraction, but I found focus. Whatever happened, I whispered thanks to myself and sat up straight.

My phone sits on the coffee table, dead, offering me no clue as to whether anyone is about to call me. I picture Phillip coming out a meeting, checking his phone, smiling, tapping my name. It's him or the 3.20 at Carlisle. I grate and grate. Doubt, distrust, imminent defeat: they fall in flakes until I can't see my feet. I want the couch to cradle me, stroke my hair, hush me to sleep and get me ready for the funeral. It's all coming together though. One race. Coming together. One win. Cmiong tohetger.

The clock on the wall won't stop turning. Every little sound it makes moves me closer to tomorrow morning. I grate and grate, clawing through my brain for the good stuff, the serotonin that will see me through this ordeal, but it's hiding; it's afraid of the ticking, the tocking.

Tick

                                                              Tock

Tick

                                                    Fucking Tock

FUCKING TICK

                                          FUCKING TOCK

FUCKING TICK

FUCKING –

I leap up and tear the thing off the wall, stamp on it, feeling satisfaction surge from my heel as the glass shatters. All I want to hear is silence. It's not an easy thing to find. When I'm underground in a box, then there'll be silence. I don't know when that's coming though, what will put me there. No one does. Lighting bolt; blood clot; chip pan fire; meteorite; snake bite; train derailment; self-harm; plane crash; poisoning; drowning; bombing; hanging; lethal injection; accidental amputation; aneurysm, influenza; malnutrition; dehydration; diabetes; dog bite; electrocution; epilepsy; heatstroke; heart attack; shark attack; strangulation; renal failure; bee sting; overdose of anything; cot death; gunshot; baseball bat; cancer of the prostate;

cancer of the kidneys; cancer of the bone, the breast, the bladder, the balls, the thyroid, the colon, the skin, the eye, the liver, the stomach, the cervix, the brain being eaten away by rogue cells that devour the living parts of you, immune to the radiation that makes you sicker than the cancer itself; plane crash; car crash; collision with a vehicle; eleven years old and on your way to football: cause of death, massive trauma; causes of death: fast car; not looking; leaving the pitches at sixteen minutes past and not seventeen; liking football and not rugby or running or cycling or swimming or any other fucking sport that wouldn't have put you in that particular place at that particular time.

I take a sip of gin in the hope that it'll stop the tears. One splashes into the mug and for a moment I bask in the melodrama. Matthew's ruin.

As I sink deeper into the couch Phillip comes towards me. He could be anywhere – driving up the M6, his phone out of reach in his jacket pocket, cursing himself for forgetting to put it into the hands-free; at a meeting with his publisher, a client, a prospective backer for our business plan. He could be in fucking Australia already. No. He's here. Working on our business. I keep grating, imagining scenarios where whatever is happening is for my benefit and not my detriment. I grate until I'm invigorated.

I stand up, hungry. I've had nothing to eat aside from the sausage that was sneaked into the garden – and even that abandoned me.

There's cornflakes and next to fuck all else so I fill a bowl and top up with milk that comes out the bottle in congealed lumps not too dissimilar to the spew I left in the butcher's doorway. If there was anything left in my stomach it would be joining the filth in the bowl. I throw the lot in the bin.

Taking the box with me, I fall back into the couch and begin to claw at the flakes. I'm back where I was before Woody broke in. There has been progress though. Twenty grand has become ten. I am half way there and I've not left the house yet.

The cornflakes are drier than an empty ocean and my throat rejects them before my stomach even gets a chance.

At least I have my silence. Even outside, it feels like someone has turned the volume down. A cannonball rolls back and forth inside my stomach, its weight keeping me lodged in the gap between the couch cushions. If I don't get up I wonder how long it'll be before the door goes, whose finger will be on the buzzer. What would they do if I didn't answer? How far would they go to find me? How cold would my corpse be before the hinges were barged off the door? The cannonball rolls.

The first time I felt fear was the day of my dad's funeral. I'd been scared before – a barking dog is scary, falling off your bike is scary, but frights and fears are not made of the same stuff.

I was ten when Dad died, old enough to know what that meant but young enough that it remained some phantom element of my own life. That changed in the crematorium. It changed when the curtains closed and Mum stood with me and Pete either side of her, hands shaking so hard that when she touched my back my teeth chattered. Fear clung to me so tightly it's never really left.

The morning of the funeral, Mum had told me I still had to do my homework, but the jotter had vanished itself. When I told her she didn't fuck about. 'You can't just lose things, Matthew. Things are precious. You need to learn to take responsibility now and you need to learn fast.'

My ear buzzed all the way up the stairs. It was still hot and ringing when the car came to take us to church. I thought it was odd we weren't going to the normal church. Mum explained that there was a special church for funerals. She said sorry for clouting me. I said it was fine, it hadn't hurt and I'd found my jotter. It had and I hadn't.

The crematorium felt pretty much the same as the usual church, I remember. It was like the school library but emptier, as if there was more room for the musty smell to play in. I didn't listen to the minister. I just watched his mouth and imagined the words tumbling out, marching over the box and trying to nudge Dad back to life. The minister talked about Dad as if he wasn't in the room.

That's when the fear came. The words didn't creep into the coffin, they crept into me: Dad 'was' instead of 'is'. Past tense. Passed away. He was gone. Those words burrowed into me and my bones began to tingle. I let them, the way you tease a cramp into curling your toes before you stand and stretch it into submission.

They say the only two primal fears are falling and loud noises.

84

Everything else is psychological, a factor of our experiences. Once fear arrives, it stays there, marching with us as sure as our feet do. I can feel it on my skin at times, when a plane takes off, when a threat is made with intent, when I think of that summer day we said goodbye to my dad and filtered out of the room in a slow, sobbing mess. Strangers hands pressed against my sweaty palms at the door and their owners told me how sorry they were, how I'd have to look after Mum now. And as this cannonball swelled in my stomach, heavy and dark, all I could think was *what now? What now?*

Later, after I'd washed my sweaty palms and eaten my fill of steak pie at the Golf Club, the minister told me it was just as well I was a big boy because Mum would need me to do some of the things Dad used to do like take the bins out or hug her when she was sad. He said I had to take responsibility. As the minister sat opposite me, his finger waggling and ale on his breath, I could see Pete with one of our cousins; they were playing hide and seek under the tables, heads poking out every few seconds. I was fucking ten years old. I could barely look after my school jotter. Fear crawled all over me then and it's doing it again now.

Fuck fear.

I run the bathroom tap until it turns hot then scrub my face and shave, using a new razor blade. When I'm finished I slap the mixer tap from hot to cold and push the plug down, watching the sink fill. I dip my face deep into the water, closing my eyes and holding my breath until I feel my heart scream for air. That's when I begin to count, slowly…. to five….

then ten….

Nicky…

Fifteen…

Siobhan…

Twenty……

AndthenIcomeupandsucktheairfromeverycorner…………of …….the………….room,……..my chest rising and falling until

85

oxygen is everywhere and the dull weight of the cannonball is flushed away, its heaviness absent and my mind clear enough to reach for the towel that will dry my hair before I dress, splash on some of that good aftershave I got in duty free, and grab what I need to win the day. There's no time to wait about for phone calls and horse races. They will come to me. I will go where I need to be.

Yes. Fuck fear.

***

Underneath an umbrella is a place so privately snug that it offers a level of comfort normally sought in sunbeams. I'm leaning against a wall, nicotine easily overpowering nerves, the brutality of the rain having diluted the ping of my morning whiskies and gin, which probably isn't a bad thing. Under here I'm not missing a brother, I'm not missing £10,000.

I watch as people pass, a thousand footsteps lost in individual worlds. Somewhere across town Pete is listening to how much it hurts to lose a son, guilt likely bearing down on him but without sufficient pressure to provoke action; Bradley is dictating his empire from a quiet corner of luxury; Turnbull is laying foundations for a future brighter than any this city can provide; Nicky is at peace, waiting patiently for me to find him. He knows I'll get there, that in less time than it takes for the Earth to rotate on its axis we'll be together again. Even as I stand here, I am in perpetual motion. We are always moving forward.

Siobhan is not a woman who leaves herself time in the morning to pack a lunch and so some time between half twelve and half one she'll emerge from the building opposite me, head to one of the many sandwich shops surrounding this part of town and pick up something ridiculously overpriced without bothering to count the handful of change she'll get from a tenner.

I always told her she was destined for the big time – from way before she met me. She was born into a happy family – Mum, Dad, big sister, all doting on her. She moved from Perth to Glasgow to study law and spent every second weekend going back to see her mates and family, her existence never ruffled by trauma or fate at its cruelest. On our first date we met in a trendy

West End boozer and slowly got drunk as we tried to impress one another. She admitted she had ditched another date to come out with me that night.

'So what's he not got that I have?' I can remember asking her.

'I'm bored with straight lines,' she replied. 'You don't strike me as someone who walks in a straight line.'

I played off the fact that I was just back from living in Barcelona. Six months in a flat share with Darren from Norwich, both of us learning the lingo and working for ex-pat marketing companies, pushing day trips to people who just wanted some peace and a sun tan. I made it sound more impressive than it was. I never told her about the time Darren gave me a handjob while a girl we knew watched us, transfixed, before getting involved herself, coke packed into our arteries, pumping thickly through the mess of bodies. My tamed version was enough to impress her into a second date. We built something solid enough to hold our weight within a few months. She tried to make me walk in a straight line and I drove her round the bend. We worked. Then we didn't. Then we did. Then we didn't. The first time she broke up with me I could see in her face that her heart wasn't really in it. I'd lost a record four jobs in six months while she'd just had her first promotion, made associate, whatever it was lawyers called it. It was as if we were playing snakes and ladders and everything I touched slithered me back to square one. Eventually she had had enough, let me go, told me I needed to make more of my life. It felt like being sacked. I spent two months running my CV through my mind - from the Union bar that fired me for my 'one for you, one for me' policy on pouring drinks, to the countless pubs that followed, pouring the pints that fate demanded of me, spending time on the opposite side of the bar and building resentment in place of a nest egg; the travel agency that I lied to about the scale of my employment in Barcelona, which ended when I was asked to translate a Spanish website; selling bespoke bathrooms, timber floors, extended warranties on white goods and tellies, insurance policies, selling anything but myself, one job leaking into another as I walked out in apathy or was asked to leave in polite tones of displeasure. I always wondered what would have happened if I'd finished uni, or if I'd not come home from Spain. Every time I tried to look forward I saw past regrets. Then came the letting agency. I don't know whether it was the fact I'd lasted a few months, or that I was wearing a suit every day, but Siobhan let me back in. For a while, at least. The six months that I'd class as our second honeymoon were the happiest of my life – me working steadily, her bringing home a packet, the flat being decked out in nice gear, a holiday to Barcelona to show her my old haunts. The safety of contentment.

And then I see her, safely shaded from my eyes by the brolly she's huddled under with a colleague. I can't see her face yet, but those are legs I've spent the best years of my life admiring and parting, and I know they're hers. I head for them, my own brolly lurching wildly in the wind and almost taking the eye out of some old guy who glares at me as if I'd unsheathed a fucking Claymore.

I catch them up and dunt their brolly with my own, unfortunately sending rivulets of water down her pal's jacket – inside and out.

'Watch where you're…oh,' says the pal. Veronica.

At least she used to like me. We got on well. I made her and Siobhan brownies once and delivered them to their work while they grafted through some acquisition papers that forced them to dispense with sleep for two nights. I say 'made'. I bought them in the supermarket and transferred them into my own Tupperware. It was the thought that counted.

'Shit, sorry, Ver,' I say, wincing.

Instead of replying she just looks at Siobhan, her eyes telling me everything I need to know about her opinion of me. Siobhan has a fringe. She's not had a fringe since she was a student.

'What are you doing here, Matt?'

I smile. She doesn't.

'I needed to chat to you.'

'You chatted to her earlier,' says Ver.

'Sorry, Ver, this is important. Properly.'

'Pick an umbrella,' says Ver to Siobhan, who hesitates before stepping from underneath her friend's to mine.

'I'll see you upstairs,' she says.

They wave at each other.

'Matt,' shouts Ver, turning back. 'I'm sorry to hear about Nicky. Really, really sorry.'

I say thanks. She means it too. Everyone means it. No matter how much they hate me, they find compassion in the fact I am minus a brother. Every time I hear the tone guilt seeps deeper into me. I hope he doesn't know what's happening.

'Let me buy you a coffee, I promise this is important,' I say.

'Ten minutes, Matt. I was only running out for a sandwich.'

The coffee shop is packed, full of suits not stopping once they've grabbed the mass-produced sandwich they think is artisan. We grab a table at the window just as another couple leaves. I wonder if they're in as big a mess as Siobhan and I.

There is no Siobhan and I.

I watch her while I wait in the queue. Her legs are crossed, tanned tights visible to just above the knee, where her beige skirt hugs her thigh. I want to watch her take it all off – tights first, before peeling off her pants and hitching up her skirt. I wonder what colour underwear she's got on. My cock stirs, reminding me of what she can do to it, reminding me of the whore that sloppily sucked it soft on my thirty-first birthday last month while Siobhan was off getting a fringe cut in. I leave her with her skirt and turn to the chiller full of sandwiches. I lift a tuna thing for her while attempting to find something without mayonnaise for me. No joy.

When I take the tray back to the table she's on her BlackBerry. She forces a smile as it's put away. 'How's your mum doing?'

'She's in fucking tatters. All over the place. She'll never come back from this. It's just a matter of keeping an eye on her.'

Siobhan has that sad look that people have. 'And how are you?'

I feel like this is a questionnaire. 'I'm about the same. Though at least I've got youth on my side. I'll be okay. It just won't, well… y'know.'

She lifts her sandwich and takes a bite. She suits the fringe but I'm fucked if I'm bringing it up. Break up haircut or whatever it is they call it in the movies. 'I can't go through this with you. I'm sorry, but I'm getting on with work, and… well, my life.'

I begin to question why I came here. I could have gone to Mum's, got Pete back onside, got something to eat that wasn't coated in mayonnaise. When we're troubled we seek out those we love the most. Whenever I had something to shout about I'd want her to hear what it was, to see her face soften as the burden split itself in two. I take a short, sharp breath. 'I need you, Shiv.'

'Matt, come on.'

'Since Nicky, things have changed in my head.'

She does that nodding thing that people do. It's not quite patronising, but it's in the same part of the dictionary.

'I've not been honest with you about something,' I say.

She stops nodding and puts the sandwich down. 'What have you done now?' She looks beyond me, towards the counter. Her eyes are fresh, like she's sleeping well. Hopefully on her own.

'Do you remember Phillip Turnbull?'

She closes her eyes, sighs.

'Yes, Matt. I'm fully aware of who that arse is… are you still fawning after him?' There's anger in her tone, just a dash, but there's plenty more in that bottle of bitters.

'We've got close. He made me see something in myself, something more than… this.' I point at myself.

Siobhan stirs her latte.

'He said that us meeting each other was a sign that things were changing for me.'

Her legs move. She's thinking about standing up, going forever.

'Please,' I say, raising a hand. It's time to put the right words in the right order. 'It was bullshit I know, but then he told me his idea. His book was selling massively in Australia and he'd signed a deal to do a six-month tour there but was worried it would leave his brand vulnerable here.'

Siobhan coughed. 'You've held me back long enough.'

'I just need one more minute.'

'I don't mean just now.'

'Let me explain. Honestly, this could make us.'

'Jesus. Ignoring "brand Turnbull" ...' she flaps her fingers in exaggerated air quotes. She knows this winds me up, '... what do you mean, "us"?'

'This is it for me, my chance to be a businessman.'

'You've as much chance of getting a lucky hand of cards as making it in business, Matt.' She checks her watch. Like whatever is waiting for her at work is more important than this. 'How much did you give him?'

I take a long glug of coffee and burn my tongue. Even with

everything between us I try to look aloof when I place the mug back down, as if nothing had happened, as if I'm not a complete fucking tool. 'Right, the basics are that Phillip and I have become partners. I'm co-founder of a new company.'

'How much money, Matt?'

'We've been in talks for a few months – since before, you know, us, you… me moving out. And I should have told you but I wanted to surprise you when it was time to announce it.'

'And today is the day to do that? The day before – '

'Death puts life in a fresh perspective. We've got a life to live. Together. Our scars are different shapes, but they make us who we are.'

She looks me in the eye for the first time since we sat down. 'You know what, I don't want to know how much you've given this guy. I'm bored telling you how pathetic you are. I don't have the energy.'

I wonder what she'd do if she knew I had five grand in my pocket. 'Please, this is for us. It's going to work. That's what I wanted to tell you.'

'You're pathetic.'

'I thought you didn't have the ener – '

'Enough, Matt. That'll do you.'

She gets up and raises a finger when I go to speak. 'I'll see you tomorrow morning. Whatever you do with the rest of your day, I genuinely hope you're okay. And don't be duped by a man who manipulates people for a living. He's got you right where he wants you.'

She just doesn't get it, but I'm not going to get any further today. The seed is in the ground though.

She pats my shoulder and as her fingers trail off I wish she hadn't. It felt exactly like it ought to, which isn't how it should feel now. She holds the door open for another woman and even with her back turned I can see the polite look on her face, the way her smile will turn up just a fraction on the left side and her head will dip a little, not in a nod, but in subconscious submission. Then she's gone: back to work, back to her life.

There are beers in the chiller on the row below the orange juice and kids' smoothies. I pull out the change in my pocket and start counting.

10

Counting back to the moment he committed himself to Barton, because mental arithmetic was one of the few stress relievers Peter could rely on, almost 602 days had passed. The calculation had taken just under five seconds to come together, re-imagining the scene slightly longer.

Peter had been sitting at his desk, a half eaten duck wrap spilling its insides on a report. His phone was pressed to his ear, the air around him humming with an upturn in the markets. Giddy traders were chomping down on designer sandwiches, plotting their afternoons with more confidence than Peter had felt in a while. Finally, there was a *Hello?*

'Cillian, Peter Fletcher. You recovered?' He tipped his wrap into the bin, along with the report. Boring shite anyway.

'Shotgun. What a weekend that was, eh? Great craic. Great to see you too. How can I help you?' His tone was professional, friendly, exactly what Peter had expected.

'We talked about some trades, I'm just reaching out, seeing how that was progressing?' Peter had resisted calling Cillian for almost a week, but curiosity was a devil that didn't stop tapping.

'Nice timing. I'm back in London next Thursday. Need to go and see my ma that weekend but let's have a pint after I've been over there. I'll mail you.'

The line went dead and Peter turned to his screen, keeping a close eye on a couple of numbers that he reckoned were about to peak.

Thinking about it now, as he sat on Nicky's bed, that call to Cillian was the very moment he bought into Barton. One year, 236 days and twenty-two hours ago, 14,446 hours, 886,760 minutes… Peter toiled for a moment with the seconds. He closed his eyes. 52,000,560. All of them gone. Never to be relived.

Cillian had emailed before the end of the day, suggesting they meet in Covent Garden. Peter picked a gastro pub he and Helen used to go to for a drink after the theatre, before the twins arrived.

A week later, Peter strolled through the pub's front door and was bear-hugged by Cillian, who was two-thirds of the way through a lager.

'I knew you'd come good, Shotgun.'

'I've not come good yet, pal,' said Peter, slipping off his jacket and sitting on the wooden bench that passed for a chair. The pub was bright and airy – all exposed concrete and untreated pine. It was packed with shoppers and PR people talking bollocks. 'How was the homeland?'

'A fucking shambles. Jaysus. It's like I channel the energy of James fucking Joyce every time I set foot on the island. Plane touched down around six and by half eight I was…'

Peter drummed his fingers on the table. 'No offence, mate, but we've got bigger things to discuss than your no doubt impressive bar tab in some backwater shithole.'

'You asked the question.'

'I was being polite. "Good, thanks" would have done.'

Cillian took a drink and sat back in his chair, his eyes scanning the pub. He looked like he was trying to be offended.

Peter couldn't help laughing. 'Since when did you get so sensitive? I'm just fucking with you.'

'London. Man, it's the rudest city in the world.'

'Compared to New York? Don't give me your crap. Business first, then we can compare weekends. Deal?'

'Okay, let's get an ale and burger and go through the details.' Cillian signaled to the waiter and ordered.

Peter did the same, a fresh orange instead of a lager.

'You've changed, man,' said Cillian.

'You were about to tell me about this Barton character.'

Cillian came back to life, leaning forward, arms punctuating every sentence. 'Okay, when I said this hedge fund had plenty of capital I wasn't fucking kidding. It's all Barton's too. I met the guy on some jolly a while back somewhere upstate New York. We got talking. He told me his plans. By this point Bernie had already told us about the Miami move so I didn't fuck about in selling myself to this Barton fella. Wouldn't you know, he made me an offer that actually convinced me to move back to this imperialist hovel as opposed to staying in NYC. He's a funny one for a hedge manager. Rude, bit like you, but he's not a playboy. A real fucking serious character and big enough that he could have been a rugby player. Maybe he was, I don't know. Intimidating mix anyway. Voice that could silence a trading floor as well, but blunt as fuck. And every time you say something to him he looks at you as if you've just told him he's got cancer.'

'So where do I fit in?'

'Like I said, he asked me for a trader I could trust. Now, I don't trust any of youse cunts, but when I saw you in Miami, I remembered that you see numbers the way I see them.'

'And how's that?'

'Quickly.'

The food arrived and they both began to dig into sloppy cheeseburgers. Cillian smothered his in ketchup, the way Sam would do to anything when she was in a restaurant *sans* her mum. It was banned in the house.

'The wash trade is a test,' said Cillian, the chewed up meat rolling across his mouth. 'As much for me as for you, I think. I'm not going to lie to you. He wants to know if you're onside and if I'm capable of pulling off what he's wanting.'

'Onside for what?'

'Look, don't think too much. He wants you to cradle his balls while you rub the shaft of his billion dollar cock, and when he spurts his load of solid gold nuggets, they'll land right in your eager mouth.'

'It's a risky thing to do to prove loyalty to a guy I've never heard of.'

'Think of it as insurance. Things are going to happen that you're not going to believe. You're here, which makes me think you've already made your mind up, so how about we cut the shit and get rich?'

Peter took a slow sip of his juice, wishing he'd ordered a pint. 'What's the stock? I take it he just wants to create a bit of momentum.'

Cillian's head bobbed from side to side. 'Well, something like that. Mr. Barton has found himself with a sizeable chunk of Valitech.'

Peter didn't like where this was headed. Valitech was a Spanish mob who had made their name with a series of mobile gaming apps that hit the zeitgeist square in the balls, real toast-of-the-City stuff, but tech was fickle and fleeting and Valitech had just reported losses running into hundreds of millions; something they didn't have nearly enough collateral to cover.

'How much is sizeable?'

'Nominal in the grand scheme of things, but he doesn't like losing money.'

'Well, he's going to. It's a distressed asset, mate. They're fucked.'

'Hence the reason we need to get a little momentum behind it. I'll call you with the instructions, just play along.'

'Dead cats don't bounce, Cillian. No matter what people say.'

'Look, you buy it, you sell it, you buy it, you sell it.'

'I know how it fucking works, Cillian. I'm saying if I'm caught – '

'Risk and reward, Petey, boy. That's what the City's built on, after all. Look, you won't be standing out there with your cock in hand. We've got a few guys working this so there'll be a lot of movement, which means the algos will pick up on it in no time. When you notice that happening, you can go and buy a fucking sandwich or something, pat yourself on the back. Job done. It's not a big enough company to pique anyone's curiosity.'

'That might be so, but what happens when the net value gets pumped up by the algos? If he sells everything before the asset crashes, it'll get traced back. Fuck's sake, if he's that deep in it, they'll need to notify the exchange.'

Cillian shook his head, his grin widening. 'Nothing gets traced back to Barton. I've learned that already. He's like a fucking drone. No one knows what his position is, but it's always exactly where he wants to be.'

Both greed and desperation could motivate people to cross dark lines but it was conscience that determined the course of action. A trade he could retire on? Well, that was a carrot that needed a big fucking bite taken out it.

He finished his burger and drained his juice. 'Let me think about it, yeah? You're asking a lot here, mate.'

'It'll be worth it, Peter. The start of something wonderful. Now, can I get back to me story?'

It all went smoothly in the end. Cillian called Peter a few days later and Peter put an order in for a small volume of Valitech.

When he put a sell order through simultaneously it was instantly picked up, at least proving Cillian had been true to his word and Peter wasn't having the piss taken out of him. Over a couple of hours he kept buying and selling and it didn't take long before the underlying value of Valitech started creeping up like a slowly stroked cock. He was making zero commission because the price he was trading at wasn't moving, but if Cillian was to be believed the payday would follow. By lunchtime the algorithms had got involved and the price was inflating. The stock was still fucking worthless in real terms, but Peter had walked by that point, focusing instead on trying to make some genuine positions. He'd spent all fucking morning distracted and his P&L was practically blank.

Two days after the wash trade, Peter still hadn't heard from Cillian. He hadn't heard a peep from Tom either, which was a victory in itself. He'd been keeping an eye on Valitech stock and it was back in the toilet. He doubted whether Barton had even held stock to begin with. Whatever, if it was a test, Peter wanted to know if he'd passed.

Kim was in the midst of a treatise on how brokers continually seemed to mistake female traders for high-class hookers. Stuey had mentioned that she shouldn't dress like one when out with brokers and they might not think it. The banter was good-natured with just a hint of malice. Peter was enjoying the distraction when his phone rang. Cillian's warm Irish accent greeted him. 'Peter me boy, I'd like you to take a short position on Taylor-Caraway.'

Short selling on Taylor-Caraway was suicidal. The company's results were due out the following day and talk was that they were going to post record profits. Peter quickly brought up the price and it was trading up 2.2 per cent for the day and would only go up the following morning. Taylor-Caraway was a financial services company that constructed algorithms for computerised trading. They were huge and getting bigger, with almost 9 per cent of all trades in London carried out by the firm's systems. Unless those systems were about to fail their shares were only going to go one way. Peter's vision narrowed as pain tightened inside his skull. Surely not?

'Are you there, Peter?'

Peter blinked hard, exhaled the pain out into the room as he looked around. It was a moment he captured, a single frame of omniscience. It felt beautiful. 'What sort of volume are you looking at?'

After taking the details, Peter got to work. He borrowed two million shares in Taylor-Caraway which he then sold on to the market. Tom questioned the trade and had to be appeased by Peter's talk of hunches and trust. Over the course of the day the price continued to rise, and when the FTSE closed at 5pm, Taylor-Caraway was up 2.8 per cent and Peter was in the hole for more than he had collateral for. His night was uneasy, sleep broken with visions of Miami strippers, Cillian's chunky lines of coke and that Irish cackle. Had he been set up?

The answer arrived the following morning. Taylor-Caraway had indeed posted record profits and the firm's share price continued to rise. The graph began to look like the side of a fucking mountain, with Peter standing at the bottom in his bare feet. He waited, confidence in Cillian waning by the minute.

And then it happened. Something somewhere went off course. Nonsensical trades started appearing at astonishing rates, sending random share prices spinning. Peter watched the whole thing as the floor around him flapped. It was insane, as if the market was on acid. The volume of voices grew and swirled through the air. No one had a clue what was going on, except Peter. The algorithms had gone rogue - and it was no accident.

Within ten minutes Taylor-Caraway had got everything under control but covering the losses of the trades it had made would cost tens of millions. Peter held off long enough to avoid suspicion before buying back the two million shares and returning them without a word of gratitude. He'd earned enough in commission to pay his mortgage off. Some fucking hunch, Tom had said, beaming. The rest of the floor were seething – there was plenty of chatter about Peter hacking into Taylor-Caraway's system, but he rode it all. He felt safe, the scale was so unimaginable that no one would ever think he was anything other than lucky. It might not have been enough to retire on, but it was the single most profitable day in his life. And it was all thanks to Barton.

Peter stood and smoothed out the bed sheet. He had to get back downstairs, but not yet. He opened Nicky's wardrobe. Clothes hung, redundant. It was awful. Little jeans with elastic waists, jumpers lined up in order of colour. They'd all go to the charity shop, probably. A job for Matt. Peter thought of the ache that his brother would be feeling. He closed the door and retreated to the window, flicking through his phone book until he found Cillian's number. His thumb hovered over the name. He swapped his work phone for his personal iPhone but didn't have a personal number for Cillian. Fucking amateurish, but what did it matter? He was stranded, his allies abandoning him. Cillian would be looking out for his boss, the fucking mystery man with the City in the palm of his hand. Stuey would be looking out for himself, and Tom? Who knew what was going through Tom's mind. He'd started the company when he was in his twenties himself and had guided it steadily, never pushing it too far, never allowing it to grow into something he couldn't control. He never got involved in prop trading and he kept the firm private, with a select few investors the only people he was answerable to. Until now. Now he'd be answerable to the Financial Service Authorities, to the police, and all he'd done was trust Peter.

Fucking hell.

The future was foggier than ever. All Peter had ever wanted to do was make his family secure. He had been doing a remarkably good job of it too before fucking Barton came along. There was the house in Putney, five minutes' walk from the river, excellent schools, nice cars, Tuscan villa, disposable income aplenty. No worries. It was in sharp contrast to his brother's world. He would occasionally hear reports from his mum about whatever fucking catastrophe Matt had attached himself to in any given month. Peter was beginning to wonder if their similarities outshone their differences.

He started flicking through the books on Nicky's shelf. Kids stuff: football annuals, comics, Roald Dahl. The bedroom was a shrine to possibilities that would never come to be. Once again, he found himself drawn towards the window. When he was little, he and Matt would lean out into the night and talk. There was something exciting about it; if their parents had caught them there would be have been bother, but that never happened. He couldn't remember when he and Matt began to drift apart. There wasn't a pinpoint moment, but everything changed when their dad died. Matt paid less attention to their mum, treated Peter like a child rather than a pal. Then Craig came along and everything flipped again.

Looking back on it now, Peter could imagine how nervous Craig must have felt. Peter was eleven, in that glorious summer between primary and secondary school. It had been four years since his dad died, and the memories he had of him were mostly recalled through stories Matt told. With photos of the man banished, he eventually forgot what his dad looked like. Matt had stronger memories and more of them.

Then one night she told them about Craig. She had met him at the travel agents where she worked. He worked for a holiday company and would come in to tell the staff about the hotels his company represented. She told them that he made her laugh, and that they'd been out a few times, for a drink (so she hadn't been working late!), to the pictures, things that adults did. She told them he was coming round for dinner because he really wanted to meet them. Matt had kicked Peter under the table when he began to protest.

The next night the boys set the table as Betty sweated over, what was it again, Bolognese? Lasagne? Something Italian anyway, one of Peter's favourites. She was a good cook. Still was, probably.

When the door went Betty shoved her apron in the cupboard and checked the boys' hair.

'You look pretty, Mum,' said Matt.

'You're such a suck up,' said Peter after she'd left the room. 'I bet he's a dick.'

Matt nodded. 'Probably, but that doesn't mean we need to be dicks, does it? Come on.' He grabbed Peter's shoulder and marched him up the hall.

Standing just inside the front door was this lanky man with a beard. A beard. Only teachers and paedos had beards, thought Peter. Or so he'd been told by Matt.

'Hi boys,' said the man. 'I'm Craig. Thanks for having me over.'

'We normally just use the side door,' said Peter, pointing to the more frequently used entrance.

'Peter Fletcher, that's no way to greet a guest. Say you're sorry,' said Betty, before apologising herself.

He said sorry as if reading from a script.

'That's okay,' said Craig, taking a big black coat off and handing it to Betty. 'So if you're Peter that must make you Matthew?'

'Matt,' said Peter. 'He doesn't like Matthew.'

'Matthew's fine,' said Matt, slapping the back of his brother's head.

'Let's have a welcome drink,' said Betty, leading them into the kitchen. Her voice was shaking and Peter couldn't understand why she was nervous.

'Hey you, take it easy.' Matt had stopped him before they entered the kitchen. His finger prodded Peter's chest. 'Stop acting like a spoilt prick. You're better than that.'

All Peter wanted to do was run upstairs and unleash a flood of tears into his pillow. The Craig guy would think he was just a kid though, so he took a seat and politely asked him about his job, if he got to travel a lot, if he got a discount on holidays like they did. He didn't give a shit about the answers, but he didn't have to. He didn't fully understand what he'd discovered that night until much later, but as long as he asked the right questions and retained the right information provided by the answers, he would give the right impression while ensuring he worked out what made a person tick. It was a gift he still used.

By the following spring Craig had moved in and Peter had realised the only way he could get away from him was to do well enough in school that he could move elsewhere. The irony was that Craig left first, but his legacy was screaming the house down on a constant basis. When the time came, the fact Exeter had a great reputation for maths courses was secondary to the fact it was about as far away as he could get from Glasgow without learning a new language.

It might have broken her heart in the end, despite Nicky coming out of it all, but the fact that Peter could remember Craig but not his dad was something he laid at his mum's feet. In turn he wanted a steady home for Sam and Jess. Two parents. Always.

And they had to be friends as well as sisters; he had to be a friend as well as a father. He couldn't do that from prison. Fuck, he couldn't do anything anymore. Downstairs, he heard the doorbell ring. He could answer the door. That was something.

He bounded down the stairs, pain piercing his head. He arrived in the hall as his mum was reaching for the front door.

'Don't worry, Mum. I'll see them in,' he said, ushering her back into the living room.

He was worried it might be McAllister, come to spill his conscience onto the living room carpet. Through frosted glass he could make out two figures, neither of which looked anywhere close to McAllister's Big Fucking Giant height.

As the door opened, a strange mix of perfume and aftershave hit Peter – one too musky, the other too sweet. Standing there were a couple who looked like they'd stepped off the cover of a straight-to-DVD film about plastic surgery gone wrong. The guy wasn't too ridiculous. His tan had no place in Scotland though, and he seemed to wear his aggression as comfortably as his black suit. He had a well-manicured goatee that was whiter than the hair on his head. What stood out was the botox-flattened forehead that gave his brow a look of fright that was at odds with his alpha-male body language. Standing there, chest pushed forward, he had the demeanour of a man who slept flat on his back, ball naked and unencumbered by the stresses that came with life. The woman was another thing. She was at least ten years younger, and had she left herself alone, would still have been stunning. As it was, her face looked permanently frozen in a polite smile, while her skin was the colour of cheap Indian takeaway and clashed badly with her garish yellow hair, a shade that Peter couldn't possibly have called 'blonde'. Her cleavage, bursting from a powder blue dress, demanded attention that would likely lead to a slap if the husband witnessed it. It was him who held the enormous bunch of flowers.

'Hello,' said Peter.

'You must be the brother,' said the man, stepping into the hall without invitation. 'I'm sorry to hear of your loss.' He stretched a hand out. 'I'm Bradley, a friend of Matt's.'

11

The pile of notes feels thick in my pocket as I stagger onwards through town, trainers kicking up water in a steady rhythm as the bones inside my legs feel like they're beginning to crack and splinter under the strain. One of these puddles is going to be six feet deep and when I sink into its depth the money will weigh me down like a brick. I will plunge far beyond the grasp of winning horses or missing coffins or business opportunities with a swift and significant return on investment. All that will be left is me and Siobhan, galaxies floating apart in an expanding universe: her scent, her single-dimpled smile just before she laughs, her slender fingers as she grips my cock or pushes her hair behind her ear – even they will drift from view as if they never existed. I need to watch her waken every morning, become aware of every new grey hair and wrinkle. It's the only way it can happen. *It will because I will it to.*

I suck manky air into my lungs and cough as my feet splash through the city centre. I shouldn't have gone to her. Today is not a day for stupid moves. Patience, Matt. Patience and pressing matters. I quicken my pace. Since finishing my beer and leaving the coffee shop, I've developed an assumption that today is the day I'll be mugged. *Empty your pockets, pal* they'll say, knife pointed, their hands hungry for a phone and a fiver. I can see them exchange a glance when they point to the inside pocket of my jacket and an inch thick pile of notes makes itself known.

Too much negativity creeping in. Turnbull's in the future, with Siobhan. Even Nicky isn't in the here and now. The only thing I need to worry about this second is the rain. As long as I keep the notes dry then they will multiply. I picture a horse crossing the line, Woody's smirk, McAllister's relief, Pete's surprise. I'm buying a fucking umbrella.

A problem is a challenge, is a goal, is a prospect of success. That's what Phillip Turnbull told me the first time we sat down together. The positivity I'm clinging to is all down to Turnbull's teachings. This is a man who's had books published on the subject, who can bring out the best in anyone.

If I'd left that first lecture after Phillip took his bow to a smattering of applause I wonder where I'd be right now. I didn't though. When he left the stage, I headed for the hotel lobby where I queued with twenty or so others to buy a book with a personal inscription. He asked my name and it felt like he was looking through my eyes, peering right into my brain. The book instantly inspired me. Maybe it was because I'd been at the lecture, and so could hear him speak as I read, maybe it just happened at the right time. It doesn't matter. What matters is that I had my hands on a solution. I tried to get Siobhan to read it. She laughed it off as nonsense, said he was a man who preyed on the weak. We disagreed in raised voices.

When he went back on tour later that year I pre-ordered my ticket, took my seat, listened intently, waited in another queue to buy his second book, *Your Mind is Not Your Enemy*. He smiled and signed his name again, yet it wasn't enough. There were too many questions, like how can you focus when stress muddies your mind, like how to deflect negativity as it sweeps towards you like a landslide, like how to believe you can do the things you need to. The night of the lecture I took a gamble, had a drink in every bar in every five-star hotel in the city. I was half-pissed by the time I found him, sitting alone, nursing something clear and pretending to watch the news while he gazed at a woman perched on a bar stool. He laughed later, when I told him this, saying I'd cost him a shag. The thought that she wouldn't want to sleep with him was one his mind was incapable of forming.

I bought a pint, asked if he minded a bit of company, explained that I recognised him, that it was strange we were staying in the same hotel. He didn't believe me, said he admired my tenacity, that I had his ear for the evening – reward for my effusive efforts, he said. He listened more than he spoke, asked questions about me with a warmth that went beyond good manners. He actually gave a shit. We spoke until the barman made it evident he wanted his shift to end. Phillip gave me his number, said that he had a duty to help others stare in the mirror and see what he saw. That was the start of it all, the start of a better me. I don't know how

I'd cope with a day like today before Phillip came along.

Patience and serenity are the binding roots of confidence, he told me once. *With them, ideas become achievements*. Yeah, and achievements stay out of reach when ideas stagnate and unsettle serenity. Where the fuck is he? I phone him again, straight to voicemail. I don't bother leaving a message this time. It's been six weeks since we poured over the business plan, agreed on the schedule and parted with a handshake. He did tell me the following few weeks would be crazy busy – a book deadline (his third, *Life Means Live)*, a couple of radio shows, a six-date tour of Sydney and Melbourne to test the water – but that momentum was with us, that the balloon was rising. I remind myself I was content enough with the plan before Bradley decided to be a cunt. We are still on schedule. It is Bradley and not Phillip who is trying to pop a pin in the balloon.

I get to Central Station and take my place in a taxi queue full of suits and old dears feeling flush enough to avoid a soaking at the bus stop. I hitch my collar up tight. The queue goes down quickly as a steady stream of Joe Baksis turn into the rank. I jump into mine and give him Mum's address. It's coming good, man. It's coming good.

'Some day for the rain, eh?' says the driver, his red face breaking into a smile that reveals perfectly white teeth. They look ridiculous.

'Must be a good day for you,' I say, thinking of him dragging this humungous tip jar into his dentist's.

'It's as if punters are scared to get wet or something.' He chuckles again.

I lean back, stretching my legs out. My jeans are stuck to me. I unzip my jacket and subtly check the cash. It's not dry, but it's not wet enough to be an issue. The car is one of those old style Hackneys, made in the days when suspension was a luxury.

'What is it you do yourself, pal?' he asks.

I want to slide over the wee window thing between us, but you're never in any control over the conversation in the taxi. They just assume you want to share your views on the world, that you give a fuck what theirs are.

'This and that.' It's all I'm giving him.

'Lot of money in "this and that"?'

'It has its moments.'

'Not enough for a brolly, but, eh?' He laughs again and slows down for a set of traffic lights. 'Tell you, pal, see if I had my way, I'd be ferrying folk from Palma airport to their hotels. That's the job I want. She won't have it though, says she'd miss her sister. Your sister can come and visit whenever she wants I says, but it's like talking to a brick wall, you know what I'm saying, pal? You married yourself?'

I shake my head, try to let my mind drift, but I'm bouncing along, his fat specky face a constant in the rear-view mirror. He's got the heater on full bung; it's a dry heat full of cheap air-freshener and a hint of his BO.

'Aye, well. Tell you, sometimes I think I'm just going to head to Spain myself, and it'll be up to her if she follows. You been to Spain?'

'I lived in Barcelona for a while,' I say, inexplicably. He looks at me as if I've told him I fought against Franco. The correct answer was 'no'.

'Did you? Now that's something. You enjoy it?'

'It's a good place.' This is what they do. Questions rain down like arrows and eventually your shield slips.

'What did you do there?'

And without them even realising it, they win. 'Funnily enough, I picked folk up at the airport. Not folk staying in the city, but ones heading down Costa Dorada. There's a load of wee villages, private villas and stuff. I'd drive them down, sell them day trips on the way.'

He takes this in, thinks about it for a while, probably imagining himself doing the job. It gives me a chance to get my phone out. I tap on the web browser and as he makes his way to Mum's I go back to studying the form for this afternoon. General Catalyst still looks good. Numbers run through my head as I weigh up the risk and reward. My five grand will get me back enough to keep Woody happy, with a bit more besides. The driver says something but I don't hear him. I'm staring at my phone as if I'm reading.

Seconds later my arse slides across the back seat as he swings a left at the lights.

'Where you going, mate?' I say. The cannonball swings round with us.

'Murder up ahead. Pensioners driving too slow in the rain.'

'I wanted you to stick to the main road.'

'Don't worry. We'll just head up round here, past the football pitches, over the main road and in that way.'

'I'm not wanting to go that way, mate. Can you just go back onto the main road please?' I lean forward now, my voice getting louder. Fucking taxi drivers.

'Just relax, pal, you know what I mean?'

I go to say something else, but he's only trying to help. He doesn't know. He doesn't

I sit back and stare at my phone. My eyes can't focus so I close them, just blank it all out, concentrate on the sound of the engine revving, the old leathery smell of the back seats. It's making me feel sick. Christ knows what's in there to come up, but it's not far away from putting an appearance in. That would serve him right.

Fuck it, I can't help but clear the condensation as we approach the pitches. I wonder if people in plane crashes look out the window on the way down.

The driver clears his throat. I know what's coming. I am not prepared for this.

'You hear about the wee boy got killed here last week? Fucking tragedy.'

I ignore him.

'I heard he just ran out into the road, poor guy never saw him until it was too late. Stupid, these kids. They need to be careful. Still, at least – '

'Just drive, will you?'

'Poor boy died before he hit the ground, I heard.'

I lean forward, gripping my phone tight. 'Is that right? How do you know?'

'Easy there,' he says, slowing down a bit. His voice is calm. 'I'm just saying there was an accident here last week, on this road. Wee boy ran in front of a car.'

'So you said.'

'Look pal, I'm just – '

'Were you here? No. So, you don't have a fucking clue what happened.' I slap the Perspex panel. I want to smash it, choke the bastard, ram his whitened teeth down his fucking throat until he bites his tongue off.

106

The taxi comes to a sharp halt. The driver turns around. 'What's your problem, pal?'

'Just let me out.' I try the door but the red light remains on.

'Look, did you know the boy?'

'Open the fucking door.'

'Look it's pishing down, let's just get – '

I start rattling the handle. 'Fucking move.'

'All right, calm down. Here you go. Fucking nutter.'

The door light goes off and I open it, breathing in the rain as I step out. I throw a tenner back inside.

'I'm sorry if you knew him. I never – '

I slam the door and hunch up my collar again. At least I've got clothes at Mum's.

The driver speeds away. The meter was only at £4.60 as well. Fuck this. I gaze up into the sky and watch the rain come down. I want to scream, but don't. Instead I clench everything, my jaw, my legs, my fists, until I begin to shake. I can't be here. Even when Mum came down I stayed away, told her I was sorry but I just wasn't ready. This street is in my mind forever anyway; I've run its length more times than Nicky ever did, football boots over my shoulder by the laces, sweat pouring off me but never getting tired. Nicky would have been bounding down this very pavement. He'd have crossed the road diagonally to save a precious second, he'd have seen the car, just long enough for his wee brain to process what was about to

I start to walk, then stop. I sit down on the kerb then stand up again. Ridiculous thing to do. My arse is soaked. I'm outside someone's driveway. They're probably watching me, wondering why I got out a taxi but don't seem to be going anywhere. I start walking again, ignoring all the twitching curtains. Across the road the pitches are shielded by a hedge. In front of the hedge is an iron fence, painted green so it can blend in. I know I'm going to see them before I do. At the gates of the park, where each weekend morning scores of kids run towards their pitch, eager to get their boots on and start playing, there are two dozen bunches of flowers tied to the railings. Stuck to each one will be a card with my brother's name on it.

The cannonball drags me across the road. The flowers are wilting in the rain. There are carnations, roses, plenty of others

I recognise but could never name. It's the cards I really don't want to see. The first one is in a child's scraggly joined-up writing, the blue ink running:

> Nicky,
> I'm sorry that you were knocked down.
> It's not fair. I'll miss you.
> Darren.

Darren makes me cry, he makes my cheeks puff up and redden.

> Dear Nicky, I hope you're playing
> football with the other angels.
> Lots of love,
> Emma

Emma makes my legs buckle. I grab onto the railings as I stumble. Who is Emma? Do you have girlfriends at eleven? I remember fancying Kirsty Fleming. I thought I was in love. Maybe Emma loved Nicky, in that way kids do. Maybe she's been crying every night.

The wee man wasn't a crier himself. He was made of a strong stuff – even as a baby he wasn't that bad. There was the odd night I can remember when he just wouldn't fucking quit it, usually when Pete had deigned to visit us, but for the most part he was content. From wide-eyed tot to curious toddler to a young boy who just consumed information. He was always smiling, his appetite for life not diminished by the fact his home was so different to those of his friends. They had their families, their siblings; he had this Mum that was as old as a Gran, and nothing much else. They were a good team. He never once questioned why he never had a dad. Maybe he would have in time, maybe he'd have wanted to find his prick of a father and ask him outright why he did what he did. Maybe he would have been a good enough wee footballer to hit the big time. Or golf, or tennis, or acting; something to put him in the public eye and draw Craig out into the open to claim the credit and tell the tabloids how much he loved his son. Who knows? Behind every tragedy there are so many unfinished chapters.

I stand up straight and look beyond the flowers to the field of pitches. It's deserted. I wish the taxi had just stayed on the main road. I run my hands through my hair. I need a towel. Jesus. The money. I check my inside pocket and sure enough the notes are beginning to get a bit too wet. It's a fifteen-minute walk, but I used to be able to run it five. I begin to jog steadily, getting further away from the flowers with every step. I concentrate on my breathing, following the route Nicky would have taken had his day gone like any other. I brush past the hedgerows and take a left. An old guy out walking his dog gets a fright and I apologise with a wave. The dog barks. Hell of a day to be walking a dog, but I guess you can't keep them cooped up just because it's pissing down.

I cross the road, dodging out between two cars as they pass. I ignore the horn beeping, my head down, chest beginning to lift more evidently. A stitch appears at my side. The whiskies with Woody won't be helping this. They say you shouldn't exercise when you've been drinking but you never see anyone drop dead running for the last train. I turn right and pick up the pace a bit, trying to run through the stitch. It feels as though it's pushing against my kidneys but I'm past caring. I imagine I'm Nicky running home after football. My team has won three-nil and I scored the last goal. I'm dying to get home to tell Mum, to phone my big brother Matt and describe how I picked up the ball from a thrown-in, turned inside my marker on the edge of the box before feigning a pass, moving forward a yard or two and drilling it into the bottom corner. What a goal! My teammates swarm around me. Only five minutes to go and the game's in the bag.

Maybe he did run out without looking, maybe the taxi rank gossip was right. I keep on, ignoring the weight of the cannonball. Pain grips me, but I welcome the distraction, pick up the pace until there's nothing but the burn in my thighs and the stitch in my side. I feel flab wobbling around my midriff. I cannot think of one thing in my life I don't need to change.

I slow to a walk at the corner of Mum's street. By the time I reach the house I've just about caught my breath and I don't even know what's sweat and what's rain. I am serenity. The stitch fades as I gulp at the wet air, and within a couple of minutes I'm ready to face them – my family.

12

'So what is it you do with yourself then, Peter?' said Bradley, taking a long slow sip of tea.

Peter was standing by the fireplace, Bradley closer to him than was necessary, his stare relentless. Peter had made drinks for everyone while Bradley and his wife – Heather, with a kiss on both cheeks – were introducing themselves. Bradley's voice had boomed into the kitchen, his lack of tact becoming apparent by the comments that peppered his conversation – terrible way for a boy to die, he'd said, as if there was a fitting way for an eleven year-old's life to be taken. Heaping sugar into the man's tea as he heard this, Peter had decided on the spot that Bradley was the worst sort of wanker – the man who believed his thoughts were gospel. This had only been cemented since Peter returned to the living room. Bradley may have had the ability to silence the twins, but his attempts at small talk were painful. He'd complimented Peter on his family, asked where he lived, and had now moved onto the third strikingly obvious question. What was next, asking where he went on holiday and giving him a fucking haircut? That aura he had around him though, something that rested between school bully and headmaster – coupled with the fact Betty had taken a liking to his flattery and flowers – meant that Peter was reciprocating.

'I work in the City,' he said.

'What, the city centre?'

'No, the City of London.'

Bradley's face was blank.

'It's what people say when they work in finance, I guess.'

'Another world that London,' said Bradley, taking a sip of his tea. 'Up here, we just say what we do, not where we do it.'

Unsure whether Bradley was winding him up or trying to get a measure of him, Peter just smiled and drank his tap water, deciding that his mum was getting an espresso machine for

Christmas.

Over on the couch, Heather was holding Betty's hand like a grief counsellor while Helen looked on. The contrast between the two wives was stark. Heather's lack of class shone brighter than the ridiculous diamond on her finger yet this stranger was the one stroking his mother's hand and nodding as she heard what a lovely boy Nicky was, how he didn't have a selfish bone in his body. His mum's voice was wavering, but she seemed pleased to be telling someone new about Nicky. Or maybe she was just pleased not to be alone with Helen.

Out in the hall there was a clatter followed by the sound of the door closing.

A strange smile crossed Bradley's face, disappearing as quickly as it arrived. 'That likely to be your brother then?' he said.

Before Peter had a chance to reply, the door opened and a sodden Matt stepped into the room, his face as pink as a pig's. He kicked the bottom of the door and threw his head back as if he'd just walked into it, causing the girls to squeal with laughter.

'Hello ladies,' he said, as they leapt from the couch. It was just as they crashed into his legs that Peter saw his brother's expression change from puffy-cheeked eagerness to something resembling the result of being told your plane is going down.

'Here he is, the star of the show,' said Bradley, moving towards him. 'How you bearing up, Matt? It can't be an easy time.'

'What the fuck?' Matt stepped back and clattered into the door, causing a vase on the TV unit to wobble. Bradley grabbed the piece and steadied it.

'Careful, pal,' he said.

His mum jumped to her feet. 'Matthew, watch your mouth!'

The twins, reeling from exposure to the naughty word ran towards their mum. Peter wanted to freeze time, get the fuck out the room and leave them all to it.

'Sorry, Mum, I just wasn't expecting…'

'It's okay, mate,' said Bradley. He hugged Matt tightly and seemed to whisper something in his ear. Whatever his words of comfort were, Matt was mute in response.

Heather stepped towards them, looking at her husband as if seeking permission to offer her condolences. Bradley even nodded at her, a single flick of the head. Only the colour of her make up and cut of her dress set her apart from a geisha.

'Matt, I just wanted to say how sorry we are,' she said.

Matt mumbled something Peter couldn't hear.

'We'll leave you to it,' said Bradley. 'We just wanted to pop by, let Matt here know he's in our thoughts.'

'Please, finish your drinks,' said Betty.

'I'm sure you've all got a lot to be getting on with,' said Bradley.

'We're so very sorry,' said Heather, stepping towards the door. She seemed in a hurry to get going now Matt had arrived.

'Apologies we won't be able to make it tomorrow, Mrs. Fletcher,' added Bradley. 'But I'm sure Matt here will ensure everything goes as smoothly as it can.'

He squeezed Matt's shoulder then offered his hand to Peter. 'My condolences.' He said it in such a tone that Peter wasn't sure whether he was referring to Nicky or Matt. It could have been either.

He wondered if this Bradley character knew something about Nicky, but the thought passed quickly; the guy was ballsy but he didn't seem to have the mind of a megalomaniac. It was more likely Matt had tried it on with Heather at some point, even if Bradley seemed the sort who would rip the limbs from anyone whose fingers or toes had been anywhere near his wife.

Whatever unsaid words were flickering throughout the room went on their way with the happy couple, leaving something close to a hangover in their wake. The girls were clinging to their mum. All adult eyes were on Matt. His plane was still crashing.

'Well, you made it,' said Peter, patting Matt's back. His brother's eyes were glazed, as if he'd been drinking.

'Why wouldn't he make it?' said his mum. 'Come on, Matthew, get your coat off, it's dripping all over the carpet.'

'Hiya, Helen. You well?' said Matt. He laid his jacket over the back of the couch.

Helen smiled. She didn't deserve what was about to land at her feet. 'Sorry to have to see you like this, Matt,' she said. 'It's just… awful.'

Matt smiled at the girls, coaxing them out from behind Helen's legs. He knelt and hugged them both, one arm around each, gripping them tightly. Too tightly.

'Okay, Matt, that'll do,' said Peter, but there was no

movement, no noise. And then from deep within the huddle, a wail. Matt's shoulders began to shake. The girls drew back but couldn't release themselves. Peter moved in and prised Matt's fingers away.

'It's okay, girls. Uncle Matt's just upset.'

Without the protection of the twins, Matt fell to the floor, palms pressed against the carpet, head down like a wounded animal. He was weeping loudly. Peter felt like kicking his ribs. He'd often baulked at the news when some disaster befell a developing nation and those mourning their dead would cry to the heavens, piercing the fucking sky open while the TV camera focused in on their grief. Those moments of extreme intimacy should be carried out in privacy, just as Matt should have kept his tears to himself. In front of Helen as well – as if she needed further ammunition. She hadn't even taken the girls from the room; allowing them to witness this breakdown was calculated. Peter didn't blame her – determine what you don't want your children to become and engage with a bit of positive reinforcement whenever the chance comes along. Solid parenting in his book.

'Come on. Up you get,' he said, grabbing Matt's arm only to have his hand swiped away. Fucking baby.

'Easy big boy, come on. The girls are waiting.'

Matt looked up, face red and wet. Rising to his knees he forced a smile at the girls as he dried his eyes with his sleeve.

Jess skipped over and patted his head. Sam joined her and together they tried to pull him towards the couch. Soon enough they'd learn that fun Uncle Matt was nothing of the sort. Helen was about to stop them, but Peter put a hand up. What was that thing about children preferring to play with kids their own age?

Matt sniffed and wiped at his nose. 'Have you pair been behaving yourselves?

The girls nodded, smiling like they would for a clown.

'Are you sure?' he said, tickling their bellies.

Invigorated by their laughter, he scooped them up, one under each arm and swung them round, just about keeping steady. Disturbing him could be just as dangerous as leaving him to it but he began to turn with them, speeding up, his steps wildly off balance. As the girls came round for a third rotation Sam's head just missed the fireplace. Helen screamed and Matt staggered back, banging into the coffee table. He'd stopped moving, at least.

'Put them down,' said Helen. 'Idiot.'

'All right, calm down,' said Matt, the words merging into one. 'You ladies not want a twirl from your Uncle Matt then?'

Having rushed into their mother's protective arms, they were gazing at their uncle as if he was a pet who'd just shat on the carpet. Matt slumped into the empty couch, spreading himself across it.

'Maybe you should head upstairs, sort yourself out,' said Peter.

'I don't need sorted out. What you talking about?' He squinted his face and looked at Helen, who was ushering the girls towards the kitchen. Betty had already left the room.

'Sit down, Helen. Matt's leaving,' said Peter.

He hauled Matt to his feet, straightening up his collar with the unfortunate delicacy demanded by an audience of children. 'I need to speak to you in kitchen,' he said.

'What for? I'm busy. I've not seen my nieces for months.'

Peter leaned in closer, as if offering a hug, his lips almost pressing on Matt's ear. 'Get the fuck away from my children.'

Matt twisted away. 'Eh?'

'Kitchen, now.' Peter began frog-marching Matt into the next room, managing a quick rabbit punch to the back of his head. Matt shook his head but didn't otherwise react.

'Uncle Matt's tired, girls. He gets just as grumpy as you when he's tired.'

'I don't get grumpy,' said Sam.

'Yes you do,' said Jess. They paused, then both laughed.

Peter shoved Matt through the doorway just in time to see his mum throw plates into the sink with a clatter.

'I was going to ask where you'd been but it seems fairly obvious,' she said.

'I had stuff to do. I meant to phone,' said Matt.

'Well, you weren't feeling very well earlier, so perhaps that's why you forgot to phone.' Her voice cut through the room and Peter half expected her look to give him a black eye.

'You're drunk,' she said.

'No I'm not.'

'Do not lie to me, Matthew Fletcher.'

Matt's lies were just part of who he was; they came out as naturally as the air from his lungs, and probably just as frequently.

'Mum, seriously. I just ran here to get out of the rain. I've not been drinking. Jesus, what is it, lunchtime?'

'You're a liar and you're a bloody mess.'

Matt raised his hands in defence, his tricks the same, their impact weakened through overuse.

How many family feuds had been decided in that kitchen? All three of the lives Peter had led before leaving had used the room as its headquarters – each of them with Betty in the matriarchal hot seat. There was the family Peter had felt part of, the one with a dad and a big brother who hadn't quite worked out how to be a cunt yet. Sure, they kicked each other under the table and Matt's hilarious running gag of flicking peas on the floor and blaming Peter had caused more tears than laughs, but it was their room, the one where the telly didn't dominate; the weekday rush and the weekend calm, when cereal was replaced with pancakes and sausages. It was still their room after Dad had gone. They were all quieter for a while, but it was still theirs. Then Craig moved in. At first it was the occasional weekend morning, their mum chirpy and the radio louder than it normally was. Peter would trudge in for his breakfast and sense the smiles before he saw them. Mum by the grill, Craig sitting reading The Daily Record and drinking coffee (his breath always stank of coffee). It had to be the kitchen where she told them. 'You're going to be seeing a lot more of Craig. Not just at weekends, but all the time.' Peter had cried. The need for companionship was not something he could comprehend at the time. All he saw was betrayal – of his dad, of him. Craig had no right to sit at the table his dad had paid for, or climb the stairs his dad had fixed when they squeaked and splintered. Craig gave the impression he was committed to family life though; he never tired of trying, until his own child was on the way, at least. It couldn't have been easy, forever buying three tickets for the football or the pictures and only ever needing two. It was only as an adult that you could see the harm you were capable of causing as a child, the hurt you could administer with a few words you didn't understand. And then he was gone. When faced with fatherhood, real fatherhood, he'd reached for his running shoes. Fucking pathetic. He would never know that the son he abandoned was dead. Well fuck that, he may have never been a father, but Peter was going to make sure he felt the pain of losing a child. As soon as he dealt with Matt he was heading for 'the box', the hidden biscuit tin that was home to the folders where his mum kept her life. Some of Craig's details may still be there, and a private investigator could turn a ten year-old bank account number into a present day address.

'Where have you been then, Matthew? Enlighten us,' said his mum. 'You ran off without a word three and a half hours ago.'

Shit. Always get your story straight. The one piece of advice Matt ever gave Peter that stuck. In fact, it may have been the only advice he'd ever dished out. 'I told you, Mum. He had stuff to take care of.' He stressed the last three words in the hope she'd think he was talking about Siobhan and not pry.

'Stuff? The only stuff he's been taking care of comes out a bottle.'

'Can I have some water?' said Matt.

His mum poured a glass and handed it to him. Her hand was shaking. 'Your father would be ashamed to see you like this, today of all days.'

'What? That's a fucking terrible thing to say, Mum.'

'Watch your tongue, you.' Peter slapped the back of his head. Matt reacted as if a wasp was loose in the room.

Their mum began to sob and dabbed at her eyes with a dishcloth. 'What's the matter with you, Matthew? You think you're the only one affected? Please. Just go.'

'Go where, Mum? This is where you need me today.'

'She doesn't need you anywhere near her like this, mate' said Peter, putting an arm around his mum's shoulder. He wondered if this was how bomb disposal experts felt as they crouched over a volatile device, never sure how it would react to their movements, always wary that an explosion was imminent.

Matt nodded his head, a grin forming on one side of his mouth. It made him look like he was having a stroke. 'I wondered how long it would take.'

'For what?'

'You know fine well what.' Matt nodded at Peter's protective arm.

'Why don't you just go and take care of whatever it is you need to do,' said Peter, refusing to take the bait. If Matt would just get the fuck out the house, squeeze someone for the cash, fucking Siobhan even, and reappear when it was time to do up his tie properly the following morning, Peter could at least focus on his own problems.

'You'd like that, wouldn't you?'

'Yes, Matt. I'd like it very much. As would everyone else, I'm sure.'

'Well, everything's in hand. Don't you worry. I'm here for lunch with my family, but if they don't want me then that's fine. It's cool. I can deal with that.'

'What's in hand? What are you talking about?' said their mum, shrugging off Peter.

'Nothing, Mum,' said Matt. 'Everything's fine. Just you make sure you look after Pete. You might not see him again for six months.'

'This isn't the day for shit like that, Matt,' said Peter.

His mum slapped him on the arm. 'You watch your language.'

'What the fuck, Mum? Jesus,' said Peter, fending off another slap. 'Shit. Sorry, no. Fuck's sake Matt.'

Peter's voice had risen to the point Betty stepped back. 'Deep breaths,' she said.

'Truth hurts,' said Matt, his face twisting grotesquely.

'Is this how it works Matt? Crawl around looking for someone to hand you the life you feel you deserve, finding nothing but empty bottles and then coming round here to agitate Mum until you feel better about yourself?'

'At least I'm here.' Matt prodded himself in the chest. 'Me. I'm the one that's here, dealing with everything. Dealing with going to hospital and identifying him, dealing with – '

'Matthew, please no.' His mum covered her mouth and stepped back against the sink. Behind her, the lawn looked so vivid against the dark grey sky.

'No, Mum. He needs to hear this. He's got no idea. Down there in happy ignorance of everything that's gone on here since the day he walked out on us.'

'I went to university, I didn't walk – '

'You walked out and you know you did.'

117

If there was one thing Peter hated it was being confronted with a truth he denied. Of course he walked out. Why the fuck would he have stayed, with a screaming baby in place of the fake Dad that had disappeared? 'You don't know what you're talking about. You need help,' he said.

'Maybe I do. I wonder what they would say was wrong with me. What do you think, Pete? What's my downfall, eh?'

'Please, stop it Matthew. Just stop it.' Their mum's face had reddened, mourning temporarily replaced with a more recurrent emotion, though Peter wasn't sure if it was outrage or embarrassment.

'I told you, he needs to see the damage he's done. How many years has it been since you walked, Pete? Ten? All those years without giving a sh… a damn about your actual family.'

'My *actual* family is in the living room, unless they've got in the car and driven as far away from here as they can.'

He saw the look on his mum's face before he could change the direction of the sentence. It was the same one he'd seen when he said he was moving to Exeter. She'd been expecting him to go, but to another part of Glasgow, Edinburgh at the most. Not four hundred and fifty miles away.

'You're still my family, Mum. You know what I meant.'

'Family? Ha.' Matt spat the word at him. 'When was the last time you invited her to London? When the last time you took her off to your posh gaff in Italy?'

'Look, you don't understand.'

'I understand fine. You don't care about us. This entire trip is an inconvenience to you. There's bound to be something infinitely more important going in your world.'

If only you fucking knew, thought Peter. He turned to his mum, who was contenting herself staring at the floor. Her roots were coming through; it was as if every part of her was slowly malfunctioning. Seeing her only a couple of times a year, Peter still pictured her younger than her fifty-three years, and was always surprised when he saw her – crow's feet, arms losing firmness, slower off the couch than she was once. And that was before Nicky's accident. 'Nothing is more important than me being here today,' he said. 'And tomorrow. Okay?'

'And I'm the liar. You couldn't make this up. Are you listening to him, Mum? Or it is just me that lies?' He turned back to Peter. 'You left and if you had it your way you'd never need to come back. The odd trip to appease Mum and hand over a present to Nicky. Well, one down, one to go, eh?'

'Right, that's fucking it.' Peter grabbed Matt's arm and dragged him towards the back door. 'Outside, now.'

'You can't punch your way out of this, fatty.'

'You think so? Mum, we'll be back in five minutes.'

He opened the door and shoved Matt outside. He turned back and mouthed an apology before closing the door. He wasn't entirely sure what he was apologising for but Matt's attack had wounded him where he hadn't expected, right in the heart of his conscience.

13

Back in the pissing rain. Here we go again. So soon after our last dalliance. I step out of the grasp of Pete's big stupid hands and spin around. 'What exactly is it you think you're playing at, wee brother?'

'Don't talk like that in front of her.' He's standing tall, bravado to the fore. Pete the Protector. Always acting, always playing a part.

'Truth hurts, eh?' I look inside the kitchen and Mum's just standing there watching us. I give her a smile and she shakes her head, her mind made up the second his car pulled up outside. He'd have been as well arriving in a Superman costume.

'That old cliché was bullshit the first time you used it,' he says.

I want to give him that denial-ain't-a-river-in-Africa patter you see in films, but fuck it, I'm not in the mood. 'Then let's stand here and find a cliché that fits as well as one of your tailored suits, 'cause I just wasn't fucking wet enough.'

'Does that chip on your shoulder give you back problems?'

Shite patter. The patter of someone surrounded by Yes Men. He's got the cheek to turn away from me as well, as if that was a clincher. Is he going back indoors? He can't lock me out my own fucking home as if I'm a disobedient dog. I just need a drink of water and something to eat and I'll be fine. A wee lie down next to the fire wouldn't go amiss either right enough.

He heads towards the garage, takes the latch off the side door and ducks his head as he steps inside. Was lunch really too much to ask?

I follow him, knowing there is much to discuss – hopefully not including a Q&A on the life and times of Bradley. Fuck was he playing at, coming here? He's bold, the cunt, I'll give him that. Drinking tea, smiling away, hugging me, having a wee word in my ear. *Tick fucking tock, Matt.* I should've pumped that Heather when I had the chance. He'd never have found out.

It's dark in the garage, stinks of mould. And it's freezing. You could lift it up, Wizard of Oz style and drop it in the Mojave desert and it would still be fucking freezing. At least the rain would have stopped rattling on its roof I suppose. The only window is clouded over by webs, which gives it an eerie half-light that fades into complete darkness at the opposite end. Garden tools lie rusting along the wall, redundant aside from one little shelf where Mum keeps the bits and bobs she still uses to keep the garden in check. There are mousetraps dotted around two huge white spots on the concrete floor that at least reveal the source of the mouldy smell. I told Mum to leave the mice alone, but no, she didn't want Nicky being bitten. She should have had the thing knocked down years ago. Back in the day, Dad used to give its frame a coat of creosote every summer. It was the smell of school holidays and hide and seek, but there's not a note of it left. Everything rots eventually.

'What are we doing in here?' I say. 'I just want a fucking sandwich and to get on with my day.'

'We're keeping you the fuck away from my children. Christ, Matt, did you leave the undertakers' and head for the nearest off-licence?'

'I'm hardly pissed.'

'You're hardly sober.'

'Fuck off. I had a whisky to calm my nerves. It's been a bit of a morning.'

He doesn't say a word, just stares at me. I shouldn't have opened the gin.

'You can't talk like that in front of Mum,' he says, eventually.

'Why? In case your cloak of invincibility slides off your fat shoulders?'

He walks to the far end of the garage, where the main doors are, where the light doesn't reach, and vanishes. I can hear him trying to push one of the old doors open but the wood is warped and he quickly gives up.

I consider telling him who Bradley is, allowing the shock to knock him off track and get him off my case.

'You don't get it Matt,' he says, stepping back into this dimension before I can make my mind up. 'All you're doing is upsetting her.'

'All you're fucking doing is upsetting her. You think she likes knowing that Helen's folks practically live in your gaff in Italy and she's never once been invited?' My legs can't take this anymore. I flip a wheelbarrow onto its back and sit on it. I didn't even know we still had a wheelbarrow. 'Why did you never fly her and Nicky out there? Can you imagine how much they'd have enjoyed it?'

'It's not as simple as just – '

'Of course it's that simple. "Mum, fancy a week in Italy?" There. Simple. I can't be bothered listening to your bullshit, Pete. You want to know where I've been? I've been to where it happened. I've read the messages on the flowers pinned to the fence at the pitches. Highly recommended reading. You might finally begin to waken up to what's happening here. Imagine it was Sam or Jess, out riding their bike, deciding to cross the road because someone waved at them – '

'You think I've not done that? It's right fucking here.' He taps his head a bit too dramatically.

I spin the wheel of the wheelbarrow, allowing its creaking rotations to replace our voices. For now, it's just this rhythmic squeaking and the pattering of rain.

Pete stops pacing, his hand moves to his pocket but he changes his mind. 'What happened to this place? It never used to be so dark,' he says.

'That's what happens when you don't pay attention to things.'

His selective memory serves him well. The garage has been fucked since Dad died, a good decade before Pete left. Craig never really gave much of a shit about the garden. I think he always felt like he was taking over every aspect of Dad's life and so he let that one be. Mum should have moved house when Craig moved in. I don't know why she didn't, hasn't.

'You never made it easy for him, you know,' I say.

'Who, Nicky?'

'Craig.'

'What's he got to do with anything?'

'I'm just saying.'

'Well don't just say.' He's started padding again.

I need to keep him off the hot topic, and if it's not Bradley that's going to do it, I've got just the man for the job. 'Craig never tried to replace Dad. He just wanted to be part of our lives.'

'Why are you bringing him up?'

'He left Nicky, you left Nicky.'

'It's hardly the fucking same, Matt.' He stretches a foot out to stop the wheel turning. I start it again, look him square in the eye while I do it.

'I saw him once.'

He pulls back, eyes widening. 'What? When?'

'I was in town. He'd left Glasgow, he said. Was only over for a wedding. I remember thinking 'over' could have meant Edinburgh, but his tone suggested further afield. Maybe. I don't know. It was awkward as fuck. I saw him pass me and I tried to keep going, but something wouldn't let me, so I turned back, overtook him and passed again to make it look like an accident, you know. He said hello, all sheepish like. Holding hands with a woman, so he was. She was younger than Mum. His age.'

'When was this?' Pete looks fucking deranged. If I ruffled his feathers earlier, I've plucked them out now, exposing him to a reality that's making him shiver.

I stretch my legs out. My knee's aching from the run. 'Five years ago. Maybe six. Nicky had started school anyway. I asked him how he was. He said fine. I told him that he might be interested to know he had a son, that Mum still stayed in the same house. You should have seen the look on the woman's face. I just got on my way. He never appeared, obviously. Fucking horrible. I tell you, every time I run that conversation through my head I say different things, put him on the spot, demand a fucking answer.'

'Then why compare him to me? Just to score a point?'

I look at my feet. My trainers are for the bin. 'Because he was a cunt for leaving, but he was all right when he was here.'

'He was a cunt full stop.'

For someone so clever Pete's not so good at reading between the lines.

'Would you rather she never had those few years of happiness?' I say. 'Rather she never had Nicky?'

He doesn't say anything. If there were ropes in here, he'd be leaning on them.

'I saw your face in there. You don't… didn't even see him as a brother. What was he to you? A distant cousin?'

'Don't do this, Matt.'

'Just fucking admit it then.'

He moves back into darkness and kicks the door. Warped wood splinters, light cuts into the garage in daggers. I jump to my feet. It's opened enough for him to stick his head outside, but he doesn't. Instead he turns back, the open door casting light across half his face. It's chilling, like a poster for a horror movie. I hope he's not about to ring the bell for round two of this morning's pathetic spat.

'You know something?' he says. 'I feel alien when I come back here, but at the same time that I belong. It's fucking bizarre. I never think about this garden for example, but just now, before you brought the circus to town, I was up in my room looking at the height of the birch tree.'

'Nicky's room.'

He brushes the correction away with a wave of his hand. 'Yeah, Nicky's. Anyway, when I left for uni it was level with the upstairs window on the house across the back lane. Now it's beyond the chimney. It looks exactly the same, but it's kept growing, no one taking any notice.'

'Okay. So Mum's been neglecting to climb sixty-foot trees to prune them. What's your point?'

I'm starving, cold and just want out of here. He's not going to recognise we've both got our faults. Maybe that's the way to go, never admit any wrongdoing, any flaws. Is that a marker for success?

'I read once about a plant called a Rafflesia,' he says. 'From Indonesia or some fucking place. I'm sure it was Indonesia. It's not like a tree. It's not got any stems or leaves, doesn't even have roots. It just sticks itself to something else and goes for it. A fucking parasite that sucks the life out its host. The weird thing is, it's got the biggest flower in the world, up to a metre across. It's beautiful, the colour of strawberries. But here's the thing. It smells like a rotting corpse. That's how it attracts insects. Locals even call it the "corpse flower".'

'Thanks for the horticultural lesson, but what are you getting at?'

His eyes look like they're searching for something he'll not find in here. 'The birch out there doesn't bother anyone. Just gets on with things. This corpse flower looks as though it does the same, but probe deeper and you can see it sucking the life out everything around it.'

I step forward. 'I think you best watch what you're saying.'

'Don't flatter yourself, Matt.'

'What does that mean?'

'It means the world doesn't revolve around you. It means your problems are of such little fucking concern to me that there's no room for them in my head.' He puts his foot on my wheelbarrow as if he's posing for a sculptor. He'd probably like to see his bust cast in bronze. He is ridiculous, and I've got things to be getting on with. This conversation was always going to be about him.

'So Nicky's my problem?' I say.

'Look, you've got three options. The first is you continue to kid yourself on that you can do what needs done here. Now if you want to get serious, get me a sort code and account number and I'll transfer it over to whatever scumbag you've fallen in the sewer with. I suspect that's not how these things work though, so option three, if you need cash, I can get it, but I'll likely need to go to the big branch in town, and pretty fucking soon.'

Fuck him. I'm not a parasite, strawberry coloured or not. Woody's right – Pete's not like us and he's got no business trying to assume control of this like some sort of hostile takeover. If he flashes his cash here I'm beholden to him forever and even if we never cross paths again, even if we're on opposite ends of the world, he'll forever be here, in this rotting garage, telling me he's fixed things as if he's talking about putting new batteries in a remote. I have my game plan and I'm sticking to it. If I can move beyond the gall of Bradley turning up, I can sidestep this cocksocket in front of me.

'Keep your money warm. I don't need it.'

His eyes roll. 'Bullshit, Matt. Where are you going to find twenty grand?'

'Like you say, my problems are of no concern to you.'

He just looks at me. He's always had to know the intricate details of everything he's ever involved with. The bits people don't find important are the bits he's drawn to.

I laugh. 'You can't cope, can you? Can't get your head round the fact I don't need you. Man in your position should know better than to make assumptions.'

He looks dejected, like he's lost something. His fucking marbles judging by that last rant. His forced snigger fades into a smile. 'You know what, you're right. Bang on the fucking money. And you know what else? Good on you. If you're not at the wind up then you're having a better fucking day than me.'

The listlessness in his voice is taking the shine off the moment. Something's burning in paradise, as sure as a shite follows a fry up. So that's why he got all biscuit-arsed in the kitchen. All this really is a distraction for him, for whatever deal has gone awry in Petetown. It's time the curtain was lowered on this particular scene.

'Look,' I say. 'I don't have time for lunch. Can you – '

'No one's going to ask why you're not there. No one cares where you are.'

I want to tell him he's not better than me, that our genes and the chemistry in our heads might have moulded us into different people but we've still got the same blood. I could walk out the garage and never see him again and my life would not suffer as a result. His wouldn't either. I want to ask him why we're both okay with that. I want to put his finger in a mousetrap. 'I'll see you later, Pete,' I say.

'You seriously don't want this money?'

'You can get back to being the hero tomorrow.'

'This isn't something to piss about with, Matt. You leave here now and there's not going to be a funeral. You're going to ruin what's left of her.'

'Stay out of my business.'

His hands go up in surrender. 'Sure. Whatever you need. Like you say, it's your problem.'

I leave him in the garage to lament his Rhodesian flower or whatever the fuck he was on about. I look in the kitchen window and it's empty so I head indoors, quietly. I can hear a kids' TV programme in the living room. I grab my jacket from the coat hook in the hall and head upstairs.

In my room I take the cash out my pocket and rest it on top of the radiator. By the time I take a piss and change into fresh jeans, the notes are a bit drier and going crinkly on the edges. I've gambled again. I could have taken the twenty Pete offered, given Woody half and used the other ten plus my five to start again, renting fucking bikes on Phuket beach or something. Fifteen big ones would last a while in that world, but not long enough for me to forget that it was Pete's money that took me there.

I hear the toilet flush, the tap running. I stick my head against the door. Footsteps. They stop along the landing.

'Where are you?' It's Helen's voice. A pause, then, 'Well get back inside.' Another pause. 'Of course she's upset. Is he gone?' And another, longer this time. 'He's an alcoholic, and he's not coming near the girls again.'

Clueless bitch. There's a difference between an alcoholic and someone dealing with the most inconceivable fucking stress. I grip the hip flask in my pocket, take a swig of whisky, enjoying its warmth as it slides down my throat. She knows nothing.

When her footsteps have faded I head downstairs. The back door clicks behind me as I make my way along the side path. Before I'm even on the pavement I can feel my jeans press against me as the rain resumes its assault. There's no way I'm going to fail today. Fuck lunch. The reality of the morning is being swept aside by the possibility of the afternoon. Just south of the border, General Catalyst has his head buried in a bag of oats, a stable boy brushing him down. The big bastard better be in the mood for it.

14

The garage window was clouded over with too many years' worth of stour and spider webs. It was from this perspective that Peter watched what could have been an apparition of Matt close the back door behind him and head down the side path.

The M74 had never held more appeal and as soon as the wake was over Peter would be heading south as fast as Helen would allow him, away from whatever mess Matt was about to create and towards... he didn't know what.

Long after his brother was gone, Peter continued staring at the path. The concrete was cracked in places; too many footsteps, too much rain. He pictured Nicky running between back garden and front, playing with pals either real or imagined. At least Peter had Matt to chase him round in circles when they were younger. Nicky was an only child in many ways – his toys his own, always to be found where he left them. Peter had often dreamt of a life without Matt. No one to tease him, to trample his sandcastles or administer Chinese burns. Just him and his mum. At least he'd not had to endure a parental split. His dad's death was hardly comparable to divorce, and with Craig it never felt like losing a parent. Fucking Craig. And Matt had seen him? Actually met his fucking eye and told him about Nicky. Peter wondered if it was only parents themselves who couldn't fathom the concept of abandoning a child. He wondered if Matt had told him Nicky's name. *Over for a wedding.* That meant he lived in Europe now, maybe North America. Craig, Barton, whoever, wherever: people should face consequences – and if Peter had to then so would every other fucker.

In the dim light, he began pacing the length of the garage, his phone pressed to his ear. 'Tom, it's me again. Just checking in really, seeing if there's anything to report. Give me a phone when you can.'

He slipped the phone back into his pocket. He had to assume

that every call could later be played in a courtroom and so had tried to sound as relaxed as possible.

The garage stank of damp. The wooden frame was cold and wet as rain leaked in through the corrugated iron roof. It was a deathtrap, a cell, a foretaste of the future. It needed demolished. It was also fucking freezing and everyone would be wondering where he was.

In the kitchen he heard a voice he didn't recognise from the living room; female, friendly enough but sharp. Lunch was already well overdue thanks to Matt's pissed-up tantrum and if he knew his mum, she'd be getting anxious. The constant stream of sympathetic well-wishers would be comforting, but exhausting. He wondered what horror she saw at night when her visitors had left and she was alone with her heartbeat. It was how she would always be now.

He poured a glass of water and began rifling through every drawer and cupboard in an attempt to find some painkillers. In among the tins of beans and sweetcorn – because where the fuck else would they be? – he unearthed something soluble and a packet of prescribed Co-codmol. He added two tablets to his glass and stirred with his finger to speed up the effervescence. When the tablets were barely dissolved he placed a Co-codmol on his tongue and washed it all back. Showtime.

'Hello little ladies,' he said, marching into the room.

The twins were sat on the big couch with Helen, while Betty shared the two-seater with an elderly woman who looked as though she'd died a few years back but had refused to stop chatting. Was that…? Fucking hell, it was. Mrs. Carter – wicked of tongue, knifer of footballs, killer of dogs. Okay, the last one was unproven but rumours had been rife. She was one of those women that had been in her eighties since the dawn of time, the only thing keeping her going her hatred of school kids. She was dressed for church, dyed hair tightly curled and wearing a dark crimson dress that would have had a bull stamping its feet and snorting.

'Is that you, Mrs. Carter?' said Peter. The painkillers were doing nothing yet.

'Peter, hello,' she replied and stood up, putting her glass of wine on a coaster. Fucking wine? Now that was an idea.

She hugged him tightly, her skinny frame pressing so close against him that Helen would have stepped in were the old cow not just bones strung up in a leathery, kidney-spotted bag of skin. Mothballs and cheap perfume flooded Peter's nose and he coughed just as she planted a clown's kiss on his cheek, catching enough of the side of his mouth that he could taste her lipstick.

He wanted his life back.

'I was just saying to Betty how sorry I was to hear about Nicholas. I didn't like to knock the door, but it's the thing to do, isn't it? I'll be there tomorrow and I wanted to let you all know that you're in my prayers.'

'That's very kind of you,' said Peter. Nobody ever called him Nicholas.

Mrs. Carter had taken hold of his hand and was stroking it back and forth. 'Such a handsome man – to think I used to watch you running up and down the street out there.'

Peter laughed. He tried to withdraw his hand only for her to grip it tighter.

'Where's your brother?' said his mum. Her tone was flatter than it had been all day. Peter suspected Mrs. Carter was about as welcome as Matt.

'He had to nip out, said we should just eat without him, if that was okay.'

'That boy, he never stops,' said Mrs. Carter.

Peter whipped his hand away and scratched his neck. 'Are you behaving, girls?'

They nodded and smiled. They almost always smiled. There were tears of course, the odd tantrum, but on any given day they'd spend ninety percent of it happy, collisions with drunken uncles aside. Helen was an incredible mother. They were lucky on that front. He moved behind the couch and squeezed her shoulders. She'd been unsure about giving up work, she was a good events manager, but with Peter's salary he'd been able to give her the choice. It depends if you'd prefer them to spend their days with a nanny, he'd said. She never went back.

She'd maybe have to start looking for work. The villa in Tuscany was in her name so that was safe, the house was paid off and there was no way they'd go after that anyway, not when there was so much cash and stocks available. The only things that would change were the income and the lifestyle – his more than hers; at least she'd have more than an hour a day outdoors.

He shook his head; the negativity needed coughed up and flushed away. In all his years of trading worst case scenarios rarely came about. Even 2008 could have been worse.

'Is it time for this family lunch we've been planning then? I'm starving.' he said.

His mum stood up. 'Yes, it is. You can help me, Helen.'

Helen had never once leapt to her feet on Betty's command. In fact, his mum had never once commanded her. Peter felt an unspoken conspiracy stir as they both headed for the kitchen. Helen smiled at him, eyes bright with hidden laughter.

Mrs. Carter was shaking her half-empty wine glass. 'Wee top up, Betty, to help the sandwich down.'

So the prompt for her to fuck off had been treated as an invite. Of course it had. Stupid.

'Beautiful girls,' she said, as Peter took a seat between the twins.

He lifted both onto his lap as a sort of shield. Within seconds their weight was crushing his thighs. They weren't slow in getting big. 'You hear that, girls? Mrs. Carter says you're beautiful.'

The girls looked sheepish, smiling at Peter but rooted to the spot. The old witch had cast her spell all right. Bad news for the girls. And for Peter's quads.

'Cath, please. You're not a wee boy anymore.'

There was something Craig always used to say about her. Cath Carter. It always cracked his mum up. Even Peter had laughed. He couldn't remember what it was. The little things fade eventually. In twenty years time would he even remember the conversation he was having? He fucking hoped not. In twenty years he'd have made enough to pack it all in, spend more time in Tuscany than in London – the girls visiting for long weekends when they could get away from work. Barton would be a forgotten figure, nothing more than a memory that would occasionally surface over a late night Limoncello. It was all possible.

At the end of his second year at uni he called his mum to explain that he'd picked up a job in a small accountancy firm for the summer and wouldn't be home. She'd fallen out with him.

Nicky was still just a baby and she'd been expecting his help. They hadn't spoken for a month, until Matt appeared in Exeter one random afternoon and urged him to go home, for a week at least. When Peter returned from Glasgow, mentally battered by the experience, he'd headed straight to the pub with his housemates, where at the table next to him a group of girls were settling into a session. Helen had been the one to say hello.

They never really decided to move in together. It was just that neither considered an alternative, and so on a hot summer's day they drove up the M5 with Peter's Golf stuffed full of everything they owned. He was set to commence work with AMJS two weeks later.

They rented a flat in Clapham – tiny place that at least had a separate bedroom. The living area had space for a two-seater couch and a TV unit along with a ridiculous plant that Helen insisted sat in the corner. The plant was the only thing that made the move to Putney with them.

When he got his first month's salary, he booked a table at the cocktail bar in the Ritz and ran up a £200 bar tab. This is how we're going to live, he told Helen. She slurped her cocktail and he burst out laughing.

He heard Mrs. Carter cough. 'I said, how are things in London? I hear snippets, of course. Betty says you're doing well. Lovely car outside.'

'Thanks,' said Peter. He had an urge to literally pick her up and deposit her on the pavement. There was no inclination to expand his response so he left the word hanging and began to twist a lock of Sam's hair around his finger. He marvelled at how straight it was, so delicate. He wondered at what age they would begin to cut their hair differently. He hoped they wouldn't be one of those sets of twins that still dressed the same in their sixties. He pictured an old woman lying in an open coffin and another in an identical dress standing over it, weeping. Coffins again? What the fuck was happening to him? Where were the fucking sandwiches?

'So, can you?'

He was aware Mrs. Carter had said something. 'Sorry, what?'

'I asked if you could remember Mr. Dougan, from number forty six.' She was terse with her reply.

Peter began to wish the girls weren't there. Good manners were to be encouraged at all times. He could remember Jimmy all right. Decent old guy, always telling stories about his days as an amateur footballer. 'No. I don't remember.'

'Oh. It's just, he passed on last month.'

Poor old guy – probably had had enough of Killer Carter's dynamite chat. 'I think I'll go and see what's taking those sandwiches so long. You pair look after Mrs. Carter, okay. She's a guest.' He bumped the girls off his knee with an astonishing surge of guilt and shot through to the kitchen.

When he opened the door, Betty and Helen turned quickly, their cheeks puffed up with suppressed laughter. Peter's tension broke into a stupid grin.

'What is she doing here?'

'She's making herself at home,' said his mum. It was the first time he'd seen her smiling all day.

'She's pissed,' he added.

'Language, you.' She hit his arm with a dishcloth.

'My shift's over. Your turn,' he said to Helen, whose head was shaking before he finished speaking. 'The girls were asking for you.'

'I'm sure they were,' she said. 'Okay. You can finish these. And be quick about it.' She flashed a rare smile at Betty and headed out the room.

Peter looked at the counter top. Eight slices of white bread with too much butter on them were awaiting fillings from a selection Betty was currently dividing up. Helen would have been horrified. She really was a saint.

'There's too much butter on these, Mum.'

She threw her knife into the sink. 'For God's sake. I can't do anything right, can I?'

He was taken aback by her tone. She'd looked so contended a second ago. 'I just – '

'I'm sorry. That woman. She's no business here other than picking up gossip for her bloody club. She'll be taking in every last detail of anything you say or do and drawing the wrong conclusion from it. Just help me finish these and we'll get moving. Sooner we eat, sooner we can get her out.'

Peter began to scrape butter from the bread then lift slices of ham from a packet and lay them on top. He wondered if this was the sort of laborious work that happened in prison. No. He wasn't going to fucking prison. Again he chastised himself. He would win; that was what he did. There was no time to lament the decision he'd made in Miami. Besides, he hadn't stopped to consider his actions while the trades from Barton kept coming.

After the Taylor-Caraway storm, Barton vanished. He'd given his performance and left the stage as the applause was still ringing. Peter continued to pitch the odd bit of business Cillian's way but he was always dismissed with that same fucking cackle. Weeks later Cillian called with another instruction that seemed out of the ordinary. A pattern began to emerge: Peter would execute the trade, then something unusual but inconspicuous would happen to the stock. Barton had a handle on acquisitions no one expected; he could speculate on the oddest fluctuations and walk away with a win every single time. For Peter, the slaps on the back from Tom and the growing commission kept him from thinking too much about how Barton managed to have an oracle's grip on the markets. Ignorance was innocence. The car was upgraded; a new Maserati Granturismo Sport arrived, soon followed by the Range Rover for Helen. On their first weekend in the villa, Peter opened a bottle of Cristal and raised his glass into the warm Tuscan air to the phantom fund manager who had made it all possible. When they returned, the girls were enrolled at a highly reputable public school. It's not that he wouldn't have achieved those things, Barton just accelerated the process.

All he had to do now was work out how to get the better of a ghost who had ears in every office.

'Ready then,' he said to his mum, cutting the sandwiches into triangles.

She nodded. 'Though I'd like to get her out the house and eat as we intended… Matt aside.'

'Come on. It'll be fine.'

They transferred the sandwiches onto a tray before returning to the living room to find Mrs. Carter in a full on rant at Helen. Something about bin collections. At the sight of the sandwiches a bored looking Jess jumped from the couch and ran towards him.

'Jessica, watch,' said Peter, just as she swerved past Mrs. Carter and knocked the glass of wine over. The old dear leapt off her seat and started kicking at the air in an attempt to get wine off her shoe. It was more the look on Jess's face that made Peter laugh. He tried to capture it, but it was already loose in the room. He could almost see it wrap itself around Mrs. Carter and spin her into a daze.

'What exactly is it that you are laughing at?' she said. Incredulity was spread across her face as thick as her blusher.

Peter sucked in his cheeks. He considered what he was about to say, weighed up how easy it would be to just apologise and get on with the day. 'Tell me honestly, did you once kill a dog?'

His mum's hand covered her mouth, an exclamation just about slipping out.

The noise that emerged from Mrs. Carter was far more primitive. It was the sort of sound he imagined an elephant would make if you trod on its tail.

'I'm asking because I'm curious,' said Peter, as relaxed now as he'd been all day. 'You seem very curious about me, so it makes sense that I'd be curious about you too, doesn't it? My curiosity is channelled though.' Peter was gesturing with his hands, actually enjoying himself. 'In fact it's almost exclusively focused on whether or not you're a dog killer. You must have heard the rumours? Killer Carter? The Dog Burier?'

'Peter, that's enough,' said his mum.

Peter's hands protested. 'Like I say, I'm just curious. Look girls, Mrs. Carter's face is the same colour as her dress. Perhaps she should go outside and see if she can cool down.'

'Monster,' said Mrs. Carter. 'I never took your children for monsters, Betty.'

'Just get out,' said Peter.

His mum began guiding Mrs. Carter towards the door, muttering apologies. Her witchy fingers were getting nowhere near the fucking sandwiches. Any win's a victory, as Tom always said.

'What's got into you?' said Helen. 'That was beyond rude.'

'She's rude. Did you see the look she gave Jess? Nosy bisom.'

'What's a bisom?' said Jess.

'Actually, yeah, what is a bisom?' added Helen.

The Scots ran deep, thought Peter. 'Mrs. Carter is a bisom.

You ever hear the word again, just picture her.'

'Bisom,' said Jess, trying it out.

'And if I hear you saying it again, there'll be bother. It's not a nice word.'

'Then why did you – '

'Because Mrs. Carter is not a nice lady. She was upsetting your gran, and she was about to shout at you. And no one shouts at you except me and your mum, okay?'

He heard Betty clear her throat in the doorway and was about to apologise for the sake of lunchtime serenity when he saw McAllister standing beside her. His mum's face had fallen, any trace of the smile he'd seen in the kitchen having long since faded.

15

Even my cigarette's getting wet. I smoke quickly, before it disintegrates. The walk through the estate from Mum's cleared my head at least. Always Matt's fault. Always accountable. I can't be fucked with Pete anymore. If ever a day needed a hero it's today, and it's not going to be him. Before turning onto the main road I sneak a quick nip from my hip flask. I'm going to need my wits about me in here.

Back when I was wee, I had to wait outside the bookies when Dad disappeared into the smoky fog. He'd occasionally emerge, jacketless and grinning, and hand over a quid to me and Pete to buy-some-sweets-and-get-back-quick-without-stopping-anywhere-but-the-sweet-shop-or-else. Then he'd disappear again. I always wondered what magic lay inside.

The days he left smiling, he'd have a sneaky fish supper and keep us quiet with a pickled onion each. How he managed his dinner afterwards I still don't know. Greedy bastard. Most times when he came out though, there was no grin. He would walk home so quickly we had to jog to keep up. It was the only time I ever saw him in a bad mood, the only time he didn't kiss Mum before he sat down for his dinner. If I noticed these things, she must have too, but she never said anything.

Bookies might look brighter now, they might have windows and vending machines, but most days the punters still go home too pissed off to kiss their wives. Not me though. Not today.

I've had sex that's left me breathless, I've had pills that left me sure the meaning of life was within my grasp, but nothing comes close to a big win. Nothing. First time I got the buzz was at my dad's Golf Club. It was the year before he died. They had a Ladies' Day in the summer and the clubhouse was open to all, women and children allowed to openly mix in the monastery of misogyny for one day a year. Not that I appreciated such gender inequality at the time, of course. I was only fucking ten. Dad bought us all tombola tickets and when it came time for the draw I was transfixed. One of the senior members rotated this battered wooden box as it sat on a rudimentary stand. The crowd cheered every time he stopped, and his wife plucked out a ticket. The room fell silent as she announced each number. On the table next to her were bottles of whisky, massive chocolate bars, ornaments; all manner of pish, and one by one folk would shout their number, put their drink down and walk over for a prize, ticket aloft. The whole place felt more alive than it had all day. About ten minutes in, with just a handful of prizes left, my own number came out the box: 34. It's still my lucky number. I cheered and ran up to claim my prize. I picked out a wee toy monkey and bounced back to Mum, Dad and Pete. Something surged through me and I felt like I might just float off. I didn't care that the three of them were already clutching their booty. Every nerve ending revelled in my delight. It was a glow that only I could feel the heat from. Everybody won that day, but I felt like the only winner.

A few days later, when I bet Andy twenty pence he couldn't hit the blackboard with a bit of chewing gum, the glow returned. He got a hundred lines and I got a little richer. It was as though the sun was swelling in my stomach and its beams were radiating into the heart of every piece of me. That haze, man it was fucking beautiful. It faded all too quickly though; by the time I got home it was gone. I made a bet with another kid the next day – twenty pence again, on heads or tails. When I saw the Queen's head wobble against the playground concrete I sunk beneath it, a black hole greedily consuming me. A precursor to the cannonball had replaced the starlight, but it was worth it compared to the possibility of the glow. The potential high was worth the low. It still is. Watching that little white ball bounce across a roulette wheel, no one knowing where it's going to settle. Red. Black. Starlight. Cannonball.

I've sunk so low that I thought I might never feel the glow again, but luck changes, that feeling returns. It always will. And you never know when.

I never much enjoyed poker. I preferred the honesty of roulette, the binary beauty of triumph hanging on odds or evens, red or black. Or the educated approach to sports betting that reduced the risk and worked the odds away from the house. There was something about poker, the way it was more about your opponents than you. I'd played a few times, lost a few times. That was before The Treehouse, before Simon the landlord asked me if I fancied a game and curiosity opened a bright shiny box of potential.

I was living with Siobhan in the West End and working for a horrific short-term letting agency. The pub near the office was always good for a sharpener to ready me for the bus journey home. It was one of those pubs that was always quiet, to the point you wondered if it was a front. I got to know Simon fairly well as he had fuck all else to do but shoot the breeze with the few folk who did keep his hands busy. One night when I'd stayed for longer than a couple he asked if I fancied a game of poker, after closing. Politeness coupled with curiosity and the effect of the pints had me nodding in agreement. At finishing up time, he bolted the door, leaving me and three other boys who had been lingering over their pints. No one said a word.

Simon led us up a narrow staircase to a big office space that had a round green baize table in the centre. It was only when they took their seats among a few others who were already sitting there that my new acquaintances began to chat. A couple of scary-looking sorts sat on comfy armchairs not saying much, but their looks providing sound advice on what was expected in the room. One of them introduced himself as Woody, the other stayed silent. The good-fucking-nutter, bad-fucking-nutter routine. I learned later that it was Woody who gave the room its nickname of The Treehouse because the trees at the back of the pub did an admirable job of blocking the view, should anyone wish to pry as to what was going on.

No one seemed tense other than me so I tried to relax, helped no end by Simon when he handed me a bottle of beer from a fridge. He winked at me and took a seat with Woody and the other heavy.

I didn't win that night, didn't get near it, but the following week I headed upstairs again after seeing how big the pot could grow and realising how satisfying the win would be, how bright the glow. On my commute and in quieter moments at work I read up on the game, learned how to play, how to read faces –

the twitches and direction of gazes. The week after I didn't do as badly. I was patient, studying the eyes of these strangers who sat around me. I learned when to be bold and when to fold. Eventually I was playing twice a week, confident of standing up with more than I'd sat down with. Over the weeks the bundles of chips grew; some nights I left with hundreds of pounds, walking home with the glow trailing out behind me like a million fireflies. Some faces stayed the same, others changed. There must have been two dozen of us on Simon's team sheet, but only ever eight on any given night. If you turned up and the table was full, tough shit.

Occasionally, a man in a suit would appear. Wide-shouldered and immaculately dressed, he would only ever observe us. Emotionless and silent, he would sometimes leave before we finished, other times he'd still be standing there as we left. All I'd ever exchanged with him was a nod and a smile. Then one night I won big, over seven hundred quid in the pot. That night as we got our coats and headed downstairs, he said hello.

'You been playing a fair bit, yeah?' he said.

I nodded.

'You play anywhere else or just here?'

It had never occurred to me to find other games, and poker tables at casinos were too heavy duty for me. 'Just here,' I said.

He offered his hand. It was thick, the ridges of his knuckles barely distinguishable. 'That's a big win tonight. Well done.'

'Thanks. Sometimes you just get the right cards.'

'Yeah. And sometimes maybe you make sure you get the right cards.' His hand squeezed mine. Pain gripped me; the glow faded under the weight his shadow cast in the bar's dim light.

I looked down at my hand, tried to wriggle free. 'I don't know what you mean.'

He pulled me towards him, spoke into my ear. 'Course you fucking do. I ever hear you've been cheating, you'll have your legs broke. Understand?'

I nodded. My bladder relaxed and I clenched hard to stop myself pissing right there in front of him. 'You seen the way I hold my cards? I wouldn't know how to cheat.'

'You being fucking wide? Everything a joke, eh?'

'I'm not joking. I'm sorry. I just – '

'I'm Bradley,' he said, releasing his grip. 'It's good to meet you.'
'Matt.'

'I know. I'll be seeing you. Matt.'

He nodded at Simon and headed out into the night. Everyone else had already gone.

Simon went behind the bar and poured two whiskies, sat down at an empty table. He kicked a chair out.

'Drink.' He clinked one glass off another. 'He's all right is Bradley. It's his pub. One of God knows how many. There's not many further up the chain than him. Don't worry. He's taken an interest in you because that's a lot of money you've won. It's better to be anonymous at times, but keep on his good side and you'll do okay.'

So I did. I engaged Bradley whenever he appeared, always respectful. We got drunk one night. I didn't know at the time, but it was a test. No cards, just an endless flow of liquid and conversation. As the sun was creeping in the windows, Bradley offered me some work. He said he'd put me in touch with Woody, who looked after 'operations'. I said it sounded interesting, but that unfortunately I couldn't commit, that my own work was keeping me too busy. He shrugged, said it was an open offer. Truth was, there was no way I was risking Siobhan finding out I was doing anything on the wrong side of the line. She was a lawyer for fuck's sake. She knew I played cards; she didn't like it, but let it slide. I wasn't pushing it.

My luck changed after that night, as if Bradley controlled the hands. I lost more than I could afford, chased it, fell into Bradley's debt. Always give a mug credit, he said to me once. I owed him £1,500 and had to come clean to Siobhan. She bailed me out, but that was the day we began to rot. I stopped visiting The Treehouse, started going straight home after work. I never spoke to Bradley again, not until Turnbull came along, not until the banks said no.

I wish I had time to head to a bookies in town, where there's less chance of meeting someone I might have once known. Out here, back in my old stomping ground, there's more chance of someone taking an interest in the sizeable nature of my bet. Suburbia is nosy and five grand is a lot of money to be sticking on a horse on a wet September afternoon.

See if I was a horse and I saw the amount of money that was being stacked on me being able to run faster than the horse next to me while some wee guy skelps my arse with a whip, there's not a fucking chance I could handle the pressure. It's good for them to be ignorant, literally blinkered as to what's going on around them; the deals and the odds, the despair they can bring and the fact they can make a man that's never so much as patted their nose want to kiss their big stupid horse lips. That man is me. I know what I'm capable of because I've done it before. I tap my pocket, feeling the weight of the cash, remembering how good it felt when it first dropped into my pocket. I've won before and I can win again.

As I walk, I plan. *Visualise and reprise your desires until they become real and true.* Here's how it goes. You walk into the bookies. You wipe your feet on the mat because your feet are soaking, in fact, if you're not mistaken there's a fucking leak in one of your shoes and your sock's getting wet. Inside, you take in the reek of Eau de Pensioner and wonder not for the first time why so many of the folk inside are under forty when there's plenty of good job centres they could be hanging about in. You stare at the bank of TVs – Sky Sports News; some football match in Australia or Japan or some fucking place; a greyhound race that two old punters are keenly observing – enjoying would be overstatement when they look as though their pensions are riding on a dog's ability to chase a plastic rabbit. One screen has an interview with a jockey and trainer as they get ready for the race that is going to decide your future. They are laughing, relaxed. You are not. You are shiteing yourself and considering the casino. Betting red and watching black come up would be painful, but quick. Not like this. Not like the torture of leading then dropping back, pushing forward, not quite gaining momentum, but then bursting late on and

TVs everywhere. And slips. Every spare bit of a wall has been displayed with slips for football, for racing, for picking the winner of fucking I'm a Celebrity ballbag. Step right up folks, deposit your earnings here, we won't even tax you if you win. If. And then there are the gaming machines. Arcade casino terminals in the more informal surroundings of your local bookmaker. It's no coincidence that the machines that make the most money are in the poorest parts of the country. Simple social experiment: take someone with fuck all, give them next to nothing and the chance to lose it and watch the queues form. There's a reason you never see a millionaire feeding a fruit machine.

You put these distractions behind you, knowing that losing focus could lead to the loss of everything. You wish they still allowed smoking in these places. Not because you particularly want a fag, but because the dampness of the young malnourished guy sitting nursing a can of Coke is permeating the entire room. You wonder if he knows he smells so bad, if he's in the country legally.

YOU CANNOT ALLOW YOURSELF TO BE DISTRACTED.

So you make your way to the HORSE RACING section, where that day's races are pinned to the walls, splashes of coloured cartoon busts indicating the jockeys' jerseys, and next to them a wealth of information on the horse and rider – useful if you understand that sort of thing, which you do. You ignore the pre-loaded sheets that make backing a horse as simple as entering the lottery. You grab a blank slip, old school, and lift a pen from the box. Tiny wee red thing. It reminds you of a schoolboy joke: cock like a bookie's pencil. You snigger. You wonder when they switched pencils for pens.

YOU NEED TO FOCUS.

On the slip you write

Carlisle 2.45
General Catalyst 6/5. to win
£5,000

He is the favourite for a reason. Favourites don't always win right enough. Maybe one in every three races, just how the bookies like it. General Catalyst looks solid though. Two seconds and a fourth in his last three races; ground conditions ideal; a jockey that's won on him before. And it's a four horse race so you know the favourite is even further ahead of the field, the odds of an upset reduced to a point where hope becomes

143

expectation. £5,000 becomes just over £11,000. Simple maths. Simple. You take the slip to the desk. On the other side of the counter sits a pretty blonde who looks good now but will likely still be sat there in a decade, three kids worth of weight on her hips and the backchat from a million unhappy punters having long since killed her smile. Her work shirt looks cheap and half a size too small.

'Just this, thanks,' you say.

She takes one look at your slip and says: 'Just give me a sec, I'll need to get my manager.'

A minute passes and behind you one of the old boys starts shouting.

'Go on, go on, run ya fucker, run!'

His mate is shaking his head, mouthing ,'Useless bastard dug.'

The girl is still away. The old boy is shouting 'comeoncomeon comeoncomeoncomeoncomeon' until it sounds like a train passing. Then he screams: 'Go on number four, go on ya wee shite. Yes. Yesssss. Ya fucking dancer.'

'You can get the pints in,' says his pal.

'With pleasure, Jim. With pleasure.' The winner is grinning like a schoolboy. His teeth have seen better days.

'Cash?' says a male voice. You turn to see a tall streak of piss with two days worth of stubble staring back at you.

You reach inside your pocket and withdraw the notes, pass them under the gap and watch, hypnotised as the manager counts them. Twentyfortysixtyeightyonetwentyfortysixtyeighty twotwentyfortysixtyeightythreetwentyfortysixtyeightfour... and so it goes until his hands are empty. Then he repeats it, moving in a blur.

'Chelle, there's a queue,' he shouts behind him, not losing count. There are two dodgy looking sorts so close you can feel their smoky breath on your neck. It would be just fucking typical if today was the day the place was held up. Bookies don't have it easy. Take Chelle there. She doesn't get paid to deal with some jumped up twat deciding he

FOCUS

The manager hands over your slip, you thank him and wander over to the bank of TVs. The race starts shortly. You've done your bit. The whole thing will take just five minutes. Three hundred seconds to determine which direction the rest of your life will take.

I run this sequence of events through my head time and again, thinking of the horse approaching the line, a half-dozen lengths to spare, taking me out of Bradley's debt without so much as a sheen of sweat on its coat.

I turn onto the main road and the smell of oil from the chippie reminds me I've still not eaten today. There will be plenty of time to eat soon; full fish supper, just like Dad – I'll even throw in a pickled onion for old time's sake.

I walk past the chippie, the charity shop, the newsagents. I don't break my stride until I'm wiping my feet on the bookie's mat. My sock is wet. I think there's a fucking hole in my shoe. This is it. It's beginning.

16

What the fuck was McAllister playing at? Peter's eyes were locked on the old man's, hidden as they were behind those gold-rimmed glasses that hung on his beak like they were supposed to make him look trustworthy, comforting. If anything, they made him look like a child catcher. And now he was here, in the family home, where Peter's children were trying to wrap their hungry, developing minds around the concept of death – not of some ageing grandparent from McAllister's generation, but one of their own.

Both McAllister and Betty remained in the doorway, the silence somehow preventing them from stepping into the room. Peter felt Helen at his shoulder; he was becoming aware he was staring the undertaker down, while the undertaker sized him up. Probably literally.

'Mr. McAllister, hello again,' he said, eventually, extending a hand and drawing the man in.

McAllister's handshake was mild, not limp, but far from the sort of grip that earned respect. 'Mr. Fletcher.'

Peter leaned in to give him a hug, something that McAllister seemed utterly bemused by, until Peter got his lips close to man's ear. 'Not a fucking word out of you.' He whispered so quietly he didn't hear the words himself but each syllable would have tickled the old cunt's ear just enough to resonate.

'Mr. McAllister said he wanted to run through the details of tomorrow morning,' said his mum.

Did he fucking just? 'We were just about to have lunch too,' said Peter. 'Mr. McAllister should perhaps have phoned to see if it was a convenient time.' Peter was surprised McAllister was still holding his gaze. Fight in the old fuck yet.

'I was passing, you see. I thought it easier to pop in,' said McAllister.

'How unfortunate that we're about to eat then,' said Peter.

146

He felt Helen prod his back.

His mum shuffled towards the dining table. It was as if the undertaker had cast a spell on her. 'I'm sure Mr. McAllister will join us, won't you.'

I'm sure he will, thought Peter, glad at least that Cath Carter was stumbling back towards the cavern she dwelled in. McAllister would follow.

'That's very kind of you,' said McAllister. 'I failed to find time for lunch earlier,' he shot a look at Peter, 'so a sandwich would be most welcome.' He started to remove his coat. Making himself right at fucking home.

'I'm Samantha Fletcher,' said Sam, appearing from somewhere with her hand stretched out.

McAllister bent down to shake it. 'Well hello, little one. It's very nice to meet you, though a shame that we convene in such dire circumstances.'

What the fuck sort of way was that to address a child? Sam looked up at Peter and then hid behind his legs.

'Children, they often seem alarmed by my height,' said McAllister, directing his comment at no one in particular.

They're alarmed by your medieval banter, never mind your lanky frame, thought Peter. Temporarily defeated, he introduced McAllister around the room and led him towards the sandwiches, which were laid out buffet-style on the coffee table. Peter lifted one of the ham and cheese salad monstrosities he'd put together and took a big bite. He chewed it slowly, all the while staring at the undertaker. 'Well, it took us long enough to get here, but the sandwiches get pass marks,' he said, swallowing it down in a thick paste. 'Fire in, everyone.'

He felt someone pull at his sleeve and turned to see Helen drag him away from the queue that had now formed around the table.

'What is going on?' she said, when they were safely in the kitchen.

'I don't know what you mean.'

'The funeral director. You look like you're about to attack him.'

'Really?' It was about all he could offer.

'Yes, really.'

'You know what I'm like when the markets are moving without me.' Even as Peter spoke, he knew Helen was far too intuitive

147

for such a trite excuse.

'Or, possibly being back here has made you realise how much you loved Nicky and it's beginning to hit you harder than you thought.'

Fucking hell. She'd never been that far off the mark before. He kissed her. 'It's not easy,' he said.

'What happened with Matt? Your mum said you went into the garden.'

'Nothing. He just crossed a line. He's out the way, for now.'

'I don't like this. Something's amiss. Is everything okay with Nicky?'

'Well, no. That's why we're here.'

She slapped his arm, thankfully unaware she was throwing punches in the right places. 'Don't be a shit, Peter. That's not funny.'

'Look, nothing's amiss, I promise. Don't let Matt get under your skin, okay?' He squeezed her shoulders, waited for his smile to be returned, which took its fucking time coming. 'Let's eat. I'll be nice.'

In the living room McAllister was sitting with a plate on his knee, piled high with sandwiches. The girls were opposite him, transfixed. It reminded Peter of how they'd reacted to their first sighting of the giraffe enclosure at London Zoo.

Peter wanted to know if the old boy had any news (doubtful), or if Matt had been in touch with him (doubly doubtful), but for now, he was left with little option but to decorate his plate with the last two sandwich quarters and commence the sort of idle chit chat that made him want to take a fucking fork to someone's eye. He could have been at work; buying, selling, making progress.

'I was just telling Mr. McAllister that he's welcome to join us at the Golf Club tomorrow,' said Betty.

Fuck Matt for his jabs about the price of the Range Rover and the villa. Peter had earned them – and plenty more besides. Everyone had an opportunity and anyone who thought otherwise had wasted theirs. This perception that only the wealthy stood a chance was a socialist myth concocted by people who could have been out doing something meaningful with their time. He'd done it; all it took was aptitude and dedication. Too many were content to drift through life with Government-approved blinkers on, following a trail of TV executive whims until they were no longer able to control their own minds, and eventually, their bladders.

'Again, I'd just like to extend my sympathies,' said McAllister. 'It's just… tragic isn't enough to describe it.'

People's minds were numb. It made them incapable and that gave them no control over their lives. Control had always meant something to Peter. He dictated the direction he took. Or rather, he had, until Barton gripped his hand and led him merrily into the woods.

He took a bite of his sandwich. McAllister and his mum were discussing the quality of the Golf Club catering, how the new chef was doing the business or something. Maybe they were saying he was shit. It was all so irrelevant.

Since the Reuters hack Peter had spent hours on Twitter, scanning through newswires, marvelling at how this new world had been established. People didn't even need the news to tell them the news anymore. Like Barton's 'assassination' of the Prime Minister. It hadn't been difficult to piece together: Barton had some computer geek on side, someone with a moral disability who was both capable and content to hack into anything Barton demanded. The poor fucker probably got a few quid as a kickback with no idea of what he was about to cause. The whole chain of events that morning had been dictated with minute precision. It was genius in its cunning, but something was missing. In order for Peter to become the prime suspect in rigging a complicated algorithmic meltdown, Barton needed him to profit from the crash, otherwise it was just a bomb going off in the desert, something to put the shitters up him and get Tom asking questions. Okay, so he had profited, Tom had asked questions, but his trades on the day were nothing to do with Barton – he could just as easily have lost millions. It didn't fit with the meticulous calculations Peter had come to recognise. Revenge was not an act left to chance.

Peter looked at Sam gnawing her way through the last of her sandwich. Barton was risking his family's future, and all because he'd lost a dance partner. It was fucking deranged. No one was ruining what Peter had built. Not fucking ever.

McAllister had put his plate on the floor and was nodding

along to whatever story Betty was telling.

'So, you said you came to talk about tomorrow Mr. McAllister?' said Peter. His Mum looked hurt that he'd cut her off mid-flow but enough was enough. He needed to think, and that couldn't be done with this stick insect in a suit nosing about.

'I, eh, well…'

'You'll appreciate this is all very sensitive for my mother and as Matt isn't here at the moment, I assume you won't mind discussing things with me, in private?' Peter stood up and rubbed his hands together. It was high time this coffin carrying cunt was back out in the rain. 'Mum, I'll be as quick as I can with Mr. McAllister, okay? By the time the tea's ready I'll be back,' and he'll be trying to drive his car home with a fist rammed up his arse.

Peter held the door open for McAllister and followed him out into the hall. What a fucking day it was turning into. What a fucking week. Peter smiled at the women in his life before closing the door.

'What exactly are you doing here?' he said.

'I've heard nothing from your brother. Nothing. I'm frankly at the end of my tether. Your poor mother in there.'

'You let me worry about her.'

'And what am I to do in the meantime?' McAllister's face was covered in uncertainty; he had no idea which way he was facing or which way he ought to be.

'You're meant to do your job. Which if you'd done in the first place would have saved you a lot of grief, don't you agree?'

'Have you even spoken to your brother?'

'We're not doing this here.'

If McAllister wanted to play on Peter's turf, he would play by his rules. Peter wanted him exposed, utterly uncomfortable before facing the questions that only shock had prevented him asking earlier.

He began to climb the stairs, motioning for McAllister to follow him. At the top, he turned into Nicky's room. In here, he could wring the truth from McAllister with the effectiveness of a waterboarding.

'He felt safe here, as you can imagine,' said Peter, forcing the undertaker into the middle of the room while he stayed by the door. 'The morning of the accident, Mum said he was being lazy, wouldn't get up, even though it was for football training – which if you have any grandkids, you'll know is about the most motivational thing in life.' Peter had no idea if this had actually happened; it was doubtful. 'She wondered if he was feeling unwell, but she nagged him and he eventually got up and dragged himself down to training. You know what happened on the way home so I don't need to go into details.'

McAllister was biting the tip of his thumb. 'I am aware of my responsibilities. It's just… unbearable. My father would be turning in his grave if he could see what was happening today.'

'So to speak, eh? Maybe he wouldn't have taken his eye off the ball and let a coffin be stolen on his watch.'

'I undertake every duty with the same diligence as my father.'

'The cock couldn't have fallen far from the cock tree then, could it?'

'I have never in my life met so rude a man.' McAllister seemed to look around the room for somewhere to sit, his eyes resting on the bed and then moving on swiftly, as if his mind was telling him just how outrageously out of bounds it was.

'How did they get in?' said Peter. He'd been called worse things than rude.

'We have yet to establish the point of entry.'

'You didn't phone the police, you phoned Matt. Why?'

'I told you this morning, to protect your family, and frankly as time – '

'My family, or yours?'

'I don't think I like what you're implying here.'

'I've got two theories. Would you like hear them?'

'I believe it's time the police – '

'Firstly,' said Peter, raising a finger to silence McAllister. 'It could be one of your staff. Whoever these fuckers are that Matt's been stupid enough to dick about, they have funds, ways of doing things. I'm suspecting your staff aren't millionaires. A few hundred quid to leave a door unlocked doesn't sound too fantastic a story does it?'

'And your second?' There was bite in his reply. A bit of a kick left.

'That it's not your staff that have had their palms crossed.'

McAllister didn't reply. He just stood there, his head only just avoiding the lampshade dangling from the ceiling. Peter didn't believe for a second what he'd just proposed but give someone an unpleasant alternative to an unpalatable truth and they'll soon accept reality.

Peter measured his breathing. He felt drowsy and was regretting the second batch of painkillers.

A creak on the stairs startled them both, but it was Peter who flinched first. He opened the door to see Jessica turn into the hallway.

'Hello,' she said.

'Hiya, toots,' he replied. 'You going to the bathroom?'

She nodded then hid her face with her hands. McAllister had emerged behind Peter.

'It's okay, you can go on ahead.'

She shook her head and ran back down the stairs. Maybe she could see something he couldn't. Maybe he really was a child-corpse-catcher and Nicky was never going to be seen again. Time was being wasted.

He moved aside to let McAllister out of the room. 'If it's not you, who is it?'

'I think you've made your point,' said McAllister. Defiance had drained from him as if it was his dying breath. Result.

'Then you'll deal with your staff?'

'I will summon everyone when I return to the office. If a culprit exists, we'll find him.'

'And no more friendly visits.' Peter took a business card from his wallet and slipped it into McAllister's breast pocket before prodding the old man's chest. 'Now, off you fuck.'

Peter followed McAllister down the stairs. The desire to kick him in the back was so faint it was disappointing, a feeling Peter put down to the numbness of the painkillers as opposed to any sense of pity. The old fucker had come looking for an answer and was leaving with one. Perhaps when he arrived he really didn't believe his staff were responsible, maybe he was just consumed with concern. Whatever, someone had to have been paid off and if McAllister could find out who, Peter could squeeze them, reach out to whoever had Nicky, get him back without Matt being part of the equation. Cost was not the issue, fucking Matt was.

He led McAllister into the living room for a short round of goodbyes, shepherding him back out into the hall before he got comfortable again. He opened the front door and stepped aside.

'I'll be in touch,' said McAllister, offering his hand.

Peter looked up at the old man's eyes and closed the door.

17

I make my way through the bookies towards the counter. I've not been in this particular establishment since I was a student throwing away a fiver on the Grand National. It's opened right up, a big bright box of a room with harsh yellow lighting, a coffee dispenser that's hissing in venomous fashion, and a bank of casino gaming terminals that provide a clanging ambiance. The smell is predictably stale; the smoking ban must be the worst thing that ever happened to bookies.

Half a dozen people flit about, filling in slips or eyeing the TV screens. Old, unemployed or illegal. The stink could be coming from any one of them. Like I'm better. Like I'm any different. Showers don't make people clean. There's a lesson to live by.

I grab a slip and write down the name of General Catalyst followed by a five and three zeroes. I move quickly, my arm protecting the slip from curious eyes. This is easily the biggest bet I've ever placed. The cannonball lurches back into my stomach.

Deeeeeeeep breath.

I will leave this hole with eleven grand. It's already here – locked in a till on the other side of the counter. All I have to do is liberate it. Then give the lot to Bradley. More money than I've ever seen. To fucking Bradley. The rapist of morality. It's not right that my fighting fund is being obliterated like this. A deal is a fucking deal and I've done nothing wrong. Twenty fucking grand? I only borrowed ten in the first place. The world turns on a toxic axis – cunts like Bradley and Pete sucking the rest of us dry.

I head for the counter and place my slip down. The brunette girl serving looks around thirty; pretty eyes, bad skin. No name tag. No smile. She's worked here too long, her manners lost in the fury of torn up fortunes.

'Just this?' she says, picking the slip up. I nod and watch her feed it into her scanner, waiting for her eyes to widen.

Pete flips forward in my mind, his twenty thousand sitting on a silver tray. 'Wait a second,' I say. I wouldn't even really need to pay him back. Bradley off my back for good? My own stash safe and well and ready to swell when my life as a respectable businessman begins? Who gives a fuck what Pete thinks of me.

I step back from the counter. No. No. Fuckinghellno. Bradley's debt and my balls in a vice is preferable to going back to Pete. I will not owe him a moral debt. 'Sorry. I'm good to go,' I say. But then my hand touches the cash in my pocket. Five fucking grand. This is my money. 'Actually, could you… just a minute.'

The slip hangs there limply between her fingers. 'Are you wanting the bet on or not?'

I want my wee brother back and I want my fucking money. I earned it. It is not Bradley's to just take.

'Put it in the bin,' I say. There is another way, a better way.

I watch her scrunch up the slip and discard it, utterly unaware of what she's become compliant in. She looks beyond me, indicating someone else wants served.

I nod at the guy as I pass him, notice a pile of smash in his hand. It's all about playing the odds. The important thing to remember here is that if Woody hadn't paid me a visit I'd still be looking for twenty. Twenty solves problems. Ten just delays them.

I head back to the racing section and grab a clean slip then scan the sheets pinned to the wall with info on today's races. I'm looking for trainer names, looking for form, for the right races. Yes. This is working. My foot taps too quickly, an old guy growls at me with his eyes. Fuck him as well. I can turn this five into something more solid. I am having this. *Visualise and reprise your desires until they become real and true.* There's a 3.10 at Yarmouth that could work. *Visualise and reprise your desires until they become real and true.* I don't even know where Yarmouth is. The favourite is 4/5. Two seconds and a third in its last four races. Rich Reef it's called. Numbers start turning in my head. If I leave with twenty I can give fifteen to Woody, keep my five and maybe convince Bradley to waive his coffin-thieving fee on account of him being a soulless cunt.

Fuck it. That sounds good to me. I scan the 3.30 starts, but there's nothing and as I move through the afternoon nothing jumps out until four o'clock. Newcastle. Careful Hue. 11/10 favourite. Fucking stupid name, but there's a science to this: he's from a good stable, decent form, hungry young jockey. 4/5 on the first race is nine grand carrying onto 11/10, which would give me about… fuck, just under nineteen. Not enough money, coming too late in the day. My eyes keep moving, looking for something better. There's a shout of 'Go on!' behind me. Shit. The 2.45 is about to get underway. General Catalyst is good to go. There's no need to be greedy – with the cash or the countdown. Woody will just need to wait; he'll be better off for doing so.

I begin to write out the new slip

<u>Yarmouth 3.10</u>
Rich Reef 4/5 to win
<u>Newcastle 4.00</u>
Careful Hue 11/10 to win
Double

I stare at it. *Visualise.* A worthless scrap of paper that in half an hour could be the most valuable thing I've ever owned. *Reprise.* It looks good. *Real.* Feels good. *True.* I spin round on my stool and scan the bank of screens. There's a wide shot of the 2.45 riders, General Catalyst among them. I stare at my slip again, the cannonball swinging like a pendulum. Fuck. One bet. One simple fucking bet on a dead cert and I had Nicky back. I force myself to look at the screen. General Catalyst's not won yet. This could prove to be a masterstroke.

I wander over to the screens. The four runners are close, but the General soon begins to position himself in front. Just half a length, but a gap's been established. The others jostle but he's holding firm. I've got work to do. The General's race is none of my business.

At the counter, the cannonball is making me sway as if I'm drunk. My ping has long since faded, left shivering in the garage along with Pete's sanity. I need a pint or a whisky or something. A bag of fucking glue would do the trick.

The same girl awaits me. She's still searching for her smile. 'How much?' she says, eyeing my slip.

'It's on the – '

'You've not written a stake.'

She pushes the slip back over the counter. I laugh louder than I should and she looks at me with enough contempt to vaporise any tip that might have been coming her way.

Underneath the word *double* I write a five, pausing before drawing the three zeros, each one an escape, each one a noose. These other folks sticking down a quid here, a fiver there; hundreds of transactions every day, all of them forgotten as soon as the next punter comes along. Every now and again she'll get one to remember. She'll be telling her mates about me down the pub on Friday, they'll ask her how much I won, if I was worth a lumber. She'll say –

'Money?'

'Sorry?'

'Money. I. Need. Your. Money.'

Cheeky fucking cow. I lift out the wedge of notes and feel them one last time. It really was a great hand of cards. I pass them over and she begins to count. No smile. No manner. She does it methodically, as if I'm not to be trusted. I'll miss the fucking race at this rate.

There's a cheer behind me as an old guy gets up off his stool. I glance at the screen where there's a close of up General Catalyst. As the guy punches the air I watch a ghost beside him fall to his knees, grinning manically. He gets up and hugs the old man, who seems a bit taken aback. The ghost turns towards the teller and I feel him brush past me. He hands over a slip and the teller counts out two tree's worth of notes. The ghost stuffs them into his pockets and leaves, his world brighter, the biggest problem he's ever had about to be over. In four hours' time the ghost will be in a quiet restaurant with his family, making small talk and sipping wine slowly enough to stay sober, for the ghost has a big day tomorrow and he needs to be ready for it.

The girl tears off the bottom copy of my slip and places the pink copy into her drawer before handing me the white copy. No smile. No manners. No big deal.

Five minutes until the first race. I scan the TVs until I find the one broadcasting from Yarmouth. Just as they're lining up, the old guy that backed General Catalyst sidles up next to me, too close for comfort.

'What one's got Yarmouth, son? My eyes are fucked.' His skin is thick and loose, eyebrows wiry and creeping over the top of his glasses. There's a confidence about him that's veering towards cockiness.

'They're good enough for you to see your horse coming in,' I say.

He chuckles. 'Ach, I can make out the shapes, the colour of the jockey's top, but it's my cataracts, everything's a smudge. Fucking murder, so it is. I still like watching them come home though, know what I mean?'

He nudges me with his elbow and at least the mystery of who stinks is resolved. I direct him to the screen where the Yarmouth riders are gearing up for the start.

I can't stand still. 'I'm going for a coffee, old yin. You wanting one?'

'Aye, go on son. A tea would be grand.'

He stares at the screen, hand not moving towards his pocket.

I wait for the drinks to drop out of the machine, fully aware of how foul the coffee will be but content with the peace provided by the errand.

The ghost has gone back to his family to reclaim what's been stolen from him. It's just me, the cannonball and two horses. If you keep throwing dice in the air, eventually everyone gets a double six.

In the bookies, I hand an old man a tea. In Yarmouth, six jockeys signal their horses to go, and go they fucking do.

'What's your name son?' says the old boy.

'Matt. You?'

'I'm Davie. Ta for the tea. Who you backing?'

'Rich Reef.'

'Shite odds. But I'm on him as well. Got a wee treble the day. Just waiting on this one to come in and I'm good for £8.20 off my pound. How's he doing?'

The nags are neck and neck, one of them edging ahead, just. I don't know its name. If I'd tracked Davie, I could be walking out of here with forty-odd grand.

'Come on ya big fucking reefer bastard!' he shouts.

Rich Reef has nudged his head in front, but it's still close. Hot Jazz is the name of the other horse, according to the commentator. These two are pulling away, but Hot Jazz is more than matching the favourite.

'Come on,' shouts Davie. 'It's our day, son. I'm telling you.' He puts his arm around me, the smell rising into my nose. He should spend his winnings on soap and a box of Daz, the old bugger.

He's right though; Rich Reef has pulled himself ahead, almost half a length. Hot Jazz is pushing, jockey on his feet whipping its arse, but the nag's not got the legs for it. Rich Reef does. He's pushing harder, getting whipped himself. Go on. He's ahead now, a length, two lengths. Go on. I can see the line and he's going to do it and he's doing it and yes, yes, YES, HE'S WINNING, and Davie is as close to jumping as a near-blind pensioner can be. He's practically hugging me.

'Go, go, go on son,' he shouts, and as the horse passes the line he actually does manage a wee jump. 'You beauty! Ho ho!'

There's a round of applause behind me from two other old boys that have appeared.

'Well in Davie,' says one of them.

'Aye, good wee win that,' he says. 'Think it's time for a celebratory pint before dinner.' He turns to me. 'Much you up?'

'Still waiting on one more.'

'Well, I told you mind. Our luck's in today, son.'

Visualise and reprise your desires, until they become real and true. I smile and he trots off towards the teller. The brunette hands over his winnings with her flat, grim face unwavering. For fuck's sake. The old guy is over the moon and she's got nothing for him. He's a winner. I'm half a winner. Right now my slip is simultaneously worth nine grand and nothing. Careful Hue, your time is now. I will name my first male child after you. I will pay great heed next time I choose a colour to paint the flat. Whatever it takes to get you over that fucking line.

People are milling about, filling in lines, filling their plastic coffee cups and talking utter shite. There are fifteen minutes until the race and my feet are getting itchy. I can't just stand here. Time can be the biggest tease of all.

159

I go to the teller and ask her if she knows what pub Davie drinks in. She begrudgingly tells me. Outside I turn in the opposite direction. It's not like there's a shortage of pubs round here.

Four doors up I head into a bar which on a normal day I wouldn't be caught dead in. Today, as I'm repeatedly reminded, is not a normal day. The place is dull and dark, smaller that it appeared outside. There are only four people in. It could be the grimmest place in Glasgow. It smells worse than the bookies too. I do my best not to catch anyone's eye. It's one of those pubs where there's a right way and a wrong way to look at someone, and in my experience, in situations like that it's best to look at no one at all. Except the barmaid.

She's done well for herself seeing as she looks as if she was born on a fucking farm. Jesus, she'll not get much trouble in here, the sort that calls everyone darling until they've had one pint too many at which point she'll pick them up under her arm and turf them out the door with a heel to the nuts.

'You look lost, darling,' she says when I'm still six feet from the bar.

I manage a nervous laugh and order a pint.

Some old guy crouched on a bar stool with his face buried in the newspaper looks around. He's dressed completely in black. His eyes are so dark it looks as though the pupils are one huge black mass. When his gaze catches mine I feel cold, his stare so hard it feels like he's taking an X-ray of my soul.

'How's it going there?' I say, forgetting my own rules.

He rolls his tongue around the inside of his mouth and sniffs before returning to his newspaper. There's no indication of whether or not I passed whatever test he was subjecting me to.

My pint arrives with all the appeal of piss water but tastes not too bad. The first quarter of it vanishes in a thirsty slurp and I carry it off to a table, mumbling a thank you to the barmaid on my way.

'Don't be a stranger,' she says.

For some perverse reason my mind starts imagining sex with her, those giant sweaty paws gripping my cock as my hands claw inside her bra. Dirty big ride. I take a seat as far away from anyone else as I can, making sure the guy at the bar can't see me,

160

and take a long sip at my pint while trying to think about anything other than what's about to happen in Newcastle. I relax into the fantasy. The barmaid falls to her knees and begins to slurp at my cock, taking slow, deep mouthfuls while squeezing my balls. She begins to stroke my shaft while circling the wet tip with her tongue and looking up at me, her eyes… her eyes turn black and then she's not the barmaid at all, but the old boy at the bar – his dark stare consuming me, tar-like spit dribbling from his lower lip onto my

Fucking hell. I kick out at the chair opposite me. The clatter draws the attention of another drinker. He scratches his nose with the back of his thumb and stares vacantly in my direction.

I need to clear the fog. Turnbull flits through my mind. That'll do. It's a year from now and he's due back in the UK after extending his Australian tour. We're meeting in London; the plans are to celebrate with an expensive meal and get outrageously drunk. Even the WAGs are coming. I'm getting Siobhan a new dress. Things have been going well since I moved back in with her. I'm so busy with work that there's no time to be distracted by card games, and drinking has become a celebratory pursuit carried out on Saturdays alone.

I'll look back on today, on this very hour, as the moment things turned, when a horse crossed the line and showed me that I am capable of making the right decisions. Nicky's funeral will be a memory, the ordeal that preceded it nothing more than a lesson in how not to live life. *Harnessing positivity from the past can fuel future fulfillment.* Repeat: I've won before and I can win again. I've won before and I will win again.

It was my mate Sandy's birthday. Despite only lasting six months at university I kept turning up at the pub until graduation, so was still part of the crowd that a decade on met with decreasing regularity. Having rounded off everyone's thirtieths with a shambolic four days in Antwerp, it was agreed that quiet dinners and a couple of pints would be the extent of our debauchery from then on in. It was like a social half-life. We were all getting older, some of the boys had kids, most were married. Boys' benders were something you did in your twenties. I called this for what it was: defeatist pish, but I was a lone voice in a crowd of screaming babies and parents with earplugs.

161

So, for Sandy's thirty-first he booked a decent Italian place where half a dozen of us divided up too many pizzas and not enough lagers. I was content to watch it descend into farcical hi-jinks and see who was standing after the last train left Central Station. Turned out that just Sandy, Fraser and myself were prepared to go the distance. Sandy had an all-night banter pass; it was his birthday after all, and Fraser was the only other one of us still single. We made for an odd trio – Fraser being a bald indie hipster and Sandy a former rugby player. They were about as compatible as a Belle & Sebastian album at an end of season piss up.

With the debate on where to go next likely to have lasted until dawn, I suggested the casino – open late, good bar, plenty of ogling to be done. It was an easy sell and soon enough we were standing with bottles of overpriced imported beer watching chancers and chumps move from table to table. With Sandy settling down to dick about with fifty pence chips at roulette, I headed for a blackjack table and lost fifty quid in a matter of minutes. With only a tenner left in my pocket I headed back to find the boys. Fraser had started chatting up some girl in a black dress who was so far out his league she was playing a different sport. To be fair, he had more chance of success than Sandy, whose pile of chips was severely diminished by the time I squeezed in next to him. As he spread his chips across the table I placed my crumpled tenner on black and winked at him. A minute later, I lifted £20 from the table and patted him on the shoulder, whispering *mug* loud enough to make him jump. A second blackjack table proved more to my liking and I went on a crazy run of four winning hands, turning my twenty into a hundred. Just as the glow was beginning to warm me up there was a change in dealer so I walked away. By then, Fraser was standing at the bar, the black dressed girl – who must surely have just been trying to piss off her boyfriend – laughing at something he'd said. Sandy was slumped in his seat, fiddling with what little he had left to play with. The glow was making me bold. I whispered *red, red, black* in his ear and put £100 of chips on red. He tutted, murmured something and proceeded to execute his tried and tested method of inevitable failure. Red came up. Sandy scraped in about £2 from covering a quarter of 34, while I doubled my money. I left it sitting there, radiant. *Are you mental*, said Sandy. I just laughed. Where he saw £200 I saw a tenner. That was what I'd had left, so that was all that was ever at stake. Sandy put his last fiver on black and when that beautiful little ball landed on red thirty-six he walked away from the table. As I pushed my £400 onto black, a woman sat down next to me. She was tall, middle-aged with sweeping blonde hair, dressed in a white gown that touched the floor. Fucking bold look, but good on her. The boys were nowhere to be seen; it didn't matter. White Dress didn't even matter. My focus turned to that wee plastic ball. Around me, the other players decorated the table with chips. The croupier waved his hand over the table to signal the end of betting. I had nothing left but a fifty-fifty chance of complete illumination.

The ball wobbled and bounced and slid across the wheel… it leapt like a lamb in the morning sun, wrecking and granting my dreams as it was propelled onwards… and onwards… and onwards…. it bounced meekly in its fading throes, settling into red seven… but there was one final kick… it jumped up and dropped into black twenty-eight. Black. BLACK. BIG FUCKING BEAUTIFUL **BLACK.**

As the wheel slowly turned, parading its result, the room lit up. I began to breathe again and golden rays burst from deep inside me. White Dress smiled and rested her hand on the edge of the table. I looked over her exposed shoulder into the body of the casino. Lights flashed and dazzled in harmony with electronic beats and victorious hollers, but no roar was as loud as mine.

I swept up my chips and brushed my way from the table towards the bar, past jealous looks and nonchalant smiles, past White Dress and all she had to offer. The boys were nursing beers and bruises from their respective bouts, their eyes indicating it was home time. The glow was as close to perfect white as it had ever been though. It had bigger plans. I ignored their protests and headed for the poker room, just for a look, just to see what was happening. A tournament was beginning, there was once place left. Entry was £500. It was fate. Twelve players and a full five grand to the victor. Even if I lost I'd be leaving with £300 – maybe £600 if I turned back to the roulette table. Sandy stropped off with Fraser at his tail. That was fine; if I'd wanted cheerleaders I'd have bought White Dress a martini.

The private room was quiet, the throng silenced by thick glass walls. It was as though we were on display. I paid my fee and took a seat at a table with five others. Two would be eliminated and the other three would join three from the adjoining table in a winner-takes-all final. We were playing Texas Hold 'Em. Two cards dealt face down to us, and five in the middle of the table, which the dealer would reveal with each round of betting – three at first, to let us see what was on offer, then the turn card, which separated players from spectators, and finally 'the river', the card that fortunes hinge on.

I watched the actions of everyone as they placed their bets – how they looked at me, at their cards, how they pushed their chips in, how they reacted when they saw what they'd been dealt. A couple of the guys were solid, another couple clueless, like they had too much money for Glasgow but not enough for a long weekend in Vegas. Still, I treated them as equals, eyeing their reactions as the dealer turned three of the community cards face up for everyone to feast on. I had plenty of time to gaze at what had been dealt, but only one shot to gauge the tables' reaction. That's what I loved about it all – no matter who we were, where we were from or what we were worth, we were equals around the table, only luck and the courage of our convictions to separate us.

It was like I had hit the big time after months of training at The Treehouse. I moved easily through to the final, learning a thing or two about my opponents along the way. The glow had forbidden me a drink and so with a ginger ale I took a seat, repeated my well-practiced observations. I played safe, considered every move, folded when I wasn't confident and watched on as three of the table squandered their chips on cheap hands.

With just three of us left and the heat of the glow keeping my cheeks warm, I followed the dealer as he whipped cards out from the deck. I glanced at my hand, just the corner of each card. A King and a Ten. The community cards unearthed another Ten, another King and a Five. This was it. I bet clever, drew in the table by exuding the look of a man who was bluffing, all the while praying they weren't doing the same. One folded, the other raised. The dealer played the turn card, a Jack. The man opposite me – an Asian boy with an intense gaze and a half-smile that told me he was playing for pleasure more than cash – led the charge, pushing all his chips in. I called him and the dealer turned over that final, fateful card. When that second King revealed itself I sat still, not thinking of my own hand, but on what could beat it.

Full house, kings over tens, said the dealer. The Asian boy flipped over his cards and I caught a glance at a pair of a fives before losing focus. It was only when he started to laugh and leaned over to shake my hand that I let the glow consume me. Its intensity almost broke me apart. Even later as I stood in the pre-dawn twilight, holding a cigarette in a shaking hand while waiting for a taxi, I knew this was as fierce as it would ever shine.

From nothing, we build. I drain the pint in three swift gulps and return the glass to the bar with a thank you. The barmaid's smile is kind. She probably does give good head. I shiver. Black Eyes is still there, behind his newspaper, yet crawling all over me. He will not pry this positivity from me. You hear me, Black Eyes? I know you're listening, wanting me to fuck up, to come back in on my knees. Fuck you. You get nothing – this glow is mine.

Back onto the street and I light a fag, inhaling deeply before the rain gets near it. Even with the memory of those cards and the five grand they earned for me, I can feel him on me, those black eyes taking me in, his fingers gripping his paper like giant spider's legs tightening around my throat. I check my watch; it's almost time. One more draw on the fag and I throw it into the gutter. I will forget that man ever existed. When I reflect on today he will not be a part of it.

18

Somehow it was getting on for half three. With McAllister on his merry way, Peter considered calling Matt, just out of curiosity, but the less interference with his brother's plans, the more illuminating the fireworks would be. Anyway, there was work to do and Christ knows who'd be at the door next. Somewhere in the house lay a link to Craig. Tomorrow would be too chaotic. Identifying windows of opportunity and climbing through them as quickly as a cat burglar was a necessary skill in Peter's wide arsenal. He crept back up the stairs, knowing full well the next time he stepped into the living room Helen wouldn't let him leave again.

Opening the door to his mum's bedroom, he felt a flurry of guilt, as though he was trespassing. It had been years since he'd been in her room – there was never any reason to go there – and it felt strange. Not just the colour of the curtains, or the flat-packed wardrobe that had replaced the rickety old thing he remembered hiding in as a child while his dad counted to one hundred, but the atmosphere itself. It wasn't like Nicky's bedroom, where everything was different; this was almost the same as it had always been, but not, like walking into the wrong class in school.

He trod warily across the carpet, automatically remembering which floorboards creaked loudest. Beneath him, the polite chatter would be continuing, Helen getting increasingly annoyed at his constant vanishing acts. He had to be quick.

Opening the door of the internal cupboard that once housed the old water tank, Peter was met with the scent of clean laundry, each shelf piled with more bed sheets and towels than his mum could possibly need. At the floor of the cupboard, was a ledge that had supported the old tank. Peter stepped onto it, burying his face in the linen spilling out from the shelves.

Breathing in, he stretched himself fully and reached up beyond the top shelf until his tapping fingers touched metal. Bingo. He clawed at the corner of the box, coaxing it towards the edge, from where he grabbed it and stepped back into the openness of the room.

The old biscuit tin was battered and the illustration on the lid of Victorian children playing some shite looking game was faded – as it had been the day he first saw it. The memory was stark.Peter and Matt had stood silently when their mum showed them her hiding place. It must have been a few months after their dad died. She'd wriggled herself into the cupboard and used an old poker to retrieve the tin: 'This is where we keep our important things – the things you'll need if anything ever happens to me.'

It had carried an ominous undertone, even back then. The thought of his mum dying was something Peter had never contemplated, despite what had happened to his dad. Later, as he had searched for sleep, all he could see was him and Matt, alone in the house, fighting over the last scraps of food, unable to reach the box.

The lid was stiff but with a bit of persuasion it squeaked open. It was rammed full of papers – official looking documents, statements going back years, long-expired insurance policies. It wasn't going to be as quick as he thought.

He tipped the entire contents onto the bed and began to sift through them. Among the documents were a number of letters – eleven in total. They had been opened carefully, with a knife by the looks of it, the familiar address Peter once called home written in the same stumbling handwriting on each. The postmark on the first one he lifted was stamped in Hull back in July 2008. Most had Canadian stamps on them though. Each was dated in July, every year including the current one. Only one letter had a Glasgow postmark – the oldest, from 2006. It was the only one addressed to Betty and not Nicky. Peter tore a hand-written letter out of the envelope, his fingers shaking.

Dear Nicky,

You were born and I wasn't there to
see it. I can imagine your cries though,

and your eyes opening for the first
time, the mad rush of it all. It's a shame
we can't hold onto that memory, don't
you think? Our introduction to the
world. I'm sorry I had to miss yours.
What you need to know is that your
mum is already an amazing parent, and
she'll do just as good a job with you as
she did with your brothers, if not better
with all the practice she's had! She's at
her best when being a mum; I saw it in
her every day. I hope that by the time
you read this you'll be old enough to
appreciate that not everyone is cut out
to be a parent, that sometimes by being
there they make things worse. I don't
know if you'll ever be able to
understand, but it was for your own
good that I had to leave…

Peter was pacing the room as he scanned the letter. It was a
single sheet, both sides filled with lament and a pathetic self-pity.
The utter utter cunt. The letter explained how Craig had never
intended to have children, how when he tried to be a father to
Nicky's big brothers he found himself wanting. He felt he didn't
have the capacity to be a father and his presence could only be
damaging to Nicky's long-term well-being. He even talked about
how he wasn't able to talk to Peter. The fucking audacity. It
wasn't even written to a child, but to an adult, the reason for
which confused Peter, until he reached the final paragraph and
discovered that Craig had instructed Betty to give the letter to
Nicky only when she felt he was ready to read it. He'd even
signed it with a fucking kiss.

He tore open the next nearest letter. Dated two years later and
sent from Hull, it was longer, running to five pages – its tone
more contained, more factual, packed with trivial information
about jobs and observations on the small world Craig was
inhabiting at the time. It asked rhetorical questions of Nicky,
whether he was walking, talking. As Peter scanned its lines his

headache sharpened.

The next letter was dated on the same day, Peter remembering Nicky's birthday through a process of deduction rather than reminder. As this sank in, he began tearing each one out of its envelope, scanning for clues. It was only when the pile of papers were strewn across the bed that he realised how careless he'd been, how much time had passed, how he should have locked himself in the bathroom in case she came in. She. He swiped a hand across the bed, scattering betrayal after betrayal all around him. One letter remained buried in its envelope; correspondence from father to son that was just two months old and sent from an address in Toronto. He dug it out and used his phone to take a picture of the sender's address.

So she knew where he was. She'd always known. She'd replied to that first letter, told him the boy's birthday, his name for fuck's sake. And she clearly had always planned for Nicky to know too. Peter imagined the talk, the bundle of letters lying on the kitchen table – because where else would a conversation of such magnitude take place – as an elderly Betty explained to an adult Nicky that his absent father may not have to remain a stranger, that the decision was his. He wondered how Nicky would have reacted.

Footsteps. Fuck. He began to gather the papers. The door creaked. Shit.

'What are you doing?' Helen stood in the doorway, looking unsure if she wanted to know the answer. Peter wouldn't have blamed her for leaving, for driving all the way back to London, speed cameras flashing like paparazzi.

'Just give me a minute,' he said.

'What's going on, Peter?'

'Nothing.'

Her eyes were looking past him, to the mess of papers decorating the bed. A twist of her brow and she was back on him, focused, screaming for an answer without uttering a word.

'Look, there's some shit that I need to deal with,' he said.

'Your mum is all you need to deal with today.'

'Believe me, she's the last thing I need to deal with right now.'

'What does that even mean? You're being ridiculous. She's getting upset, asking what you're doing and I can't deal with listening to how much pressure she thinks you're under while you're up here... what is it exactly you're doing?'

'Just close the fucking door, will you?'

She complied and stepped into the room, her finger pointing right between his eyes. 'This is not your work. I am not your colleague. You forget that too often.'

Just two more fucking minutes, that was all he had needed. 'Sorry,' he said.

'Sorry's not just a word, Peter.'

He didn't need this. He didn't ever need it, but that moment, just as walls wobbled on defective foundations, was the perfect time for something else to be happening.

'This is important, so let me explain or leave me to it,' he said.

Helen folded her arms. 'Okay, explain.'

'Read this,' he said, holding out the first letter.

As she read he began to fold the others into the box, not bothering to put them back in the envelopes. It wasn't like he wouldn't be bringing it up.

'Is this meant for Nicky?' said Helen.

'It's from Craig. One sent every birthday. She evidently decided to keep them for him, for when he was older.'

Helen sat on the bed. Peter watched her eyes flick across the page. No histrionics, no bombardment of questions on how he'd come to find them, what he'd been looking for. 'She will have her reasons.'

Serenity often highlighted a lack of comprehension. 'After tomorrow, she can fuck off.'

'Don't be so ridiculous.'

'Ridiculous? Are you forgetting who we're talking about? He walked out on her, on Nicky. She's no business letting him walk back in.'

'Do you not think Nicky had a right to know his father?'

'Nicky's father had no right to know his son.'

'And he won't, and that's tragedy enough, so forget you ever found this.'

He might never know his son but he sure as fuck was going to find out what it was like to lose him. That was something Peter could ensure. Nicky would never get the chance to make Craig feel like he deserved to feel. It was a proxy role that Peter was happy to inherit. It wasn't about protecting his mum anymore; she was complicit in maintaining a relationship that had no right to exist. It was about respecting the innocent when everyone else was guilty. That was something even he'd failed to do that day, something he could resolve with ease. So what if it gave Matt an easy way out, it wasn't about Matt, it wasn't about Peter, or the money, or even their Judas mum. It was about a boy who had only been half a brother, half a son.

'You're right. I need to find Matt, get him sobered up, get us all round the dinner table tonight. Let me call him and I'll be right downstairs.'

Another lie. Another betrayal.

Helen kissed his cheek, her hand resting on his head. She stood up and pointed at the letters. 'Put them back wherever they came from. And be quick.'

When she'd closed the door behind her Peter reached for his phone. Exhibit A. Still no messages. He began scrolling, past Cillian, past Matt, until he found the number he was looking for.

19

Back in the bookies and there's more of a crowd around the TVs. I jostle my way to the front and scan the screens for the right venue. The cannonball feels denser than it ever has before.

'This your next race, son?'

Davie's back. Just when I thought my nose had cleared. I imagine Turnbull's face when I tell him about Davie. He'll laugh, apologise again for not getting back to me quicker. He'll never tire of me repeating the story.

'Thought you were off to the pub, Davie,' I say.

'Aye, I came back in for my bunnet. Who you backing?'

Leave me in peace, Davie. 'Careful Hue.'

He nods. 'Not a bad horse, that. Due a win. Don't know if it'll come today right enough. You couldn't help me find my bunnet, could you?'

'The race is about to start.'

'It's my eyes you see. I cannae make much out. It's two mile plus anyway, is it not? Plenty of time to give me a hand. It'll sort your nerves out.'

What the fuck does he know about nerves? I glance at the screen. The cannonball expands. There's less than a minute until they're underway and I want to watch without him grumbling in my face. I head to the counter and interrupt a young guy placing a bet.

'Has anyone handed a bunnet in?' I ask the brunette.

'Hey, there's a queue,' says the guy getting served. Young, reedy boy that looks as though mealtimes mean an extra cigarette. There's an aggression in his tone though and the cannonball reminds me I'm not in a nice part of town.

I go to apologise but behind me there's a cheer as the race gets underway. The girl shakes her head at any rate. So, as the horse that will alter the course of my life one way or another begins to gallop, I start scanning the floor of the shop for Davie's fucking

172

bunnet. I move quickly between the punters, eyes focused on the floor – dirty trainers, stool legs, crisps packets, coffee spillage. No bunnet. I check the TV. Careful Hue is in the pack – a white horse with a red-jerseyed jockey has pulled away, but early breakers are always caught in a race this length.

The floor is free of bunnets. I run my eyes around the perimeter of the shop, along every shelf. There's nothing. I turn back to the telly and see them pass the mile mark. Red jersey is back in the midst of the pack, but I can't see the orange and black of Careful Hue. It's like he's not there. I have a glance at the coffee machine, but there's someone in the way. I step away from the TVs and… Fuck this. Wherever the bunnet is I've done my bit and there's a race to watch. I start scanning the horses but the camera keeps cutting and I can't get a fix on him. Where the fuck is he?

A horse buried in the pack moves to the outside. The jockey is resplendent in a rustic yellow that could pass for orange. This is it; he's making his move. I'm struggling to focus they're going that fucking fast so I close one eye over. The breakaway horse is up to fourth. The jersey is definitely yellow though. I'm sure he was meant to be orange. With black fucking sleeves. Shit.

'Here mate, can you see Careful Hue?' I ask a boy next to me; it's the nutter from the queue. The yellow jockey is on his feet now, whipping like mad. The boy scowls at me and turns back to the race. 'Where's Careful Hue?' I repeat and don't even get a scowl this time. I'm about to grab his shoulder when an old codger grabs mine.

'He threw the rider, son.'

Everything stops. The room, the race. My heart. I step out of time and turn around. The old man looks concerned, his face solemn, a big purple nose dominating a face covered in ridge-like wrinkles.

'Say that again.'

'He got himself in the lead early on, a good length but he froze. Something spooked him, jockey went flying; looked a sore one.'

The room accelerates as time catches up with it. Everything's louder as the folk in front of the TV start shouting at it and it's as if there's an army here, and then there's me, staring at the screen, unable to take it in and there are flashes of red and yellow and pink and green, purple and orange and blue. And orange? He can't be right. I look for the orange top. Orange. Orange. Come on. COME ON. The winner crosses the line, then the placed horses. One, two, three, four. The rest will follow but the camera cuts away from the finishing line, not to the winner but back to the track where paramedics are treating a body lying on the torn-up grass. The bookies falls silent. It doesn't look good. Next to me I see Davie take his bunnet off and hold it over his heart, bowing his head. I go to speak but feel like I've channelled Hue's jockey.

'No way that boy wasn't trampled,' says a voice.

'Hooves hitting the ground at that pace – aye, you're not walking away from that without a few broken bones,' says another.

'As long as that's all it is,' says Davie. 'As long as that's all it is.'

'What happened for fuck's sake?' I manage.

'Did you not see it? Terrible throw,' says Davie.

'No, I was looking for your fucking bunnet.'

'Well, doesn't matter now. I found it.'

'I can see that. What happened to my horse?'

The younger guy that scowled at me earlier turns towards me. 'Watch your mouth, mate.' His tone is more threatening, his frame still isn't.

'Mind your business. I'm asking a civil question.'

He steps forward. 'No. You're not.'

In my pocket I clench my fist around my slip. A worthless scrap of paper. The room begins to narrow, my vision darkening. Fuck this. I snatch Davie's bunnet from his head and throw it across the room. It's fucking cursed. I shove the scowling boy out the way with both hands, just to make a path to the door. He trips over a stool and stumbles back. I try to sidestep him but see an arm appearing from somewhere and have to duck. Davie's thrown a fucking punch. I pull back, but the gap between me and the door closes as Scowler gets back on his feet. Davie comes at me again. I weave out his path and slap his arm down. Old cunt.

'Get back to the pub before you get hurt, Davie,' I say.

'Bad loser, son. That's all you are. A bad loser.'

Scowler is in front of Davie now, and another boy has appeared. I back away, not fancying my odds so much now there are two of them. Well, three if you include Davie. I turn to get my bearings and there are another three behind me, circling. They look about twenty. Wee neds. On the TV screen a pensive looking reporter is speaking to camera. The jockey can't be in good nick. I get the feeling I'm about to join him.

'You're going nowhere, pal, not yet,' says one of the guys behind me.

The manager appears just in time; a great big fucking lump of a guy, full of fat that used to be muscle. 'What's going on here?' His voice tries to boom, but it cracks as if he's speaking through a broken megaphone.

Scowler doesn't flinch – no fucking wonder – and I know that nothing the manager says is going to prevent this. I need to get outside, fucking pronto.

I lunge forward, waving my left hand at chest height as if I'm dancing. The instant Scowler glances at it I throw a right hook. It catches him on the chin as he throws his head back. It's doesn't floor him, but it knocks him off balance for long enough that I can charge forward, away from the hands that are grabbing at me from behind. I turn around but the three of them are standing close together, ready for me. Davie's stepped back, arms folded. Scowler is straightening himself up. I need to act. Now. There's no way I can make it out onto the street so I knock over two stools and run for the toilet, speeding through the door and locking it behind me. I press my body up against it as the hammering starts. The door shakes, but holds.

It smells like Davie lives in here. Manky bastard. He cursed me. Him and his fucking bunnet. Arms folded and standing there like a gangster. Fuckfuckfuck. How the? Careful fucking Hue. Wonder what the odds were on him murdering his jockey.

The toilet floor is soaked in a puddle of piss. I slam the lid but catch a glimpse of dark brown smears on the bowl before it closes over. The cannonball pushes its way up into my throat and it feels as though it's going to choke me. What a shitemare this is.

The hammering on the door stops with one final onslaught. I climb up and sit on the cistern, my feet on the lid. Outside, threats fill the air. In the background pleas from the manager make for a pitiful refrain. Hopefully they'll take it out on him, or some other bastard that isn't me.

I take the slip out my pocket and feel the tears come before I've unravelled it. I stare at what should have been £18,900 if my maths is right. I have nothing.

Everything is exhausted. There is no plan but Pete. The debt must transfer from Bradley to my brother. General Catalyst will be chilling out somewhere, resting his victorious legs. This is the end of it. I tried. I did my fucking best.

I wipe my eyes with my sleeve, grateful that the snot is blocking my sense of smell. The light flickers as one of them thumps the door again.

I fold the slip into quarters and drop it in the inside pocket that my five grand spent the morning in. I will frame it one day; let it remind me of what rock bottom looks like. As the thought forms, an idea appears alongside it.

My hands shake as I pull my phone out. There's another massive bang on the door. The light flickers again, goes off for long enough to turn the room black before flickering back on.

My thumb moves clumsily across my phone.

**Can you meet me in The
Clachan at 5pm? Need your help.**

I press send and stare at it, waiting for the reply. The door takes another hit. It sounds more like it came from a toe-capped boot than a hand this time. Perhaps five o'clock is optimistic.

20

The call to the bank was straightforward enough. When Peter gave them so much to look after, they were compelled to look after him. He explained that he was in Glasgow, that there was an emergency and he needed £20,000 in cash before closing. He'd waited for the anticipated protests to pass and repeated the urgency with which the transaction had to happen, and the frustration he would feel if it didn't. In less than two minutes he'd been asked to make his way to one of the big branches in the city centre where the manager would carry out the withdrawal personally, and with the required sensitivity. Why the manager had to get involved, Peter wasn't quite sure, but fuck it, whatever got the job done.

It was the most straightforward moment of the day since that initial drive from the hotel to his mum's. That short journey now seemed as though it had occurred in the distant past, before his brother's revelation, before Stuey's call.

Peter walked back into the living room and sat down with the girls. They were focused on a cartoon playing on the TV. Whatever his Mum and Helen had been talking about, they stopped when he appeared, his mum no doubt keen to know why he'd spent the bulk of the afternoon alone when the whole purpose of the day had been for them to huddle together. He could barely look at her. She and Matt could do as they pleased from here on in. What chance did Nicky ever have? He had an urge to blurt it all out – the letters, the coffin, the whole fucking caboodle. Let her see what it felt like to be betrayed.

'How about I get that tea?' he said, standing back up. 'Can you give me a hand, Hels?'

In the kitchen, he asked Helen to close the door.

'Did you get hold of him?' she said.

He nodded. 'There's been a mix up with the payment for the wake. Whatever he's doing with his afternoon, he says he can't get up there, so I need to get to the bank and just pay them in cash. Can you hold things together here?'

'I have been holding things together, Peter.'

'Look, it's complicated.'

'Your brother needs – '

'Whatever you're about to say, I've thought it at some point today. Forget him. Just, I don't know… let her help you book a restaurant for later if she's up to it.'

'And the letters?'

'They'll keep for another day. Let's just get through this one. By tomorrow night we'll be back where we belong.' He kissed her forehead, her nose, her lips.

'We'll be fine,' she whispered, her lips vibrating against his. He held the kiss that followed, wet his lips a little. Even after all these years she could still empty his mind of everything.

'I'm sorry,' he said.

'It's not your fault.' She kissed him again. He wished she knew what he was apologising for.

It would be after four o'clock by the time he reached the bank. Time – it never gave anybody a fucking break.

'I'll be back soon, okay? We can go to the hotel, change, go out. You're a superstar, Mrs. Ellison-Fletcher.'

Helen leaned in for a hug. 'I don't know what we'd do if anything ever happened to the girls. Your mum might be their gran, but we forget that she was just like us too, until last week.'

'I know,' he said, brushing his hand through her hair. Nicky felt more like a brother than ever before. He stepped back and clapped his hands. 'Right, action stations. I'll need to sort this nightmare out.'

There was one more kiss before Peter swept through the living room, planting wet kisses on the girls and smiling thinly at his mum.

The Range Rover started up and Peter flipped on the wipers. As he made his way along the arterial road into the city centre he thought back to the days when he'd take the bus in on a Saturday morning with his friends. Friend, singular, if he was honest. He and Adam were thrust together thanks to no one else really giving them the time of day. Peter was Matt's brainbox wee brother, and Adam was just, well, strange. They were close nonetheless, a shared interest in hating every one of their classmates ultimately providing them with a kinship that would last until Peter left for Exeter. He'd lost touch with Adam by the end of the following summer. When he grudgingly returned home for that week of baby Nicky screaming and shiteing, he hadn't bothered calling Adam for a pint. While Peter had matured and seen what the world had to offer, their occasional phone calls indicated that Adam had become even more withdrawn.

As he drove past The Barras market his anticipatory grimace faded. Where he recalled grotty shops, greasy cafés and counterfeit traders he saw the beginnings of gentrification – arts venues, a run-down church converted into a bar, students and hipsters and middle-class couples seeking out vintage furniture mixing with the less salubrious bargain hunters, whose idea of a good sale was probably still five pairs of sports socks for a pound. They came together though, this combination of what the city had been and what it had become.

He turned right, passing some arches that looked home to various car garages and crossed High Street into the Merchant City. When he was younger he and Adam would head into the old Candleriggs market before hitting the main shops. He couldn't be certain he was even looking at the same place. The corners of the old market building housed stylish bars, the cobbled streets feeling quaint rather than antiquated. The whole area could have been deposited in the west end of London and not looked out of place. Past Merchant Square he kept going; more bars, restaurants, designer boutiques. He had to actually spend time in the city, come up for a weekend that involved more than running from a hotel to his mum's and home again. Show Helen another side of the city he always derided. Helen's folks could look after the kids for the weekend. Might be good to reconnect.

He twice circled George Square, keeping an eye out for indicators on parked cars while pedestrians ducked between the slow-moving traffic, brollies held out like jousting lances. On the third lap he headed straight on, into a one-way system that felt foreign. Remembering the street the bank was on had been pedestrianised, he pulled up on double yellows close by and got on his way. If he got a ticket, so be it. There was no time to fuck about looking for a multi-storey.

A short walk later, he hopped up the stairs and into the old bank building. He shook the rain off his collar and took the place in. It had retained many of its classic features; huge high ceilings and ornate stone carvings, but a cheaply erected mezzanine with a maze of partitions ruined the illusion of grandeur. There was a short queue at the tellers but Peter headed straight for the customer service desk and explained he had an appointment with the manager.

Retail banking was something of an oddity to Peter, the straightforward process of deposit and withdrawal, managing savings and loans. It was surely a job that people did, but not one that many could like. It wasn't like trading, where every day could have you higher than a bag of Columbia's finest or lower than hell's own inferno.

When it came to Barton, Peter was hitting new highs. The trades were neither frequent nor consistent, but every other month Cillian would call with instructions and Peter's bank account would swell. Whatever the means of Barton's market manipulation, Peter was content to see himself as an innocent processor. It was when he was calculating his assets one Sunday afternoon while the girls played in the garden that he began to realise gluttony was now a factor in his accumulation of wealth. Greed was one thing, but gluttony was a more ugly word and nothing in Peter's world was ugly. He'd opened a beer, taken a break to kick a ball around with the kids and begun to think.

The following morning he phoned Cillian first thing. 'C-bomb, we've been reappraising some of our dealings here, just, y'know, internally. Bit of a spring clean. So, the thing is, Barton – '

'Yes?'

'Yeah, we're going to need to cut the account.' Peter lurched in his chair as he spoke. It was as if by even saying the words, Barton had dropped a cannonball into his stomach.

'Not sure I follow, Shotgun.'

'I can't do trades for your hedge fund anymore, Cillian. That's the official line. Like I say, we're doing some internal reorganisation.'

'I hear you, Peter. I'm surprised, but thanks for the forward notice.'

Cillian hung up and seconds later Peter's iPhone buzzed. He headed out into the corridor.

'Are you fucking insane, man?' said Cillian.

'It can't go on, C. There's a trail leading right through the forest to my front door.'

'There's no trail. He doesn't leave a trail.'

'I leave a fucking trail. If anyone ever questions me, ignorance is not a line of defence that will stand up. So no more. I'm out.'

'Peter, you're a buddy. I'm not telling you to keep this up because I like the way you do business, but more because I like you.'

'I appreciate that, but – '

'If you appreciated it there wouldn't be a fucking "but".'

'There must be plenty of others who can do what I've been doing. Your contacts list must – '

'You remember Taylor-Caraway?'

'I should have deleted your number the day that happened. No offence.'

Peter saw Kim coming towards him, heels as high as her arse. She squinted at him, but kept walking.

'He won't walk away into the night like some ghost you've exorcised,' said Cillian. 'This was never an opt out deal.'

Peter pressed his phone tightly to his ear. Kim was sharp. Everywhere he looked he found reasons to abandon this madness. For the first time, he even considered leaving AMJS. Helen had always wanted to live in New York. They could set up there, keep the house in Putney for the summer holidays. Yeah, that could work. Fresh start. Flawless.

'I need to think about my family, the repercussions of this coming out.'

'If you were thinking about your family you'd be a million fucking miles away from this decision.'

'I'm sorry,' said Peter. 'I've made my mind up. How can I keep working with a man that won't even meet me?'

'Whatever happens next is nothing to do with me. Know that. I'll not speak to him until tomorrow, give you time to reconsider. You don't know what he's capable of. I think you should spend some time with your family, think about how much they mean to you.'

'Don't you fucking threaten me.'

'Christ came through the window. I'm not threatening you Peter.'

'I'll speak to you soon, for a catch up, for stability. Other than that, I'm sorry.'

Peter hung up and launched his handset the length of the corridor. He watched as it bounced on the floor, crashed into the far wall and smashed. He wandered over to pick it up just as Kim emerged from the bathroom. She looked to the source of the noise, then back to Peter. She said nothing.

He hadn't considered Kim in his equation. The less contact he had with the office the better, but with Stuey and Tom still silent, he needed someone to tell him what was going on. Maybe not a phone call. Maybe... Just as he reached for his phone he saw someone come down the stairs from the mezzanine. The man was obese, his suit one size too big for him, sleeves down his knuckles, tie swinging as low as his flies. How the fuck was this guy a bank manager? The talent still flocked south, he thought, as the man greeted him with a sweaty handshake.

'Mr. Fletcher, I'm Darren Henderson. It's a pleasure to meet you.'

I bet it is, thought Peter.

'If you'd just follow me, Mr. Hamilton is in the middle of something but shouldn't be too long.'

Was this prick having a laugh? Where was the manager, and why was Peter being left to deal with some fat fucking secretary or whatever it was this effort of a humanoid did to occupy his days. 'If there's a hold up can you not just get me the money – I explained it was emergency.'

'So I gather. Just this way, thanks.'

'You'll be familiar with the term "emergency"?'

'He won't be a moment, sir.'

Fatty led Peter up the stairs before pointing at a row of empty chairs and trampling off down the corridor. Probably to have a bag of Monster Munch after dealing with the stairs. Wouldn't want to burn off too many calories too quickly.

Peter calmed himself by admiring the ceiling. His own work building was new; it was glossy, but this place had class. Back in the days when it was built there was a skill to the construction, a real art form. People had pride in what they did. Where the fuck was this manager? He began flicking through stocks on his phone. It hadn't been a great day, the FTSE was down, Wall Street had opened and dropped a little. Nothing remarkable. Most importantly, it had been six hours since Stuey had called – compliance might work longer hours than the markets but if something was going to happen, they would have phoned. The following morning felt a little further away. It was as if an hourglass had been turned.

'Mr. Fletcher, sorry to have kept you.'

From nowhere, a boy who looked as if he was on work experience had appeared next to Peter. At least his suit fitted him.

Another handshake, another introduction. The Hamilton boy was impressive though. He stood tall, had an air about him that left no doubt about who was in charge, despite him being two summer holidays away from his first shave. He could go places, and acted like he knew it. He directed Peter into a dull, soulless office that was empty save for a desk and a piss-poor print of a butterfly on the wall. Waste of a good building.

The boy at least apologised for the delay, even blew smoke up Peter's arse by saying how he was more than happy to comply with the request given Peter's strong relationship with the bank. There was no fucking about, no inane drivel about how much it was putting them out, which suited Peter absolutely fine.

'If you'll give me five minutes, I'll prepare the withdrawal.'

Hamilton left the room with another smile. Peter pulled out his phone but the office's thick walls had killed his reception. He stood up and walked over to the butterfly print. He couldn't understand why anyone would hang such a thing on a wall. It probably came from a high street shop, thousands of the things on thousands of walls in every part of the country. It should have carried a tag saying 'this is not art'. He stared at it until the black and orange wings melded into a single blur. The day before he'd been sitting in his own office, working to minimise losses after a tough day's trading. Everything had been normal. Tom was on good form, gearing up for a dinner with some Japanese.

It had been a week since the banking world watched the arse

fall out the markets in the wake of the PM's momentary demise. Tom hadn't been wrong when he'd told Peter there were questions to answer; it was procedure. Truth was, they'd both been expecting a call from compliance. Peter had explained that Barton was a fund manager he'd never met and given what had happened he'd told the guy's dealer to set up a meeting, put them all in a room together. The 11.27 phone call, he'd said, was a mystery, but one he would endeavour to resolve. He played down the influence he believed Barton to have; there was no mention of insider trading, of the wash trades. He convinced Tom it wasn't unreasonable for outsiders to accept Peter had just got lucky, that the phone call didn't need to become public knowledge. Tom had acquiesced with a grunt. So, while Peter had been awaiting a call from compliance, what he hadn't been expecting was a fucking raid on the CEO's office. There was nothing compliant about a raid. Like he always did when a problem required a solution, he channeled his inner mathematician, the part of him that could think laterally, that had lifted him from Glasgow and made him something better. And something wasn't tallying.

Facts: Peter hadn't been contacted by compliance. Nor had he seen compliance raid Tom. While distracted by Matt, and Nicky, he had accepted Stuey's version of events without giving it further thought. Stuey would wait to stamp on his carcass sooner than give him a drink of water if he found him in the desert, therefore, logic dictated that Tom hadn't been raided. Fuck. Tom was likely playing golf with the Japanese, his phone off due to on-course etiquette. He was an idiot for letting Matt get under his skin. An idiot for not writing a cheque at nine o'clock and concentrating on what really mattered.

He stuck his head outside the door. There was no sign of Hamilton. He sat at the man's desk and dialed a number on the landline.

'Good afternoon, AMJS. How may I direct your call?' said a sunny voice.

'Stuart Anderson, please.'

'Putting you through.'

Some soothing classical piece was broken seconds later by a familiar voice saying good afternoon. Peter hung up. So, Stuey was there, which meant he was blanking Peter's calls. What the fuck was he playing at? Stuey was a prick, but this made no sense. Unless. Unless…

The sound of the door opening jolted Peter. He shot to his feet just as Hamilton entered the room. Peter focused on the stupid butterfly picture, attempting to look impressed. Hamilton's brow indicated something was amiss, but he was a pro. 'Freedom,' he said, pointing at the painting. He was carrying a cloth bag.

'What?'

'To me, the butterfly represents freedom. *What joy awaits you, when the breeze hath found you out among the trees, and calls you forth again.* Wordsworth, I should add, not me. The butterfly reminds me that we must work for a better world, that we all have the capacity to emerge from a challenge in better shape than we began it.'

'Okay,' said Peter. The boy was an idiot. No one was free. That's what butterfly nets were for. Stuey was fucking dead. Little larva prick. Working with Barton this whole time? Still, if Barton was planning on driving Peter from the City he'd need more than a few scare tactics from a limp fucking patsy. He wondered if Stuey knew about Taylor-Caraway, about the PM Twitter hack, and realised it made not a solitary fuck of a difference. Game on.

Hamilton sat down and lifted four bundles of notes from the bag. He placed them on the desk.

'It's been counted twice, but if you'd – '

'I'm sure it's all there,' said Peter. He lifted the notes and stuffed two bundles in each of his overcoat's inside pockets.

'I appreciate your assistance today,' he said, standing. 'I'll be sure to mention it to Robert next time I see him.'

'It's been a pleasure,' said Hamilton.

They walked to the stairs together before Hamilton's handshake indicated they were done. Peter thanked him again and skipped down the stairs and out onto the street with purpose. He just had to get back to London. Stuey was naive, arrogant. Peter could work him; make him slip up without him ever knowing he was being manipulated. Fucking lickspittle. On top of that, Nicky was as good as paid for. All Peter had to do was find out where the fuck Matt had gone. He wanted back to the car before phoning him though: the street was busier than when he'd arrived and with the cash in his pockets he was feeling utterly exposed. Every face was a mugger, every hand in every pocket was a weapon about to be drawn. He picked his pace up, a nervousness grasping him. His feet splashed through puddles, the leather soles of his brogues beginning to feel slippery. He kept going, avoiding eye contact but taking in as much information as he could on those he passed; students, shoppers, workers on an early finish interested only in keeping their hair dry on the way to the station.

He rallied himself. The money was fine. People had as much interest in him as he did in them. He had to focus. Barton's minions were fucking with his mind. The man had near omniscience in the City, that much was evident. If Barton wanted compliance to target Peter, they would have arrived the day of the flash crash. It made his acceptance of Stuey's bullshit about Tom being raided all the more galling.

He thought back to the morning it happened, the same morning Nicky died. The only reason Peter had made so much from the Twitter hack was because he'd sold short the day before to hedge against the position taken by the new fucking client. A position so odd it leapt off the pages of Barton's playbook and yet was missed entirely by Peter thanks to his preoccupation with imagining how fucking high his reputation was soaring having been hand-picked to carry out the trade. *You have fun out there now, you hear.* Cillian's words echoed deep into Peter's consciousness. There was an assumption of what would follow, the perfect execution of Barton's revenge plan. It wasn't perfect though. Barton might have guessed that Tom would haul Peter in to discuss the 11.27 phone call, that Peter would subsequently be distracted and so act on instinct when Barton's insider sent the algos all the way to fucksville, but those sorts of assumptions could fill the Grand Canyon. Barton didn't get where he was by leaving things to chance. Every move was calculated. Peter might have been exactly where Barton wanted him to be, but Barton didn't programme him and he didn't programme Tom.

Peter stopped with a start, so dizzy he lurched forward as if on a boat in rough seas. Blood rushed to his brain, flushing out the fear and confusion. What he could see now was shining on the horizon with unimaginable clarity.

'Watch where yer goin, pal' said a voice behind him. A hand was on his shoulder, then gone again. Peter stepped back and staggered, stumbling into two women huddled under one umbrella.

'Sorry,' he said.

There was no call from Barton before the crash.

'Are you okay?' said one of the women.

There was no Barton.

'What? Yeah. Fine. Sorry.'

Tom was Barton.

It came together, each piece being sucked into a black hole. Tom knew Peter would short sell to hedge his position, he was the one who mentioned the time of the crash before it happened, he was the only man who knew Peter well enough to know exactly how he'd respond. He'd controlled it all. Miami, the strip club, Cillian's invitation: he was already onside, running Tom's private hedge fund. Tom and Lieberman had history too, so placing Peter and Cillian in the same room was hardly a stretch. But why?

He spun away from the women and continued towards the car, cold rain whipping around his head, taking his breath from him as his soles slid through puddles.

If he'd turned down Cillian's offer of a wash trade there would have been no recourse. Life would have continued as was, Tom safe in the knowledge that his top employee was righteous and beyond reproach. Everything he'd earned he would have earned eventually. Tom once told him the first million was the hardest to get your hands on. Peter was there on paper, if not in cash. Without Barton he'd be on the same road, just not as far along it. The first rule of futures trading was to ensure as much of your exposure was hedged as possible, and without him even knowing it, Tom had been hedging his relationship with Peter all along.

No wonder he never questioned the questionable trades – it was fuck all to do with his faith in Peter. He could corrupt the City through a proxy that was always in his line of sight, keeping the company he'd founded in the clear. There was no prop trading; AMJS was untouchable if all it had on its hands was a single rogue trader.

It was all just a matter of contacts, years of networking and grooming enough of the right people to build a team of shadows. The algorithm catastrophe at Taylor-Caraway – a trial of what would follow; all Tom had needed to do was reach out to someone of a suitable disposition in GD's IT department. Tom had followed the introduction of algorithmic trading like a priest follows God, yet he swore himself against the technology. All the time he'd been ensuring its designers were on his backhand payroll, kickbacks disguised as consultancy fees. One man to push a few buttons and spin the market into turmoil, and if he had a man who could cause an entire company's trading system to buckle, he sure as fuck had someone capable of hacking into a Twitter account. Christ, Tom had netted a fortune through his AMJS dividends while ensuring the firm had zero exposure to his actions. Peter was a cash cow milked at Tom's whim. Until the day he said no. *You don't know what he's capable of.* Those were Cillian's words. The bastard. Phone records no longer mattered.

Thumbs soaked and shivering, Peter ducked into an office doorway and dialed Cillan's work mobile, knowing he'd have been expecting the call for over a week.

'Peter, how's it – '

'You were fucking planted in Miami, weren't you?'

'Whoa, whoa, whoa, what – '

'When did he bring you on board, Cillian? What's your cut?'

'Hold on a minute, will you…?' there was silence, then a muffled hiss. Peter pictured Cillian heading for the nearest empty toilet. 'What the fuck do you think you're playing at, phoning me at work and throwing accusations around?' Cillian's voice echoed, intensifying the aggression in his tone.

'Fuck you, just answer the question.'

'I warned you. I told you what would you happen.'

Peter was calm. The call was about confirmation, not conflict. 'I know it's Tom.'

There was no reply, not even the sound of breathing, just the static in the atmosphere between their respective spots on Earth and a satellite six miles above them. Peter hung up. Shitting fuck. He had nothing. He was finished at the firm and Tom would make sure he was finished in the City. Whatever allies Peter had,

Tom's friends were in higher places. He knew enough that there would be no prison, but that was small comfort now. Through the flash crash he'd been given a golden parachute, even if it's strings had been cut before it was packed.

His legs felt heavier, the money like stones in his pockets as he walked into the rushing tide. The last remaining truth was that there was no one else to blame.

He rounded the corner and took the car key from his pocket. Where was the fucking car? He looked across the road, but nothing. As he was beginning to think he'd turned off the pedestrian zone too early, he looked up the street in time to see a pick-up lorry turn a corner, a sleek black 4x4 on its back. Peter looked down at the double yellow lines. The attention he'd avoided since leaving the bank was now fully on him as passers by turned in the direction of the screams.

21

Shaking. My legs. My hands. My fingertips as they fumble for my phone. I feel as though the cannonball could sink me. The walls, dirty from the handprints of many a constipated pensioner, close in. This could be my coffin. No silk lining, no Sunday suit. The hammering on the door has stopped, but the voices haven't. They're quieter now though. Plotting. Only pish and shit can escape from here. Drowning in a bookies' toilet was never part of the plan.

I look at my phone. I've developed a compulsive habit of checking to see if Phillip has replied. Every plan is failing. Phillip is gone. The money is gone.

Nicky is gonegonegonegonegonegonegonegonegonegone

Fucking Bradley fucking jesus what sort of man can steal a just where the fuck can you hide a how do even get out of this it's a bookies toilet a fucking bookies toilet and I'm here and Nicky's where where Jesus I'm sorry Nicky I'm sorry pal you know it's not my fault not my he killed the jockey killed he wasn't ready for it wasn't ready at all WHERE ARE YOU?

A scream. From inside the cubicle. It must have been me. Above my head a pipe creaks and the lightbulb flickers again. I suck in air. I can breathe without gagging now, the stench diluted by my exposure to it. Shake my head, slap my head. Concentrate. On getting out, on the voices outside. One sounds calm, but the words aren't penetrating the door. The manager will be aiming for damage limitation. A second voice is louder, more aggressive. Scowler. I wonder what the girl at the counter is thinking, if she's scared, if she feels for me, if she's able to be the calming influence. They can stand out there longer than I can sit in here. At least I'll not be forced to piss myself.

Inaction absolves you of willing reaction. Turnbull says that by making the first move we can all dictate the direction of our day. It's been over eight hours since McAllister sat alone in his office and pushed my mobile number into his phone. Five minutes later Bradley did the same. Two people dictating my day, taking action while I stared at the ceiling and imagined, what? Irrelevance. That's what. I've done fuck all but fuck up.

I get off the cistern and my shoe splashes into the puddle of piss. I push my ear to the door, but still can't make out what they're saying, which at least means they've moved away from the door. I slide the lock open and pull gently on the handle. The voices stream in with the light.

'He can stay in there all fucking night if he wants. I'll be back in the morning.'

'The lassie said he had five grand on that horse that threw his jockey. No wonder he was upset.'

'Well, if he can put five grand on a horse, he's bound to have plenty more. Compensation, know what I mean?'

Voices without owners. The second one sounded older; it could be Davie. He had sway, the old bastard. Commanded respect. If I got him onside I'd be all right. If I can get to the front door the city is an open field. Action.

'I've lost my brother,' I shout. 'It's his funeral tomorrow.'

I peek my head out and see a group of men turn towards me, their faces growing into frowns. Scowler is nearest. He runs towards me and I slam the door, flicking the lock just as he tries the handle. He rattles it, kicks the door.

'Fucking get out here!' he shouts.

'Billy, please, let's not do anything we regret,' shouts someone else. The manager?

'In here, outside. Either way, he's fucking getting it.' The voices are clear enough now.

I slap the door. 'Look, I'm sorry, right. I lost more than I can afford to lose and I shouldn't have snapped,' I shout. 'Just let me leave.'

The door gets punched again. And then there's silence. I punch it myself. I try to imagine what Turnbull would say, what words would diffuse the situation. If the sentence even exists it's not going to come to me here.

In the midst of this silent standoff, the room explodes into laughter, and then a dog barks. It barks louder and claws at the door. A dog? Where did the fucking dog come from? Jesus. This is not fucking on. It snarls and claws, unrelenting, angry enough to tell me it wants my leg for a snack.

I scramble back up onto the toilet seat, ducking so I don't hit my head on the ceiling. They're still laughing. If the dog's the joke, I'm the punchline. This is all Davie's fault. Him and his fucking bunnet.

A growl rumbles under the gap at the bottom of the door.

'Did you say it was your brother's funeral tomorrow?' says a calm voice. It's vaguely familiar. Not Scowler or Davie though.

'Yeah. Why?'

'What was he called?'

I pause. I don't want his name said in this shithole.

'Is that you, Matt?'

I jump down from the toilet seat. 'Who's this?'

'It's me, Andy.'

I step back and clatter against the toilet, grabbing out at the wall as my balance wavers. I wipe my hand on my jeans. 'Andy?'

'Come on out,' he says, then shouts, 'it's fine, he's my pal.'

'Is that wee Andy that was barking?' I say, going nowhere near the fucking door.

'He's just looking after his old pa, aren't you boy?' He laughs. Wee Andy says nothing. He's probably licking chocolate off Andy's trackie bottoms.

'How do I know they're not going to shove you out the way if I open the door?'

'Ah, they won't. Good folk. Decent. It's stopped raining, you know.'

They're using him. They must be.

'My Uncle Davie says you lost a lot of money.'

Fucking 'Uncle' Davie – unbelievable.

'You shouldn't take it out on other people, Matt,' he says, lecturing me like we're still fifteen. 'That's why he was angry. Dead angry. He's a grumpy old bugger. Haha! You took the shine off his win. Not so shiny now. It's fine though, it's fine.'

I slide the lock and tease the door open. Andy's standing there, stupid grin on his face.

He points at me and turns around. 'It is him, look,' he says. 'It's Matt. My pal, Matt. The one that saved Wee Andy.'

Davie, Scowler, they're all standing there, no one moving.

192

'Twice in one day, eh Matt? Twice in one day. Not seen you for years either.' He laughs again.

I laugh back, pathetically. There are five of them, feet facing the TVs, eyes facing me. The rest of the punters have gone. Can't blame them. No one says a word. The manager is at the back wall, arms folded, impotent. Wee Andy is lying at Andy's feet.

'Come on,' says Andy. 'Let's go.' He clicks his fingers and Wee Andy lifts himself up and trundles after Andy. I look down at his dark eyes, his black coat that's greying around the jowls. It can't be the same dog that was an inch of wood away from tearing my leg off.

I slowly follow Andy towards the door, staring at my feet.

'You're fucking lucky. Prick,' says Scowler. I say nothing. My feet shuffle. I backed the wrong horse. Actually, that's more likely to be my fucking epitaph than any pithy line of my own. *Here lies Matthew Fletcher. He backed the wrong horse.*

'Wait,' says Davie. His bunnet is back in place. Again.

Andy stops. 'It's okay Uncle Davie. Honest.'

'You shut it before I change my mind and set the boy on him.' Davie's voice is fierce. He's a different person, a someone.

'Listen, you,' he pokes me in the chest.

I'm surprised his bony old finger doesn't snap. Something inside me twitches, but I don't react. Can't react.

'The boy's right. You are lucky.'

I smile, almost snort.

'You don't think so, eh? You lost your money. You lost your brother. That's tragic. I heard what happened to him. Just a lad. He was unlucky. Your jockey, he was unlucky as well. You're walking away from this, so you're the luckiest cunt of all. Because see if Andy hadn't walked in, if Wee Andy there had stopped for a shite on the pavement, that door was coming off its fucking hinges. So next time you're thinking about acting the prick, remember this. Got it?'

I have this incredible desire to headbutt the bastard, knock his bunnet right off his self-righteous head and spread his nose across his face.

I don't. I nod. 'Well done on your win earlier,' I say.

'Aye, well. Mind you're the lucky one.'

I think about my five grand sitting in the till. I nod again and head out into the street before I decide to reply.

Andy follows me out and we stand there, not quite sure what to say. Even if you make the right decisions you still need luck to make the right things happen. I'm luckier than Nicky, I know that much. Turnbull says luck doesn't exist. Fate, he says, is a figment of our imagination, but that can't be right. Our life is determined as much by the decisions we make as what the world decides to do with them. My bad decision on the horses, my good luck Andy came in when he did. We rely on so much to just keep breathing.

'Thanks, Andy. Really. I don't know what would have happened there.' There's nothing else to say. It's easier speaking to strangers than former friends.

He slaps my arm, this man that was once my best mate. 'I do.' He punches his open palm. His laughter fills the gulf between us.

I forgot Andy's family was connected. It's why he never got much grief in school, despite his general idiocy and vulnerability. I wouldn't be surprised if Davie or that dick nephew work for Bradley somewhere down the line. Andy's old man was always arse deep in something dodgy, a brother was in jail at one point. Can't mind what for.

I bend down and tickle Wee Andy's ears. I wonder what he'd have done if he'd got hold of me. Would he have seen his one time saviour and licked my face, or is the command of his master everything? If he doesn't make his own decisions then how is his life dictated? If he's not lucky, then what exactly is he? I am beginning to think Turnbull is full of shite. Six weeks. I mean, how can you be in business with someone who doesn't call you for six weeks? His face appears, suntanned, mouth slightly open in a snigger. If he's fucked me over then… then even beyond Nicky, it's all been for nothing. I need to pause, give my mind time to settle.

'You fancy a pint, Andy? On me?'

'Is the funeral not tomorrow? You need to see your mum, Matt, see if she's okay.'

'Yeah, that's all in hand. My brother's taking care of things. I've got time for a quick one.'

He looks down the street and then at Wee Andy. 'I'd love to, love to. It would be good, but I've got to get some messages for my mum.'

I think about the blue plastic bag he had on the bus and know he's lying. I look at my watch. 'I'll see you around, then. We'll get that pint one day.'

'Hope so,' he says. 'Come on, Andy.'

The two of them trot off, not even checking which way I was going. He couldn't get away from me quick enough. He could have given me his number on the bus, but he never offered it up here either. I check my phone and see a text message – this is more like it. One last crack at the title.

It takes ten minutes to walk to The Clachan. Ten minutes nearer the end of all this. The plan is coming together at long last. The pub's faded red carpet and wood panelled walls remind me of my first legal pint, when Craig took me down here for a birthday treat. He never really worked me out, but he tried, for a while. He'll live the rest of his life imagining what his son is doing with himself, never aware of the desperate truth. Poor Nicky: abandoned by his father, forsaken by his maker. Fucked over by his brother.

I order a pint and take a seat in full view of the door. All I can do is wait. The lager tastes good. Local pubs are always better than trendy bars. They give a shit about the quality of the product. In town, it's all about the fucking wallpaper. As you get older, you realise the wallpaper is the one thing that doesn't matter. With all that carry on in the bookies, I'm as sober as I've been since breakfast. I gulp at my lager, draining a quarter, feeling its coolness line my throat. The barmaid had no idea who I was, that this was once my local. She smiled and poured my drink then went back to staring at her phone. I doubt she's got a real worry in life. Her every day will end with a contented kip. I've stopped at that station. I know what it's like to smile into my pillow. Now every thought I have is a sleep-bothering catastrophe-in-waiting.

A fortnight after I last saw Turnbull, Bradley summoned me to his office. I'd only ever been to his house once before, when I picked up the cash. His gates had an intercom, and beyond them a white flag-paved driveway led up to this great old sandstone mansion. Externally, it was stunning, built for a tobacco baron who knew the importance of status every bit as much as Bradley did. Inside was a different story. Heather had clearly been given *carte blanche* and the result was a tragic gaudiness that literally stung your eyes. Bradley's office, by contrast, was like an oasis. In there, sitting behind an old wooden desk, he looked less dangerous, which somehow made him more so. Woody was lingering at the back of the room, looking sheepish.

'We've got ourselves a business agreement, Matt,' said Bradley, before my arse was on the chair. 'And when I have business agreements with people, I like reports.' He poured two whiskies from a bottle of 21 year-old Aberfeldy, filling the glasses two-thirds of the way up. I remember wanting to explain to him that wasn't how you drank whisky, especially from a hundred pound bottle, but Bradley has the sort of aura where even polite urges are suffocated before they're allowed a breath.

'Now, it's been, let me see,' he flicked through a notebook for effect, 'two months since you came to me with a proposal. Have I got my dates right, Matt?'

I nodded, and took a gulp of whisky. It was impossible to sip something that resembled a glass of apple juice. Christ, it was good stuff.

'I'm asking, because under the terms of our agreement, I gave you £10,000 on the promise that I would be paid back at a rate of a thousand pounds a month for a period of fifteen months. Have I got that right?'

Sanctimonious prick was sitting there like a bank manager. 'I explained at the time it would be a few months before I could start the repayments. You said that was okay.'

'A few, Matt? That's a very vague term. You think I got where I am without focusing on detail?'

'No. Not at all, it's just, that's what we agreed.'

He locked into my eyes for a second longer than necessary. I held it, trying to appear relaxed when I was pretty sure he could see my heart beating through my jacket. Bradley took a sip of whisky and grimaced.

'Fucking whisky. Piss water. Get us a vodka and orange, Woody.'

When Woody left, Bradley stood up.

I shifted back in my seat. 'You said it was okay, Bradley. That was the deal. I would never have taken the money if you hadn't 'cause I knew I wouldn't be seeing a return for a while.'

He slapped me hard across the cheek with the back of his hand. 'Keep talking, wanker.'

Gasping, I pressed my hand into my face, thankful my fingertips were cold. 'It was an investment, I explained that. Look, I can give you five hundred the now, but that's it.'

He raised his hand again, and I swung back in the chair. He sat back down, laughing.

'I tell you what, you can keep your five hundred for now, but you better hope that wee investment starts working for you, because if you don't start paying me back next month you'll force me to take action. I don't like taking action, because it makes me seem like I'm a cunt, which I'm not. I'm not a cunt, Matt, am I?'

'I don't think so, no.'

'You don't *think* so?' He put a hand on the table, leaned forward a touch.

'You know what I mean, Bradley. Of course you're not.'

'I can be, if people don't settle their debts. I can be a right cunt when I have to. Do you think I'm capable of being a cunt?'

I selected my words carefully, conscious of the syllables I stressed and where my eyes were looking when I said them; just above his, watching the wrinkles on his fat fucking forehead: 'I think you're capable of being whatever you want to be, Bradley. You wouldn't be sitting where you are if you couldn't.'

The silence threatened to choke me. Until he laughed. It was one of those laughs that can only come from the lungs of a psychopath. He took another gulp of whisky.

'Fucking Scotch. Is this meant to be good stuff?'

'It's pretty fucking good if you ask me.' I almost drained my glass. It burned, a waste of decent malt, but it did what it needed to.

'Come on, Woody tells me there's a game of cards at The Treehouse tonight. We've not seen you for a while. I'll give you a lift.'

I lost a hundred quid that night. I didn't care. I knew it was the last time I'd sit round that table. I'd have paid double to get the fuck away from the place half an hour earlier.

Two weeks later I was standing in that taxi queue outside the casino, five grand bulging in my pocket. That money wasn't Bradley's though. I'd worked hard; I deserved a saving pot. Bradley would be paid as per the conditions of the agreement. Which he would have been if Turnbull hadn't fucking ruined everything. Captain Hindsight swoops in and tells me I should have paid Bradley enough to keep him from wondering if I'd pay him at all. I should have done a lot of things.

The cash is gone, but the memory of that five grand night retains its value through the lesson it taught me: we don't always know when we're going to win, but knowing that we can is enough to keep us moving forward. That's one I should give to Turnbull.

It's important to remember days like that on days like this. It keeps us believing that the glow is brighter than the cannonball is heavy.

Something blocks the light and I look up.

'I didn't know if you'd actually show up,' I say.

22

'Well, I'm here now, aren't I?' said Peter.

Matt looked like shit. Worse, he somehow smelled of it too. None of your metaphorical shit either; this particular bouquet was unquestionably the genuine article. He was half-slumped on his seat, eyes red as if he'd been crying, though possibly that was purely down to the fact he was still half-pissed, and had possibly fallen in dog shit. They were together though, they had the money and according to the last text Matt had sent, whoever they had to give the money to would be arriving imminently.

Thirsty and feeling as though his brain had been fed through a mincer, Peter stood by the table. 'I'm getting a pint, you want one?' He pointed at Matt's glass, which although half full – or in Matt's case, half empty – would doubtless need replenished. Matt's nod confirmed this and Peter made his way to the bar. He hoped Matt's liver had a better work ethic than its owner.

The girl serving was buried in her phone. The contempt with which some service staff treated their customers astounded Peter. He coughed twice before she looked up. Her smile was huge, utterly untroubled by concern. Maybe there was something to be said for taking the easy route.

He ordered the two lagers, handed over a ten and told her to keep the change. That earned him another smile. This time he smiled back. He wondered how she would react if he told her his entire world had fallen apart, that those who he had trusted had lined up with knives sharpened and ready to plunge into his back, his chest, his fucking throat, while he was doing their bidding.

'Cheers,' he said, chinking Matt's now empty glass with his pint. He sat down and tapped his overcoat pockets; who knew how quickly pickpockets worked. It was paranoia, of course, no one had been anywhere near him.

The pint tasted pretty good, all things considered. Krug, a 1982 Bordeaux, 40 year old single malt; sometimes a pint of cooking lager was the only thing that hit the spot. Peter felt oddly invigorated. At university, he could spend weeks working on an equation and the elation of solving it would last days. That was what he did. He found solutions. Well there you fucking go, X equals Tom.

'So, how's your day been?' he said, distracting Matt's gaze from whatever he was looking at.

'Great. Yeah, fucking fantastic. Can't wait to get the pictures back.'

Peter took a drink and waited. He genuinely wondered what Matt had been doing since stumbling out of the garage and heading off to find a fucking money tree. What he did know was that enquiring would only lead to more lies. The series of texts had begun with Matt's request for Peter to head for The Clachan of all places. When Peter eventually replied to say he had the cash, there wasn't a word of gratitude.

> Seriously? Get to the pub then.
> I' ll tell the contact to meet us
> here.

Peter might have wanted Nicky back with minimal fuss, but he was fucked if he was going to be the one to address the obvious.

'So where's this money?' said Matt.

Of course. It couldn't be polite, couldn't carry some sort of shame in its intonation. Defiant to the end, with the guarantee that whatever it is, it's someone else's fault.

'It's in my pocket.'

Matt spread his arms out, doing an impression of a plane coming into land. 'Superpete to the rescue.'

There was a strong argument for just smacking him in the mouth. It's not as if they wouldn't hand over Nicky just because Matt was bleeding; if anything it would probably speed things along.

Matt began to laugh as he if he had read Peter's mind. 'I'm sorry, I'm being a dick. I'm glad you're here. Family should be together on days like today.'

'No one has days like today, Matt.'

'How's Mum?' Matt sank a quarter of his pint in one long gulp.

'She's fussing over the girls.'

'Good, good. They're some size getting.'

They both took a drink.

'So what now?' said Peter.

'You've really got it?'

Peter nodded. Matt shook his head.

'What?' said Peter.

'It's that easy for you. Half the fucking country doesn't earn twenty grand a year yet you can just rock up on any given day and make a cash withdrawal for it.'

'I had to pull strings, Matt. It's not the sort of thing you can just do on a whim.'

A glimmer of life sparked in Matt's eyes. 'That's my whole point – you can pull those strings. Normal people can't.'

'Normal? We grew up in the same house, dickhead.'

'That might well be, but we didn't have the same upbringing.'

Where was this fucking contact of Matt's? The sooner he arrived the shorter the impending rant would be. Matt was probably the type of fisherman that would cast his bait then stand up to his thighs in freezing water for a week and blame the fish for not allowing themselves to be caught. Peter relaxed into his seat.

'You don't know what it was like for me after Dad died. There were expectations. I wasn't allowed to be a kid.'

It was a familiar script, one that Peter, oddly, never seemed to have time to hear. 'What's happening with the money? Where's your guy?'

'From the day he died I had responsibilities.'

'Focus, Matt. We're here for Nicky, not to lament the childhood you think you lost.'

'That's in hand.' He waved the request aside with his arm. 'It was all right for you, playing games and doing whatever it is you did.'

'What do you mean, "in hand"?'

'Just listen will you, for fuck's sake.' Matt slammed his glass down.

Peter could feel the pub's eyes on them. He patted his breast again. 'Whatever it is that's biting you, pack it in. Do what you need to do and let's get this over with.'

'Whatever it is? We've lost our brother, Pete and you don't seem to give a flying fuck.' Matt was leaning in, his voice lower, but its tone sharper.

'Don't use him. That's low, even for you.'

'What's it like up there? Sanctimonious prick.'

'If I had a pound for every time you said that it would make fuck all difference to my vast wealth.'

'Laugh it up. You'd be nowhere without me.'

Was delusion permanent? Whatever, it was the first time Peter had laughed properly in days. He leaned forward. 'See when you were out getting pissed and trying to put your hands up girls' jumpers, I was in my room studying. Remember you used to tease me, remind me I had no mates? You'd come in on a Friday night, stumble up the stairs and get me to make you a sandwich so Mum wouldn't see you were pissed. Was that you bringing me up, or did something else happen that I've forgotten about?'

'Fucking plenty happened.'

'I must've been working too hard making something of myself to notice.'

'That's what you do isn't it? Look after number one.'

Peter shook his head. 'No. There is no number one. Me and my wife and kids are all huddled onto the top step on the podium. Speaking of which, how's Siobhan?'

'You're an arsehole.'

'Drop the fucking attitude. You're making a tit of yourself. Where is this scumbag fuck we're waiting on anyway?'

'How do I know?'

'Well, it's your situation.' There was only so much Peter could swat away before going on the attack. He looked at his watch. Fucking hell, it was quarter past five. Whoever had Nicky was taking the piss. Tick-tock you degenerate cock. On the plus side, it was also almost an hour since the London markets closed, which further confirmed that compliance had no interest in him. Their silence, given the nature of the trade, led Peter to think Tom could have even them onside. That meant he could unleash them at any moment. He was confident the complexity of the twitter crash and what it could unearth about Tom meant it would enter folklore without either of their names attached to it, but investigations into any one of a dozen other trades was enough to get him disbarred. The next week wouldn't be any less challenging, but on that front at least time – for now – was his.

'This isn't my life, okay,' said Matt. 'This is one incredibly fucked up man showing me how powerful he is.'

Silence fell, worlds collided. Power was relative. So were problems. 'In another life, you could have come to me for the loan. If you genuinely thought whatever this fucking guru guy was doing was worth investing in, I could have helped. We don't have that though. You know why?'

'Yes, but I'd love to hear your take on it.'

'It's like those nights when you were pissed and I was working. I saw what I wanted and went for it. Did you have a better laugh in your formative years, drink more, shag more? Course you did. And the worst thing is, time moves slower when you're kid too, a year feels like it's never going to pass. But it does. So I worked, and I got where I wanted to be. And you know what I did then?'

'Kept being a boring prick, I would imagine.'

'That's it, exactly. I worked harder. Fuck me, I worked hard. And look at us both now. Here's me with my fucking honey-scented harem, fifty pound notes for wallpaper and barely enough room to roll onto a cool corner of my silk sheets for all the golden-skinned supermodels lining up to suck Champagne out of my arsehole.'

'Very good.'

'You just waited for the knock on the door telling you everything would be okay, and here's that job you want, we think you'll be very good at it, sir. You've no idea how to earn anything.'

'It's not easy getting work just now. Your lot made sure of that.'

'And so we come to it.'

'To what?'

'The failings of society being the sole responsibility of the banking system.'

'Well, it's fucking true isn't it?' Matt's fingers were jabbing the air as if he was bursting invisible balloons. 'Gambling other people's money until there was none left then turning with your palms spread out to the Government saying that if you can't shore up the breaches you've just lost in a bet then the whole system will fail and poor wee Mr. and Mrs. Every Other Cunt On The Street will lose everything.'

'It's not as straightforward as that.'

Matt laughed. 'Of course it's not. You say that because you're one of them. You act with impunity, sitting there at your desk every day, rolling the dice with other people's money, mopping up if you bet the right way and not even bothering to apologise if you don't.'

Peter thought of his actions since Miami. He'd undone all the work that he'd just been talking about. He'd utterly abused the position he'd catapulted himself into in the most underhanded way. Everyone acts on an insider tip now and again, even your average punters who invest a little of their savings in a stock because someone at the gym or the golf club or some fucking place lets slip that a merger is on the cards. They don't even know what they're doing is wrong most of the time. Ignorance was not a plea that Peter could use. But he could still defend the ninety-nine point fucking nine percent of clean trades he carried out.

'People invest their money through me because I know more about where to put it than they do.' He began prodding the table. 'I am an expert in this stuff and every penny I earn comes from making the right decisions at the right time, every fucking minute of the day.'

'I'm not talking about the decisions you get right, I'm talking about the ones you get wrong.'

'It's called hedging, Matt. You mitigate your losses by covering the exposure elsewhere. I could not even begin to explain to you the sheer fucking complexity of my company's balance sheet.'

'We're the same you and me, that's the crux of this.'

'We are not the same,' said Peter. *One incredibly fucked up man showing me how powerful he is.* 'We're just fucking not.'

'I'm going to level with you. I had five thousand pounds when I woke up this morning. My own wee treasure chest. I earned that money, not like my normal wages pulling pints or selling lets, but by gambling. The best hand of fucking cards in my life, and I played it perfectly. Today I had to gamble that money again to get my brother back.'

Peter rested his elbows on the table and rubbed his forehead. 'Fucking hell, Matt.'

'I bet. You bet. Sometimes we win, sometimes we lose.'

The door opened and a figure walked into the pub, trailed by the grey beam of light now illuminating the place. Dust danced in the air around the figure. When the wind whipped the door closed and the dust disappeared, Peter saw a middle-aged man scan the pub. Matt hadn't moved. The man narrowed his eyes slightly upon seeing Peter look at him, but he moved on, waved towards the bar and called out something barely legible.

Peter's heart pounded in rapid dull thuds. He turned back to Matt. 'Sorry, are you saying you spunked five grand today?' Jesus fuck. No wonder he was upset at how easy it had been for Peter to get the cash. He felt his headache sharpen. He tried to think of the girls, swimming in the pool in Italy while he sipped a beer and gazed out into the Tuscan countryside. The serenity of it all countered anything his work had ever thrown at him. He wasn't going to lose it. He could be in Italy by next weekend. Fuck it, he would be. He didn't have a job anymore; where better to plan his next move?

'I look down on you, you look down on me,' said Matt. 'The difference is that I know what I am.'

It was fucking hopeless. Give Matt an hour in McAllister's basement and the corpses would be ready to kill him. 'And what's that?' said Peter. A fucking shite gambler is what you are, he thought. So fucking stubborn he would rather lose everything he had than ask his brother for help.

'A man that tried.'

'Fuck that. You're the opposite of a trier. You're lazy, Matt.'

'Eventually the system beats you down.'

'Am I hearing this right? I suppose I'm part of this fucking system? You'd change places with me in a heartbeat. You're jealous. You've been jealous of me since the day Mum asked you to help with the house because Dad wasn't there to do it anymore. You were older than, me. Of course she was going to ask you first. You could have reacted, made the most of it, learned how to succeed. But all you did was ball it up into an excuse.'

'I don't make fucking excuses.' Matt shouted again.

'Keep your voice down.'

Matt reached into his pocket and swigged from his hip flask.

'For fuck's sake,' said Peter. All Matt ever did was make

excuses and the way he was going, he'd soon be concocting one to explain why Nicky wasn't at his own funeral.

'Don't judge me.'

'I don't need to judge you. The people in your own life do that. You never told me how Siobhan was doing, by the way?'

'She's fine. We're going to be fine. You can ask her yourself at the funeral.' Matt was spitting his words out now. If he'd managed to sober up before arriving in the pub, he was gone again now.

Peter knew he should force Matt to call his contact, but not yet. The antagonistic prick needed told. 'What you don't seem to realise, Matt, is that some sins are worse than others. Greed and envy are not comparable. Yeah, I'm greedy, but I am motivated by greed – it drives me to achieve more than whoever I'm standing next to because I don't just want what they've got, I want fucking more, and I'll do whatever it takes to get it. Whereas you just want what they've got and complain that you don't have it. I don't envy anybody on Earth. I pity them because they're up against me.' Peter thought of Tom as he watched his brother's eyes. How fucking dare he? Peter had given everything to AMJS. Loyalty was supposed to be reciprocal otherwise it was nothing but servitude. 'You don't even know where the fight is, Matt. You've lost before you get out your pit on the mornings you even fucking bother.'

'Life's not about winning, it's about living.'

Peter slammed his palms down on the table top, the left one catching some ooze that seemed to want to keep his hand. 'Bullshit. A loser's charter, that's what that is.'

'You're not happy, Pete. That's what this is about.'

'Oh I'm happier than you, dear brother.'

Matt began to smile, as if something important had been revealed to him. 'You can never be happy, because you'll never be content.'

'You don't get it, do you?' Peter swept his hand around the pub. 'This is what you've got, you and everybody else in here.' He lowered his voice. 'This is life's basement. The view I've got is so fucking good I'm as close to happiness as anyone can be.'

'So relativity doesn't come into it?'

'What do you mean, relativity?'

'You want to use this pub you think you're too good for as an example. Look around – it's a Thursday afternoon, it's pretty quiet, but if you were to stop listening to your own voice for a minute, you know what you'd hear? Chatter and laughter and all the things that make the passing of time more pleasurable.'

'It's fucking empty, Matt. There's about four people here and they're all reading the paper.'

Matt looked beyond Peter into the bar and took another gulp. 'Well come back tomorrow night then, I bet it's packed. There's millions of people content with their lot in life – they've got decent jobs, they raise their families as best they can in warm homes. And I'm not just talking about being able to afford to pay their gas bill. Millions of people are better off than you. Money's not a measurement of contentment for everyone.'

'You want to talk about contentment? Are you content?'

'I'll get there. It's a better thing to aim for than riches.' Matt's eyes were glazed over, focused on nothing other than some memory playing in his head. Perhaps not a memory, but a future where his wishes are granted with the flick of an imperial wrist. Matt was the sort of person who found it easier to bury himself in imagined worlds that were safe from the demands of reality. The sneer on his face made him look genuinely ugly. Right now, the only thing he needed was Peter's riches; that was something he seemed to have forgotten.

'Do you ever regret what you've become?' said Peter, beginning to ask himself the same question.

23

I take a slow gulp from my pint and leave Pete's question hanging. I am not being drawn into this. It's none of his business who I am or where I've found myself. Fucking contentment. All very good when you're not clinging to the edge of every day, hoping that there's enough strength left to survive until tomorrow.

'We've all got regrets, Pete, but I'd rather be outside the machine than part of it.'

A frown cracks across his forehead. Clueless. Pete is floating through calm waters in a custom-made yacht while the rest of us cram into a canoe and try to avoid the rocks. Well, if he doesn't need his life jacket, I'm sure as fuck not going to let it go to waste, not now he's just presented it. The plan has changed in the most generous fashion. Ten grand to Woody, ten grand to me. Nicky back and enough left to get me to Vegas. It'll be as if I'd never given Turnbull a penny. Bradley can fucking whistle for the rest. I'll deal with my conscience in due course.

'You could have been so much more, Matt.' He takes a drink. Doesn't look like he's enjoying it much. Probably because it's not Champagne.

I wonder what I'd have done with the chances he got. At least he took advantage, I suppose. Dad would be proud, I think, and so should I be proud by proxy? I've never once asked Mum how she feels when his sports car or his fucking jeep pulls up outside.

'Matt, are you listening?'

Whatever he's achieved though, it's changed him; made him think he's better than me, than that solitary pal he had at school. What was his name again? Pete would cross the road to avoid a guy like Andy, sneer from a distance. So would Turnbull, even Bradley. It's Andy's kind that props up the rest of us.

'Matt?'

Take away the generous and kind and humanity would crumble

under the weight of its own arrogance. Maybe we need everyone to stop giving a shit. But if everyone did collapse, Andy would be first to his feet, rescuing the likes of Pete then wondering why he gets stamped on when there are enough people standing.

'Matt, fucking pay attention.' He's shouting, demanding to be heard, speaking because he thinks he ought to, not because he should.

'I sometimes wonder if you'd be as selfish if you'd come first,' I say.

He looks over his shoulder, into the middle of the pub, for what I do not know. Two guys at the bar are deep in a conversation that doesn't carry this far. The barmaid is back in her phone, planning her night, her escape.

Pete turns back around, leans in. 'You came first and you came last, eh Matt? A head start and you're still trailing behind.' His elbows are hunched on the table, hands clasping his glass tight enough that he could shatter it. 'That's how you see the world isn't it? You've had so many chances, and you keep fucking it up because you over think things.'

'So what am I thinking now?'

'You believe there's an order and that your place in it is predetermined. All that does is give you an excuse.'

I slap the table. He's riling me now. 'That's bullshit. You've no idea the determination inside me. Just because I'm not in your shoes doesn't mean I've failed. I'll only be a failure if I don't get where I want to be when I keel over and die.'

'But you're not going to get there by being who you are.' Pete slaps it back. The liquid in his glass jumps and a thin head forms. 'You sit and wait for things to happen. Same parents, same house, same school. The only difference between you and me are the choices we made.'

'Poke, poke, poke. You want me to go and get you a stick?'

'Fucking grow up. I'm trying to help you.'

'Some help.'

He checks his watch. 'Look, where is this guy? What's happening?'

This is it. You can only hit the snooze button so many times.

'He's not coming here.' I'm remarkably calm when I say it.

'Then where is he? What the fuck are we doing here?'

Pete's yacht has run into a storm. It's almost satisfying to watch him flap.

'Do you think we're all just going to meet up in the pub and do a swap? Jesus. I need to go to him.'

'Are you fucking serious?' Again he looks to the door, as if Woody is going to miraculously appear.

All I can do is nod. 'It's in hand.'

'If you've to go to him then can I ask what in the cunting name of Christ you're doing sipping a pint like it's a Friday fucking night?'

He's shouting now. Daft prick. If I had twenty grand in my pocket I'd be quiet as a statue and twice as still.

I remain calm. 'I'm waiting on a phone call'

'Why didn't you say that before?'

'I've told you it's in hand.' I take a drink, just to noise him up. 'Trust me.'

'You're aware we've got a restaurant booked in less than two hours.'

This makes my lager go down funny. 'Who gives a fuck about dinner? This is about Nicky,' I stutter out between coughs. My stomach rumbles at the word dinner, but my point remains.

'Yes, and we need to have Nicky back before we go out or she'll realise something's amiss. Or, if we don't go out, she'll realise something's amiss. Plans are in place. Are you getting up to speed here?' He's talking to me like I'm one of his kids.

'You don't get it, do you? She doesn't want to go to some fancy restaurant. She wants to sit in her dressing gown and not have to think.'

'This isn't about the fucking dinner you dumb alcoholic prick. You just said it yourself, it's about getting Nicky back. Or the way it's going, it's about you stumbling in later and having to tell her just how much you've fucked up today.'

I should tip the table over for a remark like that but I'm fucked if I'm giving him the satisfaction. 'You offered me a pint before I had a chance to say.'

'A fucking pint, Matt? We've been sitting here twenty minutes. You could have said at any time "I meant to say, Peter, the guy that needs the twenty fucking grand that you're giving me out the goodness of your heart doesn't know what's happening – I

210

better him let know".'

His impression of me is shite, the voice too slow and deep. And angry.

Some old boy's newspaper shuffles.

'Keep your voice down,' I say.

'You really would be the star attraction at a museum of fuck ups,' he says. He reaches into his inside pockets and puts two fat envelopes down on the table. I open one and look inside. Jesus, it's a lot of cash. The other one is the same. One for Nicky, one for Matt. Pete just stares. He's become the statue now. I don't even think he's breathing.

'It's a lot more complicated that you could imagine,' I say.

'Try me.' He snarls back to life.

'Look, I've not eaten all day. I'm fucking starving and tired, and I just needed a rest before I finish this thing. I'll phone him in a minute to give him an update.'

'Thing? It's a thing, is it? I shouldn't even be here. I've got so much shit to clear up you couldn't possibly comprehend. Why was he running across the road anyway? Who told him it was okay to do that?'

If I tipped the table now, it would force Pete's chair to fall over, the weight of the table thudding down on his chest. I could stand over him, bring my own chair down on his head, watch as the wood splinters against his skull and… what the fuck I am doing? Who the fuck does he think he is? 'Don't you fucking dare comment on his upbringing. Mum taught him almost everything he didn't learn at school, all right? I filled in the rest. I taught him how to hit a decent corner kick, how to make sure he got a heads every time he tossed a coin. You know what else – he taught me stuff. Last month he showed me that you can see Jupiter in the night sky. It's not always there, but it appears now and again and I know that if I live until I'm ninety, I can look up into the sky and see a planet that's five hundred million miles away and remember that the happiest, care-free eleven year-old in the world pointed it out to me one night in our mum's garden.'

Ah shit, the tears are back. I wipe them away, puffing my cheeks up.

'I get that, just – '

'What was your brother's favourite film?'

211

He sighs. 'Look, I'm not – '

'Answer the fucking question, hot shot.'

He shakes his head, eyes buried in his glass.

'His favourite subject at school? His favourite dinner, toy, trainers, dinosaur?' I let them all hang there a second. 'We don't need you, Pete. You patronise Mum with you annual trip, never letting her into that glam world of yours. You don't need us. We don't need you. If you'd had the patience to wait at the front door this morning you would never even have known about this… this…fucking mess.'

He lifts up the envelope, waves it in the air. 'And where would you have got this from?'

I've never wanted money less. 'You want to win? Well done, you win.'

'We could have done this five hours ago.'

'Have you ever thought about how this makes me feel?'

He leans forward, his mouth actually falls open a little as if I've said something ridiculous. 'You've got one chance to take this money or I'm walking away, telling her everything.'

I think about Nicky, Woody, Bradley, Vegas. They're all there in front of me yet none are in focus. 'Don't you fucking blackmail me. You're far too wrapped up in this to be innocent. Mum will know you could have helped.'

He smiles. It unnerves me. 'And maybe yesterday that would have bothered me.' His eyes sharpen, the frown closing them over slightly. He sniffs and folds his arms. 'Today, given I just found out she knows where fucking Craig is, I owe her nothing.'

'Bullshit.'

'He knows all about Nicky, writes to him every birthday. She was saving the letters for when he was older.'

'What are you on about?'

'Did he look surprised when you met him that time and told him she'd had a boy? I bet he didn't. You see, I was thinking about him earlier, how he deserved to suffer as much as Mum is. So I checked her biscuit tin, looking for a clue so I could track the cunt down. I didn't need to look far.' He gets his phone out, shows me a picture of an address. Toronto. 'She's always known, Matt, always kept a wee bit of herself for him.'

'Fuck you.' The words cut a tie that's lasted a lifetime. I have no brothers left and that's not right, but life does the most unexpected things.

Maybe's it's the way I say it rather than what I say, but he picks the money up and stuffs it back in his pocket. 'Good luck,' he says. 'Now fuck off and phone your guru – see if he can conjure up what you've just thrown away.'

The cannonball comes with me when I step away from the table. I grab my jacket and swing it over my shoulders, but can't find the arms. The barmaid is looking over. Is she laughing at me? I stumble back and hit my thigh against the table. I think I shout out. Beer swirls around my stomach, the cannonball spinning faster and faster and it's as though the beer is gushing into my veins and being pumped to my brain… and the room…. moves…and spins…and Pete's laughing, but not moving… a statue…everything I could have been…I turn away…faces at the bar… more laughter…yellow teeth…cracked grins…I hear her say something…who…what…don't fucking talk to…the door opens…and rain…and cold…and…and it hits me and I'm sick. And sick and

Sick and…

Choking me.

KciS

Sick

kciS   Sick

     kciS   Sick

        kciS   Sick

          kciS   Sick

kciSSick

Sick fuck

Fuck him

Fuck him

I stand up straight, using the building to steady me. I wretch, but nothing comes up. A pool of lager and not much else lies at my feet, my trainers covered in it. My entire day swimming about in it. No more of this please. I've had enough now. Please.

I breathe in cold air, visualise it filling my lungs. Even in the gloom, it's bright enough to make me blink as my eyes adjust from the pub's darkness.

It takes a minute of breathing, maybe longer, but I realise if it's not dark yet then the day isn't over. I straighten up and just stand there, allowing the rain to cool me. There's a bang from inside the pub; something's smashed. I need away from here, from him.

My feet begin to move, quicker and quicker until I'm out of breath, my muscles doing what's demanded of them despite being starved. Everything comes together. My body does what it has to do. Just because Pete's unexpected invitation to bail me out changed the plan doesn't mean the plan won't work: the belief that the money exists can be just as important as its existence. Fuck Pete. Time is wasting.

24

Peter stared at the empty chair opposite. He wanted to break it, smash it against the floor and give his pounding heart the sacrifice it demanded. Violence as remedy.

Matt's undignified departure had already drawn the attention of those who'd been lost in their pints and papers. He could feel their eyes on him now, wondering what he'd do, how long he'd wait before standing. Fuck them. Fuck it all. He swept his arm across the table, sending both pint glasses spinning off into the musky air. They smashed in tandem, glass and beer spraying across the floor and choking what little ambiance there was. He was ready for the barmaid's squawk. It came quickly, before the fragments had even settled, a long roar of disapproval.

Peter stood and raised his hand. As he approached the bar he lifted five twenty-pound notes from his wallet. 'This should cover any inconvenience,' he said, gesturing over his shoulder. 'Where's the toilet?'

'It's…' She pointed towards the back corner. 'Wait a minute, you can't – '

'What is it you think you're playing at here, pal?' Some guy had stood from his bar stool, defending the pourer of his pint. How fucking chivalrous.

'It's fine, Alan. He's leaving,' said the barmaid. Mop up. Moan. Facebook update complaining about the glass-smashing prick, with no mention of the hundred quid he gave you. It wasn't exactly difficult to read these people.

'She's right. I'll be away in a minute,' said Peter.

He headed for the toilet without waiting for a reply. Four middle-aged farts sipping their pints on a Thursday afternoon posed little threat. He'd been too bold but the tantrum had calmed him at least.

The toilet, unsurprisingly, stank. Peter began to piss, watching steam rise from the yellowed urinal thanks to the chill from an open window. With Matt gone, any chance of a deal with the kidnappers, body snatchers, whatever they were, fucking Nickynappers, had gone with him. Withdrawing an offer was just part of Peter's world though. Parameters shifted. If one deal didn't happen, another would. Nicky would not need to miss his appointment.

McAllister's compromised staffer and the great minds of Scotland's finest law enforcers was the only option that should ever have been considered. He needed to get to the funeral parlour, buddy up with McAllister. If the undertaker had flushed out the rat, things would move quicker with Peter directing proceedings; there was still a whole night for the police to spend scouring Glasgow. He couldn't believe he'd fallen for Matt's provocation earlier, wrestled him to the floor for fuck's sake, put him exactly where he wanted to be – right in the centre of everyone's eye line. Peter was out of practice dealing with his brother's scams, that was the problem. It was time to put things right. His mum could always phone Craig for comfort when the story got out.

He washed his hands under water so hot it almost peeled the skin from his fingers. He'd never set foot in this hovel again. It was horrific; lowlifes with literally nothing else to do on a Thursday afternoon than sip away at cooking lager as though it were some sort of elixir.

The reality of how Matt had outmaneuvered him all day was coming more into focus as Cillian's silent admission sank in. Matt was right in one respect, Peter had let greed cloud his view of the world. But not in the way Matt thought. Trades he would have carried out on Monday would never take place now; his desk would be empty while the floor went about its business. While he sat in some shithole pub in the corner of nowhere wheels would already be turning. Cillian would have been straight on the phone to Tom. He wondered how his boss, his former boss, would play it. He thought of Stuey, being too smug, being reminded of his place. Peter would set a rabid bear on Stuey, but he couldn't afford to be angry with the King of the Jungle yet. Shock was one thing, but anger clouded judgement and there had to be a chink somewhere.

Contrary to what the media would have the masses believe,

traders didn't get rich on quick, risky deals. The safest and surest way to make money was to buy long, wait patiently for the market to rise. Even on bad days, when it looked like defeat was the only outcome, a good trader would look beyond the red numbers before executing the deal at exactly the right moment.

Peter headed back out and saw that the barmaid had almost finished mopping up the spillage. A hundred quid in less time than it took a customer to a take a piss. Not a bad result.

'You're barred,' she shouted as he walked passed, which at least got him laughing. He almost gave her another twenty.

Outside, he began to look for a taxi. He should never have met Matt in a pub. The undertaker's was always a more sensible venue. He'd bought a round of drinks for fuck's sake. Sat there sipping away like everything was resolved and he had nothing better to do on a Thursday afternoon. It was shock. It was Barton's fault. Tom's. Barton's. Tom. Barton. Tom. Fucking Bartom. He was a ghost all right. The fucking audacity of it all.

For the first time that day Peter welcomed the rain. The headache was sharper than ever. Stress, the doctor had said. Fucking stress? If he was lucky he wouldn't explode before bedtime.

He stopped at a set of lights and watched wearisome traffic make its way home. Whatever days these people had endured they were likely forgettable, stories told over the dinner table that night quickly fading from memory as plates emptied. By tomorrow morning they'd get back in their cars and buses and start again. That's how things got done. There was a role to play for everyone whose alarm went off. So where were the fucking taxi drivers?

When the lights changed Peter crossed and picked up the pace, zoned out of his current environment and into a space where no one but Tom was waiting. His mentor, the man he held in the highest regard of all. For years Peter had stood diligently by his side while others moved jobs, becoming rival traders, brokers or even actuaries. The latter was something Peter had considered once, in the dark days when months would pass without the market moving in his direction. That was when he'd learned the importance of patience. It always swung back towards him. Always. Tom had sacrificed him because he was the best, not in spite of it. If you needed someone to risk their reputation breaking laws and manipulating markets, of course you'd want your best man on the job. If you were going to throw someone to the fire it was going to be the man who could dampen the flames quicker than anyone else. The only thing Tom had misjudged was that Peter would call his own conscience into question and bring the affair to a halt. It was unparalleled disloyalty, even if Peter hadn't known whose loyalty he was betraying. He was oblivious, but Tom knew exactly what he'd been doing. That left Peter something to hedge. All he needed was somewhere to make a trade. Like a storm moving across a clear blue sky, the thought gathered momentum until there was nothing left but the sensation of raindrops and an answer.

25

My pace is quick as I dart between the few people left out on this miserable afternoon. I pick it up some more. There is a single objective now. From here, it's all about getting the right words in the right order before the clock runs down. No way that's happening, buddy. You're coming home with me. Promise.

I phone Woody, pressing the handset close to my ear to stop the wind whipping into the speaker. At least being sick has stopped the spinning; brain and cannonball are Zen-like, man. The words they will flow.

'Where have you been? Time's a ticking,' says Woody.

'I've got the money, all twenty.'

There's a slight pause. 'Your brother?'

'Does it matter? Just get me my other brother, the one I actually give a shit about.' I am confident, my voice strong and authoritative. Just like Turnbull taught me, the fucking parasite.

'Your nag let you down then?'

I say nothing.

'You definitely got it, Matt?' he says.

'Come on, Woody. Make the call.'

'You need to make it.'

'Eh?'

'You need to do it. He wants to speak to you before he tells me anything.'

I hang up without another word. Fucking typical Bradley. All-consuming control. I keep walking as I redial. There's a row of shops ahead of me. I don't even know what way I'm walking. I need a fucking destination here or I'll wear the soles of my shoes down. Breathe. My words must be perfect: in order, in execution, in tone, in

'Matthew, my good man. What news have you got for me?'

'I've got your money.'

'Please, Matt. We are business acquaintances. Business can't be conducted without manners.'

I stop walking, squeeze my phone. 'No more fucking games. I've got your –' and I stop talking because I realise he's hung up. Those weren't the words I needed. Idiot. I redial and it rings five, six, seven times. He's fucking at it. He'll pick up.

Sure enough, he does. 'Shall we try that again?' he says.

This time, I'm as bright as the North Star. 'Hi Bradley, I'm just calling to let you know I've got the money, as you requested.'

'Excellent. I knew I could count on you. Now, what you need to do is go to McAllister & Son's funeral parlour.'

As soon as I hear the words, I change direction, break into a jog, forcing my muscles into labour they are ill-prepared for.

'Across the road from the entrance is a white van. Now, Woody's got the keys, but the door will be unlocked. Get in, phone Woody, tell him where you are. He'll come to you. Give him the money, he'll take you to your brother. If you're nice, he might even give the pair of you a lift back to the parlour. You got it?'

It's all I needed to hear. 'I'm on my way.'

'I'm curious, Matt. Where did you get it?'

The cannonball swings, but it feels connected now. In my mind cogs are turnings and weights are lifting. And then it appears. The end of all this. I can see tomorrow morning with all the clarity of a sunrise. Mum's tears, the minister's words filling the room. And Nicky. I can see Nicky and I can see exactly how I'm going to get him back. 'Does it matter?' I say.

'Your brother give you it?'

I say nothing, but don't want to hang up.

'He fucking did, didn't he? I bet you went crawling to him, begged him to sort you out.'

'Fuck you. General Catalyst, 2.45 at Carlisle. I took it from there.'

He laughs. Roars. I can see tears forming in his pinprick eyes. It's all been a game. Someone fucked him over, he wanted to make himself feel better and he remembered I owed him.

'I'll be in touch,' I say, and hang up.

My thighs are burning but onwards I march. Everything changes today. For me anyway. After the funeral Pete can get back in his car and his perfect life can carry on. He'll never know how I got the wee man back but he'll never stop wondering. We'll never see each other again; I'll be so far away he'll forget what I look like, but not that I did it all without him. Woody's going to do the right thing, break free from Bradley's chokehold as easily as getting on a plane. My emergency credit card can handle two tickets down under. Off we'll soar, a comfy seat and plenty of those wee miniatures from smiling hostesses. Maybe one of them will take a shine to me, invite me to join that mile high club. Oh yes, that would get the trip off to the right start. When we find Turnbull, I'll get what's owed plus interest. Fifty grand apiece for me and Woody. That's more than Pete was handing over. It's enough to set up in a town where the sun in the sky is the only reminder I'm on the same planet. A single line email will take care of Bradley: you can't spend your life swatting bees and not expect to be stung. I can see his face when he opens it. Even when he's old and too decrepit to stop his empire crumbling he'll know he could never find me. Over here fucko. No, not there, here. Right fucking here. Buzz, buzz, buzzing in your ear. Prick. Mum will miss me, maybe. Siobhan won't miss me right away. But here's the thing, in time she will. She'll go on some date with some wanker and spend the night imagining my reaction to his shite chat. The next morning she'll consider emailing me, sharing the joke, but she's stronger than that. It'll get her thinking though, about the times we laughed and the times we fucked. The memories will make her smile. From then on, when she checks her email in the mornings before showering she'll look for my name, cursing herself, fighting it. One day there will be a message, just an address and a boarding pass. If it wasn't meant to be it would never have happened in the first place.

The rain is getting heavier again. I don't know why I ever came back here. Fucking raindrops. They fall, they get swept into a sewer and rush out to sea in a hurry to be sucked back up into the clouds, just so they can sail across the sky until they're right over my fucking head again. Well let it all come down on top of me. 'It's your last chance, you big bastard!' I shout up into the sky.

I pass an off-licence and duck inside. Everything's in hand. It's all good, man, it's coming together. Matt's making history today. The shop is empty, one of those horrible places with grilles on all four sides, making customers feel as though they're in a cage. A distinct whiff of BO makes me wonder if that old fucker Davie's been in for a celebratory carry out. Then I see the wifey working the till. She's sitting on a stool reading the paper. No chance anyone's stealing from her; if anything the cage is protection for the customers. I stand at the opening like a monkey waiting for his feed, my eyes scanning the shelves for something decent. Bananas man, they'd queue up all day for one, those fucking monkeys. Well that's not for me. I need something with a bit more bite. They've got half bottles of Glenfiddich, which is a right bonus as I thought I'd be lumbered with one of the cheap blends in a hole like this. I give her my last twenty and a smile. Even the middle classes must be feeling the pinch if you can buy single malt in half bottles. I suppose that's something to thank Pete and his banking chums for. She gives me the bottle and slips a pile of change through the grille with a smile that would make children run for cover. I'm back on the street in under a minute.

There's a taxi sitting at the lights, its amber beacon flirting with me. Bonus. I dive in and give the driver directions. As he revs away he begins to pepper me with questions. Not again. Not a fucking chance. I just gaze out the window, crack the cap on the bottle and let the golden waterfall gush down my throat, cleansing my palate and bringing back the edge I need to see this through. By next week Glasgow and all it offers will be nothing more than fragments of my past.

The driver has one last go, some vague attempt to find out what team I support. When I don't answer he turns up the radio. There's a country song playing, one I don't recognise. Some boy pained about something though, taking it all out on his acoustic guitar. If I ever hear it again I wonder if it will bring back memories of what's about to transpire.

As the taxi turns into the street I see the white transit, just where Bradley said it would be. I'm sure it's the same one that was there when I stepped out of Pete's car nine hours ago. I wonder if someone was there earlier, calling Bradley with an update when we arrived at McAllister's, then again when Pete left on his own. I hand over a pile of pound coins, this time waiting for the change. See you later, driver.

222

As the taxi turns out onto the main road, I move slowly towards the van, keeping an eye out for any sign of Woody or another of Bradley's goons. I don't like this. The street's too quiet. I have a suspicion that I'm being followed, that Bradley's been aware of my every move. I take another glug of whisky. The van's empty. The street's empty. I'm in control.

The van is fit for the bin. Dents line its side and rust is advancing over the wheel arches like a cancer. I look inside the driver's door window. The black vinyl seat is torn, yellow sponge oozing out. Stour and dust coats the dashboard, empty juice bottles are stuffed into the door pockets, along with cloths and notepads. I try the door and it opens, but I don't get in. Not yet, man. Not yet.

Across the road the lights are still on in McAllister's. He'll be sitting at his desk, waiting for me to call. I'd have heard quick enough if he'd phoned the police – Pete at least has been persuasive enough on that count. McAllister deserves more than he got this morning. Odd that he should be the one I feel an urge to make amends to. Time for that later. There's a focus now, an end point that everything else is rushing towards. I wonder if this is how Pete sees the world.

I call Woody, my foot tapping against the kerb. Where the fuck is he? He must be expecting me. Jesus, fuck. Come on. Fucking answer. I cross the road and tap my foot on the opposite pavement before spinning round and heading back. Tap. Walk. Tap. I only stop when he picks up.

'What's the fuck's going on, Woody? You said you were out the loop.'

'I said I didn't know where your brother was. I don't.'

'Then why is Bradley telling me to phone you?'

'Where are you? Are you at the van?'

'Yes, for the all the fucking good it's doing me. I don't like hanging around with this sort of money on me. If I get mugged before you get here, you better still hand him over.' Right words. Right order.

'Calm down. You're not going to get mugged. I'm on my way.'

'And then what?'

'I honestly don't know. I've to phone Bradley back when I'm with you. He won't give me directions until I see the money.'

'Why the fuck not? Does he not trust you?'

'He doesn't trust you.'

'What's not to trust? He tells me where Nicky is. I bring the money. A fair exchange is no robbery, Woody.'

'Have you met Bradley? How should I know the way his mind works?'

'How far away are you?'

'Just sit tight, I'm coming.'

He hangs up and I stare into the sky. It's like a spaceship, man. This huge body of grey bearing down on us all. It's intense, man, brooding. I have to remember what this sky looks like because one day I'll miss the rain.

I climb into the passenger side. The urge for a cigarette threatens to choke me but I've none left. I open the glove box in the vague hope of finding anything with tobacco in it. There's a manual, a few cassettes. Fucking cassettes? It's only then I notice the van is old enough to have a tape deck. There's a lighter, but no fags. Beneath the seat I feel around for one that might have been dropped and discover a chip wrapper. It's lying on top of what feels like a pile of tools. The paper is cold and slimy. I wonder who bought the chips, and where. Whose van is it? Why is it part of my day?

Rain drums against the window; it's a nice beat. You could drift off to that sound. I sip from my bottle and focus on the raindrops, watching them race each other down the windscreen. I can't sleep. Can't allow… my eyes… to… Wait. Waitwaitwait. Hold on a fucking jiffy. There's one phone call I still need to make.

It rings out, as it always does. This time I don't imagine where he is. I hear his voice as he repeats the greeting message I could recite in my sleep. I see his mouth move, I see the image he projects and I want to shatter it as though it's made of glass.

'Hello Phillip,' I say. 'I know for a fucking fact in ten seconds time you'll be listening to this, judging the venom in my voice and tut tut fucking tutting at the negativity. You've no idea what you've caused, but you're going to find out. I'll tell you just before I take back what's mine and a bit more besides. I don't give a fuck what corner of the world you're strutting about in. One day, you'll walk into a bar, get on a yacht, or come home from a day of feeding horseshit directly into the mouths of people just desperate for a better fucking tomorrow, today, and I'll be there, my smile projecting an image of complete victory. I am coming for you, cunt, so don't – '

The message times out. So fucking typical. I consider calling back, but the point has been made. Right words, dickhead. Right order.

The last time I saw him, I could never have imagined it ending like this. We were sitting in a hotel lobby in London, white floors and high ceilings giving it the very air of luxury the architect was aiming for. Phillip had paid for my flight. Expenses, he said. We were sitting on opposite sides of a table for four, his laptop between us, so we could both see the screen. He was drinking his green fucking tea and I was guzzling my third black coffee. He told me how close everything was to lift off, as he put it; he showed me the artwork for the 'Help Yourself to Help Yourself' starter packs; we worked on the presentation I'd give to delegates; we shook hands when we were finished. He told me that the day in the doctors' when I saw his advert was not a coincidence. *Look at where it's brought us,* he said. *Think about where it's taking us.*

My ten grand is sitting in the cunt's bank account, slowly accruing interest. A copy of that presentation is saved on my laptop. I'm going to print out the title page and frame it next to General Catalyst's betting slip. When I go to Vegas, they'll come with me.

The light's still on in McAllister's. His day has lasted a decade. Poor bastard. Jenny the receptionist answers and sounds friendlier than she did earlier. She puts me through, even says she hopes I'll be back soon.

'Have you any news, Matthew?' He sounds greyer than before.

'I just wanted to say I'm sorry.'

'Have you any news?'

'Did you hear me? I said I'm sorry. But don't worry, it's all in hand. All in hand. Can you still get him ready for tomorrow?'

'That depends on what time you return your brother to us,' he says. The tone is weak; he's nothing left, but he'll work all night if he needs to.

'I'm on my way to get him. It's all good, won't be long.'

225

There's a knock on the window and Woody's face, glum and wet, stares up at me. Everything is in hand.

'I have to go. I'm sorry, really sorry.'

'Just bring your brother back in one piece.'

I hang up as Woody climbs into the driver's seat. He rubs his hair and wipes his hands on his jacket, which is as wet as his hair.

'I'm sick of this fucking weather,' he says.

I can offer him sunshine. He just doesn't know it yet.

'You'll be looking forward to getting home, eh?' he adds. A new bandage on his hand looks as though it's been put on professionally.

I stuff the whisky bottle into the door pocket, but not quickly enough. He shakes his head.

'It's not been a very nice day, no. I've been running about since half eight this morning when I should have been looking after my mum. I've spewed twice, been in three fights. I'm not sure if I'm half cut or sober and I'd literally kill you in the face right now for a fag. On top of that my brother's once again reminded me just how much better he is than me, and that's not even taking this fucking carry on into account.' My finger twirls around the van. 'So, yes, I can't wait to get home and get my balls felt for being AWOL all fucking day thanks to your cunt of a boss.'

'Easy, pal. Come on.' He reaches into his pocket and produces a packet of cigarettes. 'You're nearly there.'

I feel a twitch of greed and grab at the pack. The lighter I found doesn't work though. Of course it doesn't. Woody hands over his Zippo, a well-worn thing with a picture of a chequered flag on it that reduces it from classic to tacky. I flick the flame to life and take a long draw, enjoying this last moment of calmness.

'Right, where's the cash?' he says.

I suck hard on the cigarette. 'I've got a plan, Woody.'

26

Peter flicked through his contacts until he saw the name he was looking for. He dialed and slowed his pace so his breathing wouldn't sound so much like a sex fiend's.

An old voice that still had power round the edges answered.

'Is that offer still on the table?' said Peter, in response to an abrupt welcome.

'Who's this?' There was a brief silence, during which Peter asked himself what the fuck he was doing. 'Is that Peter Fletcher?'

'Hello, Robert. How have you been?'

'Are you running, dear boy?'

Fuck's sake. He wasn't in the middle of a marathon. He stopped nonetheless. He had to get back to the gym, pronto. This was no use. Ease off the midweek red and bedtime whiskies. It might even help clear the headaches.

'I'm not running, no, but I wouldn't mind talking to you about moving,' he said.

Robert Cumming laughed. He rarely laughed. Maybe it was something to do with being CEO of one of the listed investment banks. There was a certain degree of pressure that went with a job like that, shareholders as demanding as hungry children, as savage as hungry dogs. There was also the salary that made it look as though Peter was on minimum wage, and the shareholdings and long-term incentive plans that literally made him richer than some countries. Maybe the laughter would be more forthcoming when he gave it all up. Not that he looked like doing so any time soon. Cumming had seized power of Duke & Standard in 2009 when the firm came out of the recession with some angry shareholders. He'd helped it grow since, with shrewd management and canny acquisitions, to become a top fifty global investment bank with a $40 billion market capitalisation.

Peter had met him at a few functions back when Robert was CFO and they'd always got on well. He'd offered Peter a job after he'd settled into the hot seat, but Peter had explained that his loyalty to AMJS was absolute, although he valued Robert's backing and considered it a great honour to have been asked to join his firm. It was a generous offer, and maybe the old man with the most famous moustache in the City had plans for Peter that would have taken him from the trading floor to the boardroom. He couldn't leave Tom's side though. Wouldn't consider it. Not even when Robert's second offer arrived. The last time they'd spoken, six months ago at Cheltenham races, Robert had reminded him the offer was always there. Tom had been standing nearby and Peter nearly kicked the old man. He'd laughed then too, leaving Peter with the distinct impression he was fodder for Cumming's amusement – a couple of years earlier Duke & Standard had tried to buy AMJS, and while initial discussions had gone well, it had turned ugly, with hostilities continuing between the two CEOs long after D&S had walked away.

Peter didn't appreciate the public gesture and so had drawn back from Cumming. Not that six months counted for a long time in the City, even if a single afternoon could change a trader's life forever.

'The offer is where it's always been Peter. You know I'd love to have you here.'

'If I do this it's not going to be easy.'

'You mean it'll cost me?'

'No. Well, it will, but that's not what I mean. This is about more than money.'

'I've got a meeting in fifteen minutes. You've got my attention until then.'

Peter started walking again. He found a rhythm that suited both his thighs and his lungs. His capacity for rhetoric had helped set him apart from the other maths geeks he'd studied with. Peter could hold a room if he had to so gripping one man on the other end of the phone was never going to be troubling, especially not with the fucking blockbuster material he was working with. He knew it was a landline, that there was a chance his words were being recorded and could be used at any point. On one hand he felt like he was framing himself, but it was insurance. Tom had power, and while his pockets might have been full of bankers who'd stuck with his warped sense of warfare, he was leading a small nation next to Cumming's superpower. If Peter had the weight of Duke & Standard behind him he could maybe survive.

The tale unfolded, from Miami, 'horrible place,' said Cumming, to Cillian and the Taylor-Caraway algorithm disaster: 'Are you fucking telling me Matheson was behind that?' He saved the best until he knew his time was almost up. The plan was to move onto the Reuters hack just as Cumming needed to get off the phone. If Peter could force him to delay his meeting then he had him.

It was a minute to half five when Peter delivered his final line. He spoke swiftly, without giving his one-man audience a chance to interrupt. He placed Robert back in the moment the market plummeted on news of the PM's assassination, commenting on how every open trading floor in the world would have experienced the same panic.

'I have zero doubt that Tom was responsible. How much did your firm lose that day?' said Peter. He was nearing the railway bridge, just minutes from the parlour.

Cumming had been patient throughout, murmuring on occasions, gasping on others. 'You know I could take this information straight to the FSA, have you both barred from the City, God, jailed, for this?'

'Me, yes. You could do that in the morning. But Tom? You can't get him. He's pulling so many strings that I doubt anyone really knows who they're dancing for. I know him though, I know how he works, how he thinks. I can bring him down, but I need a big defensive line behind me.'

The rain had got heavier. Peter had lost the feeling in the fingers holding the phone. His shirt was wet through his jacket, and he had puddles in his shoes. None of it mattered. He stopped when he reached the railway bridge and took shelter, shielding his phone from the chatter of the pigeons perched on the beams above.

'I'll need to think about this,' said Cumming.

'Of course.'

'If I do it, what do you want?'

'I'm not looking to benefit from this. Same package I'm on just now. I'll bring as much business as I can with me.'

'You'll need to go to the beach for six months, maybe a year.'

In the grim darkness under the bridge, with bird shit covering the pavement and pissing rain fifteen feet either of side of him, Peter laughed silently. The term was one the banking world had adopted as a suitable upgrade from gardening leave. It had always tickled Peter, and its context now couldn't have been more apt. Robert wouldn't be talking about it if he wasn't in the midst of convincing himself to go for it. Peter had one last push. 'It would give me plenty of time to work out how to end him,' he said.

'I'm interested, Peter. But like I say, I have to think. You know you're tainted now.'

'Only on the inside, sir.'

'I'll have my secretary call you. Give me a week. We can head down to my place in Nice for a couple of days, talk properly, away from the scene of the crime, as it were.'

'I'd love nothing more, Robert. Thank you.'

'Don't thank me yet,' he said. 'I must go, I appreciate the call.'

The line went dead. Peter puffed his cheeks, exhaled and started walking. If he could get in front of Robert he could sell him anything. That was what he did for a fucking living. And he wasn't wrong about the year spent going after Tom. With Duke & Standard's weight behind him, he could knock Tom out of his orbit. Peter would be untouchable; he'd make sure he was.

He put two fingers to his neck as he emerged back into the light. His pulse was charging, the resonant beat of victory. Rain battered his face, but so fuck. In a week's time he'd be making plans for a trip to Nice. It'd still be plenty warm this time of year. Canada would have to wait – Craig wasn't absolved or anything, but all Peter's efforts would have to go into crushing Tom.

He turned the corner and refocused. One more fuck up to flatten out before he could unwind. Across the road from McAllister's someone was lying on the pavement. Peter stopped. Whoever it was, they weren't moving. Further ahead a white van was making its way up the street, plumes of smoke spitting from its exhaust.

Peter slowly began moving towards the body, unsure whether or not it was Matt. He wasn't entirely sure if he wanted it not to be.

27

'What do you mean, you've got a plan?' says Woody.

I don't say a word. Not yet. I want him to want to hear this properly. Instead, I think he might be about to throw a punch. I consider the space between us. Vans are roomier than cars and if he does go for me, he'll never get near me. I'll swipe down on his arm, pulling him in and throwing a left hook. That'll push him back against the window and I'll have time to get out of the van before he comes back at me. It's good to have a contingency plan.

He backs down quickly, kneads his temples. 'You don't have the fucking money do you?'

I shake my head. In spite of the whisky, I'm focused. Because of the whisky, I'm focused. Pete is history, lounging about in my past with Turnbull and Bradley.

'Let me guess,' he says. 'Your horse came second and your brother told you to piss off.'

'Close. My horse killed its jockey and I told my brother to piss off.'

His head shakes. He looks at the floor. 'Fucking hell, Matt. What are you playing at?'

'Hear me out.'

'Believe me, mate, it's not in my interests to hear you out.' He puts a cigarette in his mouth and beckons for me to give back the lighter. I don't.

'Please, Woody.'

'Don't be a prick.'

'I'll give you it if you promise to listen to my plan.'

He sighs. 'This isn't playground politics, Matt. You're in too fucking deep here. Forget for a minute that Bradley's got your brother's coffin and picture your own.'

'Fuck Bradley. He changed the rules, man. It wasn't cool what he did. He was going to get his money back. It's fucking twisted.' I punch the roof of the van. 'You work for him, you know him

– why did he do it?'

'Why do people in power abuse it? Because they can. I'm going to need to phone him now, you know that, right?'

I take a deep breath and know the next thing I say is about the most important thing I'll ever say. Even now, as I want him destroyed, I think about how Turnbull would do this. I begin by opening my palms and turning so that my chest is exposed. This will illustrate to Woody that I trust him without him even realising. So much of what we see is subconscious. We're just fucking animals after all.

'Of course you need to phone him,' I say. 'But you don't ever need to be beholden to him again. Tell him you've got the money.'

When he scoffs I raise a hand, slowly, and he stops. He's gazing out the windscreen, staring at I don't know what. I take a long draw, the nicotine sharpening me up, readying me. The cab is filling with cigarette smoke. This is it, man, my moment.

'Tell him you've got it,' I say. 'He'll tell you where Nicky is. You owe that much to fucking humanity. Tomorrow, after the funeral, we'll drive to London. My credit card will take us to Australia. We'll find Phillip Turnbull. That's where it'll begin. I don't want my ten grand back. I want him fucked up. Fingernails, toenails; I want his fucking teeth. Then I want his money. He's rich. We get fifty grand each, me and you, then we shake hands and fuck off into the sunset. We never see him again, we never see Bradley, we never see each other.'

I take a final draw and stub the end out on the manky floor. Woody says nothing. Seconds pass. Time finally feels like it's slowing down, just as I need it to pick up the pace.

'I'm a businessman, Matt,' he says. His breathing is deep, as if we're running low on oxygen. 'I provide a service, and in return I am more than adequately paid. There's a fair bit of risk involved in my job, not all of it's above board, but my boss recognises that. He has done for years, ever since he plucked me out of a cell and gave me a chance. I've worked for him for nearly twenty years. I've been to his kids' birthday parties. He is a bad bastard, you know that. Your mistake though, is believing I'm not.'

'Woody – '

'Not a fucking word.' His voices carries menace. He looks at the end of his cigarette and stubs it out on the dashboard.

'There's not going to be a funeral now, Matt.'

As he reaches for his phone, I shift in my seat, getting into position.

He turns, his face a question mark of confusion. 'Don't be stupid,' he says, not budging. He is completely composed as he taps on his phone. Misplaced confidence in his reputation. I had him in my flat, and I'll have him again. When he lifts the phone to his ear I reach below the seat for the wrench amongst the tools I clawed at earlier. I grip it tight and before he's managed to work out what I'm doing I bring it down with everything I've got onto his kneecap. He screams out and drops his phone. Twisting forward he tries to grab the wrench and tend to his knee at the same time. His instincts have let him down. I swing again, at his head, knowing he'll block it with his forearm. He does, but another blow comes, and another. He's moving towards me, trying to overpower me. I back off, budge myself up against the door where there's less room to manoeuvre. This will go my way. It can go no other way.

When he's close enough, I use my free hand to squeeze his kneecap. I can feel two separate pieces of bone and when I push down they move apart. He shrieks, a high-pitched desperate plea that makes me squeeze harder. He tries to twist away and finally lets his guard down to protect his knee. I swing the wrench one final time. The thud against his skull reverberates up my arm. I'm thankful I don't hear a crack, more thankful when he slumps forward. I push his shoulder so he falls back into the corner.

Poor Woody. He never asked for any of this. At least his knee's not hurting him for now.

I get out the van and go round the other side, opening Woody's door and almost collapsing under his weight as he slumps out. I realise my mistake and try to close the door but he's falling now, falling fast, an avalanche of solid muscle and musky aftershave rolling towards me, and all I can do is step forward and brace myself, let him hit me, do whatever I can to make sure the daft prick doesn't land head first on the concrete – something I just about manage, only through the good fortune of my thighs giving way, leading me to hit the pavement first, Woody thudding down on top me and thankfully rolling off before I'm crushed. It wouldn't have taken long. 'Sake, man. The

233

few parts of me that weren't soaked are now fucking ringing wet.

I pick myself up and think about giving him a kick in the ribs for almost battering me while unconscious, but I refrain and go through his pockets instead. The van key is there, along with his fags. His wallet has £120 cash and a couple of bank cards. I go back to the van and pick his phone off the floor, check his text messages, call history – Bradley phoned after he spoke to me. While I sat in the van, they plotted. Cunts. Bradley is at the top of the text list too. I click his name.

> Anything from Matt?

> I've not heard from him all day, boss.

That's it. The last message. Sent at the back of four. Woody lied about meeting me earlier. He was on my side, for a while at least. Fucking hell. It means nothing now. Nicky's whereabouts are in his mind, not his pockets. Fuck. Fuck. Fuck. I rifle through his pockets again, looking for anything, half a clue of what might be going on. There's a receipt for a sandwich and bottle of juice and that's it. Fuck me.

I slap his face, lightly. When his head moves, I see blood pooling on the pavement. Shit. His hair is wet, thick with blood, but the wound's not gushing. I softly press down on it; there's a lump swelling where I hit him, but the skin's not broken as badly as it could be. I slap him harder, once on either cheek. Nothing, then a groan, so quiet it's like he's dreaming. I slap him again, sharper this time, stinging my hand a little. His head slips to one side and I catch it, straightening him back up.

'Wake up, Woody. Come on, mate, wake up.'

He groans again, his head moves slightly of its own accord.

'Wakey, wakey, it's a beautiful morning.'

His mouth opens at the same time as his eyes. A silent scream emerges, then a cough. He groans again, louder. With a bit of effort I peel off his jacket and roll it into a pillow, tuck it behind his neck.

'My knee,' he spits, his lips sticking together.

'Don't worry, just tell me where Nicky is and we'll get you an ambulance.'

234

His eyes close again. 'I don't know.' He tries to sit up but I put a hand on his chest and he falls back into his jacket-pillow with ease.

'Easy, Woody, don't sit up. You've had a nasty knock.'

'My fucking knee,' he says, his voice weak.

'Where is he, Woody. It's easy. Just tell me. I can go and get him while you wait on the ambulance.'

'I don't know,' he says again, a smile breaking out. 'He won't tell you, not without the money.' He feels his head, his hand shaking. 'What have you done? You stupid fuck.'

I stand up. The cannonball tells me I've done a terrible thing. Serious assault. That's jail time. I don't know how much. I'm not a criminal. I don't keep a tally of these things. Fuck, a harsh lawyer could push for attempted murder.

'Are you feeling okay?' I say. He has to be; he must be.

'Fuck you, Matt.'

I look towards the main road. Cars pass quickly. A single pedestrian crosses the street. They don't look this way. I can't afford for anyone to look this way. I put Woody's wallet back in his pocket, keeping the fags and lighter. I roll the van key in my closed palm.

'Sorry, Woody. Really. It shouldn't have come to this.'

'I'll fucking come for you, Matt. Whatever you think is going to happen is nothing compared to the reality.' He swallows hard. His breathing remains shallow. He doesn't even have the strength to fight off the rain, which is beginning to soak his hair, his clothes, his wounds.

I drop his phone and stamp on it, shattering the screen. My foot comes down again, and again. When it's smashed open and its insides are exposed, I pick up its pieces and drop them down the nearest drain. I take one last look at Woody. He's slumped back now, his eyes closed; he looks calm. Someone will find him soon enough.

I get back into the van and start it up. It struggles into life and I pull away with a grunt. At the end of the street I turn left in to the traffic and join the commuters heading back to their families for dinner and tales of their day.

28

Whoever had dealt the unconscious figure at Peter's feet such a savage beating had disappeared around the corner in the most dilapidated getaway vehicle imaginable. Any clues about what had transpired on the street in the minutes before Peter's arrival had gone with them. Not that Peter was much interested in the squabbles of Glasgow's underworld. All he knew was that the person before him wasn't Matt. He considered heading for McAllister's, leaving whatever this fucking mess was to whoever caused it, but the guy looked in bad shape.

Peter knelt down, his knees cracking onto hard, wet concrete. He shouted hello a few times, getting close enough to the man's ear that he could smell the fruitiness of his aftershave and see the jutting angles of his stubble. No response though. There was a worrying amount of blood leaking from his head. Blood. Again he thought of Nicky.

He stood up, stepped away from the body.

Nicky. Fuck. He really was lost. No tannoy announcement to call out his name. No cuddles at the customer service desk when he toddled along, eyes wet and cheeks red, clutching the hand of a kindly stranger. He was gone, and he was gone. Peter had never stopped to wonder if the boy he couldn't bring himself to call a brother would have turned out more like him or Matt. One thing he did know was that Matt wouldn't leave someone bleeding in the gutter.

He leaned in and gently shook the man, this battered action-figure baddie whose limbs and neck were limp. His chest was moving though. Peter pressed two fingers against the man's thick neck. There was a strong pulse. He shouted again and thought the head might have moved voluntarily. He shook harder until he heard a grumble from deep down in the man's throat. He shouted louder, kept shouting until the man's eyes opened. His breathing was heavy and slow, but he lifted his neck as if awakening from a nightmare and winced.

'Easy there, back you go.' Peter noticed for the first time that the guy's head was resting on a makeshift pillow. Who left somebody for dead but made sure they were comfortable? 'You stay here, just relax.'

The man began to mumble, but it was just loose syllables unable to bond with their companions. Peter again reassured him, taking backwards steps until he felt far enough away that he could turn and run across the road.

The parlour door was locked so he began to hammer on it with both fists until he heard movement from inside. A girl opened the door an inch, her face confused and verging on fearful. It was the blonde one, from earlier.

'Phone an ambulance,' said Peter.

'What's happened?

'Right fucking now,' shouted Peter.

The girl ran back behind her desk and made the call. He heard her give the details but begin to stumble.

'A man's been attacked,' he said. 'He's out there on the pavement. Tell them to hurry up.'

The volume of Peter's voice drew McAllister out of his office. 'Peter?'

'What the fuck's been happening out there?' said Peter.

'Whatever do you mean?' said McAllister, looking over Peter's shoulder and out the open door.

'I'm fucked if I know, but if an ambulance doesn't get here soon you've got the shortest pick up in your history.'

McAllister grabbed his coat from a hook and ran outside.

'A cloth, do you have a cloth?' said Peter.

The girl stood motionless.

'A cloth, a towel, something? Come on.'

She disappeared into a room and came back with a dishcloth. Peter snatched it from her and followed McAllister into the street.

He arrived to see McAllister towering over the man. He was trying to sit up, and probably wouldn't be feeling any better with the embodiment of Death looming above him. Peter bent down and pressed the dishcloth into the head wound. 'Hold that in place,' he said, directing the man's hand towards it.

'What's your name?' asked McAllister. 'Can you remember?'

'Of course I can remember my name. Derek Woodburn.'

Sharp tone for a man whose life was in your hands, thought Peter.

'Derek, what happened?' said McAllister.

'Where's the van?'

'Which van is this?' said the undertaker.

'The van. The fucking van that was sitting right there.' Derek shouted and screamed out, kicking his good leg into the air.

Peter couldn't remember ever seeing anyone quite so angry. Tom's vein-stretching outbursts were placid by comparison. He kept quiet. This wasn't the sort of street where normal business took place.

'There's an ambulance coming,' said McAllister.

Derek puffed his cheeks. 'He fucked my knee. Jesus, it's sore.'

McAllister took his coat off and placed it over Derek. 'There you go. You stay as warm and as dry as you can in this abysmal weather. I shouldn't think you'd want to move with that head wound. I'd recommend you stay put until the professionals arrive.'

The blood that had been pooling on the pavement had trickled towards the stream of rain and was working its way towards the gutter.

Derek nodded. 'No one calls me Derek. It's Woody.'

'Well, hello Woody. I'm Arthur.'

Fucking Arthur? All day Peter had been dealing with McAllister and hadn't got past Sunday names, while this boy got the old pal's act within seconds.

'Do you recall what happened?' said McAllister.

The guy shook his head. 'I was in the van, I think. I don't…'

'Don't push yourself. It'll come back.'

'Arthur, when you've finished making friends, we need to talk,' said Peter.

'I should imagine we do,' said McAllister.

'Will you be okay here for a minute, Woody?' said Peter. 'We're going to check up on where that ambulance is, get you a cup of tea or something.'

Woody lay back down, muttering about his van. That was the least of his fucking problems.

'We can't leave him here,' said McAllister.

'He's not going anywhere,' Peter replied, beginning to drag

McAllister back across the road.

Inside, the undertaker slumped into one of the reception seats, his dignity having been chipped away over the course of the day until any pretense of professionalism had abandoned him completely.

'Jenny, could you be an angel and make a cup of tea? The man across the road calls himself Woody. I think he would thank you for one.'

Jenny disappeared and Peter sat opposite McAllister.

'Have you spoken to your staff?'

'I have my suspicions,' said McAllister, sitting up. 'He's denying it of course. This business was my life. It was everything.'

Peter noted the tense. Everything moved from present to past in the end. Nicky had been his brother. He hadn't made anything of the opportunity that had been presented. Maybe he would have in time; invited the boy down for weekends in the big smoke, his nieces showing him the sights. He might have moved there eventually. Sometimes endings crept up on you. I work at AMJS. A phrase he'd said countless times over the years. He'd planned on saying it for many more, but would never utter the words again.

'I used to work at a company called AMJS,' he said, trying it out.

'Pardon?'

Peter smiled. 'Nothing. We move on. We all move on. Your business will be fine though as long as you want to keep going. If anything people will be sympathetic. You had a rogue employee who sold you out. It happens everywhere, every day. Make sure you deal with it publicly, hang him high. Tell the papers who he is and what he did. Try and find out how much cash exchanged hands and double it when you tell the story. They'll like that sort of detail.'

'I thought you didn't want it getting out.'

'It has to get out. That's the only way we'll get him back.'

'I appreciate your candor, Peter, after... everything.'

'You want to make the call then?'

'What about your family?'

'My mum's going to need to suck it up. And my brother's a lost cause. He's not part of this anymore. He never should have been. It's up to the police now.' He looked at his watch. 'We've got at least twelve hours, so you never know.'

Peter swung his jacket off. It was soaked through. He dipped into the pocket and lifted out a pile of notes. It looked like a novelty sponge.

McAllister fixed his glasses, peered in closer. 'Is that…?'

Peter flicked through the bundle, feeling something not far off the consistency of papier mâché. 'It was. Any chance you've got a tumble drier back there?'

'I'm sorry. I wonder if…' McAllister walked towards the reception desk, just as Jenny reappeared with a tray of mugs.

'I just got one for everyone,' she said. 'Thought you all might need warming up.' She nodded at Peter's jacket, a kind smile spreading over her face.

They both lifted a mug from the tray. Peter gulped at the tea. He couldn't remember the last time he'd had tea. It was remarkable. He felt its heat line his throat. Then he heard the siren outside.

He headed back into the street with his mug, leaving the money lying on top of his jacket. The ambulance had pulled up and two paramedics were already leaning over Woody. Poor fucker. Whatever he'd been caught up in, he'd come off second best.

'Was it yourself that made the call?' said one of the paramedics.

'Well, she did,' said Peter, pointing to Jenny. 'But I found him. He was lying unconscious. He's had a sore one in the head, but he was complaining about his knee.'

Peter stood with McAllister and Jenny, drinking tea and watching the paramedics load Woody onto a gurney. They were about to roll him into the back of the ambulance when he gestured with his arms.

'It was Matt!' he shouted. 'Where's fucking Matt?' He was rocking on the stretcher, trying to get up.

Peter handed his mug to Jenny and ran over. Had Matt done this? Was this the cunt he'd been on the phone to? Someone had to be waiting for the money, someone who would know exactly where the funeral parlour was. 'Did you say Matt did this to you? Matt Fletcher?' He leaned in close. The cut on Woody's head looked sore. Peter felt like pressing his fingers into it, seeing if he could pull the fucker's brain out through the gash.

Woody nodded, settling back down. The painkillers were

kicking in. 'Do you know him?'

'I'm his brother.'

Woody squinted. 'The rich one?'

'Well, I'm not the fucking dead one, am I? The one whose coffin you fucking stole.' The paramedic put his hand across Peter's front.

He swiped it away. 'Did you hear what I said there? This fucker – '

'Sir, getting this man to the – '

'Where is he?' said Peter, pushing the paramedic away. He leaned over Woody.

'I don't know. The van, the van.'

'What about your van? Did he steal it?' Peter was lost.

'Nicky,' said Woody, his voice becoming softer. 'Nicky's in the van.'

Peter stepped back into McAllister, who gripped him from behind. It was the only thing preventing him from keeling over. When he looked to the sky he saw flashes streak across his vision. He blinked, hard, swung himself away from McAllister.

'If that's quite enough, we need to go,' said the paramedic, brushing past Peter.

They pushed Woody inside and as one man jumped in beside him, the other closed the door and ran round to the driver's seat.

Peter watched them, unable to respond. At least the police would know where to find the fucker.

The siren kicked in as the ambulance pulled away, its blue lights echoing out into the darkening sky. Matt had Nicky. They'd done it, and it hadn't cost a penny.

Peter grabbed his phone but could barely punch the buttons that would bring up Matt's number. He screamed out to steady himself. With measured breaths he managed to dial and as his brother's phone began to ring in his ear he thought of that hellish summer, Nicky screaming through the night as Peter padded around the kitchen whispering mathematical theories into the baby's ear, hoping the noise wasn't carrying up to his mum's bedroom. Just four days later he would meet Helen, perfect Helen. He pictured the twins, sleeping in their bed, sunrise brightening the room not nearly as much as Helen's smile.

29

It doesn't take long to get away from the city. Traffic lights and junctions make me nervous, but nicotine smooths out the road and the whisky sands down the corners. No one will be looking for me yet.

The van's gears are stiff, the stick long and awkward. I haven't mastered being able to change without lurching forward. The wiper blades squeak and shudder as they attempt to do what I've asked of them. Coupled with hazy vision from the booze, I'm not feeling entirely confident on the road, but I can cope. Since leaving the motorway and crossing the Erskine Bridge I've felt lighter, as if outside the city boundary gravity is weaker. I don't know how many times my phone has rung. Pete on repeat. He won't have told Mum yet, but it's only a matter of time. I'm okay about it; she deserves to know.

Someone will find Woody, maybe it'll even be McAllister. The police will arrive with the ambulance. They'll ask questions, he'll answer them, lead them to Nicky. He'll not have a choice. He'll be fine, they all will. No one would judge me for swinging at him after what happened. I'll get in touch with Mum later, try and explain. Turnbull might be the responsible party, but the blame will stick to me. It'll be okay though. Everything's okay.

The traffic has thinned out as I head north on the A82. The light is beginning to fade. Funny how cloud cover can bring the night forward. It's a bit early for twilight but when the rain comes everything gets darker. I switch on the headlights and the speedometer finds itself under a spotlight. No pressure, then. I'm doing about 45mph and the van is beginning to rattle. In ten minutes or so Loch Lomond will appear on my right. With the road ahead clear, I fish into the glove box and grab the first tape I find. It's unmarked so when Teenage Fanclub's Grand Prix starts playing I begin to believe that I can get out of this.

I didn't even know where I was going until I turned onto the motorway. I picked my route based on the shortest queues, driving on autopilot until I found the van struggling with the on ramp to the M8 heading west. There's a clearing past Luss, way up in the hills where few people venture. The first time I went there was with some mates. We would have been nineteen or twenty, game for nothing more than working our way through a case of lager round the camp fire. Fucking midges were brutal right enough, always have been. I didn't know the last time I was there would be the last time. I was going out with a girl called Rachel; it was before I went to Barcelona. She had never had sex outdoors she said, always wanted to fuck under the stars. So we went up, pitched a tent, drank three bottles of red wine and fucked under the stars, my thrusting arse as round and white as the moon above us.

I count back the years through the jobs, flats and break ups and realise more than eleven have passed. I've not been there since Nicky was born. Time deceives me more than Turnbull ever did. My path is set though, I can clear my mind there, work out when to leave, how to leave, where to go, how to get there. Decisions, decisions, decisions. I'm leaving the cannonball behind. I'm going to bury it in the woods. The further I am from Scotland, the less likely I'll be to feel it thudding underground. For once I know what's best for everyone.

I take a sip of whisky and start to sing along with Sparky's Dream as it crackles out the speakers. It's tinny, but it's not the sound quality that takes you back to sunnier days.

My phone starts ringing again. Pete will be trudging back to Mum's, his anger giving off sparks that will sizzle when they land on the pavement. He'll have to sit her down and explain everything. I don't envy him that. That's why he'll be phoning; he won't want to tackle that trauma alone. The ringing stops and seconds later there's another buzz, another voicemail. I would have taken the money if he'd left it lying on the table; maybe in another world he did. Maybe every time anyone makes a choice the universe splinters, we splinter, only ever aware of the decisions we did make, only ever conscious of the world we can see, oblivious to the infinite realities thundering towards oblivion alongside the one we're anchored to. In one of these worlds I gave Bradley my five grand stash and kept on his good side, in another I stuck with General Catalyst and got Nicky back for teatime, in another Pete handed over his cash and Bradley was good to his word. In another, in another, in another.

I drive on with intent, knowing the turn off is less than a mile away. Soon enough the farm track appears. I indicate and swing left. At least here I'll have peace to make my next decision.

The van begins to bounce as it makes its way along the broken road. Within a few hundred yards the Tarmac melds into a dirt trail with wild grass growing between twin tyre tracks. I move down into first gear as the wheels spin in the mud. The engine revs high. I squeeze down on the accelerator and it fights back, vibrating up through my arm. I'm moving again though and get it into second just as the hill steepens. We're doing it; we're making it. My whole body is juddering as I urge the van forward with encouraging words. It will do this thing for me.

As the wipers clear the windscreen I see the road ahead is messier, the tracks softening into thick mud just as it forks. I'm nearly there. Come on. You can do this. I say it to myself as much as the van. I push hard on the accelerator but it doesn't bite. The van is slipping away. Smoke begins to rise from the engine. In the fading light it clouds the path. The reek of diesel fumes reaches me. Not this time. Come on. Not fucking now. I let it slide back down the hill for a few yards before pushing it back into first and revving hard. Come on, baby. Come on. The wheels spin and spin and come on, come on. Do this for me, this one fucking thing. This

The front wheels grip on something and I move forward again, spinning left into the fork, where thankfully the hill levels out. I switch to second and the van leaps forward, hungrily. It's back. We're back and we're on our way. I plough on through the mud, smoke billowing from the engine and the stench getting stronger in the cabin. Almost there though. Almost there.

A white wall that once defined a boundary comes into view. It's endured eleven winters since I last saw it and is barely standing. The initials LH are sprayed in amateurish red graffiti. Vandalism, not art. It's the fucking countryside. Is nowhere sacred? I slow the van to a halt and climb out, coughing, my chest feeling tight. I check my phone. Twelve missed calls and six voicemails. Has Pete developed a system where he leaves a message on every second call? Does he think this is what will coax me out of my hiding place? Fuck that – the day is over as far as I'm concerned. I don't turn it off though; it's too early to sever the connection to my old life.

There's no wind in the clearing and the canopy formed by the treetops above captures most of the rain. I sit down and lean back against the wall, the arse of my jeans soaking through the second it hits the floor.

This white wall marks the spot where we'd turn off into the woods and follow the trail to the campsite. Pitch a tent, open a can, fuck under the stars. Life should never need to be more complicated than that.

Smoke continues to escape from under the hood. I take a sip of whisky, but don't enjoy it. I suppose it's done its job though. For the first time I think about how I'm going to get back. I nearly think 'home' but such a place can no longer exist. Bradley will be looking for me. He's not daft. By tomorrow he'll have someone watching my flat, maybe sooner if word gets back to him about Woody. I'll have to be clever, get back there tonight, ditch the van outside of town and walk the last few miles. I'll sneak in through the back lane, pack a bag with a single change of clothes and my passport. My emergency credit card will cover a taxi to the airport and a ticket to Australia. I don't need Woody to find Turnbull. Christ, I'll have to avoid Woody more than anyone else now. I can keep an eye on Turnbull's website; he'll surface before long and I can watch him for a while, see what he's doing and how he's doing it. Then one night, when he stumbles into his hotel after a night spending my money, I'll be waiting.

Nicky has taught me I'm no longer able to live this life. The next one will be an improvement. Healthy, with a decent job in a sunny climate. Gambling restricted to Saturday nights on the Strip, the odd beer being my only vice. I'll be eternally grateful to my wee brother for allowing me to see this, for being my catalyst. If that's the last thing he contributes to the world he's left then I'll make it count.

The sound of the rain in the trees is soothing. It's loud and quiet at the same time. I close my eyes and think of everywhere on Earth it's raining at this exact moment, the sound it makes as it lands, the smell it leaves when it hits concrete for the first time in days. I think of the accident, the infinite ways his life could have gone, all the universes that won't now exist: Nicky trudging home that afternoon and leaving his manky boots in the kitchen, getting into trouble from Mum and having to clean them before bedtime, going to school the next day and learning something about science, drawing a still life of a fruit bowl, reading a passage of a book aloud in class; a year later going to secondary school and eventually discovering what direction his life would take; his first girlfriend, first drink, exams, university and playing in a band; graduating with distinction and starting a career in astronomy that would take him across the world from a quiet Scottish observatory to the Australian desert and Chilean mountains, his work bringing him as much satisfaction as his wife and kids; rising up the ladder, getting closer to the stars, his feet never leaving the ground, before retiring, sixty odd years from now in a world not too unlike this one, but just a little better because he's in it. I imagine everything he could have been and it fills me with a dread I've never experienced before. Death being part of life is the cruelest trick creation could ever have played on us. From the second we're conceived we're both living and dying; existence itself is purgatory so there must be something else, something beyond whatever this is.

I notice a thin flame snaking its way out from under the bonnet. This isn't part of the plan. I stand up and move nearer as the flame gets fiercer, the smoke turning to black from ashen grey. There's no driving home now. No way back.

I take another step forwards. Maybe I'm not meant to return, maybe my choice is to remain here. Maybe I'm meant to burn, just like Dad did, like Nicky will tomorrow. If there is an answer then they've found it. I move closer still, close enough to feel the heat of the flame. Was today ever going to end another way? What were the odds on getting him back? Who would have put their money on me crossing the line? The bonnet is blackened now, the cabin full of smoke. There are grinding sounds from the engine as parts melt or expand in the intensity of the fire. It's true what they say about flames being hypnotic. I stand transfixed, watching as they begin to devour the van. My cheeks are beginning to sting. Vegas? Who am I kidding? Like I'll be able to find Turnbull, like I'll be able to get my money back. Like I'll even be able to get this van out of here. It's gone, just like Nicky, and Dad, and Siobhan. Gone, man. Gone, gone, gone.

The cab is on fire now; the seats go up quickly with a vicious crackle. If I reached out I could touch the flames. They twist and turn in seductive moves. In seconds they'd have me, consuming me until sated. Every problem I've ever had gone in an instant, all in exchange for temporary pain. We all die in ignorance. All I want to know is the ending and everything in between, the blood I'll spill and the cuts I'll mend, the passion and the anger, the beauty and the horror, the screaming and the silence, the red and the black, good luck and bad; how the pattern of life stitches itself together, the momentous and forgettable combined in moments too quick to measure and decades too long to see.

I stare into the fire, gaze unflinching, each breath considered, each blink the last but one. The windows shatter with an explosion of glass that makes my body dive for cover I never asked for.

I clamber back towards the wall, never quite making it off all fours.

My face stings. When I touch it, my muddy hand is stained with blood.

I sit against the wall, hugging my knees, shaking, watching. My shoulders heave when the tears come. The wailing is primal, as if it's coming from a wounded animal deep within the trees. It must be, because it's a sound I've never heard before. I keep on blinking, keep on breathing.

Eventually it stops. My stomach aches, my face tingles. I reach for my bottle. It's half empty but I glug thirstily at the dram. Still the fire burns. The flames don't seem angry, just dedicated to the task in hand. Like anything in nature, the fire is simply doing what it must. We all do what we must. It's time for me to leave here.

I rub my hands on the grass and stand up, fish out my phone. I press the voicemail button more out of curiosity than a need to return to the world I'm leaving. The emotionless electronic voice confirms the six new messages. I press 1 and Pete's desperation leaps out the earpiece: *Matt, pick up. I'm at the undertakers. Where the fuck are you? I can't believe you did it. Nicky's in the van. You've got him. You've done it. That was some doing you gave that —*

I drop my phone, slump back against the wall as my legs stop working. Either my brain or my heart will be next, I just don't know which. They both seem electrified, as if whatever had been holding the cannonball in place has snapped and it's pinging its way through me like the universe's densest pinball. I try to breathe, but my lungs are refusing to deal with me. Can't blame them. I search around for air, gasping at the forest, feeling rainwater on my tongue.

It really is over now. Nothing can alter the course we have taken and there is nothing left I can do. This truth tames the cannonball and fills my lungs with air. I listen to the message again. I didn't notice it at first, but Pete sounds different; impatient and angry, of course, but there's something else, something new.

I stare at the phone then turn to the burning wreck. The flames have consumed everything now, white has turned black, and the metal work is beginning to crumple. Nicky's coffin will be gone and he'll be exposed to the fire. The petrol tank will be next. This is beyond my control. It always has been. I look up to the heavens, whatever that means. The treetops make it all seem further away. Behind the clouds the sun is turning the sky red. We see so little of what goes on in the world. I delete the message and wait for the next one.

Epilogue

Before

On a clear night early in spring when a Sunday roast had rendered him almost immobile, Matthew Fletcher – having anticipated his mum's *right then, let's get this lot cleared* call to arms – padded out into the back garden and lit a cigarette. He slowly inhaled and waited for the nicotine to snake its way into his brain. The post-roast fag challenged even the post-coital number in the satisfaction stakes.

The garden was illuminated by the warming glow from the kitchen lights but Matt remained out of sight, leaning against the pebble-dashed wall next to the window, his ears on alert. After a few seconds he heard Siobhan laughing. His mum's voice followed. 'He thinks we're daft. Filthy habit it is too. Well, he can make the tea when he gets back in.'

A fair deal, thought Matt. It was cool, but not cold. The day had been warm; the first of the year where he'd left the house without a jacket. There had to be some old wife's tale about t-shirts in March that meant

'They're looking for you,' said Nicky.

'Jesus, you gave me a fright there,' said Matt.

Nicky laughed and covered his mouth. The noisiest kid in the world still had a knack for sneaking up on you. A career in the SAS beckoned if he ever fancied it.

'Come on, let's see how long it takes them to find us,' said Matt.

Nicky nodded and watched Matt as he smoked. The boy leaned back against the wall, mimicking his brother. Then, without warning he burst from his position as if he'd been in starting blocks and ran into the middle of the lawn.

'Wow,' he shouted, his neck straining back as he looked into the sky. 'Amazing.'

'You're not very good at this hiding game, are you?'

'Come and look at this.'

Matt tutted and extinguished his cigarette. Even before he'd stepped across the path onto the lawn there was a knock at the window. He saw Siobhan smiling, waving at him, both hands resplendent in yellow Marigolds. She mouthed 'What are you doing?' through the glass. He held up a finger, mouthed back 'One minute', and pointed towards the lawn. Siobhan frowned that way she did when she was about to laugh and turned from the window, the condensation quickly turning her to a blur.

'C'mere, Matt, honest, wait until you see this.' Nicky's voice was growing more impatient, as if the night was running out.

In the darkness Matt could smell the cut grass. Must have been the first time she'd done it this year. Summer was on its way and no mistake. It was going to be a good one.

'Look up,' said Nicky.

Matt put his foot behind the boy's heels and pushed him over. Nicky screamed as he fell back. He punched out, but was on the ground quickly.

Matt fell in a heap beside him. 'There, that'll save you getting a sore neck,' he said. 'Don't say I never look after you.'

Nicky giggled and lay back straight. 'Are you watching?' he said.

Even with the noise of the city's countless lights, the sky was bulging with stars. 'I am. It's quite impressive.'

They'd need to go camping, get right into complete darkness. If this weather kept up, they could even go within the month. He was old enough now. The boy's sense of wonder was inspirational. Every month it was something new; he would scour the internet for whatever fascination was in his mind at any given time, soak it all up. Matt could vaguely remember doing the same, but with dusty library books that made him cough, and not a tenth of Nicky's retention. It wasn't what you learned that mattered, but what you remembered.

'Do you know what one's Orion?'

'Yeah,' said Matt, scanning up through the darkness for the three bright dots that someone once decided looked like belt studs.

'Right, see if you follow his left arm, right across until you see Gemini, you'll – '

'How do you know all this?' said Matt, happy to let Nicky take the upper hand.

'Duh, I read it online. Are you listening?' The boy's voice was bursting to get to the point.

Matt couldn't remember the last time he'd felt as passionate about anything. Siobhan? Maybe, but that wasn't the unconditional joy with which the kid currently obsessed over the sky. He knew that's why his mum hadn't shouted him back in. She was probably sick of being dragged outside to stare up at nothing. Well, it was hardly nothing.

'Did you know that the stars you're looking at probably aren't even there anymore?' said Matt. He could still give the odd lesson.

'Yeah, most of the stars probably exploded years ago but Jupiter hasn't.'

'What's Jupiter got to do with it?'

'That's what I'm trying to show you. Diagonally up to the left from Orion, just below Gemini's legs, see the bright one that looks a bit pink?'

Matt closed one eye and traced the path in his mind. Sure enough, there was a pinkish looking star. 'Are you saying that's Jupiter?'

'Cool, eh?'

How did he know that? There was no way his mum taught him, no way the school did. 'Yeah. That is pretty cool. You want to look at it for a bit?'

Nicky didn't say anything, but when Matt reached out and pulled his brother towards him, the boy didn't resist. He bumped over and rested his head on Matt's chest, never turning towards him, never averting his gaze from the sky.

After

As people begin to filter into the crematorium they all glance at the coffin lying in the back of the hearse. I'm standing at the boot, returning the sympathetic smiles of those who pass. I can tell everyone is dying to comment on how it's smaller than a normal coffin, but no one does. They will later, when the family's out of earshot. But we're thinking the same thing.

To me, it's just six bits of wood, nailed together. There are seven billion people alive in the world today. Now, I've read before that due to the population expansion in the last couple of centuries there are more people alive today than have ever died, but while that's a lovely sentiment, it's bollocks. We've been around for fifty thousand odd years, which means a lot of eyes have seen this world of ours before passing out of it. There are fifteen of them for every one of us. We're outnumbered by death from the moment we're born, and it's all we can do to stay on the team in second place. Nicky's luck ran out far too soon. I say I'm unlucky; I've lived three lives more than he did. And I've got years ahead of me, decades. They all start today, those moments, hours, days and nights that will make up the rest of my life.

'This is it, then.' says Pete. Peter, if that's what he wants.

I nod, look down to make sure my tie is straight and clean. Mum ironed my shirt this morning, slapping me away from the ironing board. She was more concerned than incensed when Peter told her I'd gone missing, that he'd have to miss dinner because I had phoned him, drunk and inconsolable, unable to face anyone. I wish she'd been angry, that her slap had been fiery, but we don't always get what we deserve. When she smiled at me this morning I just melted into her arms, a wee boy again. You need to grow up. That's all she said to me, her tone gentle, her aim as accurate as ever.

It's warmer than it's been all week, humid. The threat of rain hangs above us, but today it's dry.

McAllister opens the door and begins to pull the coffin towards him.

'Are you ready?' he asks us. We are the pallbearers, Peter and I. Along with McAllister and his assistant.

It was straightforward enough in the end. Peter asked if they would supply a second coffin given the fact that the theft had occurred on their premises. It was the least they could do, he said. McAllister agreed to it all, but probably hadn't bargained for what would come next. His protests were diluted by Peter's insistence that if he lost a night's sleep over what he was about to do, we would both lose a lifetime's after explaining to my mum what had actually transpired.

So, presented with an open casket, we began the process of weighing out roughly forty-eight kilos of van parts, ash and... well, we did what we had to.

After I listened to the voicemails, I called Peter. How could I not? Nicky deserved more than fate had given him. Than I had given him. By the time I got hold of him, the ambulance had been and collected Woody. The police arrived later, but Woody had apparently told them it was a random attack so Peter kept quiet about Nicky. He was still waiting in McAllister's office, for some reason hopeful that I'd return his calls, return triumphant. I wouldn't have placed that level of faith in me, but I suppose I did phone in the end.

After he gave his statement to the police he drove up in McAllister's Volvo while I waited. By the time he arrived the fire had died down.

After the petrol tank went, it calmed down a bit. As it flickered away I sat transfixed, shaking as everything poured out of me, the vision of my brother exploding burned onto my retinas. Peter sat with me and we watched the van until it was smouldering.

We're never going to be friends, we're never going to be more than brothers, but that's the bit that matters. I doubt if Peter will accept that. I doubt he even cares. But we waited, and as the Earth spun toward sunrise we talked about life before Dad died, how it changed when he did, and how the decisions made by others as well as by ourselves helped define who we both were. We reached deep into those corners of the mind that can only be opened by a scent or a shock. He told me about his work, his arsehole boss setting him up; how he had a plan. I don't doubt him and I wouldn't want to be in his boss's loafers when Peter goes looking for him. As the flames became embers, I told him my plan. He laughed until he agreed.

When we stood up my cheeks felt warm, like they do after a day of being in the sun but not realising – the cuts from the exploding window stung, but were about the only aspect of the day that didn't cut deep enough to leave a scar. My face felt warmer still after we'd used the car mats to scoop what we needed into the boot. The rain, thankfully, had dampened everything enough to prevent it from reigniting on the journey back, though it was a drive of watchful anxiety.

When we'd filled the coffin at the other end, McAllister was left with an inch of Transit ash in his boot, something he never commented on, much to my surprise. Even now, he's not mentioned a word.

'Gentlemen, if you please,' he said. His tone is muted. His eyes distant.

I feel I have to speak. 'It's better that some of him is there instead of – '

'I'd rather not discuss the situation, Mr. Fletcher. I would like to get this funeral underway without further delay.'

We lift the coffin from the car to our shoulders, me and Peter at the front, McAllister and his pal at the rear, and walk in slow rhythm through the doors of the crematorium. The coffin is far from level; even with McAllister stooping it looks like it's floating on choppy waters. I reduce the support my arms are giving my corner of the thing to allow my shoulder to bear more of the weight. As the wood sinks in, I exhale the pain. I want it to break the skin and stain my shirt in blood, leave its mark on me. From rock bottom we can only rise.

Walking down that aisle with sobs and minor chords from the organ as my soundtrack, I know I'm on my way back. If I hadn't dialed my voicemail, if I'd trudged home along the banks of the Loch and snuck off to the airport, no one would have found him until spring. He would have lain in the forest while I lounged at the poolside. I don't think about the windows exploding when they did, about the decision I didn't get the chance to make.

As we walk towards the ridiculously sized vase of flowers at the front that Mum insisted on, the organ stops and the crematorium is consumed with a silence that seems to carry a weight to it. Together, we lay the coffin down and take our seats in the front row. I can't help but glance at the mourners. Faces blanks, most wet with tears, each one etched with the shock of what they're witnessing. If only they knew.

I squeeze Mum's hand and glance at Peter. The girls are between him and Helen. One day they'll understand what all this means.

Siobhan is next to me, her perfume filling the gap between us and beckoning the cannonball. But I can't feel it anywhere. It's back in the woods, buried beneath that white wall. I don't want to say goodbye to her after the service. I've not told her I'm leaving so she won't know it's the last time she'll see me.

As the Minister talks us through Nicky's life and the tragedy that befell him, I concentrate on Mum's wailing. The Minister's words mean nothing, no offence to the guy. If he'd lived the day I'd lived he'd know there wasn't a God; that we're all in this to just try and survive for as long as we can.

Today I put my brother to rest, tomorrow I'll waken and say goodbye to Mum. The airport still awaits me. It's not safe here. At least Bradley's had the decency to stay away, but among the unknown faces at the back will be his eyes and ears, already texting confirmation that both me and a coffin arrived on time. I feel bad for what happened, but Woody made the wrong decision. If history ever looked through my eyes, it would see I tried to do right by most people.

The Minister has spoken. No one else has. We opted not too. Let's get it over and done with, get everyone out of the room and back into the world where things like this don't happen. Steak pie awaits us at the Golf Club, just like it did after Dad died.

The curtains close over in awkward stutters, as if the mechanism needs oiled. Nicky is in there, among clumps of earth, van parts and the man-made fibres that lined his coffin. His atoms are mixing with theirs like they mixed into the forest last night, changing form, starting again. Good luck to them.

About the Author

Kevin Scott

Kevin Scott spends most days trying to put the right words in the right order. He graduated from the University of Glasgow Creative Writing MLitt programme with distinction in 2013, and was subsequently shortlisted for the Sceptre Prize.

His short stories have been published in a number of magazines in the UK and US. He also previously edited the literary journal *From Glasgow to Saturn* and is a (currently lapsed) member of the Glasgow collective G2 Writers. This is his first novel.

Away from creative writing he works as a journalist, where he is a business correspondent for The Herald.

He lives in Glasgow with his pregnant (at the time of writing) wife, and son.

More Books From ThunderPoint Publishing Ltd.

The Oystercatcher Girl
Gabrielle Barnby
ISBN: 978-1-910946-17-6 (eBook)
ISBN: 978-1-910946-15-2 (Paperback)

In the medieval splendour of St Magnus Cathedral, three women gather to mourn the untimely passing of Robbie: Robbie's widow, Tessa; Tessa's old childhood friend, Christine, and Christine's unstable and unreliable sister, Lindsay.

But all is not as it seems: what is the relationship between the three women, and Robbie? What secrets do they hide? And who has really betrayed who?

Set amidst the spectacular scenery of the Orkney Islands, Gabrielle Barnby's skilfully plotted first novel is a beautifully understated story of deception and forgiveness, love and redemption.

'The Oystercatcher Girl is a wonderfully evocative and deftly woven story' – Sara Bailey

The House with the Lilac Shutters:
Gabrielle Barnby
ISBN: 978-1-910946-02-2 (eBook)
ISBN: 978-0-9929768-8-0 (Paperback)

Irma Lagrasse has taught piano to three generations of villagers, whilst slowly twisting the knife of vengeance; Nico knows a secret; and M. Lenoir has discovered a suppressed and dangerous passion.

Revolving around the Café Rose, opposite The House with the Lilac Shutters, this collection of contemporary short stories links a small town in France with a small town in England, traces the unexpected connections between the people of both places and explores the unpredictable influences that the past can have on the present.

Characters weave in and out of each other's stories, secrets are concealed and new connections are made.

With a keenly observant eye, Barnby illustrates the everyday tragedies, sorrows, hopes and joys of ordinary people in this vividly understated and unsentimental collection.

'The more I read, and the more descriptions I encountered, the more I was put in mind of one of my all time favourite texts – Dylan Thomas' Under Milk Wood' – lindasbookbag.com

The Wrong Box

Andrew C Ferguson

ISBN: 978-1-910946-14-5 (Paperback)

ISBN: 978-1-910946-16-9 (eBook)

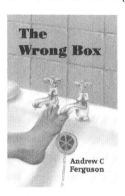

All I know is, I'm in exile in Scotland, and there's a dead Scouser businessman in my bath. With his toe up the tap.

Meet Simon English, corporate lawyer, heavy drinker and Scotophobe, banished from London after being caught misbehaving with one of the young associates on the corporate desk. As if that wasn't bad enough, English finds himself acting for a spiralling money laundering racket that could put not just his career, but his life, on the line.

Enter Karen Clamp, an 18 stone, well-read schemie from the Auchendrossan sink estate, with an encyclopedic knowledge of Council misdeeds and 19th century Scottish fiction. With no one to trust but each other, this mismatched pair must work together to investigate a series of apparently unrelated frauds and discover how everything connects to the mysterious Wrong Box.

Manically funny, *The Wrong Box* is a chaotic story of lust, money, power and greed, and the importance of being able to sew a really good hem.

The Bogeyman Chronicles
Craig Watson
ISBN: 978-1-910946-11-4 (eBook)
ISBN: 978-1-910946-10-7 (Paperback)

In 14th Century Scotland, amidst the wars of independence, hatred, murder and betrayal are commonplace. People are driven to extraordinary lengths to survive, whilst those with power exercise it with cruel pleasure.

Royal Prince Alexander Stewart, son of King Robert II and plagued by rumours of his illegitimacy, becomes infamous as the Wolf of Badenoch, while young Andrew Christie commits an unforgivable sin and lay Brother Brodie Affleck in the Restenneth Priory pieces together the mystery that links them all together.

From the horror of the times and the changing fortunes of the characters, the legend of the Bogeyman is born and Craig Watson cleverly weaves together the disparate lives of the characters into a compelling historical mystery that will keep you gripped throughout.

Over 80 years the lives of three men are inextricably entwined, and through their hatreds, murders and betrayals the legend of Christie Cleek, the bogeyman, is born.

'From the horror of the times to the changing fortunes of the characters, a gripping, historical thriller is born' – Press and Journal

Mule Train
Huw Francis
ISBN: 978-0-9575689-0-7 (eBook)
ISBN: 978-0-9575689-1-4 (Paperback)

Four lives come together in the remote and spectacular mountains bordering Afghanistan and explode in a deadly cocktail of treachery, betrayal and violence.

Written with a deep love of Pakistan and the Pakistani people, Mule Train will sweep you from Karachi in the south to the Shandur Pass in the north, through the dangerous borderland alongside Afghanistan, in an adventure that will keep you gripped throughout.

'Stunningly captures the feel of Pakistan, from Karachi to the hills' – tripfiction.com

QueerBashing
Tim Morriosn
ISBN: 978-1-910946-06-0 (eBook)
ISBN: 978-0-9929768-9-7 (Paperback)

The first queerbasher McGillivray ever met was in the mirror.

From the revivalist churches of Orkney in the 1970s, to the gay bars of London and Northern England in the 90s, via the divinity school at Aberdeen, this is the story of McGillivray, a self-centred, promiscuous hypocrite, failed Church of Scotland minister, and his own worst enemy.

Determined to live life on his own terms, McGillivray's grasp on reality slides into psychosis and a sense of his own invulnerability, resulting in a brutal attack ending life as he knows it.

Raw and uncompromising, this is a viciously funny but ultimately moving account of one man's desire to come to terms with himself and live his life as he sees fit.

'…an arresting novel of pain and self-discovery' – Alastair Mabbott (The Herald)

Changed Times
Ethyl Smith
ISBN: 978-1-910946-09-1 (eBook)
ISBN: 978-1-910946-08-4 (Paperback)

1679 – The Killing Times: Charles II is on the throne, the Episcopacy has been restored, and southern Scotland is in ferment.

The King is demanding superiority over all things spiritual and temporal and rebellious Ministers are being ousted from their parishes for refusing to bend the knee.

When John Steel steps in to help one such Minister in his home village of Lesmahagow he finds himself caught up in events that reverberate not just through the parish, but throughout the whole of southern Scotland.

From the Battle of Drumclog to the Battle of Bothwell Bridge, John's platoon of farmers and villagers find themselves in the heart of the action over that fateful summer where the people fight the King for their religion, their freedom, and their lives.

Set amid the tumult and intrigue of Scotland's Killing Times, John Steele's story powerfully reflects the changes that took place across 17th century Scotland, and stunningly brings this period of history to life.

**'Smith writes with a fine ear for Scots speech, and with a sensitive awareness to the different ways in which history intrudes upon the lives of men and women, soldiers and civilians, adults and children'
- James Robertson**

A Good Death
Helen Davis
ISBN: 978-0-9575689-7-6 (eBook)
ISBN: 978-0-9575689-6-9 (Paperback)

'*A good death is better than a bad conscience*,' said Sophie.

1983 – Georgie, Theo, Sophie and Helena, four disparate young Cambridge undergraduates, set out to scale Ausangate, one of the highest and most sacred peaks in the Andes.

Seduced into employing the handsome and enigmatic Wamani as a guide, the four women are initiated into the mystically dangerous side of Peru, Wamani and themselves as they travel from Cuzco to the mountain, a journey that will shape their lives forever.

2013 – though the women are still close, the secrets and betrayals of Ausangate chafe at the friendship.

A girls' weekend at a lonely Fenland farmhouse descends into conflict with the insensitive inclusion of an overbearing young academic toyboy brought along by Theo. Sparked by his unexpected presence, pent up petty jealousies, recriminations and bitterness finally explode the truth of Ausangate, setting the women on a new and dangerous path.

Sharply observant and darkly comic, Helen Davis's début novel is an elegant tale of murder, seduction, vengeance, and the value of a good friendship.

'The prose is crisp, adept, and emotionally evocative' – Lesbrary.com

The Birds That Never Flew
Margot McCuaig
Shortlisted for the Dundee International Book Prize
2012
Longlisted for the Polari First Book Prize 2014
ISBN: 978-0-9929768-5-9 (eBook)
ISBN: 978-0-9929768-4-2 (Paperback)

'Have you got a light hen? I'm totally gaspin.'

Battered and bruised, Elizabeth has taken her daughter and left her abusive husband Patrick. Again. In the bleak and impersonal Glasgow housing office Elizabeth meets the provocatively intriguing drug addict Sadie, who is desperate to get her own life back on track.

The two women forge a fierce and interdependent relationship as they try to rebuild their shattered lives, but despite their bold, and sometimes illegal attempts it seems impossible to escape from the abuse they have always known, and tragedy strikes.

More than a decade later Elizabeth has started to implement her perfect revenge – until a surreal Glaswegian Virgin Mary steps in with imperfect timing and a less than divine attitude to stick a spoke in the wheel of retribution.

Tragic, darkly funny and irreverent, *The Birds That Never Flew* ushers in a new and vibrant voice in Scottish literature.

'…dark, beautiful and moving, I wholeheartedly recommend' scanoir.co.uk

Toxic

Jackie McLean
Shortlisted for the Yeovil Book Prize 2011
ISBN: 978-0-9575689-8-3 (eBook)
ISBN: 978-0-9575689-9-0 (Paperback)

The recklessly brilliant DI Donna Davenport, struggling to hide a secret from police colleagues and get over the break-up with her partner, has been suspended from duty for a fiery and inappropriate outburst to the press.

DI Evanton, an old-fashioned, hard-living misogynistic copper has been newly demoted for thumping a suspect, and transferred to Dundee with a final warning ringing in his ears and a reputation that precedes him.

And in the peaceful, rolling Tayside farmland a deadly store of MIC, the toxin that devastated Bhopal, is being illegally stored by a criminal gang smuggling the valuable substance necessary for making cheap pesticides.

An anonymous tip-off starts a desperate search for the MIC that is complicated by the uneasy partnership between Davenport and Evanton and their growing mistrust of each others actions.

Compelling and authentic, Toxic is a tense and fast paced crime thriller.

'...a humdinger of a plot that is as realistic as it is frightening' – crimefictionlover.com

In The Shadow Of The Hill
Helen Forbes
ISBN: 978-0-9929768-1-1 (eBook)
ISBN: 978-0-9929768-0-4 (Paperback)

An elderly woman is found battered to death in the common stairwell of an Inverness block of flats.

Detective Sergeant Joe Galbraith starts what seems like one more depressing investigation of the untimely death of a poor unfortunate who was in the wrong place, at the wrong time.

As the investigation spreads across Scotland it reaches into a past that Joe has tried to forget, and takes him back to the Hebridean island of Harris, where he spent his childhood.

Among the mountains and the stunning landscape of religiously conservative Harris, in the shadow of Ceapabhal, long buried events and a tragic story are slowly uncovered, and the investigation takes on an altogether more sinister aspect.

In The Shadow Of The Hill skilfully captures the intricacies and malevolence of the underbelly of Highland and Island life, bringing tragedy and vengeance to the magical beauty of the Outer Hebrides.

'...our first real home-grown sample of modern Highland noir' – Roger Hutchison; West Highland Free Press

Over Here
Jane Taylor
ISBN: 978-0-9929768-3-5 (eBook)
ISBN: 978-0-9929768-2-8 (Paperback)

It's coming up to twenty-four hours since the boy stepped down from the big passenger liner – it must be, he reckons foggily – because morning has come around once more with the awful irrevocability of time destined to lead nowhere in this worrying new situation. His temporary minder on board – last spotted heading for the bar some while before the lumbering process of docking got underway – seems to have vanished for good. Where does that leave him now? All on his own in a new country: that's where it leaves him. He is just nine years old.

An eloquently written novel tracing the social transformations of a century where possibilities were opened up by two world wars that saw millions of men move around the world to fight, and mass migration to the new worlds of Canada and Australia by tens of thousands of people looking for a better life.

Through the eyes of three generations of women, the tragic story of the nine year old boy on Liverpool docks is brought to life in saddeningly evocative prose.

'…a sweeping haunting first novel that spans four generations and two continents…' – Cristina Odone/Catholic Herald

The Bonnie Road
Suzanne d'Corsey
ISBN: 978-1-910946-01-5 (eBook)
ISBN: 978-0-9929768-6-6 (Paperback)

My grandmother passed me in transit. She was leaving, I was coming into this world, our spirits meeting at the door to my mother's womb, as she bent over the bed to close the thin crinkled lids of her own mother's eyes.

The women of Morag's family have been the keepers of tradition for generations, their skills and knowledge passed down from woman to woman, kept close and hidden from public view, official condemnation and religious suppression.

In late 1970s St. Andrews, demand for Morag's services are still there, but requested as stealthily as ever, for even in 20th century Scotland witchcraft is a dangerous Art to practise.

When newly widowed Rosalind arrives from California to tend her ailing uncle, she is drawn unsuspecting into a new world she never knew existed, one in which everyone seems to have a secret, but that offers greater opportunities than she dreamt of – if she only has the courage to open her heart to it.

Richly detailed, dark and compelling, d'Corsey magically transposes the old ways of Scotland into the 20th Century and brings to life the ancient traditions and beliefs that still dance just below the surface of the modern world.

'…successfully portrays rich characters in compelling plots, interwoven with atmospheric Scottish settings & history and coloured with witchcraft & romance' – poppypeacockpens.com

Talk of the Toun
Helen MacKinven
ISBN: 978-1-910946-00-8 (eBook)
ISBN: 978-0-9929768-7-3 (Paperback)

She was greetin' again. But there's no need for Lorraine to be feart, since the first day of primary school, Angela has always been there to mop up her tears and snotters.

An uplifting black comedy of love, family life and friendship, Talk of the Toun is a bittersweet coming-of-age tale set in the summer of 1985, in working class, central belt Scotland.

Lifelong friends Angela and Lorraine are two very different girls, with a growing divide in their aspirations and ambitions putting their friendship under increasing strain.

Artistically gifted Angela has her sights set on art school, but lassies like Angela, from a small town council scheme, are expected to settle for a nice wee secretarial job at the local factory. Her only ally is her gallus gran, Senga, the pet psychic, who firmly believes that her granddaughter can be whatever she wants.

Though Lorraine's ambitions are focused closer to home Angela has plans for her too, and a caravan holiday to Filey with Angela's family tests the dynamics of their relationship and has lifelong consequences for them both.

Effortlessly capturing the religious and social intricacies of 1980s Scotland, Talk of the Toun is the perfect mix of pathos and humour as the two girls wrestle with the complications of growing up and exploring who they really are.

'Fresh, fierce and funny…a sharp and poignant study of growing up in 1980s Scotland. You'll laugh, you'll cry…you'll cringe' – Karen Campbell

22260306R00154

Printed in Great Britain
by Amazon